BOSSMAN UNDONE

BRIMSTONE LORDS MC ONE

SARAH ZOLTON ARTHUR

1

Lady Sings the Blues

I read the glowing-pink neon sign above the door a few more times, standing one foot both inside the rundown juke joint and one foot out, letting the cold air escape. *We're not cooling off the outdoors*, I hear my mother's words in my head sounding, as she normally sounded, pissed at me. Not needing anyone else pissed at me, especially not here, I move securely inside as the heavy glass door swings shut behind me.

Once the door catches, the space is plunged into darkness. The only natural light should have come from the panes in the door. But the glass has been covered over by thick butcher paper, leaving only about an inch margin of light showing through both the upper and lower sections of window, as if whoever put it there underestimated how much paper would be used. That or they just didn't know how to measure.

Remember Elise, measure twice, cut once, no matter what you're doing. You might not get the chance again.

This was something my dad taught me. I wish I'd known then how prolific those words would come to be.

I miss him.

There are a few customers hunched over tables dispersed randomly around the dark space. They look up for a moment with squinting eyes before turning back to their beers or bourbons. It's early to be in a place like this. Too early. Pretty much me and the drunks. Me and the drunks and the low, throaty, anguished melodies softly humming through the jukebox speakers.

"A duck walks into a bar," I hear, realizing someone is speaking to me.

"Excuse me?" I ask, moving closer in the direction of the voice which draws me in with the thick country twang of this area. Accents always get to me. Probably because I grew up in Michigan where we've developed the non-accent accent. It sounds fine, but no one is going to write it into a television script. His sounds smooth and sexy, and a hundred percent Kentucky.

He repeats, "A duck walks into a bar. He says to the barkeep, 'You got any duck food?' The barkeep answers, 'No, we don't got food. Especially not duck food. Now get gone and don't come back'."

"Okay," I laugh, but he's not finished. And instead of leaving, which I probably should do, I move in even closer to the man as he continues.

"The next day the duck walks into the bar and asks, 'Got any duck food?' The barkeep yells, 'No we don't got food, especially not duck food. Now get gone!' The duck leaves. On the third day, the duck walks into the bar and asks, 'You got any duck food?' The barkeep screams, 'No we ain't got food, especially not duck food! Come back tomorrow, and I'll nail your bill closed.' So the duck leaves.

"The next day the duck walks into the bar and asks, 'You

got any nails?' 'No!' the barkeep grumbles. 'I ain't got no nails.' 'Good,' the duck says. 'Got any duck food?'"

I blink once then burst out a laugh so loud, he takes a step back and so strong, I double over. It's been a long time since I've laughed with this much careless abandon, tears filling my eyes.

Once I've come down from the laugh enough to right myself, after swiping away the tears, I notice him smiling. Not many people smile at me around here anymore. And his smile, well, that's a smile worth a double-take. One that would be hidden behind a full beard, if not for the obvious trim job, allowing me to get the full effect of the crooked, yet genuine smile filled with mostly straight, not quite bright white teeth.

There's something familiar about his smile. Nothing I can pinpoint. Especially since I've blocked major portions of my life from when I used to live here. My therapist calls it a survival mechanism. For several years she's been trying to help me reach that magical breakthrough moment when they all come flooding back. It hasn't happened yet.

When I realize I've been staring, I avert my eyes, slowly glancing up until I meet his. The intensity with how he looks at me could just about knock me off my feet if I didn't have the bar to keep me upright. It's want and curiosity and friendship all jumbled together. I haven't been on the receiving end of such a look in too long a time and only now, seeing his, do I realize how much I've missed it.

First his smile, now his eyes. I want to remember him. It's in my brain somewhere, just waiting to be accessed. The stress of losing my dad, of coming back to this place, probably isn't helping the cause.

"Tried that joke several times, never gotten that reaction before."

I blink, turning my attention to his mouth. He has such a

pretty mouth and he's using it to talk to me again. I should answer him. That would be the polite thing to do. But then, what do you say to a man you've just met when all you'd *like* to do is run your fingers through his hair?

In my defense, he has the thickest head of peanut butter colored hair I've ever seen in my life. *Peanut butter hair? Really, Elise?* Maybe I need lunch instead of a drink. He keeps it pulled back in one of those super sexy man buns. That, coupled with the beard. He's simply breathtaking.

I'm so focused on the tiny stray hairs curling at his temples and the ones from his mustache trying to hide the corners of his perfect lips that it takes me a beat before I notice he's stopped talking. I blink again. The silence hangs between us and I should probably fill it.

"I guess I just didn't expect it?" I answer in the form of a question. Why? Uh... maybe because he has me completely befuddled and I'm pretty sure he can read my thoughts. Though, he's kind enough not to call me on them.

"Fair enough." He wipes down the counter with a damp rag. "What can I get you to drink?"

"Hard cider?"

"Why you end everythin' in a question?" He has the nerve to smirk at me. Oh, yeah, he can read my thoughts. *Get out of my head, hot bartender guy.*

My cheeks begin to heat. Of course, they do.

"Nervous habit?" I do it again. Damnit.

He snickers, spinning around to open a cooler where he pulls a bottle of cider from the middle shelf. Then he spins back my way, twisting off the cap, sliding it over to me in one smooth motion.

"You got a name?" he asks, filling a couple of glasses with bourbon on the rocks for an elderly man who walks up next to me. The man never even has to order. The bartender just knows. And judging by the shakes in the old man's hands when he reaches out for the glasses, I assume both are for him.

"Elise." I give the air a little punch for not asking it. "You?"

"Mark."

"Mark, huh?" I consider him, Mark with the dark eyes and beautiful smile. No matter how hard I try to place him, I'm sure I don't know any Marks.

"Yep," he cuts into my thoughts. "My mother named me after her dog."

"She *did?*"

He nods. "He had a hair lip. *Mark, mark, mark.*"

"Ooo—" I tease, taking a step back from the bar with my drink in hand. "You were doing so well."

"I was?"

"You were. Emphasis on *were.*"

He folds his arms on the bar in front of him and leans in. "What if I said the drink's on me?"

"Might get you back closer."

"Might?" Mark stands up straighter again. "Wow. Tough crowd."

And I realize within this exchange that I've not only stepped back up to the bar but slid myself onto a barstool in front of where the bottle of cider had initially come to rest. Lifting it to my lips, I salute him first before taking a long pull. It's a good distraction.

With this guy, I need a distraction. His voice sounds exactly like the bourbon he poured into those shot glasses, dark and smooth with notes of smoke-aged sensuality, even while telling me ridiculous jokes. I could fall in love with that voice alone. Good thing his face and hair and body contribute to the smorgasbord of the senses.

So, of course, right when I work up the courage to ask what time he gets off work, the door swings wide open, cracking against the back wall, straining the limits of the hinges. A woman steps inside. A horrible woman these eyes haven't looked on in years. And just like that, all the good humor sweeps out of the room as the door swings back closed behind her.

Not near ready enough to deal with the attitude she'll sling at me for coming back to town again or still breathing, I slink low on the stool, using my hair to hide my face.

The bartender sees this. He cocks his head, taking me in. I'm sure he's reading my mind again. It doesn't take a rocket scientist to pick up on my fear and loathing.

Then he moves from behind the bar, approaching her, pulling her aside, speaking in a voice low enough for only the two of them to hear.

Well, that's my cue to leave. I suck down the rest of my drink, slap a couple of dollars tip on the counter, and scurry out of the bar while he keeps her distracted enough to do so. Too bad. He seemed nice.

Nice? I have to laugh at my stupidity. Nice serves no point in my current reality. I'm here for one purpose, and one purpose only. Once that's done, I never plan to step foot in this god-forsaken state again. And the entire town of Thornbriar has let me know how much they appreciate my plan, in no uncertain terms.

I can't remember why I even ventured into that bar, to begin with, except some really great times were had inside those walls. Those, or most of those, I actually remember. There are too many memories in this town in general. Most of them are good. It's the few bad that make everyone hate me. Just because *I've* blocked them out doesn't mean *they* have.

The rumble of pipes thunders in the background, and I look up to see a motorcade of bikes traveling the road which runs along the parking lot, heading toward town. How many motorcades have I seen over the years? Once the warm weather hits in spring until the first frosts of winter fall, bikers use this route traveling from up north down to all parts south.

As my eyes follow the band of bikers, they land on one sitting alone kitty-corner from my car staring hard at me. His black, leather boots and faded denim-clad legs straddle a massive black and chrome machine. Dark shades and a black bandana with the bottom half of a skull printed on it, tied around his face from the nose down, conceal his features. But I don't have to see his stare to feel it.

It's as if he's challenging me to turn away first. His scathing death vibes suffuse the entire parking lot. My whole body begins to tremble. Though, I refuse to give in to the fear and keep standing on my shaky legs, watching. When I don't turn away, he quirks an eyebrow, nods his head, and rumbles out of the parking lot.

What was the point of that?

Bikers creep me out in general. Ever since I was a little girl. Men showed at our house one night, one bleeding profusely. My mother freaked, but my father helped them. I don't know why he helped, maybe his Hippocratic Oath come back to bite him in the ass. But I remember a giant man, all leather and chains, staring down at me through his black beady eyes outside our kitchen, where my father helped the wounded man. He ran the blade of a hunting knife up and down his calloused thumb. Every so often pointing the tip in my direction. No words. Intent clear. First and last time I kept the company of a biker. I shudder at the memory.

The door to Lady's opens. The noise pulls my attention from where Mr. Scary Biker Man tore out of the lot back to where it should have been the whole time.

Her leg, the pencil-thin leg of the one woman I not only *don't want* to deal with now, but I *don't have it in me* to deal with right now, hangs half out of a wide crack as if she's stopped to talk again before leaving. Dressed for business in the obligatory thin, beige skirt suit, even though the woman hasn't worked since college. And the only work she did then was to land her a rich husband. She's probably inside, lecturing poor Mark, the bartender, warning him if he sees me to contact the mayor's office right away. As the wife of the mayor, gossiping, manipulating, and strong-arming have become her fortes. She deals in them the way Mark the bartender deals in bourbon.

Better for us all she not see me.

I get back in my car.

Four missed texts. Two from the funeral home, two from people warning me not to linger in town any longer than I need to, and that "they'll be watching." *Great*. Not that I don't have enough on my plate this week. I still don't understand how anyone down here got my number in the first place?

That's not true, Elise. They got it from Hadley. My refusal to accept this doesn't make it any less true.

Before I take off, I call the funeral home. They put me on hold. While I'm on the phone, mayor's wife Margo leaves the parking lot, only glancing my way. Barely taking in my nondescript, midnight blue Malibu sedan, turning her nose up as she passes. Tinted windows keep her from seeing inside. Margo drives a Lexus.

Hadley, my dad's live-in girlfriend picked everything before I arrived here. His burial suit, the casket, the music, flower arrangements. Death is a racket, and she had no qualms about spending my money to ease her sadness. Apparently, my one and only job is to fund this operation since my so-blissfully-in-love father neglected to update his life insurance of which I'm the sole beneficiary. Just enough to cover taxes and the funeral. Which, after leaving me on hold for fifteen minutes, would be the reason given for why the funeral home had initially texted. They want their money.

Poor, poor Hadley. The sentiment gets repeated a good five times by the woman on the other end of the line in our short, one-minute conversation. That is, once she'd taken me off hold. Hadley is loved. Hadley is hometown, and I'm outsider. Not just any outsider—traitor, bitch, whore, or any combination of the former. Traitor-bitch. Bitch-whore. Sometimes, depending on how country they try to sound, someone will jumble the three together in a rather unintelligible *traitorbitchwhore*, which is supposed to offend or intimidate me. But in reality, it makes them sound drunk. It's hard to be intimidated by a country drunk.

As I make my way up Market Street, because every—and I do mean *every*—town in Kentucky has a Market, Commerce, or Main Street, my foot hits the break of its own will to stop in front of the scene of the crime. The place where I first met Logan Hollister. Or as he's also known, the reason I'm a *traitorbitchwhore*.

God, he was beautiful. And that day, he had eyes only for me. He and his cousin Beau were hanging out. Those two were always hanging out back then. Crew cuts, clean-shaven, expensive clothing. These guys were the epitome of the all-American boy-next-door jocks.

Beau was a grade ahead and already had his early admission to the University of Kentucky, or what everyone down here shortens to UK, for when he graduated. And he was beautiful, too. Good genes, the Hollister family. But as I said before, once Logan and I locked eyes that was it.

My dad had moved home after he and my mom divorced. It was undecided where I would live because my mom packed up and moved away from where we lived outside Kalamazoo to Denver. So either way, I'd be leaving my school and friends behind. Little did I know the impact of being born up north, in Michigan, would have on my acceptance in the community. Enveloped between the love and warmth from my father and the Hollister boys, I'd never felt the impact. Up north, we don't think it makes a difference where a person hales from. But in a small southern town, it makes a huge difference. Especially once I no longer had the Hollisters to protect me.

We met the summer before our junior year. And obviously, that one day sealed my fate. I knew, just knew where I'd be living.

And his opening line was a doozy: "You've got kind lips," he said. Big, bright smile full of *perfectly straight*, white teeth.

Flattered and completely taken aback that such a specimen of masculine beauty would even speak to me much less send off a compliment, I smiled back. "I do?"

Totally fell into that one.

"Yeah, the kind I'd like to see wrapped around my—" But he didn't finish. Waggling his eyebrows at me suggestively instead. The line shouldn't have worked. Come to think of it, I should have been mortified. It was the eyebrow waggle that did it.

And thus began the reign of Logan Hollister and Elise Manning.

Life would be so different now if I'd just used my head that day. Walked away. Moved with my mother to Denver.

It still hurts. To think of what he might have been now. What *we* might have been now. No use crying over spilled milk or dead boyfriends. The past should stay in the past.

Get in. Bury my father. Get out. It's the perfect game plan, and in order to make it happen, I have to get this over with.

Every place I pass on my way to the funeral home holds some happy feeling which doesn't fit with the way they treat me. My feelings versus their memories, I stand no chance at winning.

Mr. Delavigne, the funeral director, meets me at the door.

He graduated with my dad—and as it were, Hadley's dad. So of course, he's none too thrilled to see me. Not that my dad's death was my fault in any way. He fell off a ladder cleaning out the gutters on his and Hadley's home. But I'd stayed away all these years, since the fallout with Logan, so that made me a terrible daughter.

"Just need you to sign some papers and write the check," he says with as much curt punctuation in his tone as a businessman can without being outright hostile.

"Sure," I answer, following him in to sign those papers and write the check.

———

THERE'S NOT enough bourbon in the state to make me forget today. Being seen at the funeral home was rough, to say the least. Everyone showed up. I'm surprised they weren't brandishing torches and pitchforks to drive me out. Half the town still hates me for Logan. The other half, for my leaving my dad, even though they didn't want me to stay in the first place.

And the hits just keep on coming. I'm stuck sitting on the curb outside my dad's house waiting to see if Hadley will change her mind about giving me a place to stay. She's thus far refused to let me in.

He's my dad. I loved him even if I had to stay away. And it's not like he couldn't have come to visit me. I'd have welcomed him into my home at any time. We talked semi-regularly on the phone, but it just so happens that he went out and found himself a replacement for both me and mom in one fell swoop. Old enough to sleep with and young enough to be his daughter, Hadley didn't want to visit, so they didn't visit. Booty over DNA. She never liked to not be the center of my father's attention. Of course, this tidbit gets ignored by everyone but me. One of the perks of being homegrown.

I hang my head in my hands, defeated. She's not going to open the door.

"*Elise?*"

I look up and smile, returning the crooked smile of the gorgeous man with the peanut butter bun walking my way. *He has tattoos!* Holy wow, somehow they'd escaped my attention in the darkened bar earlier. Because let's face it, there's something super sexy about a man with tattoos.

"Hey. Mark, right?"

His crooked smile grows even bigger.

"How's it going?" I ask, wishing we had met under different circumstances.

"Ah, you know... If I was doin' any better, I'd have to be twins. How 'bout you?"

"If you're twins, then I'm a miscarriage."

2

MARK

"This your dad's place?" I take the last drag off my cigarette before throwing the butt down on the ground in the gutter, snuffing it out with the toe of my boot against the curb. Sucks to have to pretend I don't know her, at least the her from five to seven years ago. But she put that ball in play, now I have to run with it.

Elise looks almost exactly as I remember her. Still just as beautiful. Her hair's maybe a bit shorter, otherwise not much physically has changed. It was so hard to let her leave the bar earlier, but when Margo barged in very unwelcome, I really didn't have a choice. As soon as Toby showed for his shift, I hauled ass into town to find her. Not too hard in a town the size of Thornbriar.

"Yeah. How'd you know?" she asks.

"Small town, remember? I live just a couple streets over."

"Then you should remember your place, here," she says. "Or moreover, my place. You shouldn't be seen talking to me. I don't know how long you've lived here, but I'm not well-liked in these parts." I hate that she feels the need to remind me of this, but she's telling the truth. Nothing I can do about it right now. Soon, though.

"Couple streets over?" She flawlessly changes the direction of the conversation. "You live by the Hollister's then?"

"Yep."

"George and Margo?"

I nod.

"Dave and Lenore?"

I nod again.

"Anyone heard from Beau in recent years? I haven't seen him since—do you know about Logan Hollister?"

I nod for a third time, lips pressed into a tight line. Don't mean to, that's just what happens when I hear Logan Hollister's name.

"Then you should know... I'm... um... I'm the one he was dating when it happened. So you can see why you shouldn't be talking to me."

Shouldn't be talking to her? I know more than she thinks. "The Hollisters don't dictate who I talk to. And for the record, I know what happened. You are in no way responsible."

"Well, I didn't use to think so, but five years down the road, and they're still blaming me. Maybe you can call a town hall meeting, enlighten them. Because from where I'm sitting, their version of the truth seems highly contradictory."

"I'll get right on that." I tease.

When she didn't recognize me at the bar it stung, and yeah, still stings a bit now. But thinking about it, she did me a favor. It's better for the both of us if she don't remember just yet. Gives me time to prepare. What with the way my heart still pangs when I'm anywhere near her, there's a lot to prepare for. Plus, it ain't like I haven't changed completely since the last time we were together. Neck, arms, chest, and back covered in tattoos. My hair, as in, I have it now. Don't keep it shaved like I used to. My face, don't keep that shaved either.

Elise Manning is a wet dream come to life, exactly as she was seven years ago when she first rolled into town. Only then, despite her parents' divorce, she still had this sparkle in her eyes, which turned them from average blue to like, I don't know, a gemstone or something. Her face alone emanated this natural light, something which brought out a smile to folks old an' young. If she stood next to you…*shit*. No straight man in this town, married, single, or otherwise, stood a chance against her magnetism.

Now that light has been all but snuffed out. Sure, she's here to bury her father, which can't be easy. Her light, though, started fading out years ago. Everyone in town knew Logan was a train wreck waiting to happen. The kids just didn't care because he was so cool. The adults ignored the situation because he was the golden boy. Or should I say, another golden boy. Another Hollister golden boy.

She hitched her cart to the wrong horse. And then she fell in love. Love makes us stupid. Don't I know it? But Elise— she wouldn't unhitch that horse, even when it turned rabid and needed to be put down.

Toward the end of their relationship, I'm not sure if she had any love left for him, but if she did, it was residual. Maybe loved him out of habit, but she wasn't in love. By the time she made her break, Logan Hollister wasn't a train wreck waiting to happen, his train was in the process of wrecking.

What I do know, she never did what they accused her of. I knew it then, know it now. So for her to think she shoulders any responsibility—I just wanna beat the shit out of Logan Hollister. Jackass didn't know how good he had it.

"Come on." I hold my hand out to help her up off the

curb. "You can't stay here all day. Let's get some lunch, then I'll take you back to the bar. Show you why I call it *Lady Sings the Blues*."

"You don't have to be so nice to me, Mark. It will come back to bite you."

I don't say anything back. She's right again. It will come back on me. But this girl needs a friend to get through the next week, and I finally have my shot with Elise. I'm not blowing it this time because gossip mongers can't keep their noses out of other people's business.

After she took off, I looked for her everywhere, trying to reconnect. She went MIA, a social media ghost. Short of hiring a private detective, which would've just been creepy, she didn't exist anywhere. I mean, I knew she had to live somewhere, work somewhere. I worked up the courage to ask her pops once. *Elise, you'd probably be surprised to learn your dad ripped me a new one.* Doc Manning wasn't known for using the words flying out of his mouth at me that day. No one from Thornbriar could want to know her whereabouts because say, they missed her laugh or her smile. Or her kindness toward just about everyone she met until Logan did what he'd done.

I guess Doc couldn't have known how much I missed those things because she didn't know. I didn't have the guts to tell her when I should've. No point in it, she had Logan from the beginning. And then once she didn't have Logan, I don't suspect she much trusted any of us from around here.

Taking her hand to pull her up, I tug a bit too hard causing her to stumble into my arms. I couldn't have planned that any better if I'd tried. But her being so close, looking down into those eyes one more time, breathing in her uniquely Elise scent, sometimes a man can't help the physical reaction to having a beautiful woman in his arms, especially when that beautiful woman is Elise fucking

Manning. If she notices, she's kind enough not to draw attention to it.

"We can walk from here. It's a nice enough day." As we start to move, I casually adjust myself. "You still like Whippy Dip?"

She stops walking to stare at me. "How do you know I liked the Whippy Dip?"

Well... I reach in my pocket and pull out my pack of Kentucky's Choice, pull another one from the pack, put it up between my lips, cup my hands around the tip, and light the end, taking a long drag and exhaling before I calmly answer. "It's Thornbriar. Everyone likes the Whippy Dip. But you haven't been here in a while. So your tastes might've changed."

She seems to accept this answer and nods as I take another lengthy drag from my cigarette. Shit, that was close. How could I be so stupid to let my guard down this soon? She'll have to remember me eventually. But not now. Not 'til she knows how I feel, how I've always felt.

We get looks from everyone we pass on the way. Hers are for having the nerve to show up back here after all these years. Mine for betraying the town. And the Hollisters. Because heaven forbid someone ruffle those precious Hollister feathers. Don't care if she's the town pariah, I'm a shit-ton bigger than I was back in the day, and I could take on just about anyone then. That's another change. Back when she knew me, I was streamlined muscle. Running back muscle. Started gaining when I took over the bar. Put on twenty-five pounds of bulk because drunks can be unpredictable, and I couldn't afford to hire enough bouncers just starting out. I needed a certain number of bouncers to keep my liquor license. Let's face it, a bar ain't much good without a liquor license.

Still like the girl she always was, Elise don't let those

looks stop her from walking up to the window of the Whippy Dip to order. I knew that girl was still in there, despite how defeated the woman on the outside appears.

We order two Everything Burgers and a large plate of chili cheese fries to share. With so much of our worlds in flux since we were teens, it's nice to see her still get excited over chili cheese fries and an Everything Burger. Of course, even that's changed some. Instead of ordering her usual drink, she tries to order an unsweetened iced tea. Well, I don't think so.

"Vanilla Coke," I order over top of her. Now she really glares at me. Smooth move, again. Getting too excited. Showing my hand too early. *"What?"* I try to play it off. Because for a little thing, she kind of looks scary when she's pissed off. And right now, with me ordering her old favorite, she looks pissed right the hell off. "This is the Whippy Dip. Everyone drinks Vanilla Cokes. Make it two," I tell the girl taking our order, even though I hadn't planned on drinking one. My stupid mouth getting in the way again.

I was actually one of the few who didn't like Vanilla Coke. Don't matter they use the real vanilla syrup and mix them on the spot. But surely she'd remember the guy who didn't like the vanilla. *And Elise, it's far too soon for you to remember, darlin'.*

We move to sit at one of the outdoor picnic tables. She sits across from me so we can talk while we eat. I watch her take a big bite of drippy burger.

She chews on it slowly, clearly lost in thought. "I used to spend a lot of time here with Logan and Beau Hollister. I mean, I guess, everybody. But that first year, Logan and Beau were my world. The way they took me in. I needed them. Especially after my parents' divorce, which had gotten particularly nasty. Then I met those guys and decided to stay here with my dad. She didn't take it well. I'm not sure mom even really wanted me. I think she more just didn't want my dad to have me." She stops speaking to shake her head as if trying to shake away the unpleasant memory.

"Sorry." Elise bites the tip of a fry. As she chews, she double-dips the end back in the cheese sauce. "That was a little heavy for lunch at the Whippy Dip conversation."

"I think you get a pass. It ain't like bein' here's easy for you."

"No. I mean it's hard knowing I don't get to see my dad. That's a regret I'll have to live with for the rest of my life. But this place holds a lot of good memories for me, too. Your bar, Logan used to sneak us in through the backdoor. Then he'd steal whatever bottle was closest to us behind the counter. He and I and few friends would party in the banquet room. Beau did too until he went off to college. It wasn't quite the same once he left. Still, this one time we were so drunk, and it wasn't snowing, but icing out. We wouldn't have made it home. I had the brilliant idea to call Beau to rescue us." She giggles.

God, I love hearing her laugh of any sort. Her giggle, well that shoots straight to my heart. I got the feeling she don't do it near enough anymore. Seems like everything made her giggle back in the day. Now with that little burst of sound, her guards fall. Her guards fall letting me see that I'm right in deciding to pursue this with her. Knowing that happy girl is still inside just confirms it's me who's supposed to help her let go, to bring back that happy all the time.

The woman, she's still too important to me. Five years since I've been in the same room with her, and my heart gets that familiar squeeze. My mind continues to fill with *my* happy, pushing all the other shit out. I wasn't man enough to fight for her then. Damn Hollisters. But I sure as hell am man enough now.

I wanna hear the rest of her story. "Go on," I prod. "You called Beau to come rescue you."

Though instead of answering, she drops the lightheartedness from a moment ago, replaced by a serious expression as she stares over my shoulder. Then just as quickly, she shakes her head again, to clear it like, and continues. "Yeah. And he did. He drove all the way from UK in an ice storm to pick us up." Elise pauses long enough to sip from her straw.

"We had a secret parking spot only about a hundred feet from the bar," she goes on after swallowing. "Logan and I had to walk it. The idiot fell, hitting his ear. It stayed black and blue for a good week. We were frozen icicles when we reached Beau. He had this old orange Chevy pickup. Rusted out fender, wheel wells, and doors. Rustbucket, we called it. But that damn thing ran like a dream. Beau was always so good with his hands. Kept that engine purring like a contented baby kitten. It always surprised me that he opted for UK when I thought he'd be happier at one of the technical colleges learning how to build and fix expensive engines.

"Did you go to college, Mark?"

"For a while. Wasn't really my scene. Old man Galbraith who owned the bar decided to close it and retire at a time when I'd kinda lost my way. So I took my tuition money and bought it from him, cheap. He was a good man. Gave me the downhome discount." Not lying again, I love that she's interested in me, my life. Interested enough to ask questions.

"What about you? Where'd you go to college?"

"Well, I didn't. I mean, I did and I didn't. I—life got pretty hard after Logan and Beau and the town. I found it really hard to be around people for a long time, so I mostly stayed in my apartment and went to school online.

"I worked as a telemarketer for a time, which sucked, but I could do it from home, so I stayed with it until I found something else that allowed me to work from home. Set my own hours, and it paid much better."

"So, what'd you do?"

Elise avoids looking at me, wiping her hands on the napkin and moving the remaining chili fries around on the plate with her fork. "I don't want to tell you," she admits. Then takes another long sip of her Coke.

"C'mon, it can't be that bad. It ain't like you were a sex worker or somethin'."

Right as the words leave my mouth, Elise chokes on her drink. Coughing up liquid. She grabs her napkin again as pop spurts from her mouth and nose. Poor girl, her eyes water.

I jump up to pat her back hard several times so she don't die on me.

Eyes still watering, once she can catch a breath, she answers, "Phone sex operator."

Sputtering, I choke, spitting out *my* pop, spraying the ground because I'm smart enough to twist my head so she don't end up wearing my backwash.

"I'm sorry?" I finally cough out.

"You heard me just fine. Don't make me repeat it, not around here. These people already have a skewed opinion of me."

Right.

I don't want shutting down Elise. I want laughing, giggling Elise back. "Okay, so tell me what happened after Beau picked you up."

Her eyes light up again with her unspoken thank you.

"The Hollister boys—hey, do you see that?" she asks, staring over my shoulder again.

"See what?" I turn to look behind me turning my head left and right, but I don't see anything. "What am I lookin' for?"

"I thought I saw—nothing. I'm just being paranoid." She swats her hand like she's swatting away the idea. "Anyway, as was saying, I'm sure you know, they were big. Beau, a little more than Logan, though not by much. So they squeezed me in the middle of the two of them. Even being as little as I was, it was a tight fit. Beau had this dingy Navajo print seat cover. Between the pattern on the seats, being squished between two Hollister men and the full blasting heat blowing directly on me, because you should know, the rust bucket only had on and off for heat. No turning up or down option. At any rate, all that coupled with my drunken stomach—"

"You puked." I chuckle.

"No. Puke would suggest a normal amount. I erupted. Like, a high-pressure geyser. All over the seat, the dash, Beau and his steering column, Logan, the floor."

She pauses her story to pile her napkins on the burger wrapper, ready to throw them away. I watch mesmerized as she stretches her arms above her head, arching her back, which of course makes me think about other ways to get her back to arch.

"Hey, eyes up here." She laughs as catches me staring. But when she arched her back, her chest pushed forward. And Elise has a fucking fantastic rack. I'm a grown man. Grown men have these thoughts regularly. Don't want her thinking I'm an asshole, though. But, that's how I notice the other customers around us quickly turning their heads away.

Her story had an audience. Minds clamor for a look into her world. What with one Hollister father being the mayor and the other being county commissioner, along with both boys being lords of the football field, a look which included Thornbriar's most fortunate sons.

And cute, petite Elise Manning got the inside scoop firsthand.

"Let's go." I grab up our trash and walk the three steps to the trashcan before she joins me.

"Mark, I'd like to hold your hand. Just while we walk. You have very strong hands. They look like good hands to hold. Would that be okay? I can even explain it to your girlfriend in case it gets back to her, that you were just comforting a friend."

Smooth move, Elise. Shouldn't that be my line? And with more spunk than I gave her credit for. "I don't have a girlfriend."

The little coquette tips her head down, one corner of her mouth up in a playful smirk, watching me out of the corners of her eyes. "You don't?" she asks with an obviously fake innocence.

I shake my head no.

"*Boyfriend?*"

"Don't much care for one of those. No judgment, just not my thing." Her boldness earns her a smile back. "And Elise." I stop to make sure she's looking at me full-on this time. "You can hold my hand any time you want. It's yours to hold so long as you're here."

Replaced is my little coquette from a moment ago. I think I knocked her off her game because she lets out a shaky breath as she nudges at my bicep.

"I don't know why you're being so nice to me, but thank you." The woman does what she wanted to in the first place and links our fingers together.

Her hand feels right in mine. Warm. Soft. We walk back in the direction of her father's house because we'll need to drive out to my bar. We're silent for several minutes before she interrupts the stillness by speaking again.

"Okay, I didn't want to say this while so many ears were listening, but I feel like I should say it now. I'm sure you're tired of hearing about Logan and Beau Hollister. But for some reason, I feel compelled to talk with you." The warm breeze picks up, rustling her hair, sweeping a few of the strands over her cheek. Elise nibbles her bottom lip. "Why do you think that is?" she asks.

"Don't know. Maybe because I'm a bartender. I hear lots of dirty little secrets."

What's hanging between us is how desperately I don't want that to be the reason. Part of me wants nothing more than for her to recognize it, while the other half hopes like hell she don't. Not yet.

And Jesus, the lavender scent from her shampoo is kind of making me dizzy. It a smell that if she were mine, I'd be burying my nose in her hair as I held her close because that ain't the kind of scent you grow tired of.

"What didn't you want anyone else to hear back there?" I shake my head to clear it, slowing our pace to draw out our time together.

"I'm not talking bad about him, so please don't take it like that. But um—Logan was always jealous of Beau."

"What?"

"I know. Cousins—practically brothers—and best friends. But it's true. Logan and I actually broke up for a couple of days because of it."

"*Wow*. What was it about, if you don't mind me askin'?"

"Well, it was the start of our senior year. Beau had already left for UK. He'd been fixing up this sweet Mustang. The thing was a piece of crap when he bought it. Someone had wrecked it. But like I said, get Beau around an engine and magic happened. He restored it to showroom condition. He'd brought it to school with him, storing it at a friend's garage. When he wasn't in class or at football practice, he'd work on it. Already had a buyer lined up and everything. Beau and I talked on the phone all the time back then. He missed me and Logan. I missed him, something fierce. Without anyone Hollister enough to keep him in check, Logan's ego started getting out of control. We were seniors now, after all, and ruled the school anyway." She stops talking to take a breath.

But of all the Logan Hollister lore I've ever heard, this is new, even to me. "Go on." I urge her.

"The week before homecoming—Beau was our standing King and per tradition, as you probably know, would be handing off the crown to the new king, which everyone knew would be Lo.

"Beau had finished the Mustang and wanted to try it before he sold it. Man, it was beautiful. Cherry red. White soft top. I'd never wanted to take a ride as badly as when I saw him roll up with the top down. Without me even having to ask, he held out his hand. I jumped at the opportunity. Logan preferred muscle to speed in his cars. Funny, as he was the quarterback signed to play for UK the following fall. Speed was his job."

"There ain't nothin' like it."

"Right?" She agrees.

"I love the feel of the wind on my face," I tell her, and notice the brief smile which appears and disappears just as quickly.

"Then you can probably picture me plastering myself to his side from the excitement."

Yep. I could absolutely picture it. In detail.

"Logan saw us. He saw us leave. We were gone for a couple of hours, the weather had been perfect that weekend, and the leaves were changing colors. I got to enjoy time with my friend without having to put on a show. Logan loved the show. He wanted everyone to envy us. I just wanted my Lo back. Seems I'd already started losing him." She shrugs. "But he saw us come back, too. And he was pissed. That was the only day I'd ever been scared of him. Thought he might hit me."

"*Sonofabitch*," I murmur.

Her head snaps up to look at me with wide eyes and face drained of color. "Nothing happened between me and Beau," she says quickly. "I'd never have cheated on Logan. I'd never cheat on anyone."

Fuck if she don't think I consider her a cheater like the rest of the town. *Elise, darlin', that sure as shit ain't it.*

"So he broke up with you?"

"Yeah. Which let me tell you, was awkward. We were each other's homecoming date. So we went together as expected, but he was hostile to me the whole time. Only danced with me for the required dances. He was crowned king, and I'd made queen. Since he'd shown up, I spent the majority of the evening dancing with Beau. I just couldn't tell him about me and Lo. I mean, they were cousins. What if he didn't want me around anymore, either?"

"Then Beau took off back to school. He kissed my cheek and took off that night. Lo grabbed my hand and hauled me to his jeep. We ended up at this cabin the families owned off the river on route eight."

"The family still owns it." I offer because, well, she's been gone a while. It might make her feel better to hear the place has yet to leave Hollister hands. "Did he hurt you?"

"What? *No.* Without the audience, he got real lovey, admitted to me how much my friendship with Beau bothered him because it just came so easy with Beau. He was afraid of losing me to his cousin."

"Are you serious?"

"As a stroke."

"I think it's as a heart attack."

"Does it matter? They're both serious."

Touché. "So what happened next?"

Beautiful Elise bites her lip, looking to her feet, her face reddening to almost strawberry. "We um... got back together."

"That's it? Very un-climactic ending to your story." Yeah, I tease her because I gotta hear how this ends.

"It wasn't. Trust me."

We stop at the curb and wait while an old Impala with half its muffler hanging down rumbles by us leaving a trail of thick, black, noxious air for us to choke on. She uses the collar of her shirt as a facemask while we continue on to cross the street, through the smog.

"Then what happened?"

She blows her bangs from her face, exasperated. "I lost my virginity that weekend if you must know."

"But I—I mean everyone thought—"

"I know what they thought. Because we'd been together all of junior year. We'd done other stuff. I just wasn't ready to take that next step. Course, once I let him score the touchdown, it was game on."

"TMI, Elise. T.M.I."

3

ELISE

Though I'm glad to be out walking with Mark, as he's managed to turn what started out as a craptastic day into something tolerable, I can't shake this prickles on the back of my neck feeling. A feeling of being watched.

By who? Who knows? Too many people have grown tired of my presence, despite my only arriving this morning, and would like nothing more than to lay claim to being the hero who ran the *traitorbitchwhore* out of town.

What I do know, I'm here for the week whether they want to run me out of town or not. And I'd like nothing more than to let Mark help me forget, even for a short while, that it's because I have to bury my father. He's the first man I've felt such a strong attraction to since my heart was broken by a Hollister man so many years ago. And not by the one who should have. That ship had sailed. The one part to the story the town actually got right. Although I was never the traitor, bitch or whore the town accused me of being. No one would listen to the truth, no one that is, except for Beau. Too bad we had so many strikes against us.

Too bad the same goes for me and Mark. Poor timing,

poor location. We're a Shakespearian tragedy waiting to happen. He's a Montague and I'm a Capulet.

Maybe he'd be willing to visit me in Chicago. Long distances can work, right? Especially in the face of such an immediate connection. I feel it. He feels it. I see it in the way he looks at me. His eyes convey that same heart stuttering, knees buckling, hard-to-catch-a-breath sensation I've been plagued with since our first meeting. Though, it's more than that. When we talk, when I held his hand for the first time, he brings with him a sense of history aside from the obvious physical attraction. One I really don't understand, but if he were willing, I'd be willing to try too.

Scarily, it's the same kind of connection I'd felt locking eyes with Lo seven years ago, only without the history. Apparently, I'm a sucker for a bad joke. That's when it happened, I connected with him the minute "A duck walked into a bar." Thank goodness Mark's a bartender and not a comedian, or I might never get myself to leave.

Sure, I started dating again, I mean, once I actually began leaving my apartment. But most of those were first dates only. Not because any one of them came to the date with exaggerated quirks. Not a one still lived with his mother, only ate yellow food or owned an abundance of "kitties" he had to run home and tend to. Generally speaking, they were perfectly fine men, just... Sitting through dinner made me feel more like I'd been dining with a distant cousin than a potential mate. Mark's the first man I've met in five years who I've felt like touching, and not in an innocent, 'Welcome to Thanksgiving dinner, Cousin Jackie' kind of way.

I actually never thought I'd entertain the idea of sex again, either. But honestly, if Mark asked me home with him right now, I don't know that I'd turn him down. What does that say about me? Probably that I need to get laid.

As we walk back toward my dad's house, Mark pulls a

smooth, black rock from his pocket. He continues to hold my hand while flipping the rock up in the air and catching it in his other hand on a continuous loop. Or action. Whatever you want to call it, he does it.

"What's with the rock?" I finally venture to ask, tearing my eyes away from the hypnotizing movements.

There's something fun and almost naughty the way he leans into me. "It's my sex rock."

I totally stop walking. A sex rock? I've never heard of a sex rock. "What exactly *is* a sex rock?" I ask in a low voice, ready to be let in on his secret.

With his crooked smile growing, doubling in size, I wait.

The anticipation is just about to kill me when he opens his sexy mouth to speak again. I know I'm about to be let in on something big.

"It's just a fuckin' rock," he says, and he winks at me.

"Asshole!" I shout, drop his hand and stomp off, more upset with myself that I'd fall for something so obviously stupid. But I don't get far as he snags the back of my shirt pulling me to a stop.

"Wait. Wait. I was just teasin' you, darlin'."

"What did you call me?"

"Darlin'. Why?"

It's just a ubiquitous endearment, but being back here, hearing him say that—oh man, my head is messed up.

"Someone used to call me that a long time ago."

"Well, you are quite a darlin'. But if you don't like it, I won't do it again."

"It's fine. You just caught me off guard."

"You still mad at me?" He quivers his bottom lip, fluttering his eyelashes.

"No. But my car's just there." I point to the street where I'd left my car parked while we went to lunch. I wish we hadn't gotten here so soon. "I have to find a hotel before I do anything else. Had been hoping when I rolled into town that Hadley would let me stay with her. She wouldn't even let me in the house, so I really have no choice now."

"Come to the bar when you're checked in."

Mark pulls me closer resting his hands on my upper arms, not a hug but it could be if he shifted those arms just a bit more. His eyes scan my face, watching my eyes anticipating his kiss then they drop to my lips which suddenly become so dry I have no choice but to lick them. Then his gaze drops lower to my chest rising and lowering with slow exaggerated movements mirroring that same anticipation he sees in my eyes. Finally. Finally, he bends his head in a slow descent, and I just know I'm about to get my first kiss in five long years to actually mean something. Look at him, how could a kiss by this man not mean something wonderful?

But then he stops, lips hovering a good five inches from mine, he closes his eyes, swallows hard then shoves back away from me, dropping his hands from my arms and everything. What just happened?

I'm still standing in stunned silence when he clears his throat. "Right..." he starts. "Go find your hotel."

"Finally realize who you're with?" I whisper, angry now for having wanted it so badly and for allowing myself to want in the first place.

The tears forming in the corners of my eyes, they're from dust. And if anyone asks me, that's what I'll tell them. Although nobody is going to ask me because the one person in this town who acted like he cared just shot me down.

"*Elise*," he calls after me as I hurry away, but hell if I'm going to turn around. As much as I'd like him to, he doesn't come after me either.

We both know I won't be at the bar tonight or any other time. Get in, bury my father and get out. That's the plan.

I climb inside my car and wrotely buckle my seatbelt.

Instead of starting the engine, I lean my head on the steering wheel letting those *"dust"* tears unabashedly fall. I haven't even cried this hard over my dead father yet, which makes me cry even harder.

Guilt's a bitch.

The tears for Mark go on for exactly five more minutes. That's as much as I'll allow myself, and wipe my eyes—checking the level of splotches and puffiness in the rearview mirror—then turn the ignition and drive.

This town has exactly two motels. Not hotels. These are motels that haven't been updated since probably the early nineteen sixties. I don't need updated. I'm on a business trip, not a vacation destination.

When I walk into the small lobby of the first motel, I'm greeted with about five seconds of a welcoming smile before the old man behind the desk realizes who just walked into his place of business.

"Hey, Mr. Ritchie. How are you?"

"Elise," he says my name as if choking on a sour lime.

Pretending to ignore his tone I continue on as if he'd welcomed me with a bear hug. "I need a room. Just a single will be fine."

"We're out."

"Okay, I'll take a double, then."

"*Sorry*, we're all full up."

"But the sign out front says vacancy."

"Don't care what the sign says. We're all full up."

Right.

"I get it," I say to him as I turn to leave. I'm not about to fight the man over a damn motel room. It's not worth it, not here.

Over my shoulder, I hear him say, "Your poor father." Mr. Ritchie is team hate-me-for-my-dad. Can't *something* go right for me today?

Of the two motels in town I'd rather stay at the Twilight, but as that's now out my only other choice is the Daniel Boone. I should at least be able to get a room though. They aren't known for being picky about their clientele at the Daniel Boone. It's the kind of place you go if you're having an affair, shooting up, or trying to get your date out of her prom dress.

Forget about being updated, I'm not sure this place has been cleaned since the early nineteen sixties. Located on the outskirts of town, it has two stories with rooms over the lobby in the front and then a row of single-story rooms behind the lobby.

I walk past the crumbling stucco which used to be white, through the door with the frame eaten away by termites. I'm only hoping I don't leave with bed bugs as a souvenir from my time here.

A little bell jingles over the door when I enter. And a big head of brown, curly hair and boobs about a cup smaller than mine but packed tight into a white blouse about a size smaller from them and only buttoned at the fourth button down, hot pink bra showing through along with the cleavage spilling out of it, moves from a back room to behind the desk. That's when I know it doesn't matter if the bed has bugs or not because there's no way I'm getting a room here today.

She sees me before I can make an anonymous escape. "Oh, how the mighty have fallen." She sneers at me. *Sneers.*

I sigh probably my most defeated sigh since arriving back here. "Shayla," I greet her in a forced chirpy tone that doesn't remotely match the '*oh, shit*' sigh I just graced her with.

"You were never good enough for him and because of it, he's dead." Of course, she'd say that since she thought she'd almost had him before that fateful day in front of the Whippy Dip when I met Logan. She'd never almost had him. And he left me well before I ever left him. As for the dead part, what happened to Lo was tragic. But I didn't put the shotgun to his head. I didn't pull the trigger, though arguing that point now is meaningless. For the rest of her life, I'll be the whore who stole and then killed her boyfriend. "We ain't got room."

"Clearly."

She seems upset that I refuse to engage her in confrontation. I know it sounds bad, but she wanted to be me. She wanted the kind of relationship I had with both Logan and Beau. She wanted prom queen and head cheerleader. She wanted nights in the family cabin off the river on route eight.

Maybe there's a small chance that eventually she might have gotten it, all of it, if I hadn't come to town. But I did come to town and now she works the reception desk at the Daniel Boone judging me on things she really has no clue about, based solely on rumors set in motion by an unstable man who was in a bad place in his life. Period.

"You need to walk your stuck-up, whoring ass back outta town."

"I'm leaving as soon as I bury my dad."

"Well... you best leave Beau alone. Caused him enough heartache."

"*Wait*—Beau's in town?"

Shayla shifts on her hip, folding her arms across her chest, eyes narrowed on me. She thinks she's going to intimidate me? Get in line. It forms to the left.

She messed up. She knows it and she's pissed.

Seriously, is this a joke? Is her glare supposed to hurt me? Make me wish I was never born? Jokes on her, I beat her to that punch years ago. Hard to get the blame from an entire town for the death of their one-in-a-million golden boy, Logan Hollister, and all the fallout afterward, and not think everyone's life would've been easier if I'd just never existed.

With the way the town talks, one would think I assassinated the president, not that my ex-boyfriend committed suicide. Though, the ex part he liked to keep under wraps. Apparently *"good girl"* Elise fit better with the highly cultivated façade he wanted to continue to put out for the town, then the cadre of female companionship he chose to surround himself with once he decided to be done with me. All the lies and half-truths flying around, kept in circulation by Margo and Lenore. Lenore had no idea what her son put me through, what he took from me. Then because Beau had my back, I get the reputation.

I don't know, maybe it is my fault. Maybe if I'd seen the signs sooner?

Unfortunately, my name's not George Bailey, and my angel Clarence hasn't come around to set me straight yet. I thought maybe he had with Mark, but what an unfair expectation to put on a man I'd just met. And the way he pushed me away earlier, I was way off base. Or should I say, way off the 'Mark'? It probably isn't really him that gets to me anyway, it's his jokes. I'm a sucker for a sense of humor in a good-looking guy. I love a man who doesn't take himself too seriously. And it's hard to take yourself too seriously when telling lame jokes. Come to think of it, about the time we hit senior year, Lo had stopped telling me jokes. As his girlfriend, shouldn't I have caught on to that?

The standoff between us continues as I wait for Shayla to come to grips with the reality that her body language does nothing to me.

She gives first. "He's been back a few years now. Don't think I'm tellin' *you* where to find him."

"Have a nice life, Shayla." I do my best to keep my head up as I walk out the door.

If Beau's in town, then he knows about my dad, which means he knows *I'm* in town. I would've thought with our history, he'd have reached out to me, tried to get word to me through Hadley or Mr. Delavigne. It doesn't matter how long I've lived away. In a town this size, everybody goes to church or graduated with you, your brother or sister or grandmother or aunt. If he still lives here, he'd know exactly where to go to best get a message to me. Since he hasn't reached out to me, I can only assume he still doesn't want to see me.

That hurts.

He and I were so close once. Hours spent on the phone. His visits home, or mine to Lexington. When everything began to spiral with Logan, he was my shoulder to cry on. My rock. Until he wasn't.

But now there are more immediate concerns for me other than being ignored by Beau. Namely, I have no place to stay until the funeral.

The park across from City Hall used to bring me comfort when my mom hassled me, or Logan and I had a fight. So I head there. It only takes ten minutes to drive from the Daniel Boone, though it feels as if I've been transported back five years, the last time I came here with Beau. The last time I poured my heart out, and he pretended to understand. The last time Logan showed up and Beau stood behind me as I delivered him life-changing news.

THERE'S a heavy pounding on my window and I become acutely aware of the hulking figure looming just outside my door. And it's dark out now, real dark. I fell asleep and now there's a menacing figure pounding on my window. The universe hates me.

Without thinking I reach for the door to make sure it's locked. It's locked. Maybe I won't get murdered in my car.

I chance a side-eyed glance at the perpetrator—you know, in case I have to make an identification. Mark. Mark is the hulking figure standing right outside my window. He's motioning me to roll it down. And like a fool, I do.

The man makes no attempt to talk. Before I register what he's doing, his face is in my face, his lips are on mine. I tense my shoulders expecting with the way he came at me, a hard, passion-filled kiss. But that's not what he gives me. He gives me soft, strong lips, pressing gently. His tongue probing even gentler until I open for him. The taste of him on my tongue is as addicting as exhilarating. I close my eyes, giving in, letting him draw from me, giving it back and drawing from him.

All the sadness in my life melts away and I know it'll stay away if he just keeps kissing me.

The thought of which scares me because we've known each other, what, a day? It just doesn't make sense. Nothing about us makes sense. My arms circle around his neck to bring us closer, to deepen the kiss.

He breaks our connection.

Lacing our fingers together at the back of his neck, he moves them to his chest, pressing our joined hands above his heart. "Been waitin' a long time for that," he breathes, pulling our hands up to press a kiss to them, then moves them back into place.

"You have?"

"Elise, you know I have." And he's right. I know he has because no one would court the wrath of the Hollisters the way he has by simply being seen with me if they didn't have a damn good reason.

"Why you sleepin' in your car? Weren't you supposed to check in at a motel?"

"No vacancy."

"*Damnit.*" Mark leans his forehead against mine, closing his eyes he sighs as if making a decision, then he pulls back and gives my hand he's holding a squeeze. "Come on. You're stayin' with me."

"No." I vehemently shake my head. "You don't need this kind of trouble knocking on your door. Despite that phenomenal kiss or how I'd cut off Shayla's left nipple to experience it again, the fact is I'm not your problem."

"*Shayla's* left nipple?"

I shrug.

At first, he smiles that not quite white, crooked smile almost like he's holding back a laugh, but then his good mood shifts, and he pins me with a mesmerizing raised eyebrow. The challenging kind.

"Darlin'. *Now*. Follow me."

This time I give first.

He pecks the tip of my nose and turns to walk back to a massive, black, Dodge Ram pickup truck. From the streetlamp illuminating the spot he's parked under, he motions for me to start my car.

Two streets over from my dad's house—or I guess only Hadley's house now. Wouldn't you know Mark's place is located three houses down from Beau's parents, George and Margo, and two houses down from Dave and Lenore, Logan's.

It's the only tiny house on the block, nestled between the two massive ones to the left and right, looking like a small child compared to the big, expensive parent houses. He's kept it up nicely from what I can see, but it still looks out of place.

How many times did I walk past this place going to see Logan or Beau? Mark pulls into the drive motioning for me to turn in behind him. I do it, but I don't want to, knowing what he'll face tomorrow from his neighbors. They may not know my car anymore but I have no doubt on who will be the first to identify the Illinois license plate as being mine.

"Pop the boot," he tells me in his Kentucky-ese for "open the trunk."

Mark grabs my bags.

I slowly, hesitantly, climb out. He meets me at the door, the strap of my small red travel bag shrugged over his shoulder, my matching suitcase he picks up to carry, not bothering to extend the handle and wheel it.

Little bungalows like his are rare in this neighborhood anymore. Although they used to be plentiful, peppering every street in town, now buyers would be hard-pressed to find one outside River Street, which is basically the poorest section of the town proper. When the new subdivisions started going in back in the eighties, homeowners abandon tiny with character for cookie-cutter HOAs.

He has a porch when no other house on the block has a porch. Somehow it makes me respect Mark even more for choosing the Charlie Brown Christmas tree of houses.

"What's earnin' me that smile?"

"I like your house."

"Yeah?"

He grabs my hand right as I answer him. "Yeah."

The outside has nothing on the inside. Most guys his age would gut an old house like this. New. New. New. Dark woods. Granite countertops. Stainless steel appliances. But not Mark. The first thing I see are these great built-in shelves filled with books and knick-knacks. Carved arches. Refinished hardwood floors. He hasn't gutted, he's restored.

"I take it back, I'm *in love* with your house," I fawn because really, it deserves a good fawning.

And I think I hear him say, "Well that's a start." This guy... what do I do with him?

When he drops my bags next to the sofa it makes it real that I'm in Mark's house. That I'm staying in Mark's house. I could picture myself spending a lot of time here, despite being in the land of Hollister.

In two steps his hand falls gently on my hip, while with

the other, he tilts my chin up until I'm looking in his eyes. They burn. My belly flutters. Then we're touching mouth to mouth, harder than before but not more urgent. He kisses me as if we have all the time in the world. And he continues to kiss me like there isn't a town full of people wanting to run me out. By the end of the week they'll get their wish, but right now, wearing his lips, it's hard to imagine how fast that day will get here.

"I'm gonna be good." He presses his forehead to mine, lips still brushing mine. "Don't wanna confuse you."

"Think I'm okay with confusion." I'm dizzy, having fallen under his spell. Lustful pants escape me when his mouth slides from my lips slowly up my jaw.

Apparently, I've given the wrong response. He stops the kissing altogether, holding me away from him.

"Not now. Not with this," he says firmly.

I wish my body would listen. Undaunted by rejection, his voice, his touch, the memory of that kiss shoots chills over my fevered skin and I delve back in for round two.

"Elise, darlin', *no*." Neither his voice nor his consternation dampens my libido. They just up my embarrassment.

"You don't want me now," I say really to myself, horrified that I just threw myself at this man. "I'm so sorry. It's been a long time since I've kissed anyone. *Shit*."

I can't look at him. I stoop to pick up my bag, ready to change into my pajamas and sleep the rest of this humiliating night away.

Luck's never on my side. But tonight luck's really not on my side. I try to pull away to make my grand escape, he grips my shirt with both hands keeping me rooted to the spot.

"Look at me." Not a soft request, he outright orders me.

This is so humiliating. Why would I think he'd like kissing me? Logan stopped liking it. He'd kissed a hundred other girls to forget the taste of me. Beau never even tried.

Tears well in my eyes. *Oh my god, I'm a bad kisser.* Am I bad at sex, too? Did Logan fake his orgasms? Can a man fake an orgasm?

"*Elise.* Please look at me."

I shake my head no, keeping my eyes averted, waiting for him to let me go.

"*Fuck.*" He forces my face up. "I want you. I want you more than I've ever wanted anything in my life. But I can't let myself have you 'til you know everything. And it ain't time for you know everything. Couple more days."

"I'll be gone in a couple of days." I remind him.

"Not if this thing growin' between us is meant to be. And I think it's meant to be. Only reason you found yourself in my bar of all places."

"I don't believe in fate, Mark."

"Not talkin' fate. I'm talkin' somethin' which started brewin' between us years ago. You don't remember now, but you will. We got sidetracked back then by Logan Hollister. Not gonna happen again. No more sidetracking. So we gotta wait."

He has no right to bring Logan into this and frankly, it ticks me off. I wrench away from him. He tugs me back, kissing my forehead, then shoves me toward the open bathroom door. With a pat on my behind, he tells me, "Go change for bed."

"Drop the blankets on the couch." I'm still fuming. "And just so you know, I will be gone in a couple of days."

I stomp away.

He laughs.

Jerk.

4

MARK

I hear her leave the bathroom. Just as she asked, I left the blankets on the sofa. What she can't know is how fast I had to be to get them out there before she finished dressing for bed. If I ran into her again, we'd be fucking. Balls-deep, legs over my shoulders, fucking.

Don't want her? I should get a fucking Nobel prize for my restraint.

If not for the town, I'd have thrown down my claim at the bar this morning—especially when Margo Hollister paid me a visit, trying to warn me off of seeing her again. I ain't afraid of Margo or the rest of the town, only that Elise is skittish as a fucking jackrabbit. She'd run and I can't leave. I'm tied here. The only way to keep her seems to be keepin' her at arm's length for the time being.

Five years ago, I let her down. And it ain't like I don't know the shit the townsfolk say. A hundred and one reasons we shouldn't be together, and they all have to do with Logan. Elise needs to see that someone in this town will fight for her. As much as I admired Doc, even he didn't. When she finds out our truth, it's gonna hurt. My only shot is if she feels deep enough for me to see this thing through to the other side where life is good again.

An hour passes with the sound of the damn sofa springs squeaking coming at me, distracting as fuck. The flipping and shuffling front to back, trying to get comfortable. I've slept on that sofa. It's more than comfortable, it's a brown chenille cloud. 'Course, my bed's comfortable, too and I can't stop tossing and turning knowing she's out there instead of in here with me.

Fuck the plan. I pound the mattress then get up to head out to the living room to tuck her in.

Those startling gemstone eyes find me as soon as I step foot inside the living room.

"Can't sleep," she says.

"I know."

"Was I disturbing you?"

"If by disturbing me you mean that I want to fuck you so bad that I'm ready to kill everyone keeping us apart?" I ask back sarcastically. She gasps. "Push up," I order then climb in behind her pressing my back against the back of the sofa so I'm resting on my side. One arm slides under her neck, the other I drape around her waist tucking her in so snug against me, I might actually be breathing for her. Both our heads rest on the pillow.

She don't speak, but shoots me a *'What are we doing?'* look. Hell if I know. I'm winging it now, bending down to kiss her temple. Her nose. Each cheek. Then lightly brush my lips against hers. Yep. I'm a glutton for some seriously damn punishment.

Her tongue darts out as she tries to take the kiss deeper. I shake my head. This is as much as I can give her tonight.

A slight head nod, a sigh, and she closes her eyes. It's starting. She trusts me enough to sleep. Hell yeah, she does.

I follow her in sleep for a few hours, but no matter how

comfortable she had me, snuggled so closely together, the fact is my sofa ain't made for two adult bodies to sleep on. My back rests against the back cushion. My hand, my arm, and even my leg have kept her from spilling onto the floor.

As hard as it is, I extract myself from her warmth and roll her so she lays safely, rolling onto her side. Elise is so beautiful. So innocent. Knees tucked up to her chest. Hands tucked under her chin.

What the hell am I doing? Ass on the arm of the recliner next to the sofa watching her. The longer I watch, the more my resolve begins to slip. Just like earlier, I don't extract myself from the situation, she's getting fucked. Shower. I need a cold shower.

It helps some.

When I leave the bathroom showered and dressed for the day, tying my damp hair back, a noise catches my ear from outside. More than *a* noise. Glass shatters, then tires squeal.

I run out the door barefoot and seeing red. The car and people are gone when I get out to the driveway. Palms pressed to my forehead, I swallow back the shout.

Then there's a soft gasp behind me. Elise heard. Now she sees. Tires slashed, windshield shattered and disgusting words spray-painted in choppy yellow lettering so the whole neighborhood can see them set against the midnight blue of her coupe: Slut. Whore. Traitor.

I turn, capturing her in my arms, trying to shield her from the sight. Although she sags into me, she refuses to look away.

"I'm not a whore," she whispers against my shoulder.

"Let's go inside, darlin'."

"I'm not a whore, Mark," she says again.

"I know, darlin'. I know." This is me she's talking to. I know the truth.

She lets me lead her back inside, phone to my ear. Within minutes the police arrive.

Tommy Doyle walks into my house in an official capacity today. Just a couple of nights ago he was drunk, watching the game with me on my sofa. Been friends for years. Graduated together. Seeing him, *shit,* I panic he's gonna spill my secret. But Tommy was a good friend then and continues to prove himself a good friend now.

Elise sits on the sofa wrapped with the blanket from last night around her shoulders, shaking with the weight of everything that's gone down the past couple of days as he takes our statements.

"Sorry about your dad, Miss Elise." Tommy squats down next to her, placing his hand along the ridge of her shoulder. "This was the last thing you needed."

"So you don't hate me?"

I clench my teeth, fighting back the burn in my chest from how beaten down she sounds.

"Girl, we partied together in high school. I could never hate you."

"Seems you and Mark are the only ones who don't." For a woman who used to show such a strong spirit, she hangs her head low, so fucking defeated.

And it guts me. I'm letting her down again.

Tommy shoots me a confused '*Mark?*' glance. I shake my head slightly. Just enough to keep him from asking the question out loud and at the same time telling him without words, '*We'll talk later.*'

"You know," Elise continues. "They want me out of town so badly, how am I supposed to leave when they've trashed my car? I can't drive home with a smashed windshield or... or..." She takes in a gulping breath and the tears I've been waiting on finally show. "*Slashed tires.*" She actually finishes her thought.

"Wasn't very smart," I offer. Not much else to say.

"Vandalism's never smart," says Tommy. He pats her shoulder, then stands. "Well, I think I got everything I need. Any more trouble, girl, you call me. Got it? You still got friends here. I'm one of 'em. Which." He pauses. "Call Maryanne. She's worried sick about you."

"Maryanne?" Elsie murmurs.

"Maryanne. Buckley. Don't tell me you've forgotten your best girlfriend already?"

"No, no. I haven't forgotten Maryanne. I just... how *is* she?"

"Good, I hope." A smile plays across his face. "And she's a Doyle now."

"You married Maryanne?"

"Almost three years now. I'll tell her to stop by as you wouldn't have her number, come to think of it."

"Tommy, do you think it's safe for her to be seen with me? Mark's already taking such a risk."

"Sweetheart, let me tell you somethin'. I love bein' married. I love goin' to bed at night and wakin' up in the mornin' next to her. So if I plan on stayin' married, which I do, there's no way on God's green earth that I'm keepin' Maryanne Buckley Doyle from comin' to see her long lost best friend."

Tommy bends to kiss Elise's forehead and walks toward me. "*Mark*," he says. "You and me. Beers at Blues while those two catch up."

He wasn't asking. And proving himself today, he's owed an explanation. I nod.

"I'm off by six," he says. "We'll be there by eight." And then he leaves out the door.

"Maryanne married Tommy Doyle," she says. "I never saw it coming. She always wanted Beau. Always."

"But Beau never wanted her, darlin'. Tommy, however, did. And he's a good man."

She blinks at me as if registering what I've said and repeats it. "Good man."

That's it. I feel her shutting down. I refuse to let that happen. "Up. Get dressed. You and me are gettin' away for the day."

"What about the bar?"

"Peaty'll take the mornin' shift. You're more important."

"But... I don't have a car."

"Good thing I have a truck, then."

SHE STANDS at the mouth of the cave contemplating the darkness. Her back to me, hair flowing past her shoulders, a silhouette I've dreamed about just about every night for the past seven years. The cave is beautiful, but nothing in nature can compare to Elise Manning.

She turns to me. "The last time I came here was with Beau." Her back faces me again. "Spring of senior year Logan and I had a huge fight. It was right before, well everything. I needed to get away and like always, Beau came to my rescue. We came here instead of Mammoth because all the tourists go to Mammoth."

That's all she says, reaching her hand back to me, I take it and we begin our descent into Carter caves. The deeper we travel the darker our world becomes. The colder our world becomes.

Elise, on her own, moves from holding my hand to pressing herself to my side where I'm able to slide my arm around her waist. She presses her face to my chest briefly before moving us along again. She moved on her own. She did.

And it's at this point when we're at the deepest, darkest spot in the cave when we're completely without light. When I can't see her face, but can only feel her, she says, "You keep coming to my rescue. Just like him." Then she pauses and I think she's finished so I give her a reassuring squeeze. But she's not finished and what she says floors me. "Don't leave me like he did."

I can hear water dripping. I can hear her breathing. What I can't hear are my own breaths. I think I've stopped altogether. The only way I know I'm still alive is from the feel of my heart pounding out of control against my ribcage. Two days. I've had her back in my life for only two short days, and she feels it again, this thing between us. She feels it again, already.

After taking a beat to find my words, I pull her until she's flush against me, front to front, and have her locked securely with both arms around her.

This is it. Here in the dark, I feel safe to tell her how she's never getting rid of me. How it's always been her and always will be her. Only, she don't let me get it out.

"I'm here for the week. I need your strength until I go home. Please be my strength."

Then she pushes up on her tiptoes using her finger to swipe over my face to find my lips in the darkness and brushes a kiss over them. It's soft and relatively quick, but not remotely satisfying for me. I have to find a way to convince her to stay.

The urge to talk becomes obsolete after that kiss. She's mine. And maybe if I can get the rest of Thornbriar to know it, she'll know it and want to stay. Elise belongs in Thornbriar. And what Thornbriar don't know, they get in my way, try to come between me and her again, they will not like the end result.

If we could only return to living as cave dwellers. Because

being here in this spot with Elise, it feels like we're the only two people left in the world. Yet as has been known to happen, we're interrupted by the world descending down on us.

Chatter of *other* cave dwellers bounce off the cavern walls. Like I said, unwelcome interruptions.

I run my hand down her shoulder, then her arm 'til my fingers lace with hers and I pull her along next to me. As we walk, the light from outside begins to filter in around us giving peeks of stone and stalagmites.

She sucks in a long breath filled with awe when we hit the cave opening. We step outside into a lush wooded area complete with a deep, clear pond, which only became a pond thanks to a fallen tree and beaver damn. It's not quiet here like in the caves, but full of nature sounds, peaceful nature sounds.

With the temperature difference between the caves and the outside, it's like stepping out of a refrigerator right into a damn oven, but the smile on Elise's face never wavers. So neither does mine.

We leave just at the right time. More people have shown up crowding the parking lot and ticket window. The distinct rumble of engines rips through the chatter of people and squawking of birds. Definitely time to go. I usher her by the arm up into my truck. Once I'm in, we take off without looking back.

5

ELISE

"Elise fuckin' Manning! Where the hell you been girl?"

At the sound of her shrill voice, the entire bar turns to look at the tiny figure shadowed against the backdrop of streetlamps pouring into the room as she fills the doorway.

And when I've only managed to stand halfway from my stool, I get tackled by that shadowed figure who moves surprisingly fast for such a little thing.

We both fall to the sticky floor as she squeezes the breath from me. The men's laughter fills the space around us.

"Okay baby," Tommy Doyle says, still laughing. "Don't kill her before the reunion even starts." She's plucked off me and seconds later I'm peeled off the linoleum, pressed into Mark's arms.

He's all crooked smile. Tommy smiles. Then I look to Maryanne. She's even prettier now than she was in high school, if that's possible, because Maryanne Buckley was a freaking knockout in high school. Small, thin, but curved in all the right places. Porcelain skin still flawless. Chocolate brown hair with natural highlights swept over her shoulder in a long, awesome braid, a braid like Elsa from Frozen, if Elsa had chocolate brown hair.

Marriage looks good on her. Of course, Tommy Doyle being her husband, it doesn't surprise me. He was always, always, so nice to us when we were being pains in the asses of the seniors while Maryanne and I were still juniors. And he was hardly hard to look at then or now. Now even more so with that fit, ' I'm a badass cop' physique he's got going on.

Still, despite how good she looks, Maryanne is Maryanne. This means she goes from hollering redneck to crying just that fast. Since I have this rule where no one cries alone in my company, as her pretty brown eyes tear up and spill, so do mine.

"Oh shit," I whisper. "My mascara. I'm gonna look like a raccoon."

Mark presses a kiss to my jaw. He's a touchy-feely guy. And, I don't know, maybe it's because I deprived myself of human contact for so long, but I don't mind it. Being here, surrounded by Mark and my old friends, reminds me of how it felt so many years ago when I first arrived in Thornbriar. Reminds me of what made me want to stay.

Maryanne certainly doesn't mind Mark's PDA, smiling, but she turns up the pressure on her waterworks. "Holy shit!" she cries. "You two really are together... after all this time."

Tommy, still holding Maryanne, kisses her cheek, whispering something in her ear for just the two of them to know. She nods then turns to Mark. "We need drinks."

"Toby," Mark calls out to the bartender working tonight, every bit as bearded and tattooed as Mark, but with big, black gauges in his ears. They look like small drain stoppers, not the open ones. His hair is so brown it's almost black and his eyes, they're equally as dark. Being so ridiculously handsome must be a job requirement to be a bartender.

Toby walks over to us. "What can I get you pretty ladies tonight?" Mark throws a slightly playful, mostly menacing look to his employee. "Anything they want. They both have rides home so let 'em have fun."

"You got it, Bossman."

"My car was trashed this morning by vandals who want me out of town," I tell him for whatever reason. "What do you suggest to take away that sting?"

"Whiskey Sour it is." He grabs a bottle of Maker's Mark from behind him.

"Make it two," Maryanne tells him.

Maryanne and I pull up stools at the bar to sit. I'm rewarded by a kiss from the "bossman" while she's rewarded by a scorcher from Tommy before the men head to the opposite side of the bar. The last I see of him before Maryanne snags my attention is the two of them racking up at the pool table.

Toby knows his way around a Whiskey Sour. I'm happy to be enjoying a drink with an actual friend but apparently, she's done waiting on me to pony up the information.

"I'm serious," she says looking me directly in the eyes so I can see how serious she is. "What the hell happened to you?"

"I left," I say with a shrug.

"You left? That's all you've got for me? We were best friends. You called layin' all that shit in my lap. Then Logan. And you just disappear from my life without a trace. I lost my whole world. You, Logan, and Beau in one fell swoop."

"I'm *sorry*." What else is there to say? We were a Manning, Hollister clusterfuck, but over the past five years, I'd neglected to take into account how many other people we brought down along with us.

"You're sorry?" Her tone hardens as she takes a huge swig of whiskey sour. "I barely survived. If it hadn't been for Tommy, don't think I would have."

"The shit with Logan—the whole town turning on me. Then Beau turned his back on me. I was so lost. My whole world fell apart too, but I didn't have Tommy to fall back on." I want to cry but I'm so angry the tears, they won't fall.

"Did you give it up?" she asks.

Now I can't keep my voice under control.

"Give it up?" I scream at my once best friend, not giving two shits that the entirety of the place sits in engaged silence listening to my freak out. And here I am giving them the gossip. "I didn't give it up. I lost it. *The stress… The stress…*" The anger finally ebbs replaced by the crushing sadness I've been avoiding for years. "I lost my baby," I whisper, falling back, not onto the stool but into Mark's arms. I didn't even hear him come over.

"*Shh…*" His consoling word feathers against my breaking heart. "*Shh…*" he says again.

"I wasn't a whore, Mark. I wasn't. The baby was his. He might not have wanted it, but what his mom said, what his aunt said—Lenore and Margo hated me. But I swear…I swear I'm not a whore."

Some people have a higher tolerance before reaching their breaking point. Some have lower. I'd like to think since it's been five years that I'm the former. Though, higher or lower, I've just about reached mine. He twists me in his arms to full-on hold me with his entire body, warming my soul with his care.

"I'm so sorry I wasn't there for you," he whispers against my neck. "I should've been there. I promise I will never let you down again."

We keep holding on, tuning everyone else in the bar out, for who knows how long. The rest of the world building up and crumbling civilizations around us. Both of us content to remain so, at least in my mind.

"Did you know the toothbrush was invented in

Kentucky?" he asks, out of the blue, and a ninety-degree turn from the last words he'd spoken.

"What? No." I shake my head, wiping away tears with the back of my hand.

"If it were invented anywhere else, it'd be called a teethbrush."

Idiot. I laugh, loud and obtrusive, garnering head turns from people all around us. Mark chuckles around pulling a drink from his longneck. Tommy and Maryanne join in the laughing *and* the drinking, too.

"Should've given you Whiskey Sours years ago," Tommy says, then. "Glad to have the old Elise back."

"Are you, Sgt. Tommy Doyle of the Thornbriar Police Department, condoning underage drinking?"

He shoves my shoulder. "Only when it keeps my wife and my best friend from hurtin'."

WITH ALL THE heaviness behind us and three more Whiskey Sours down, Maryanne and I pivot on our stools barely able to keep ourselves from slipping off, to watch the men deep in a game of pool again.

"I wish I'd been at your wedding." I halfway slur.

"Wish you'd been there, too. I had to ask Tommy's sister Beth to be my maid of horror."

"Don't you mean honor?"

"Not with Beth."

"Oh man, I remember. She was a piece of work."

"You have no idea. She wanted us to have a ceremony right outta the puritan handbook. Should've seen her, I mean her entire face turned purple when I told her I didn't want to wear white because I wasn't a virgin. I kid you not, she fell to her knees and prayed for mine and Tommy's immortal souls."

"How do I even respond?"

"Well I'll tell ya, she went from purple to red when I told her I would not be agreein' to obey Tommy, either."

"Really? She got angry with you?"

"Yeah. Because I told her I'd stop the ceremony then and there if she tried to get the minister to slip it in. And I wouldn't go any further until he retracted it."

"That's my girl." We try to fist bump, totally missing. "Was Mark there? At your wedding?"

"Sure. He… he was the best man."

"How? We never hung out with him in school, did we?"

Maryanne's hand finds my shoulder. "Listen," she says. "What you need to know—" But her words fade, the sound of her voice drowned out by another. This one low, husky, and soulful.

We redirect our gazes to the small stage kitty corner to the pool tables and the gorgeous black woman standing atop it.

"Isn't that Whitley Burgess?" I ask Maryanne.

She only nods as Whitley begins to sing.

"He said I love you…I said 'I do'… I came home from work. What I found was you…

"He said he was sorry…Never again. Stabbed in the back by my husband and closest friend…

"I got the blues… I got those cheater man blues.

"Never again? He got that right. I ain't seen him since that very night.

"My mama, she warned me. My daddy did too. And now I'm stuck nursing my cheater man blues…"

She's sad and glorious, and I could listen to her sing the rest of the night. The live band I'd been too distracted by my

Whiskey Sours to notice setting up accompanies her bluesy riff after bluesy riff.

Her song ends. Right when I think she's about to start another, she steps off the stage allowing someone else to take her spot. When her applause dies down, the next woman begins to sing, although without nearly Whitley's ability to carry a tune. But just because her voice sounds like fingernails scraping a chalkboard, doesn't mean her words are any less heartfelt.

"That's why I called it *Lady Sings the Blues*." Mark found his way to my side again, just as stealthily as before.

"Do only women sing, then?"

"No. Men sing sometimes..." He pauses refectively. "Back then, I was lost. Used to sit here with old man Galbraith, drinkin' my problems away. He's the one who introduced me to Billie Holiday and jazz and the blues. It's sort of taken on a life of its own. Every Friday from nine to close is open mic."

"What kind of bar is it the rest of the time?"

As if taking directions in a play, the glass door opens and about fifteen bikers spill inside. I'm the only one to even blink out of place at the intrusion. Violent thugs are what they really are. How are more people not freaking out about this?

"Mark," I whisper. "There are bikers in your bar." And I tense in his arms as the mostly hairy, leather-clad men saunter up to us.

"Hey Bossman," one of the men, this one not hairy, says to Mark, eyeing the both of us standing so close together. Despite that, he's beautiful and looks as if he should be hanging with California surfer dudes from the neck up. From the neck down he's all biker, and I'm not wholly comfortable with the way he predatorily peruses my body or the way Mark smirks at him in turn. "This her?" he asks.

"Yeah," Mark answers, giving me a squeeze. "This is Elise."

"Tommy. Maryanne." The man nods respectfully to our friends, leaving me dumbstruck that Tommy Doyle, police officer, would be as comfortable as he seems to be with bikers.

"Elise, this is Chaos." Mark introduces us.

"Chaos? Did your mother not love you?"

He and the other men laugh. "It's my ride name. Bossman's birth name isn't Bossman, either." I'm piecing together what he's said when he pretty much crumbles my world with what he says next. "You didn't tell her, did you?"

As his words really sink in, of course, I look to Mark. And from Mark, I look to Chaos, the other men, and back to Mark again. Reality.

"You've got to be shitting me?" I step free from the arms of the man I felt so safe with only moments ago, keeping clear of his friends. "So what? Are you going to threaten me with a knife, too?"

"I—*huh*? Who threatened you with a knife, darlin'?"

"It doesn't matter. But this—" I move my hand between the two of us "—can't happen. Not now. My dad gets buried in three days. Shit, I thought you were one of the good ones. I've watched biker shows; read my share of MC novels. We all know how this ends for *me*." Before he can capture my arm again, I stomp off for the door yelling ridiculously loud, "I cannot *deal* with this."

Yeah, I realize that Mark hasn't been anything but wonderful with me thus far, a real friend, nor does he know about the biker from my childhood. But that incident from so long ago put the fear of God into me, at least where bikers are concerned. There'd been so much blood. A gruesome sight for a six-year-old.

Once outside, able to breathe in the crisp nighttime air

and clear my head, I concede that I probably overreacted. But hey, they aren't called irrational fears for nothing.

As I look around the parking lot, I realize something else. I'm stuck in the middle of nowhere Kentucky without a car, no one will rent me a room, and all my stuff is at Mark 'the lyingsonofa biker's house. Lying by omission is still lying.

This cannot be happening. How did I end up here?

"You're embarrassin' me in front of my club." Predictably, the burly bar owner followed me out. I sigh.

"Don't care," I call back at him over my shoulder while flipping him the bird high in the air. With my mighty salute, I keep walking.

He keeps following.

"Woman, you better stop." His command causes me to pause. But then I remember he's nothing to me and continue moving. "Get back inside." He warns through what sounds like clenched teeth.

"That's really not going to work for me. Luckily, I'm not beholden to you or any man, so I'll carry on my way. Knowing what you are, it's for the best."

"What I am, huh?" From the anger in his voice, maybe that wasn't the best choice of words. "Where will you go?"

"The bus station."

"So you're gonna bail on Maryanne again? Ditch your father's funeral?"

"Maryanne is just as much of a liar as you are and Hadley can handle things. It's her day to shine anyway. My dad was a respectable man. He'd understand."

"Your dad was a respectable man. And he was one of us."

That went too far. I spin around, pointing furiously. "You liar! I *hate* you."

"Wouldn't let *my* old lady get away with this shit," some man not Chaos calls out to Mark, and that's when I realize our entire exchange has been witnessed by a gang of bikers.

"That's it." Mark fishes out what looks like keys from his front pocket and starts for me. I, in turn, take off running away from him. Yet with the way my luck has gone these past five years, he easily overtakes me. First kissing me, and then he flips me up over his shoulder, walking toward his truck to the shouts and catcalls of our audience.

"We're not what you think," he says.

"Mmm… says the asshole carrying me caveman style."

"Looks like someone's old lady's about to be punished," another not Chaos calls out.

"I'm not his old lady," I call back to the congregated mass. "I'm not your old lady," I repeat to Mark directly.

"You are." He slaps my bottom. Actually slaps my bottom to the tune of more biker catcalls, then drops me inside the front seat of his truck. "Get out of this car, and you will be sorry."

What happened to my nice, sensitive Mark who understood me? I think about jumping out when he rounds the truck but the unpredictability of scary biker Mark keeps my stinging bottom planted where he dropped me.

And then he has the nerve to reach for my hand as he drives toward two streets over from my dad's house. I pull away, scooting as far from him and his stupid hand as I can in the small cab. He doesn't talk to me, just laughs, shaking his head. As if any of this is funny?

We pull into his driveway, and he cuts the engine.

"Listen, Elise." Listen? I refuse to listen to anything he has to say, turning my head away from him to look out the window instead. "Fine."

When Mark climbs out of the truck, I hastily lock the doors on him. He hits the unlock on his key fob. I lock it again. We go through this game three more times before he smartens up, putting one hand to the door handle and pressing the unlock with the other, opening the door before I have the chance to lock it again.

I wish he hadn't.

Tossed over his shoulder again, he slams the truck door harder than necessary, walking us up onto his front porch. The Neanderthal still refuses to put me down while unlocking the door. Or once we're inside. My shoes come off as he walks us toward his bedroom. His *bedroom*.

6

MARK

"What are you doing?" she asks when I drop her on the bed. Her voice cracks. How could she be scared of me? *You know I'd never hurt you, Elise. But how could you embarrass me in front of my club?*

I don't answer just yet, pulling an old Easyriders rodeo T-shirt from my drawer, tossing it to her.

She holds it on her lap as I pull my own shirt up over my head. And she still doesn't move to undress when I toe off each boot then let my jeans fall to the carpet, kicking them off to the corner by the laundry hamper.

Enough. "Elise put the T-shirt on or you can sleep naked. Your choice."

That lights a fire under her ass. She slides the shirt on before taking her other clothing off, pulling her shirt through the armhole then dropping her jeans.

"Bra, Elise. It's not good for you to sleep in it."

Then she does that thing I've seen her do before, back in high school. She cocks her eyebrow at me, and I swear, it takes every bit of self-control not to attack her lips.

"Bra, Elise," I order again because when I pull her against me, a barrier is the last thing I want to feel.

"You have no say in my life," she says to me, but says it while pulling her bra out through the arm of the T-shirt again. "So just leave me alone."

"Leave you alone? I've been in love with you since fuckin' high school."

"Yeah. So you say *Mark*— if that's even really your name."

"What the hell is that supposed to mean?"

"I never went to school with a Mark. You're probably that creepy, stalker guy—what's his name?" she snaps her fingers and points at me. "Gary Litman. That it? Trying to get revenge on me because I turned you down, Gary Litman?"

"I *ain't* Gary Litman. I *have* been in love with you since high school. And every man you offended at my bar tonight will be at your father's funeral to pay respects."

"They aren't welcome and neither are you."

"Woman, you're gettin' dangerously close to saying somethin' you can't take back."

"Don't you woman me. I don't want to take it back. I don't need Maryanne or Tommy. I didn't need Logan. I didn't need Beau. So I sure as hell don't need you. You are nothing but a lapse in judgment I plan to rectify as soon as possible."

She's spouted that lip one too many times. She wants me to have her lip, fine. I'll take it. I launch at her.

Elise is surprised but doesn't refuse me as I kiss her with everything in me. My tongue in her mouth. My body pressed to hers. It kills me to do it, but when she starts kissing me back, I pull away. Rolling from her. We're both breathing as heavily as either of us has probably ever breathed in this situation.

"What are you doing?" Honest to god, she sounds like she's on the verge of crying.

"Get under the covers, Elise. I'm tired."

"You don't get to order me around. I'm not your kid, and I'm not your girlfriend."

"You sure as hell ain't my kid. But you are my woman, and you know it. I didn't want this to play out the way it has, but you forced my hand, darlin', with all your judgmental, bratty behavior."

"Don't call me darlin'."

"I will call you darlin', darlin'. Now get over yourself and get some sleep. You got a lotta ass kissin' to do tomorrow."

"I'm not kissing any asses."

"Those're my brothers. You will."

"Yeah. They're *your* brothers, not mine. And I'm out of here the second my father's funeral is over. Y'all will never see me again."

"Y'all?" I laugh at her.

"Okay, so the accent might be rubbing off on me again." She rolls over, turned away from me, tucking her hands under her chin. "Yet another reason to get the hell out of Dodge."

This is getting us nowhere. Dammit, Elise.

"Naw." I run my hands down my face, from forehead to beard, so over this conversation. "Lost you once, not lettin' you go again. What's gonna happen is you're movin' in here with me. I'll put a ring on your finger and eventually, a baby in your belly."

"I'm sorry, could you repeat yourself in English? I don't speak grunting."

I wanna laugh, but can't. "Darlin' you heard me just fine."

"Listen, Mark, if you're that hard up for a woman, why not grunt at Hadley? She has an opening now that Dad's gone. Bet she'd love to be your *old lady*. Especially if she doesn't have to work."

"Turn out the light, Elise."

"Kiss my ass, Mark."

"Tomorrow."

Her head snaps around to look at me. Well, that got her attention.

"And rest assured, when I'm done with you, not only will you be beggin' me for more, but you'll be doin' it while apologizin' to all *my* brothers. Then and only then will I give you more. Now turn the light out, Elise."

What the—it worked? She reaches over flicking off the light. So yeah, I'd say it worked. But the stubborn woman stays rolled on her side putting a whole-body width between us. This is not how I sleep next to my woman.

She don't fight when I grab a handful of T-shirt dragging her across the bed until she's taut against the length of me in full-body contact, spooning us together, and drape my arm around her waist. We end up sharing a pillow just like last night. And again, like last night I've never been more content or comfortable.

Damn her for forcing me to break out the asshole. That ain't who I ever want to be around her. It ain't who I've ever been. But just because I'm not that man don't mean the club ain't full of 'em. And these are my brothers. Men who took me in at my lowest. I respect 'em. I love her and respect them, and she's gonna have to learn to respect 'em too.

Those are the last thoughts in my head as I drift off to sleep.

When I wake, I'm flat on my back with Elise's head resting against my neck. One of her arms slung above our heads while the other rests on my chest. Her fingers flat against my nipple. The best, worst part, she's pressed her crotch flush against my hipbone with her leg bent at the knee, resting on top of mine.

I'm comfortable. I was dreaming. So then why am I up? Then I hear it, why I'm awake now instead of finishing that dream. The knock coming from the front of the house.

Carefully as I can, I peel the gorgeous, sleeping woman off me and walk out to the living room. Someone wants to wake me this early on a Saturday morning when they know my Elise has finally come home, what I ought to do is deliver an ass-whooping so they remember to never make this mistake again. I throw open the door standing in nothing but my boxer briefs.

"George. Margo."

They stare. Stunned briefly. But good ole George, he don't stay stunned for long.

"For God's sake, boy. Put some clothes on."

No one comes to my home and orders me around. I push forward, pulling the door shut behind me so we're all standing on my front porch.

"Is there a reason you've woken me up at seven-thirty on a Saturday when you know I work at a bar?"

"She's in there, isn't she?" Margo bites out, nasty as ever. "The whore. What kind of man are you? Beddin' the whore after what she did to Logan."

"Call her a whore in my presence again, and I guarantee you won't be callin' anyone anything until they remove the wire from your jaw."

"How dare you talk to us this way?"

"How dare you come onto my property talkin' shit about my woman? She couldn't leave even if she wanted to. Her car was busted up all to hell yesterday, which I'm sure you know. But she ain't leavin' anyway, as I prefer my woman to live with me."

"She can't be your woman," George barks. He might be the mayor of the town, but he has no say in my life whatsoever.

"Oh, but she can and she *is*. Elise Manning is asleep in my bed right now. And that's the only place I ever plan on her sleepin' for the rest of my life."

"Did your friendship with Logan mean nothin'? Did he really mean so little to you?" Fuck this. Margo knows nothing.

"I loved Logan like a brother, but he never deserved her and you know it. He screwed up. Now I'm gettin' the life I always wanted but never went after because I *did* love him so much."

Margo gasps. It's because of Elise, she walked up to stand behind me. I feel her. I smell her. "Whore!" Margo shouts.

Then stupid George, stupid, stupid George opens his mouth. "So you goin' to sleep your way through the entire town? How many more boys you gonna screw over by gettin' knocked up?"

It's Elise's turn to gasp. Me, I don't even think, just react, slamming my fist into his jaw. He stumbles backward and down one step before he recovers.

"You will regret that decision," he threatens. The bastard has the nerve to threaten me even as he rubs his jaw, licking at the blood dripping from the corner of his mouth?

"Get off my property," I growl, which is a much nicer reaction than he deserves but I'm trying to calm down. I got a woman needing comfort.

At least he ain't stupid enough to come at me or Elise again. She hangs her head, walking back inside while I watch to make sure they leave.

"Elise," I call out to her, only once I've closed the door. "Elise, darlin'?" She don't respond, but I hear her crying in the bedroom. "What're you doin' baby girl?" I ask when I can clearly see what she's doing. She's getting her stuff together to leave.

"I can't bring this on you."

"It was brought well before today, and they know it. Don't leave me again. Not now. Not after just gettin' you back."

"They'll never stop. Get Beau's parents to show up? The

mayor and his wife ready to run me out of town. A new low even for them. You don't need this in your life. Even if you did turn into a misogynistic caveman last night."

I can't help smiling. She's right about the misogynistic caveman shit, not the not needing her in my life, because I do. Need her in my life. And I always have.

"Come on." I grab the suitcase from her, setting it on the carpet, and take her hand. We do our Fred and Ginger dance move where she matches me step for step only moving backward 'til the backs of her knees hit the bed and she falls onto the mattress.

"What are we doing, Mark?"

"Makin' up."

"But yesterday I hated you."

"That was yesterday. Today's today. And we both know you never hated me, darlin'. That was just stress-induced panic." We weren't gonna go here until she knew everything. But if she leaves me, she never will. "So now I'm gonna help reduce your stress."

"I don't think—"

I cut her off pressing a finger to her lips.

"Shh… thinkin' causes stress. So let's not think, hmm?"

Now's the time to show her why she can't leave me. I plant a knee to the mattress, then lay, covering her with my body, and peel the T-shirt up and off so that I'm looking at the most beautiful woman in the world wearing only her pink satin panties with the black lace.

Sexy. Beauty. Such unimaginable beauty.

This, our first time together, Elise deserves to be worshipped.

With my lips and hands, I begin to show her how much she means to me. With every captured moan I give her a little more of myself. It don't take us long to go from boxer briefs and panties to two naked bodies giving and receiving more pleasure than I've ever known before. Rubbing. Grinding. So much pleasure that when I finally slide inside her and she wraps those legs around me, using her heels to push me deeper in, I almost lose it completely.

She's everything.

She's everything I ever dreamed, hoped, or imagined. And she's all those things because she's mine. We're together. She cares for me. Her body and heart, they remember me even without her mind putting the pieces together yet.

I move, thrusting my hips slow enough to make her beg for more of me without rushing. Not rushing any part of this. But she makes it hard to go slow. I think the build-up while she's crying out for me to let her let go, just might kill me.

"Please, Mark," she begs again. "*Please.*"

Every please, every time she whispers my name, I thrust harder, tattooing myself between her legs with my cock. Beautiful. Sensual. Our noises fill the air. The thick smell of love and lust, and sex surrounds us as I continue to deny her what she so desperately desires. Pumping. Rocking. Touching her every place my hands can reach. Fisting her hair. Her mouth drops open. I take her tongue, swallowing her moans. We fit together. Our bodies mesh in perfect unity.

"Mark," she cries. I lift her knee over my thigh to drive even deeper, harder. "Mark," she cries again, throwing her head back, then impales *herself* on my cock, trying to take me deeper still. *Shit.* Hot. So fucking hot. I grind against her, my heart pounding, hardly taking in a substantial breath. And I feel the moment there's no turning back. My balls draw up tight. *Fuck.*

She claws at my back begging. "Please, Mark. I can't take anymore. I... I..."

That's when I let go, pouring every drop of love I have for the woman inside her. Elise and I find that sweet release together. I take back what I said before. Her face, as she comes, is the sexiest thing I've ever seen. Her arms hold me close, tight to her chest. She wraps her legs around my hips keeping me planted inside her.

"Elise," I whisper. "Open your eyes, darlin'."

She does. Those bright, beautiful eyes stare right into mine. "*Wow*," she says, swallowing. A lump bobbing up and down in her throat. "I... um... I need to apologize to your friends."

That earns her a smile and a kiss as I roll to pull out. "Brothers," I remind her.

"Brothers," she repeats on a hitched breath.

"You know when I told you that last night, I didn't really expect it to work."

We both burst out laughing. I like this. Easy with Elise. Except one minute she's laughing, the next she's as serious as I've ever seen her. "I don't understand this."

"What's to understand, darlin'?"

"*Everything*. It scares me. I'm burying my father on Monday in a town full of people who hate me because of something I had no control over as a teenager. And here you come being a friend to me exactly when I need it, telling me how you loved me in high school. But I can't remember you from high school and then I find out you're sensitive enough to own a blues bar and offer open mic night, but you're part of a biker gang."

She stops to take a breath, and sits up, bent knees, tugging the sheet up around her breasts.

"Despite all this," Elise goes on. "there's this connection between us that I haven't felt in years and I haven't been in town long enough to feel it. I certainly shouldn't be considering asking you if you'd like to try long-distance with me, yet the thought of leaving you behind is kind of freaking me out."

"That all?"

"Isn't that enough?"

Before I tell her what she needs to hear, I wrap her back in my arms where she belongs. Fuck long distance. She's here and she's staying.

"As for buryin' your father, darlin' you're still allowed to be happy, to live your life. It don't make you a bad daughter, and I know your pops would want you to find both peace and happiness. That's all he ever wanted for you." I bend down to kiss her. "And this town, you don't need to leave. Are there some narrow-minded people here? Yes. They still need to figure out their happiness. But there're good people, too. Tommy. Maryanne. Two of the best. You weren't at their weddin', but they'll sure as hell be at ours."

"There you go, saying that again. You really think you're going to marry me?"

"Baby girl, don't think it. *Know* it. I'm not sayin' it'll happen tomorrow, but now that I've had you, you really think I could let you go?"

"You don't have to let me go. We could make it work. Chicago isn't that far."

"*Whatever*," I mutter. "Back to your points. We're a club, not a gang."

"Is there a difference?"

"Fuck yeah, there is. We live with more freedom than most allow themselves, but we don't trade in guns or drugs or flesh."

"Flesh? As in *sex trade*?" Her voice rises, sounding horrified.

Since we're not a part of that shit, I nod. "We're legit. I own the bar where some of the men work. Duke owns the tow company and garage where your car is right now, and Chaos runs the shippin' business. We all own a stake in that."

"You own the bar and a shipping business?"

"How am I supposed to afford a wife and a family someday without work? You wanna live with my parents? That'd be fun." I give her a playful squeeze. "You're in the bedroom screamin' '*Oh, god! Oh, god!*' while they're prayin' for us in the living room with Billy Graham reruns playin' on the TV."

"No. I don't think I'd like that. Will I meet them, your parents?"

"Don't think you'd like that either."

"Okay."

Her face drops. *Shit*. Small town, she's met 'em. Not good people. "Not good people," I say the words out loud then take the opportunity to kiss her cheek. Her eyes turn from sad for herself to sad for me.

I can't take it, clearing my throat. "Back to your points. This is the most important, our connection. Love takes as long as it takes. People put too much pressure on themselves. Honestly, I think the people who insist it takes a long time to develop only believe that because they ain't with the right one yet. They've met someone with checks in all the other correct boxes. So instead of cuttin' that one loose and goin' for the right one, they wait it out, tellin' themselves love is cultivated over time. You might wake up tomorrow morning havin' fallen in love with me. And even if your head don't remember, you've known me a long time."

"How? Why can't you just tell me?"

Not yet. Not 'til she admits she loves me. "Get this," I answer instead of answering her question. "You're mine. I'm yours. I'll give you a good life, I promise."

"When I say I'm scared, I really mean terrified. I gave my heart away once before and look how that turned out," she admits, quietly.

"Darlin' you were young. Didn't know you were givin' it

to the wrong man. He was too young to know he shouldn't take it."

"But you were young then. If I'd have given my heart to you instead of Logan, would you have taken it?"

"Absolutely. Because when I met you, I was old enough to see that you're the right one. Benefit of being older than you and Logan, I guess."

"It doesn't change anything. I'm still heading home after my dad's funeral."

"We'll see," I warn. She smiles through a laugh like she thinks I'm kidding. Kidding, my ass. You will see, Elise.

We make love two more times, once in the bed and once in the shower before we finally make it out of the house. She said she needed to apologize to my brothers and I intend to hold her to that. But not before we stop for breakfast. Crow don't taste nearly as good as steak and eggs.

We stop at *Margie's Homecookin'* for breakfast. Street parking only. I'm glad for Mark to be driving because I could never imagine parallel parking his behemoth truck.

The only reason I know it's called *Margie's Homecookin'* is because of the fancy script painted in the front window. Most people know the place by the big neon sign hanging above the door. The sign simply says, *Eat*.

From the day I moved here to the day I left, I don't know that I realized the diner had an actual name. But what I knew then, I still know now. Margie makes the best blueberry pancakes in the county. Not that Mark would know. What's with men and their steak and eggs? Logan, Beau, and even Tommy—always the steak and eggs.

With strong coffee and light conversation, I begin to let my guard down, thawing somewhat to the town again. That is until Margie herself steps out from the kitchen.

I only have the briefest moment to brace before she calls out, "Elise Manning in my store. Missed you, girl." Not the response I expect from the woman who used to smother Logan and Beau with golden boy attention and comped meals after home games. Highly unfortunate that her greeting calls attention to the other patrons that the *traitorbitchwhore* lurks among them.

"Hi, Margie. Good to see you."

"Hi, Margie. Good to see you?" She repeats. "That's all you got for me after what? Five years? Get your ass up."

I stand. Margie makes her way over to me through the small dining room. Seems we're the entertainment for the other patrons. Seems just like old times, Margie still doesn't care for gossipers.

"Eyes on your own plates," she yells at them while just about squeezing the life out of me. "'Cept for you, baby boy," she says dripping sweetness to my date. "You can stare as long as you want—"

"Mark," he cuts in, which yeah, that seems rather odd.

I can't see the look on her face, but she pauses a beat. "I know who you are. I may be old, but I ain't that old. Been comin' in here his whole life," she mumbles to herself. "Don't think I know his name."

She releases me allowing both of us to slide back into the booth. "How long you in town for?" she asks.

Mark reaches over, grabbing my hand across the table. "I'm countin' on forever."

Margie smiles big enough at him to show all five of her missing teeth. "Bet you are." Miss Margie, she's a cantankerous old broad, and when I say old, she always liked to joke that God created her *then* dirt. Her voice is pure gravel from smoking a pack a day since conception but her heart can hold the whole town. I'd been worried her heart held the town minus one. What was I thinking?

"*Marge*," her husband yells from the pickup window. "We got back up orders."

"Seems my work ain't never done. You stay, you come back. You leavin', you come back first, you hear?"

"Yes, ma'am."

When she's safely back in the kitchen and out of earshot I ask him, "What was that about? The name thing?"

"Looked like she was strugglin' for a second. Ready to head out?"

I nod. The waitress sees me nod and thinks I'm asking for the bill because she walks over to drop it on the table.

"No thanks." Mark waves her away. "We're not stayin' for the drawin'."

She blinks looking ten kinds of uncomfortable, reaching to snatch it back. He stops her hand. "I'm kiddin'," he says, picking it up.

Now I know I had to have known him back in the day because Lo and Beau used to use that exact same line to fluster the waitresses. Tommy said it at the bar just last night.

I open my purse to pull out money when Mark skewers me with a badass man stare that screams, '*Don't you embarrass me by trying to pay.*'

"Mark, I make money," I whisper. "At least let me leave the tip."

"Touch that wallet, I spank that ass, darlin'. You're with me, I pay. Not tryin' to tread on your feminist sensibilities but we got some traditions you'll just have to deal with. I pay on dates; hold the door and I always drive."

"That it?"

"It's a start. I think of more, I'll tell you."

"Why do you always get to drive? I like to drive."

"And you can. When it's just you or you got Maryanne, or eventually the kids."

I purse my lips, uncomfortable with him bringing up our hypothetical children again. "*Again*, why?"

"Because I'm the man in this family."

"I didn't know we *were* a family."

"Didn't I already break this down for you? You movin' in. Ring on your finger. Baby in your belly."

"You know what?" I shake my head. "I can't even... that logic makes no sense. How do I argue with it?"

"You don't. You accept it and move on. These are the rules, baby girl."

"What if I don't want the rules?"

The jerk has the nerve to laugh.

"You want the rules."

I don't know about all that, but I do know I want Mark. "What the hell am I getting myself into?" I mumble to myself.

He chooses to answer me anyway. "A world of happiness, you let it happen."

WE'VE BEEN STANDING outside the clubhouse for a good ten minutes while I continue to stall, internally freaking out. The building looks like it started out life as a commercial garage that probably went out of business because it's located too far outside of town to drive a broken-down car to, even though in reality, it's only two miles out.

The property they've surrounded by a twelve-foot chain-link fence with those white strips weaving through the chain links so no one can see in from the road. Two men, Mark told me are prospects, guard the gate.

Prospects are the young guys who basically get shit on by the full members. Charged with doing everything the full members don't want to do, from cleaning the toilets to going shopping, to guarding the gates, and everything a full member can think of, in-between. At the end of the prospect period, which doesn't have a defined date, but ends once the full members decide he's earned his full membership, he'll get patched in as a full member. Which is exactly what it sounds like. He'll get the big patch on the back of his cut, or, the leather vest he wears to show membership to the club. It's all very official for a group of outlaws.

Once they let us through, I took in how the property has been sectioned off. The clubhouse standing front and center with a large parking area filled with bikes and a few pickup trucks.

To the left, a garage, like of the industrial variety, yet smaller than the initial clubhouse which was probably a former garage. My guess, it must be for personal use because I can't see regular folks venturing inside these gates to find a mechanic.

To the right, several trailers. Some singlewides, some doubles. All look to be well taken care of. The prettiest being a blue doublewide with a white wraparound porch. Flower boxes in full bloom hang off the railings. A paved walkway leads to the clubhouse and the whole thing is heavily landscaped with shrubs and bushes. Mark says that home belongs to the club president.

I'd live there. It reminds me of a grandma's house. The kind of place you'd go to sip tea on that front porch. I'd rather go there than inside to the clubhouse. Not because I'm scared of the men. I'm just not fond of looking stupid.

Now is now. I've put it off long enough.

"Suck it up, darlin'. Time to go."

I sigh. "I know. I just... feel stupid for how I acted last night."

"Which is what you're here to rectify."

On a nod from me, he opens the door. The inside looks

exactly as I suspected an MC clubhouse would look. Peeling, brown-laminate siding covers every inch of wall, darkened by years of smoke. Drop ceiling stained in several places by water damage, or, at least I'm telling myself it's water damage. A neon Budweiser sign hangs next to the pool cues above the pool table directly across the room from the front door. There's an old poker table to the left with ripped and missing sections of green felt. It has four barrel chairs with red vinyl cushions, tucked in around it. To the right of the door is the bar. And on the shelf behind the bar, someone stacked numerous bottles but only with the big four representing: Bourbon (we are in Kentucky), tequila, vodka, and gin.

The very left wall has a newer-looking flat screen, a long, overstuffed black vinyl sofa, and three matching club chairs all in various stages of wear with rips and tears, even some stuffing pulled up. Then finally to the very back of the manly space, there's the mouth to a hallway. I'm not going to lie, the whole place smells of stale smoke, overly fermented alcohol, and years of sex.

"*Bossman.*" He's greeted. I'm ignored. Not that I blame them. Every man I offended last night is in this room, plus some, who I'm sure have heard the story by the unholy glares shooting my way.

"Hey guys," I address the room. Time to man up. They turn to listen but not one says hi back. *Okay, I can do this.* "I acted like a judgmental brat last night." That gets grumbles of agreement. "I was shocked and out of sorts and used that as my excuse to embarrass someone I care deeply about by being rude to all of you. No more excuses. I truly am sorry. And I hope my behavior doesn't reflect poorly on Bossman." Crickets. Not one man reacts to my apology. Okay... I hang my head. "So yeah... that's all I've got."

Mark walks up behind me, giving my arms a squeeze, and pecks a quick kiss on my cheek. "You did great, baby girl."

"I don't know. No one really looks to have forgiven me."

"Give it time."

"Yo Bossman," a man standing behind a bar area calls over to him. "Need anything?"

"Beer."

"How 'bout you, Elise?"

"Does that mean I'm forgiven?" I whisper through the corner of my mouth. Mark smiles his crooked smile at me so I know it's okay to relax and ask, "Cider?"

Pretty soon we're chatting with the man who brought the drinks. He introduces himself as Sly. When I ask why Sly, he tells me because he is. Chaos joins us and I'm introduced for the first time to Duke, the club president.

"Don't much like hearing my men being disrespected, especially in one of our establishments. But I appreciate you coming here today to make it right."

"I'm still really embarrassed by my behavior last night. Apparently, it was stress-induced."

"Bossman never claimed an old lady before either. Seems you're the only one he's ever wanted. Because of that, he warned us yesterday that you got a spitfire personality and aren't accustomed to club life."

Claimed an old lady? Is that what I am? An old lady is the official title for a member's woman. An old lady is fully recognized by the club and is someone not to be messed with. Like a queen to the king. How's that going to work with me living in Chicago?

Still, instead of arguing my point which might lead to more alienation or outright hostility, both things I don't want, especially standing at biker ground zero, I push that thought away for now.

"No, I'm not," I admit. "And I've had a lot on my mind.

Even living in a big city, I've never actually been around a motorcycle club before. Seems there's a lot to learn. Good thing Mark is patient."

"You're inexperience is the only reason we didn't beat the shit outta your man for bringing your trouble into our club."

"You'd really do that? Beat the shit out of him because of me?"

"Actions have consequences," Mark says to me. And he shrugs as if completely unbothered by the idea.

"He claimed you as his woman." Duke attempts to explain. "We don't hit women. So by claiming you, he claimed your punishment."

"But that seems so unfair."

"You rather take a hit? He takes the punishment here, then it's up to him to decide how to punish *you*. But that's between the two 'a you in the privacy of your home."

"I mean no disrespect, but this whole concept of punishment seems... barbaric. We're all adults here. Why can't we talk it out?"

"It's our way."

And I know that's all the answer I'm going to get. If I decide to keep Mark in my life, I'm going to have to get used to these archaic rules.

"Where are all the women?" I chose to change subjects.

"At home or working." Chaos offers. "Old ladies don't usually hang around the clubhouse. Mostly for family days or parties. When we throw parties, pieces come around, too."

"Pieces?"

"Of ass."

"Ah..." *Do not judge. Do not judge. Do not judge.* "Is that the only time *pieces* come around?"

"Nah." Another man, Carver, joins us. "Pieces come around at night or earlier on the weekend whenever they feel like a little action. Most of the men are down to fuck." He shrugs. "Available pussy's available pussy, right?"

"But they aren't girlfriends?"

"They'll take whoever's here."

I whip my head to look at Mark. Pieces will take whoever? Is that what I can expect when I'm back home in Chicago? I'm not judging, but I'm not an open relationship kind of girl. If I don't sleep with other men, it's not a stretch to expect the same courtesy extended to me.

"Don't look at me like that, darlin'. You really think I'd risk us for a piece of ass? I got the woman I want, and I'm not willin' to share. Since you got the man you want, I have to assume the same."

"Mark," I sigh, trying to figure out how best to tell him the truth. "This club life has me so...so... *twisted up*, I'm not sure if I want to kiss you, kick you in the balls or take you into a coat closet and screw your brains out."

The men around us chuckle and, or, low whistle. "Don't have a coat closet, but I got a bed in back," he replies.

"You do?"

"All patched-in members do. A place to crash after a party. Keep the men from drinkin' and drivin'."

"Or getting caught by their old ladies while they're screwing their pieces," I add.

"That too."

I was kidding. He's definitely not kidding. This is all so much to take in. Of course that's when the first few *pieces* trickle in. The door opened to three of the most overtly sexy, sexualized women I've ever encounterd in my life.

"Honestly Mark, how are we going to make long-distance work when you've got all these available women shaking their tits in your face every night? How long are you going to be able to resist?" I know there have to be better old lady candidates for him. More roll with the punches, what happens in the clubhouse stays in the clubhouse. That's not me.

"Excuse us, gentlemen." Mark grabs my hand pulling me along behind him. He sets our empty bottles on the bar and says in response to us leaving, "I have to explain some things to Elise."

"Looks like she's about to get accustomed," Chaos calls out.

Mark drags me down the back hallway. I can't even chance a look around, needing my eyes to stay glued on my feet. Making sure they hit every step so I don't stumble from the way he's hurrying.

He throws open the door to his club space. I expect— I don't know what I expect. A personal man cave, maybe? His room, though, is just that, a room. A bed. No window. A closet. Even somewhat… tidy.

Queen size bed. Not the king he has back at his place. Still, it takes up almost the entirety of the room. Nightstands on both side of the bed and one long six drawer dresser across from the bed appear to be the only furniture to fit.

There's a thin hollow wooden door to the left of the drawers. I know it's hollow from the hole in the center of it just big enough to match a burly man's fist.

"Closet," he says in response to me eyeing the door. Then he tips his chin toward the only other door aside from the one we just came through, at the very back of the room. "Bathroom." Good to know he's got his own bathroom because I wouldn't even want to consider stepping foot in a public toilet in a motorcycle compound. A breeder factory for communicable diseases.

But discussing public MC toilets is not why we came in here and he's being patient. I've noticed over the past few days Mark's patience runs dry pretty quickly.

I look at him, leaning his backside against the edge of the

dresser, his feet crossed at the ankles and his arms crossed over his chest. *Whelp, time to do this.* "Did I embarrass you again out there?" I ask, trying to avoid direct eye contact without looking like I'm avoiding direct eye contact. "Because I really didn't mean to. That's actually the last thing I want."

"No. You didn't embarrass me." His voice grows soft as he snags my shirt with a hooked finger, bringing me to stand toe to toe in front of him. In this awkward stance, my knees have nowhere to go except to press against his thighs. And I fall forward, my cheek to his chest, my arms wrap around his waist to pad the fall. "But what *do* you want?" he asks me in the sexiest voice I've ever heard come from a man aimed at me. Movie star sexy. Smooth and rich. Top shelf bourbon. There's no other way to describe how it sounds, coating my body in delicious decadence.

Standing pressed together, my cheek resting against the name patch on his cut. Breathing in the smell of worn leather, his arms holding me like I matter. It's this moment when I'm able to listen to that flutter in my chest reminding me why after knowing each other for such a short time, why I want to try.

"For you to be happy," I answer, reaching my hand up to caress his jaw, then drag it back down to hold his waist. "That's what I want. But there are so many rules that I'm just not used to or necessarily comfortable with. Maybe your kind of happy and my kind of happy, aren't the same happy."

"*Darlin'*," There it is, that voice again. He snatches my hand, pressing a kiss to the knuckles on two of my fingers. "You're the *only* one. And you don't gotta learn it all in one day. You don't gotta accept them all either. We'll go over them as they come up. You'll tell me the ones you can live with and the ones you absolutely can't. Not won't, though. Can't. Got me?"

I shift my arms from holding him to a full-blown hug. Yes, I hug my biker, and not in a sexy way, either. We'll deal with his luxurious come hither in a minute after I kiss my *"maybe"* onto his cheek.

"What about when we're apart? I don't like to share. That's a can't. I'm serious."

Mark holds my stare as he gently strokes his finger along my collarbone. He muddles my mind when he touches me like that. Which, I'm sure is his goal.

Apparently, he's done talking. The finger strokes are good, but they're nothing compared to the other stuff he unleashes next.

Mark's other stuff is what my father should have warned me about as a teenager. Of course, Logan was still pretty much a boy so it's not really fair to compare, but his stuff can't hold a candle to the stuff Mark lavishes on me. The licks. The nips. Sucking. His fingers finding home inside my panties. Inside me. Rubbing, pressing down.

Um…wow.

Mark's the first man with a beard I've ever been with. I love it. The is hair coarser than on his head, but still soft and tickles everywhere it touches my skin.

I nibble gently on the bulging vein running down the length of his neck. No matter what has or hasn't gone down between us or his club, he wants me. *Me.*

We're not even in the bed. He spins, pinning me up against the wall. Yet another first. I've never been taken against a wall before. I'm aching for him, and at the same time, not sure my legs will hold me.

He touches, caresses. He rubs and grinds.

I'm top-to-toe tingles. The need keeps growing.

Mark just keeps upping his game. I thought what we'd done this morning after George and Margo left was extraterrestrial. The shower, cosmic. But as his kisses intensify, I can't imagine anything better in existence. I can't remember wanting anything more than to feel him inside me again. I think he's about to give it to me. And I'm so ready.

The grinding. *Oh lord*, the grinding. We're both still mostly clothed. Only our shirts gone. All other sensations coming from those miracle-making fingers. And it's so intense to feel him everywhere, expanding my universe. Until I don't.

Mark quits kissing me. "I can't do this," he says with his lips still pressing against mine.

I'm shocked, aching for this to happen. "Did I do something wrong?" I panic.

"No. No baby girl. I just can't do it here. Not with my brothers in the other room."

"I need you," I whine and pant all in one breath.

"That's good to know, darlin'. But I can't bed you in the same bed I've had pieces. This room was single me gettin' off when you were still gone in Chicago."

"But you've already had me."

"In my bed, in my home."

I don't understand what he's saying. He must sense it. "Baby girl, you're the only woman ever shared that bed."

My eyes close while I try to tamp down the ache of need still pulsating through my expanding universe, but the more I replay those words the easier it becomes to extinguish that ache. Or at least to dull and push it into the background as some other sensation, something I'm not ready to fully name pulses to the foreground.

But I certainly can admit something. "You *really do* care for me."

"Been tellin' you this whole time."

"I thought it was just something you said... *I didn't*... Take me to your home, Mark."

"Can't take you to my home. It ain't mine anymore,

darlin'. It's *ours*. I'll take you to *our home*. But you gotta say it first. Out loud, as a promise. I take you there, you're never leavin' me. We're Elise and…"

"*Mark*," I finish for him.

"Right. We're Elise and Mark."

Though I can't make that promise, because Elise is still heading home to Chicago after the funeral.

Did she agree?

She smiled and pressed her lips to mine. But I got so caught up with her loving on me that I didn't follow through. I never actually made her say the words. That kiss, it has to mean yes, don't it? I'm going with yeah because she feels me. She *feels* me. And it's the real me. Even if she hasn't seen me yet, she knows I'm in here. In the room. In her heart. Nothing else matters.

I keep her pinned against the wall where I can really hold her. Elise. My woman. How it should've always been. Without that hiccup of Logan keeping us apart. Seven years ago, when we met her. Then five, when she left us.

Ever since she stepped back into my life, we've been playing this game. I tell her she is my woman, she don't deny it but then some bullshit thing happens and she does, pulling away, distancing herself from me and everyone else who could be real family to her if she'd let us in.

But she came to apologize to my brothers on her own, and she admitted out loud she needs me. She's with me.

Hurdle one successfully jumped. Now for hurdle number two.

She has to hear the truth.

Leaving it out has been hard, but I stand by it was the best decision for the both of us. Slowly... slowly, I'll introduce her to all the truths until we have no more secrets between us.

"You're amazing," she says softly, her voice shaking. And it's all she says. My mouth slides into a stupid, large grin. It's the only movement aside from my rapidly beating heart, which I have no control of, as I just continue to take in all of Elise. Like her smell, it engulfs me. This delicate combination of rose perfume and hints of almond and vanilla body wash, mixed with the Tide she clearly washes her clothes in. She's more than that though, she's more than what I can smell or touch or see or hear. There's so much in this moment for my head to wrap around. For now though, our closeness seems to be enough for her, too.

We've stayed in the room long enough for my brothers to think I've taken her at least a couple of times. I don't care if they know or don't know but I realize she's done it for me.

"Okay, Mark. I think it's safe. We can go now."

"I've loved every minute of holdin' you. But darlin', we could've left any time you wanted."

She smiles again. "I know. And I love that about you. But these are still bikers, and you might not have totally lost face in their eyes, you've misplaced enough of it because of me. If I can help get it back for you, I want to."

"You said you love me."

"No, I said I loved something about you. There's a difference."

"Whatever you need to get you through the day, baby girl." I bend over snatching her blouse from the floor and then plant a long, wet kiss on her open mouth while shoving the shirt in her hands resting at my stomach.

Elise keeps a death-grip on my hand once we make it back into the common. The pieces have all arrived for the evening. I'm not embarrassed by my brothers, but having her witness this scene after what went down in the privacy of my room, it's too soon. I really wish she didn't have to be exposed to this side of the club. Not today.

She stops walking, taking it all in. Duke's on one of the sofas, arms spread wide across the back, his Levi's undone, eyes closed with a contented smile on his face as his regular piece sucks him off.

The look on her face guts me. Not judgmental this time. Pained and uncomfortable. Needing to know what's going through that pretty little head of hers, I squeeze harder on her hand, pulling her out of eyesight of what comes down to a typical Saturday night with us.

Unfortunately, I can't get her out fast enough. We see Chaos in the corner, a relatively new piece—I don't even know her name—stripped buck naked, riding his cock hard in a reverse cowgirl. Her tits bouncing while he pulls a handful of auburn hair to tilt her head back and bites down on the exposed skin like a vampire with his prey.

Chaos catches her staring and winks—the bastard. Although I see her eyes glisten from unshed tears, she don't hightail it like I thought she would but holds her head up higher and flips him a double bird as she struts slowly, confidently out of the club. She keeps up the façade until we reach the truck, and I catch the lip tremble as I help her up and shut the door.

I slide in next to her. "Okay. Out with it. What's goin' on, darlin'?"

"That was you?"

Not gonna lie to her. "It was."

"Those women are so beautiful. I doubt any one of them would take 'no I have an old lady' for an answer."

"So what're you sayin'?"

"I can't be that woman. You're talking rings and babies. All I'm picturing is my man off at the club, screwing some other woman's brains out."

"Do you trust me?"

Elise's face goes cold, expressionless, and she turns away, wrapping her arms protectively around her middle as she watches out her window. "There's a lot of temptation."

"Not what I asked. Do you trust me?" I turn down the radio, then tug on her elbow to get her to respond to me. What she says next is vital to our future together.

"I want to," she says to the window.

"That's not an answer. You're gonna have to figure this out, because baby girl, I already promised you that wouldn't be me. You'll see shit at the club you may not like. That's the life. I thought comin' here today we'd be past all the bullshit judgment."

She whips her head around, face hard, set and ready to fight. "It's not judgment," she bites. "Those women look made for sex." Then, *boom!* The hardness melts in front of my eyes, leaving pain in its wake. "How do I compete with that? I've been with exactly *two men* and you're *one of them*."

Insecurity? It's hard to imagine this beautiful, smart woman feeling the pressure from club pieces. "Darlin', Elise, you got it backward. You're the threat to them, not the other way 'round. Any man in that club would give his left nut to have a woman like you. I've been informed by a few of the brothers that if I don't want you any more to send you along their way."

"Do you think that will be an issue?"

"What?" I snap, feeling a thin stress line form across my brow as I try to figure her out.

"That you won't want me anymore," she replies.

"I've wanted you for seven years and you weren't even around for five of 'em. So what do you think?"

"I think you're a good man, but Lo started out as a good man, too. And one day he woke up deciding I wasn't enough. He went and fucked every woman he could convince out of her pants."

"I'm not Logan and he was no man. Darlin' we've gone over this. No real man does a beautiful, down-to-her-soul good woman as dirty as he did you."

"Mark…" she sighs, pressing her fingers to her forehead. "You know? I don't even know your last name. You're talking about marriage and families, and I don't even know how my hypothetical children's teachers will address me. Ms. Manning?"

"Fuck no. You and the kids will have my last name. One of the rules."

"I'm not arguing. It's just… What if your last name is, I don't know, Galise? My name would be Elise Galise. That's hideous. Or worse, what if your name is Mark Ahome? Then I'd be Elise Ahome. And that's just ridiculous."

What's ridiculous is that she's even considered those names in the first place. Probably one of the dumbest, cutest, funniest things to come out of her mouth, which means I can't help the laugh which bursts from mine. Then I lean over kissing her good and deep.

"Not even a real name," I sputter.

"It could be."

"Well it's not mine, and won't be yours."

"Then tell me."

I grip the steering wheel and sigh. "Woman, I'll tell you when it's time. When it's not time is when we're drivin' down a mountain road, so you can get all crazy and grab the wheel, sendin' us careenin' over a cliff."

"Why are you being so sketchy? What are you trying to hide?"

"I ain't hiding shit. But learnin' my last name'll probably piss you off."

"It's that bad?"

"Might be. Might not be. My strategy is to tell you while we're in bed, and I'm buried deep inside you."

"Because you're worried I'll reject you?"

"Don't think it'll happen. We got too much of a connection already. But a man can't be too careful. I tell you buried to the hilt in that tight pussy of yours, makin' you feel so good, you'll be less likely to act on any ill feelins' toward me."

"That is a brilliant plan. I can assure you, I felt no ill will this morning."

"Good to know."

She graces me with one hell of a flirtatious smirk. "Well okay then."

"So we done with this?" I start the truck, driving us toward the gate.

The prospects have them open, nodding their goodbyes and we've turned onto the road before she answers me.

"For now. I feel it's only fair to inform you that we're seated firmly in relationship limbo until I know everything. And by everything, I mean your last name and why I might not want to be with you. Until then, we'll take it day by day."

What? I had her ready to move. For once I got nothing to say. Can't really blame her. Gonna have to try and convince her.

"But I do have something I'd like to talk with you about," she says.

Good. A distraction. "I'm listenin'."

"How do you feel about me talking with Beau Hollister?" I open my mouth to say something, what, I don't know, but something. Although it wouldn't matter what I say as she beats me to it. "We both know he's going to be at my father's funeral. I haven't talked to him in years. He's avoiding me. We have a lot to discuss."

The cab stays silent while I contemplate how best to answer and she waits patiently.

"You're right, darlin'. You'll definitely be around Beau at your father's funeral, and there's a lot to discuss. I just can't tell you what it means that you'd consider my feelins with all this."

"Well, you seem to have a problem with the Hollisters, too. It's *my* dad's funeral, but... It's about respect, you know?"

"I'm goin' back to Chicago with you. We'll make it a vacation. Time alone. Just you and me, maybe hit the road for a couple of weeks. How's that sound?"

"Like heaven. Which means you've got 'til the end of my father's funeral to come clean."

Her gaze moves from my face to out the window again. Seems wrong to not be touching her after everything we've just discussed. I reach my hand over to squeeze her knee leaving my hand firmly to rest there. Her father's funeral. Don't give me much time. The woman doesn't even glance down but drops her hand on top of mine, lacing our fingers together.

When we get home, I give her knee another quick squeeze. She turns to look this time and I give a slight nod so she knows to stay put. Then I walk around to open the door for her, helping her down.

"You going to kiss me?" she asks.

I think about answering something smart but just go for it instead. Lips pressed to hers, arms resting on that rounded booty, I'm lost completely to the woman of my dreams.

And then it happens again.

Dammit. I forget where we are and that these assholes ain't clued into what's about to come their way if they don't let up. A gotdamn car speeds past us.

"*Whore.*" Someone shouts out. We both turn as water balloons launch through the windows at our feet, splashing everywhere. Soaking our feet and my jeans.

Elise shrieks. Fuck this. I scoop her up bridal style and run her up to the house, setting her down only once I've kicked the door closed behind us.

"It's never going to stop," she says to her feet. "I bought the fantasy. But that's all it is, Mark. A fantasy."

"No. This is real, Elise. *We're* real, and I'm not lettin' you use some stupid teenage prank as an excuse to run because you're scared."

"Of course, I'm scared. What if we go the distance, you think I want *that*" —She points at the front door— "for your life? What about these hypothetical kids? You want them being bullied? I need to go. You need to find someone you won't have to fight an entire town to be happy with."

"*Right.* You tellin' me you had the guts to apologize to a room full of bikers but are just gonna run from some punk-ass kids? That's not the Elise I thought I knew."

"Fuck you."

"Plan on it." And that's all I give her, shoving her up against the wall, my mouth connects with her neck. At the same time, my fingers find the hem of her T-shirt, her fingers fumble to find mine.

It's rough and hard and frenzied as she shoves her shorts and panties down her legs kicking them off once they're past her knees. I drop from her neck to suck dutifully at her pink, pert nipple.

My mouth on her and she completely forgets that she was tryin' to break up with me. Keeping her pinned against the wall, I drop to my knees aligning that perfect pussy with my face, draping her leg over my shoulder to open her up wide for me. She's dripping with desire. Smells of honey nectar. Tastes of it, too. Once my mouth connects with her center, teenagers, water balloons, everything disappears. Just me making the woman I love feel good.

She comes twice with my tongue before I stand, still pinning her against the wall, and slide inside, wrapping both her legs around my waist and her arms around my neck to take the brunt of her weight. While I pound into her, she tilts to meet me thrust for thrust. One hand holds my neck, she moves the other up to tug out the hairband letting my locks spill down to graze the first hand. She grips and musses the thick strands between kisses and moaning my name.

I love the feel of her hand in my hair, but when she drops it, clawing talon marks over my back I lose myself completely.

"Baby..." I pant. "You got... another one... in you... *oh fuck*—now's... the time."

My words in her ear, she clamps down around my pulsating cock and I explode. Thrusting a few more times before dropping my forehead against hers, both of us gulping for air.

We wait until our breathing calms before I pull out, then she drops her feet to the floor on shaky legs. It's not exactly a hardship to have to keep her in my arms a while longer.

"Okay, so maybe we can still make this work," she says to my shoulder, astutely avoiding my eyes.

"'Bout time you caught up." I tip her chin up to keep her from looking anywhere else. "So you're not leavin' me, are you darlin'?"

"What about the town, and Chicago?"

"I'll take care of it. Now *tell me*." I give her a gentle shake. "Tell me what I need to hear."

"*I'm*... we'll make it work."

"Why?" I prod.

"Because there's no denying our connection. No matter it doesn't make any sense. That I haven't been in town long enough to feel this way, I do."

"Good." I smile quick and kiss the tip of her nose. "I'll order us takeout, then we're spendin' the rest of the day in bed talkin' and watchin' movies. And if at any point you want to take advantage of me again, I won't put up a fight. That's a promise."

9

ELISE

W e fell asleep doing exactly what he said we were going to do, lounge in bed, talking mostly about club life and my time in Illinois and how I dealt with the panic attacks, watching movies, and eating pizza. All naked. He wouldn't let me get dressed even if I'd wanted to, which truth be told, I've really enjoyed our day of nakedness.

Mark's a thing of beauty. Tall and strong and his tattoos... I can't even with those tattoos.

As he sleeps, I roll on my side to admire him some more, tracing my finger over the roadmap of ink representing his life. That's when I see the most breathtaking, startling piece of artwork on his body. Small. All black. A literal heart torn in half inked over his heart. The two pieces have been held together, wrapped several times with barbed wire. But the closer I study it, I see it's not just barbed wire holding his heart together, it's me. My name.

My name in barbed wire? Love and pain? Jesus, what do I do with that?

I bend in to press my lips to his tattoo when his cell begins screaming relentlessly. Each of his gorgeous eyes opens one at a time. He smiles at me, then immediately his face drops when he shifts to stare at the phone.

"Talk to me," he answers after picking it up.

While he talks, I kiss. His chest. My name. His Adam's apple. His jaw.

"Mmhmm…" he practically moans into the receiver when I suck his earlobe in between my teeth. "*Fuuuk—*" he groans then and I hear a man's laughter. "Gotta go," he tells the man on the other end and hangs up.

Then he's on me, and he's not fooling around. I go from kissing to coming just that fast. His fingers fondle. His mouth devours. Once I'm liquid in his arms, he rams his thickened cock inside me. I scream. So beautiful. So naughty. My man is hung. Thor's mighty hammer hammering between my thighs. I lose myself as he fills me. We aren't making love. We're hardcore fucking. It's glorious. Exactly what I need to forget my life for a while.

His thrusts. My moans.

"Harder," I beg, and he gives me harder. "Faster," I plead.

He flips me onto my belly, bringing up my knees and spreading them wide. In this position, he fucks me as hard and as fast as I need him to.

"*Ohgodohgodohgod,*" I yell right before I come.

Long and hard.

He holds me once he finishes. I love watching his face as he comes, but it's the aftercare he gives me that sets him apart from lesser men. I'm practically laying on top of him. He drops a kiss to the top of my head. "That was Duke," he sighs.

"I suppose he needs you. Club business?"

He wraps my hair around his hand. "Don't wanna go. Not after this. As much as I love my club, nothin' feels as good as being in bed with you."

"Can't he ask someone else?"

"'Fraid not. You okay here by yourself?"

"Will you be home tonight?"

"You'll be here waitin'?"

"Yes."

"Then damn straight I'll be home. We share a bed. Period. I've always done runs for him. Sometimes we have shippin' issues. But we're gonna have to figure this shit out. I won't stay gone from you."

He won't stay gone from me? Does this mean he's considering relocating closer to home?

"Don't get yourself in trouble on my account."

"Baby girl, I took over for him when his wife got sick, I guess about three years ago now."

"Duke has a wife?"

"*No,*" he says. I get it. I see the pain in his eyes. Far be it for me to make that pain worse.

"Okay baby. You do what you have to do. Don't worry about me." He stares at me. "And quit looking at me like that. I haven't grown horns."

"No. But you called me baby. It's the first time you've used an endearment. I like it." Then he smiles. "And for the record, tellin' me not to worry about you is like tellin' me not to breathe."

"Those might be the sweetest words anyone has ever said to me."

For some reason, his words affect me deeply. I feel so stupid for giving in to the emotions. It's all I can do to escape and I start to roll to get away. The roll gets me nowhere as his arm tightens around me to hold me in place while he silently watches my reaction. The tears just start to collect in the corners of my eyes when he clears his throat.

It's emotion. My tears mean something. "I meant every word, darlin'."

There's a pause as we both continue to watch one another

before he gives my waist an affectionate squeeze and gets up to shower.

I throw on his T-shirt from last night and head to the kitchen. Stupid smile perma-glued across my face. By the time he joins me, there's coffee steaming in his mug and piping hot bacon and eggs just come to rest on his plate.

He rests his hand to my lower back, leaning in to kiss my cheek. "You're makin' it really hard to leave you this mornin'."

"Well, I guess now that I've had your penis inside me, I don't want you to meet some other woman while you're out doing biker things, and forget about me. Not until I know if this is going to last."

"*Elise,*" he says. So many words coming across in just my name. "One of these days you're gonna believe me. I'm doin' this biker shit *for* you. I can afford to take care of you. I'm yours. You're mine. Bossman and Elise. Period. Nobody's ever gettin' in the way of us again."

Except maybe him. But I don't tell him that.

HE LEAVES ME FINALLY. Our goodbye takes far longer and with three more orgasms than either of us mean it to, two for me and one for him. By the time I scream his name again, Duke's left a voicemail telling Mark to, "Quit fuckin' around and get to work."

I know exactly what I need to do today. Where I need to go.

Forest Lawn.

I gather up my courage and walk through the cemetery gates. His parents placed him three rows back in the family plot. I hate cemeteries, and despite how things ended for us, he meant a lot to me. I never got to say goodbye.

Without Mark muddling my brain, the world starts making sense again. He confuses me. Makes me agree to things I'm not sure I should agree to. Mark knew Logan. He knew Beau. Tommy. Maryanne. *Me.*

He's a biker with biker brothers and biker rules. They dole out punishments. They have sex in public. It's not like I'll ever forget the man with the knife. But Mark has been so sweet to me. He genuinely cares for me. I'm so confused.

Maybe if I talk to Lo I'll get a sign or some cosmic insight telling me I'm making the right decisions. I need him to approve of Mark. To tell me that he wants me to be happy.

"Hey Lo," I say, patting headstone. "Sorry it's taken so long for me to get here. But I wanted you to know that even after everything you put me through, I miss you." I pause to collect my thoughts. "Those days with the three of us, you, me and Beau, were some of the best of my life. Oh—this is Elise. I guess I should've opened with that. Not like you have caller ID on that side." I laugh to myself.

"So much has happened over the past five years, I hardly know where to begin. So I guess I'll start with this." I kiss the palm of my hand, laying it reverently back on the rough surface of the monument. "I never stopped loving you. Our love might have changed, but it was still very much there. Even if we weren't together anymore. It didn't have to end the way it did. You can't have shared what we shared and have it leave completely, no matter what you thought."

"Ain't that sweet."

I still. No one is supposed to be here. Slowly, I start to turn but I'm stopped by a calloused hand grabbing my neck from behind, shoving my face roughly against the pocked and grooved surface of the stone.

"What are you doing? Let me go."

"Let you go? Is that any way to treat an admirer, Elise?

Sweet, sweet Elise." He pulls my hair at the nape while keeping my face planted.

"Please don't do this. I'm just here to pay my respects to Lo and bury my dad."

"Butllshit. You're here for more than that, you *Hollister whore*. First Logan, now you're screwing Beau. 'Course everyone knows you were doing that back in high school when you were only supposed to be screwing Logan."

"I never screwed Beau. And I haven't seen him since I've been back in town."

"*Liar.*" He hisses, picking my face up and slamming it into the stone. My vision goes fuzzy for a second. I feel sick.

"I'm not lying," I whimper.

He grinds his erection against my rear. Grinding it and grinding it, making me cry harder.

"I promise." I swallow to keep from vomiting. "My boyfriend's name is Mark."

"*You're lying,*" he barks. "Not even you can be that stupid." He lifts my face, slamming it against the stone again.

"No." I choke on the blood from my nose. "His name is Mark."

"He tell you that? You believe it, you *are* stupid. Let me clue you in to who you been fuckin'. Beau. Marcus. Hollister."

No.

My heart drops. Everything makes sense now, why he's been so nice to me. I've got to give him credit, that's one hell of a revenge plot.

I give up all pretenses of a fight. The man keeps me pinned to the headstone dry humping me. Violating me through my clothing.

"You like that, baby? You Hollister whore."

He doesn't really care if I like it or not. I silently wait it out, my eyes squeezed shut, until he makes a soft grunting noise like he actually got off, he slaps my butt and bends down to kiss my cheek. His whiskers scrape against my neck.

"You tell your man Houdini paid you a visit today. He'll know. Just like he knows he got Logan's sloppy seconds. He tosses your ass aside I'd probably fuck you. Pussy good enough for the princes of Thornbriar must be good pussy."

Houdini lets go of me, and I hear him walk away. I don't even attempt to pick my face up from the headstone for a good five more minutes.

Beau.

It all points to one fact.

I'm an effing idiot.

The joking. The crooked smile. Why he wouldn't tell me his last name. Why George and Margo showed up on his porch. Why everyone looked at me funny each time I called him Mark. How easily we connected. I think that's the worst part, using our past against me. The bun. The beard. The tattoos. The attitude. He went from sexy football jock next door to badass biker.

I can try to convince myself that these are good enough reasons to forget. But they aren't, are they? Five years just is not long enough to forget someone I spent so much time with. But somehow, I did. Call it stress. Call it stupidity. Call it naïveté. I never saw it coming.

My face feels bruised and scraped and wet. I use my shirt to wipe away the wet and it's full of red smudges.

I'm freezing. Shivering down to my bones, even in this bright Kentucky sunshine.

Mark—I mean Beau's street is empty when I walk back, still without my car, and now without a friend. I can't even think about dealing with him right now. Not until I've had the chance to regroup, to form some sort of a game plan to get the hell out of here with as little interaction as possible. After I confront him, that is.

Under normal circumstances, I'd call the police to report my assault. But what good would it do? Tommy Doyle, Maryanne—they were both part of it. Beau even made me feel guilty enough to strut into a biker compound and apologize for being rude. They must be getting a good laugh about that.

While I wait, I pack my bag then move to the bathroom to clean my face up a bit. It looks as bad as it feels, which is pretty rough. He finds me sitting on the bed when he returns home from whatever club business he'd been up to.

"Elise?" He should've been an actor instead of a bartender, what with the way he plays the part of the concerned boyfriend so well. He takes two steps toward me when I hold my hand up to stop him.

"No, Beau. I'm fine."

His face grows hard. He has the fucking nerve to let his face grow hard. "Who told you?" he asks in a voice as hard as his face. What, he's mad at me?

"You're friend, Houdini. After he called me a Hollister whore and held me down while he dry humped me from behind. So, there's that."

"What the fuck?" He squeezes his hands into white-knuckled fists.

Apparently, someone threw a wrench in his plans.

"*Yeah...* you'd think that would be the low point of my day. But no—god, you had me fooled. Got your laugh, didn't you? Sorry to spoil your fun. See the way I figure, you and the rest of the town were really going to let me have it tomorrow, right? Way to put the *fun* in funeral."

"Elise. Stop. You don't know what you're talking about."

"*I trusted you!*" Stupid tears wet my eyes. I hate myself for showing him emotion. "You and your, 'I know what happened,' ha! You sure as hell do. Nice touch getting George and Margo to show up. Standing up for me with them. And

Tommy and Maryanne. I can see Tommy. He was always a good friend to you. But Maryanne? Hell, I guess she always did want you. Are they even really married? Maybe you're screwing her, too."

"*Stop.*"

"Stop? Know what, you're right. I will stop. All this."

I stand from the bed, pick up my suitcase and sling my purse around my shoulders. It takes me a couple of breaths to mentally prepare, but I find the courage to walk past him out of the bedroom. Predictably he follows.

The jackass reaches me as I hit the front door, trapping my shoulders. "Get your hands off me now or I go to the state police and tell them you did this to me." I threaten, lightly touching my face.

"You don't have to do this." He drops his hands at the same time he drops his head.

"No. You didn't have to do this." Opening the door, I step outside with exactly zero ideas of what I'm supposed to do next.

He watches me. I feel him watching as I walk away but don't chance a look back until I'm down off the porch and safely a house away down the sidewalk. Hands crossed over his chest, face as hard as steel, showing no emotion.

How could I let myself fall for his lies? I knew better. This town hates me and I walked right into it.

Five looks over my shoulder later, I find myself ducking behind a large black walnut tree in the park across from the courthouse at the rumble of bike engines taking up the entire street, riding in the direction of Mark, I mean Beau's house. Brimstone Lords, his club's patches visible on all their cuts.

The sight of them heading to *him* has me so upset I almost blow my cover to curse them all *to Hell*. But they are the Brimstone Lords, so they'd probably enjoy the trip.

He wanted to embarrass me. Would I like it? No. But why

did he have to break my heart? It's five years ago all over again. I hardly had any heart left, and he destroyed it.

My eyes. My throat. My lungs start to burn as I know I'm about to lose it. I know I'm about to lose it, and I know I don't want to which means once the street clears, I hump it away from the park, out of the town center, keeping a low profile the three miles it takes me to reach the parking lot behind the funeral home.

What do I have to lose? Nothing. There's literally nothing left for me to lose in this town anymore. I tug on the handle of the back metal door. It actually opens for me to walk inside. The spring on the door strains and snaps back closing me in the foyer at the mouth of a dimly lit hallway.

Situated running perpendicular not parallel to the back door, the first room I come to has a flat stainless-steel table and next to it sits an open cosmetics case. They'll most likely bring my dad in here before his showing in the morning. Lord knows I can't stay here.

The next door I open smells strongly of bleach and has shelves with open bottles of various cleaners, an industrial mop bucket with a couple of mops inside it, leaning against one shelf. Since the place is closed now, I figure they've already cleaned for the night and drop to the floor resting my back on the wall next to the shelf, pulling my earbuds and phone from my purse.

Listening to Vivaldi, trying to calm my nerves, I close my eyes and hope for sleep to find me. I'm tired. My body. My mind and my soul are all more tired than I think I've ever been in my life.

Vivaldi surprisingly does calm me enough to fall asleep despite laying on the cold, hard concrete or knowing I'm surrounded by dead bodies.

Though I don't know how long I'd been out for, I find consciousness again at the sound of a woman crying. Each eye pops open independently, foggy and full of crust. I've woken with a kink in my back, in my neck, and a severe headache.

No one sees me peek out of the closet or move down the hallway to where the crying grows loudest right outside one of the salons. When I poke my head inside, Hadley is crying over my father's body. Her tears, her pain—it's all real.

Seriously, I never thought I'd ever do this but I go to her, taking her in my arms, and just hold on while she grieves the loss of her love.

"What are you doing here?" she asks, wiping her nose with the back of her hand.

"He's my dad." I shrug. "I never hated you, Hadley. I know how much you love him. We never had to be enemies, even when he chose his love for you over me. We never had to be enemies."

She stares as if I'd grown two more heads.

My eyes begin to water. "I'm not staying for the funeral," I whisper, clearing my throat. "You don't need to deal with the town drama today. So, if you don't mind, I'll talk to my dad and be on my way."

"I'll leave you then." She moves to the doorway of the salon without making one comment on the state of my face. At least my dad found it, real, true love.

"Thank you. And Hadley…" She looks at me like it's the first time she's seeing me. "Thank you, you know, for taking care of him."

She blinks, walking then out the door without saying anything in response, leaving me to stand with my dead father.

"Hey dad," I say to him, reaching out my hand, but stop short dropping it to my side because I can't get myself to touch him. He looks like he's sleeping. Clean-shaven. Just like the last time I'd seen him five years ago. Though slightly older. We look alike. The same dusty blonde hair. The same eyes I can't see because his lids are sealed. *God, damn it. How did we get here?*

I have to grip the side of the coffin to stabilize myself and take in a few shuddering breaths to clear my head. I have things to say, and he's going to hear me out. Even if he can't actually hear. "I don't understand why it had to be her or me. You knew why I couldn't come back here. I just don't understand why you couldn't come to me, not once in five years. I lost you the same day I lost Logan and Beau. But I always thought that as long as you were healthy, I wouldn't be alone in the world.

"Never thought I'd lose you in such a freak accident. Made a fool of myself with the town again. Beau this time. So yeah, I really am alone in the world." Finally, tears fall freely for my father, but crying gets you nowhere. "Oh, and I'm considering joining a convent now, too."

Scrubbing my hands down my face, I collect myself. "Love you anyway, dad. Always will." Even though it creeps me out, I complete the reach inside the casket patting his arm before going, wheeling my bag behind me. Because I know if I didn't, I'd regret it for the rest of my life.

When I slip outside the backdoor, Hadley leans against the side of the building smoking, sucking back long nervous drags until she sees me and drops the cigarette, snuffing it out with her toe.

"If you ever need anything, call me, okay Hadley? And I mean it."

She smiles, but it's weak, and nods. "How will you get home? Heard about your car."

"I'll walk until I reach a Greyhound."

"It's too far."

"I'll be fine. You take care now."

But before I can get two steps, Mr. Delavigne stops me.

"That was very sweet of you. Jimmy, my custodian, will drive you to the bus station."

It was very nice, not to mention super helpful, for Mr. Delavigne to have Jimmy drive me to the bus station since the closest stop is the next county over. We see some of the Brimstone Lords out riding, and I can't help wonder if Beau has them out looking for me because the best part of his revenge plot was spoiled. They don't see me. Who would think to look for me in a funeral home van?

I pay for my ticket and board the bus headed for Cincinnati. Once I'm there, I'll grab a ticket for home. It sucks that I'll have to figure out another car. I'd only finished paying that one off two months ago.

Dropping another twenty grand on a new set of wheels is a small price to pay for not having to see Beau Hollister or his club ever again.

Beau... I hate that I can't stop thinking about him. Attacked because of him. My heart broken because of him. I'm the laughing stock of Thornbriar and had to avoid my own father's funeral because of him. Yet the way he held me. Like no time had passed. Like he was still *my* Beau.

Get it out of your head, Elise. He was using you.

Logically I know he was. But when does the heart ever concern itself with logic?

10

MARK A.K.A. BEAU

"Calm down, brother." Chaos orders me as I take another swing at the wall, plowing my fist through the drywall. The third hole I've made in the last five minutes.

"She won't answer her phone. No one could find her yesterday after she left the house. It's like she's fallen off the face of the fuckin' earth, and you want me to calm down? Elise is gone. What if the Horde has her? She told me that son of a bitch Houdini attacked her. He's dead. They're all dead."

Bloodhound and Carver each grab an arm forcing me into a chair.

Duke gets in my face. "I understand yer motives, but you brought this on yerself by not telling her the truth sooner."

"Don't think I know that? It don't matter, none of it matters if they have her. I'll die before I let a Horde touch what's finally mine. My Elise. After all these years."

"Which is why we already got Sneak on it shadowing Rage." Rage, the piece of shit president of the Horde, spends more time getting off and getting high than governing his club. I can't understand an MC prez losing control of his men that way. You ain't got respect, you might as well put a bullet in your own brain, because you'd be of that much use to the club.

"It's Houdini who'd have her."

"If he does, you think the head Horde won't know? Sneak gets wind of anything, we'll set Bloodhound on the scent. We'll find her. Promise, we'll find her."

I drop my head to my hands, elbows to knees, on the verge of breaking down completely. Something I've never done before. Not in front of my brothers, at least, when Duke drops a photograph of Dawna on my lap.

I pick it up, staring at the face that comforted me like a mother when I couldn't turn to my own any longer. She wasn't even a full decade older than me, but she lived and breathed maternal instincts. We were the children—the family she knew she'd never have.

"I ain't good with this soft shit," Duke says. "But do you really think she's worth this reaction?"

"You of all people gonna ask me that?" With the glare I level on him, if my eyes could shoot lasers, he'd be a pile of ash at my feet.

"Seriously? We're gonna compare old ladies here?" Duke pulls a pack of Reds from the front chest pocket of his cut. He puts a cigarette between his lips and hands one off to me before lighting up. "Fill me in," he continues. "'Cuz I ain't seen her do much more than cause trouble."

In the picture still grasped reverently between my fingers Dawna's laughing, hair rustling lightly from a breeze. Her eyes have that familiar twinkle in them, the one she had, even on her deathbed for Duke.

I clear my throat. "This shit's all my fault. I never gave her the chance to prove herself. But you don't know the kind of woman she is."

"Sure *you* do?" he asks. "Doc was a good man, and I

suppose did the best he could, but maybe this is a sign to walk away."

"You didn't know her back then, and you sure as hell ain't been alone with us. Heard the things she's said to me. Dawna was class all the way. Hard and soft exactly when she needed to be. That's my Elise. We spent ten minutes out here while she tortured herself with how to apologize to y'all. I didn't force her to come, she asked to come. She was worried about how her reaction would affect the respect I've built with the brothers.

"After only three days, she was willin' to give us a real shot. Even knowin' she'd have to spend time in a town that hates her." I shake my head slowly, and light up the cigarette Duke gave me. "Sound like a woman not worth my time? I should just walk away from?"

"We'll find her." That's all he says as he pats my shoulder a couple of times then turns to leave the room.

"I need to ride," I tell Chaos, Bloodhound, and Carver. Aside from Duke and Tommy, these are the closest men in the world to me. Brothers among brothers.

"Anywhere in particular, or we just riding?"

"Just me today."

Chaos stabs me in the face with one of his infamous Chaos looks. "Fuck that. State you're in, you're liable to lay your bike down. You go, I go."

"What about Doc's funeral?"

"We'll pay our respects when you're ready. We've got men already over there making sure Elise hasn't shown up."

"She won't."

"Probably not. But we got it covered anyway. And we have two prospects on Hadley's house just in case. So again, we riding anywhere in particular or just riding?"

"Just ridin'."

"Then lead the way, brother."

11

I t's been two weeks. Two long, lonely weeks since I arrived home from Kentucky. I'd spent the first week constantly looking over my shoulder, worrying myself sick that Beau would show up. But those fears quickly abated as I realized the likelihood of him finding me in a city the size of Chicago was next to nil. Especially considering I work from home, so no employer to track, and I sublet my apartment from my landlord whose mother died last year.

Situated halfway between Lake Michigan and Wrigley field, the building sits smack in the middle of a prime real estate market. I got lucky. The apartment stays in her name, so he can keep on claiming those social security checks each month. A small cut to his buddy for falsifying documents and *voila!* I get rent control for keeping my mouth shut. Bureaucracy at its finest. It's not my problem if he's not smart enough to realize that he'd make a killing selling the property. So much more than he collects in those checks every month.

Then there's Maryanne. We'd only spent a few days together, but my time with her reminded me just how much I missed having girlfriends to gab with. What kind of self-respecting woman goes five years without a good-natured gossip fest?

Really, the only woman I know is Livvy. And I haven't even met her in person. She works with me at the phone sex line, and we found out we were both in the same online finance class at DePaul. She's asked me several times to meet up for a drink, but I've closed myself off from people for so long, the thought scares me. Besides, what kind of conversation do you have with a woman you've had a phone sex threesome with? I've sucked her virtual nipple into my mouth. And those threesomes are strictly off the cuff. What if she thinks I really roll that way and that's the reason she wants to meet?

A person's into what they're into. I'm not judging, but that's not *my* scene. At all. Although I did find it exciting when Mark—I mean Beau—slapped my bottom during sex. Or drove me hard against the wall. I liked those. I'm not allowed to think about those. It's time to forget the numerous things I liked sexually or otherwise with that man.

Should I call? I should call. Friends are important. *What's Livvy's number?* Scrolling through my contacts, I stop when I hit her name and press the call button before chickening out. She picks up on the third ring.

"Elise?" I forgot she'd said she programmed my number in her phone. "This is a surprise. Is everything okay?"

"Sure." Now I really feel like a heel for not being nicer. Her concern sounds genuine, nothing concerning hookups. I'm an idiot. "I was actually wondering if you wanted to finally hang out."

"I'd love that. What are you doing tonight? There's this new club, Scepter, if you're into that scene. Or there's this old bar—a real hole in the wall—my brother and I used to hang out in before he moved away. Moe's. It's a dump but the booze is cheap, the people are friendly and they let you get up and sing karaoke if you know the words because it's not a karaoke bar."

"That sounds perfect," I reply, trying really hard for her to pick up on my enthusiasm without sounding too enthused. It's a delicate balance.

"Give me an hour. Will that work?" Livvy asks.

"Sure. But um—how will I know you?"

"I'll be the one with the strawberry blonde hair and a bright yellow tube top," she says.

She gives me the address before we hang up, and I jump into the shower with a smile on my face. The first smile I've smiled in two weeks.

Smokey eyes lined black, thick volumizing mascara. I let my long sandy locks fall wild in loose waves down my back. Why am I putting all this effort in when I'm just going out for drinks with a girlfriend? Maybe I'm hoping as I slide my black tank top on under the cut up to hell black cotton and lace T-shirt which hangs off one shoulder, and the miniest denim miniskirt I've ever worn in my life—a recent retail therapy purchase to help me forget Beau, which ironically looks more biker chick than anything I own—with a slip up each thigh, and my black booties, that maybe I'll meet someone who can help me forget about Beau Hollister, at least for the night.

One thing I have to give Beau credit for, he woke the sex beast which lay dormant all these years. No putting that baby back to sleep.

The cab honks outside my brownstone apartment. A tree-lined street full of small front yards bursting with lush greenery. Less than a ten-minute drive from Wrigley Field. It's safe to walk everywhere from here. Not all areas of the city can claim that.

Twenty minutes later, I'm standing out front of Moe's.

Livvy was right, it's a hole in the wall in a rundown part of town. No trees. No one out walking. Boarded-up condemned buildings pepper the landscape. It's kind of depressing, to be honest. Several bikes sit parked out front. She never told me it's a biker bar.

"You sure you want in there, sweetheart?" The cabby asks, sounding concerned for my safety.

"I'm good," I answer and pay my fare.

"Don't seem right. Nice girl like you should be down at Scepter or someplace."

"I'm meeting a friend here. Thanks for your concern, but I'll be fine."

He nods and drives away once I've closed the door.

Now or never. I step inside Moe's and part the curtain of smoke to get a look around. From the smell assaulting my nose, tobacco isn't the only plant the patrons partake of. Beyond the smoke and alcohol, there's a third layer of atmosphere, a grease layer so thick I feel it coat my skin.

Though dark inside, at least two of the overhead light fixtures hang dangerously by only the cable connecting it to the outlet, I spot her right away. Just as promised, strawberry blonde hair and a bright yellow tube top sits on a stool at the bar. A bar that yeah, is as biker as the movies portray.

More jean and leather-clad men than a girl like me knows what to do with. Twice as many of them as there are women ratio, but those women make themselves count. Bent seductively over pool tables. Rubbing their behinds against the men wrapped around them, helping aim the dart at the dartboards. Giving the green light for a whole lot of bad intentions. Biker babe chic to the max. Yet all I can think about is the chaffing from all that leather. It's a sight to behold. I'm kind of in awe, still, I'm together enough to not let my mouth gape open.

"Livvy?" I call out.

She turns, drink in hand, ice clanking against the glass.

"Elise?"

I smile.

So does she.

"You're *beautiful*." Not that she isn't, because she is, I just totally didn't mean to say it out loud.

She stands and walks over to hug me.

"House rule," Bartender calls. "Hot chicks start going at it, I get to watch."

"Shut up, Rick," Livvy calls back.

"We're not going at anything," I reply. "It's just we've never met in person before. We only know each other from work."

"You both do the phone sex thing?" His voice goes up at the end. What, like a girl like me can't do phone sex? All it takes is a good imagination or the internet when you're stuck for creativity.

"Yes... *yes*... oh yes big boy," I tease in my best oncoming orgasm voice. I notice several men in the bar quit drinking, playing pool, or talking to take notice. My antics earn me a smile from Rick, the bartender.

"You know we're an anomaly, right?" Liv tugs on my hand to get us moving back toward the bar.

I purse my lips, not knowing where she's going with this.

"Most phone sex girls are actually four hundred pound, fifty-five-year-old divorcées with seven kids, five of which have different baby daddies," she says, laughing.

Ah, there it is.

"You've ruined the fantasy forever," Rick tells her. "So—"

"Elise," I tell him.

"Elise," he repeats. "What can I get you to drink?"

"Whiskey sour?"

"I see—man troubles?"

"What makes you say that?"

"Because pretty things like you only order whiskey sours when they're trying to forget. Otherwise, it's Piña Coladas and Daiquiris." He pinches his voice higher to make himself sound like a sorority girl on the last word.

"Well, Rick. You could say I have *men* trouble. I just got back two weeks ago from Kentucky. Had to bury my dad. But I couldn't even stay to do that because of a man I used to know."

He stares blankly at me. And blinks. "I'm sorry to hear that."

"Me too. Thanks, though. Dr. Manning was a real respected member of the community so…"

"That your name, Elise Manning?" After dropping several ice cubes into my glass, he pours a healthy pour of whiskey to start my drink. Then he tops it with lemonade. I guess that makes sense since the other two ingredients are sugar and lemon juice.

"Very same." And I slightly bow my head to complete the introduction.

Rick sets the glass down in front of me where I immediately swipe it from the bar top, swirl the ice around a few times to mix it and then drink the whole thing down at once.

"Another," I cough out. "Come on, Livvy. Let's sing." Grabbing her hand, we jockey from the stools so fast she almost bites it, that is, tumbles over her feet in those ridiculously high, bright yellow espadrilles.

We start off entertaining our fellow bar-goers with a rousing rendition of Aerosmith's "Dream On." Moving next through a couple of Dixie Chicks tunes, "Sin Wagon" and "Goodbye Earl" where instead of singing, "Maryanne and Wanda," I sing, "Maryanne and Elise were the best of friends all through their high school days…" And when it gets to the chorus, of course, it becomes, "'Cuz *Beau* had to die."

Livvy laughs. My words slur as the waitress has been quite attentive. Not one man makes a pass at me.

"What the hell kind of biker bar is this?" I yell at the men after my last song, the female anthem, "I Will Survive." They only stare. "I look hot tonight and not one of you has had the balls to hit on me?"

"You done, Elise?"

Oh no, no, no.

That's so not Bartender Rick.

"Thanks for the call, brother."

This would be when I actually look around at my surroundings and notice what I should've noticed when I first walked in here. All the leather cuts with, you guessed it, Brimstone Lords. Under it, the fiery devil head and an Illinois rocker.

My. Luck. Sucks.

"Time to go home, Elise."

I pretend not to hear him. Pretend not to see him. Liv excuses herself from my side wearing what can only be described as a *"holy shit"* look on her pretty face while I stand shaking my head and wishing A: I had a firearm and B: That I knew how to shoot it.

While pretending not to hear or see him and contemplating firearm use, I turn my attention as a drop-dead gorgeous man, strawberry blond hair and big brown eyes just like Livvy, only he's covered in tattoos and has snakebite piercings and gauges in his ears, walks up to her at the bar. "Good to see you, little sis. I've missed you." The name on his cut says Bloodhound.

Why can I never shake these guys? My one female friend up here has ties to the Lords? The universe hates me. It's official. Hates me. If I've said it once, I'll say it again—

for the one billionth time...

My.

Luck.

Sucks.

"Raif," she practically cries his name. "Is it safe for you to be here?"

"I'm fine, baby girl. Small world."

Well, at least I know she didn't set me up. I could never forgive such a betrayal. Beau still watches me, but with the lull in action, I discretely move to the hallway leading to the bathrooms.

I don't know how much time passes when the door to the restroom swings open, and Beau strides in. "Can't hide from me forever."

"Was just giving you time to drop dead before I went back out there."

"Darlin', I'm beginning to lose patience." He keeps stepping forward until I'm backed against the sink. Grabbing my hips, he sets me on top of the basin, pushing between my knees. "How did you think it was okay to wear this?" He slides his hands up the slits on my thighs, completely changing the subject. "Out without your old man? There are consequences to your actions, Elise."

I'm sorry, what? "Did you hit your head?"

"What?"

"Did. You. Hit. Your. Head? Because there are not consequences for my actions. You're not my *old man*. I'm not your old lady. And I can wear whatever the hell I like, whenever the hell I feel like wearing it."

"Time to go, Elise."

"Then go, Beau."

"Woman, you're tryin' my last nerve."

"Yeah well, I was *tryin'* to get laid," I somewhat slur. "Too bad my one friend has *asshole*iations with the Lords. Guess I should've paid better attention. A mistake I don't intend to make again."

"You need to fuck." Beau turns on his sex voice. "I'll be the one to fuck you." His hand moves, sliding from my thigh to burrow inside my panties. He gently tugs and twists at the light bundle of curls before those magic fingers find my center. And in finding my center, he pushes down and strokes.

My head falls back with a long, exaggerated moan I don't mean to give him.

"That's it, baby girl. Get nice and wet for me," he whispers while using his spare hand to undo his belt and the button on his jeans.

While he's distracted, I strike, kneeing him in the groin as hard as I can. As Beau doubles over cupping his boys, I use the time for my escape. Dashing out of the bathroom I cut back into the kitchen gaining a few odd looks and choice words from the fry cook as it's a very confined space, and head out the back door. The only way my get-away will allow me to get away.

It's not a good neighborhood, but rounding the big, green dumpster carefully, this time making doubly sure not to run into any cuts since I can't seem to trust anyone, and the universe hates me *and* my luck sucks, thankfully I see a bus stopped at a stop and make a run for it.

After paying the fare, I drop down in an empty seat below the window line. We hear yelling and engine rumbles in the distance. The bus driver turns to me and I shrug. I guess that's enough of an answer because he turns back and shifts into drive. *That was close.* Alone again.

"Did you see her?" I roar, stumbling out of the bathroom, still cupping my balls and barely able to stand straight. Jesus my woman packs a bigger fucking punch than I gave her credit for. I didn't even have time to do my pants up.

"She get away again, Bossman?" Bloodhound can hardly contain his laughter as he sits at the bar with his sister, who'd incidentally, known Elise all this time, and I never knew. Bad fucking luck there. She's sexy as hell but doesn't even come close to my woman.

"I don't see anything fuckin' funny about this."

"She ain't the only snapper in the sea," Rick, the bartender, calls out to me.

"Yeah well—she is for me. Which way she go?"

"Elise didn't come out this way," Livvy tells me.

Shit.

"Let's ride, baby girl," Blood says to his sister pulling her by the hand, and we file outside moving toward our bikes. At least we know she's not with the Horde. It's not much to console my burning nuts, but it's something. Damn that woman can be stubborn when she wants to be. Won't hear me out. I've got a side, and I'd like to share it if she ever gives me the chance.

I mount my ride and just scream into the air. "*Uggghhhh!*" Then I crank the engine to life and rollout.

The four of us, Bloodhound, Carver, Chaos, and myself, along with Liv of course, who's straddling her brother's bike, head back to her apartment. She says we can stay as long as we need to.

We rumble up Lake Shore Boulevard to a high-rise condo. Nice digs. Phone sex must pay well. Well enough to get her two parking spaces. Nobody gets two parking spaces on Lake Shore unless you're shelling out big time. We roll into the attached parking garage. Livvy don't even own a car. She says she can get everywhere she needs to go by bus, L train, or taxi. Our four bikes fit in her spots no problem.

A wall of bikers, we're imposing stomping toward the bank of elevators. Even more so we stand filling it. Men and women in business suits or clubwear wave us away as the door slides open for them at each stop. We hear a lot of, "I'll catch the next one."

Apparently, they ain't used to our kind on this side of the city. Becoming more and more impatient at just about everything, I snap. "*Jesus*, How far up do you live?"

"Fifteenth floor," she says casually, completely ignoring the fact I'm being a whiney bitch right now. It's gonna take fucking forever with all the chumps ringing for an elevator. I hold down the door close button, allowing us to bypass all remaining floors.

The whole time I feel Blood's sister study me.

"*What?*" I lash out.

"You're Beau?" she asks, but I don't say anything, and she continues. "As in, ''cuz *Beau* had to *die?*" She sings the lyrics

Elise had changed. Even I have to admit that was pretty clever, if not that funny.

I nod. "But you call me Boss or Bossman. Elise is the only one calls me Beau."

She bites down on her bottom lip.

I watch, and I see Chaos watching for an entirely different reason. I gesture for her to spit it out, whatever she has to say to me to get her to quit with the lip biting because I figure Blood won't be too happy with him if he reads what I'm reading.

"It's just," she continues, "She was so angry—what'd you do?"

"*Liv.*" Blood barks. "You of all people know how this works. Not our business. Not our place to judge."

They'd grown up in this life, their pops a lifer in the Illinois chapter, 'til he was gunned down in a bar fight. Blood took his revenge but had to leave town to keep the blowback from his retaliation from hitting his sister. Found out all this when he prospected with us, came in about six months after me. The same time as Chaos.

"You listen Raif, I'm not in that life anymore. And anyway, I wasn't judging. She's my friend, or she was until your bunch showed up tonight ruining the fun. I'm so glad to see you, I've missed you. But the honest truth is I'm a phone sex girl who grew up in biker culture. I don't have many friends, and if you've just lost me one, I'd like to know why."

"Stay out of it," Blood orders her, and I got to give her credit, she don't cower. Most men cower when Blood gives them an order. "Boss has it handled."

"So then why are *you* here, again? Simply to pay your little sis a social visit after being gone for almost five years?"

"He's my brother," he says as explanation.

"And this is why…" she whispers, shaking her head in disappointment at not just him, but all of us.

When the bell chimes the fifteenth floor, I let up from the door close button, and they slide open.

She pushes past us digging around for her keys in her purse. She finds them once we've stopped outside her door.

"Your keys should already be out and in your hand," Chaos snaps. "Any fucker could catch you off guard. You gonna live in the city, Liv, you need to remember. To be smart."

"Wow. Thanks, Dad. Because I haven't been on my own for years now."

"I sure as hell ain't your dad, but I'm more than willing to spank that ass," says Chaos.

"*Brother*," Blood warns. He keeps his hands at his side, calmly walking inside.

"What? I'm just telling it like it is. You show up to the party, expect party favors."

"*Women…*" Blood shakes his head, disapproval radiating off him. "We wouldn't even be here if Boss could remember that pussy tastes the same no matter where you get it." Says the man who's exclusively fucked one woman for years now.

I can't help laugh. "Right, brother. Hannah's pussy not tastin' so sweet now?" Blood narrows his eyes on me. He gets my point. "I'll do anything I have to, to keep Elise with me, safe," I say to shut this line of conversation down permanently. "I gotta jump through hoops to get there—so be it. It won't last long. She'll get it. And when she gets it, we can move on to the parts I'm ready to move on to."

"You will never find me jumping through hoops for some bitch," he says. "I'm happy to fuck a hot mama until I die or my dick falls off."

Whatever's stunting him with Hannah, she's never been *just* a hot mama. Not from the day we rescued her from that trucker.

"Careful, Blood," I warn.

At the same time, Liv says, "Nice, Raif." And stares down her brother through hard pissed-off eyes.

Carver hasn't spoken this whole time. Chaos continues to watch Liv. Damn sure hope he thinks with the head on his neck and not the one on his cock. That's Blood's sister. Screwing over a brother for a piece of ass—even if she's as pretty as Livvy—you just don't. Period.

She flicks on the light then locks the door behind us after we've all filed inside. The place looks right out of the nineteen sixties, the walls are white but with color blocks of brown, orange, and green. And the chick seems to have a thing for mushrooms. They're everywhere. Painted on the walls. Ceramic knick-knacks. A flower vase. A rug.

But her view kills, an entire wall of windows looking out over Lake Michigan.

"There's beer in the fridge if you want a drink." She gestures to the kitchen. "Help yourself to any food. I have a spare bedroom, the sofa and love seat pulls out into sleepers. But I'm afraid two of you will have to spoon, or someone ends up on the floor. I'll get blankets."

"She's my sister, so I get a bed," Blood says.

"Calm your tits, brother," says Chaos. "I'll take the floor. Carver's been quiet this whole time, so we aren't denying him, and we're here to keep Boss out of prison if he doesn't bed his lady again soon. Just remember who's the bigger man here."

Back from the spare bedroom, Liv drops an armful of blankets and pillows onto the floor in front of the windows.

We stay up drinking beers and stuffing our faces full of nachos Chaos made from fixings he found in her fridge and the pantry. I've seen that look she's giving him before. It's the look that says she can't believe he can cook, that she's clearly underestimated what the brothers are capable of.

Yes, we like to party and we like to fuck, but we're more

than that. 'Course, I know from talking with Blood, those ain't the kind of men she'd've ever seen growing up.

About three o'clock in the morning Liv stands, stretches, and announces she's going to bed. Carver and Blood immediately start pulling out sofa beds, Chaos grabs a pillow and blanket, laying it flat over a white shag throw rug nearest the hallway, which leaves me the spare room.

I sit at the edge of the bed, pulling off my boots and stripping off my cut, T-shirt, and jeans, then slide underneath the covers. I wish I could sleep, but dammit, just thinking about fingering Elise earlier this evening has me rock hard and ready. She won't get away from me again. Hell, the woman will be lucky if I don't bend her over my bike and fuck her in front of my brothers for putting me through this.

There's rustling in the next room, then I hear through the thin walls. "Chaos, what are you doing?"

Dammit brother, don't be stupid.

"I'll be good, Liv." He sighs. "I just want to hold you tonight."

"But my brother—he's right out there."

"Said I just want to hold you. Promise I won't try anything."

"Heard that before," she answers sadly. "I'm not eighteen anymore, Chaos."

"Neither am I, Liv. And when it's just you and me, you call me Gage."

Oh, fuck. He didn't just say that.

"Why?" she asks. "It won't make a difference now just like it didn't then. I gave you your one night."

"Maybe one night with you wasn't enough."

"It's going to have to be. You of all people know why. I'm not spending my life as a club whore."

"Have me or Blood or any of the brothers ever treated you like a piece of ass?"

"*Yes*," she hissed. "when you fucked me when I was eighteen, and I never heard from you again. And don't even get me started on Blood."

"Blood loves you."

"He talks to me like our father did. *His* mom was old lady, *mine* was club whore. Half the time I wasn't even sure why the fat fuck acknowledged me as his daughter. That man didn't give two shits about me. I work phone sex because I'm good at it, and it pays the bills while I'm in school. But I'm not that girl, despite who my mother was. That was her, *not me*, and you won't drag down into that life."

"Didn't know you felt that way about the club."

"Yes, you did, *Chaos*. Of anybody, *you did*."

There's a long pause in the conversation, long enough for me to readjust and close my eyes, hoping to finally get some shuteye. Unfortunately, Chaos ain't done.

"Best not be saying that shit around Elise. You have your opinions, that's fine."

"Yeah? When is it fine for a woman, a piece no less, to have an opinion in the club? I won't say anything, though. My opinion on club life, that's a fight for the two of them. She'll see. Or maybe she won't, she's an old lady. She matters."

Liv is right. She does matter.

"Night, Liv," Chaos says softly.

I see where she's coming from. If I'd been raised in her shoes, as the kid of a whore and not the kid of an old lady like her brother, I guess I'd have animosity toward the brothers, too. But what's most interesting is what she dismissed.

When it's just the two of them, Chaos wants her to call him Gage, his given name. There's only one reason for that. The same reason Elise is the only one to call me Beau. Got a feeling a shitstorm's about to unleash onto the club. Looks like Chaos and I need to have a talk.

13

I turn down my street with a plastic bag in each hand seeing as I had to walk to the grocery store since I still haven't figured out the car situation yet.

Chili sounded good for dinner tonight. There are warm-weather foods and there are cold-weather foods. Chili though, chili can and should be enjoyed year-round. And even if I'm the only one to enjoy it, I make a delicious chili. Hands down. Garnishes of Fritos, shredded cheddar cheese, sour cream, and chopped avocado. My chili could break a mama's heart, it's so good.

But as I reach the neighbor's lawn all thoughts of chili vanish what with watching the moving van in front of my brownstone and the men loading it up with furniture. Furniture they've hauled by trampling over my newly planted summer flowers. I spent hours painstakingly plotting colors and positions to give the most aesthetic view from the street. And now the flowerbed is ruined. All that hard work down the drain.

Then every time one of the men knocks something heavy,

a credenza or dining table, against the antique brick siding, my heart breaks a little more.

Vinnie is actually moving? Vinnie, my landlord who owns the building now.

It doesn't click with me, seeing all that's going on around me that the sofa being loaded into the van looks like my sofa.

"Vinnie?" I call out. "You're moving?"

"No darlin', you're moving home."

Beau.

"Oh, come on!" I shout, just now noticing the cuts where mover logos should be. "You let them in my house?"

Vinnie looks at me, completely un-remorseful. "When bikers show up on my lawn insisting I let them in or face bodily harm, I do it, sweetheart."

"Beau, this is insanity. You can't break into my home."

"This ain't your home, darlin'. I've decided your home's in Thornbriar, *with me.*" He emphasizes by poking his thumb to his chest. "So now I'm moving you home."

No one is listening to me. They just keep loading my life into the back of a U-Haul.

"How'd you even find me?"

"How you think he got the name Bloodhound?" he asks smugly, pointing to one of the men moving my dresser.

I press my hand to my forehead, swallowing, trying to calm myself when Chaos walks out of the apartment carrying a small box in one hand. In the other, he flicks on— "Do you have my vibrator?"

"Kinky little thing, aren't you? No wonder Boss wants you so badly."

He holds that particular vibrator against his cheek. "I wouldn't put your face against that one," I warn him.

"Yeah, why not?"

"Because it doesn't go in the hole you think it does."

A couple of strangled laughs come from the guys who get it right away.

Chaos cocks his head and stares blankly at me, a look to say he *doesn't* follow. And then I see it when my words click. A big smile spreads across his gorgeous face and he calls out. "Boss, I think I'm in love with your old lady."

"Watch yourself," Beau grumbles at the same time I shout, "I'm not his old lady."

"Here we go again." Chaos sighs, shaking his head.

"I'm not kidding. I've been avoiding you, Beau. When will you get it through that thick head of yours? I'm not your old lady. I'm not moving. I don't like you anymore."

"Maybe not, but you love me."

Love him? When did I say I loved him? I might have loved Beau *years ago*, but this new Beau, we had *a connection*. That's all. Right? I couldn't have been falling in love with him again. No. It's too ridiculous to contemplate.

None of that matters now, anyhow. His arrogance needs to be taken down a notch. "No. That was *Mark*," I say snidely.

The men stop moving furniture to stare at me.

"Elise, we've been over this. You got shit to say to me, you say it in private. We don't air out our laundry in public."

"Well *Beau*, since you're too stupid to clue in that I won't be going anywhere with you in private, public will have to do."

"*Dammit, woman*," he grumbles. "You got this?" he calls to someone I don't see because I turn to walk away. Total rookie move on my part. Never turn your back on the enemy, which in my case, happens to be six-plus feet, two hundred pounds of solid muscled angry biker. Basic battle strategy. Yet I do and find myself being flung, once again, over Beau's shoulder.

I, of course, start kicking and screaming, pounding on his back and ass. Rock hard ass. *Focus, Elise. You're being kidnapped.*

He slaps my bottom. Hard. "*Ouch!*"

I scream even louder.

"Tried doin' it the easy way. You apparently get off on doin' it hard, so I'll give you all the hard you can handle."

"Beau, put me down, *now*."

To my surprise, he does. He drops me on the back of his bike. Despite bikers freaking me out most of my life, I've kind of always wanted to ride on a bike. Just to see what all the fuss is about.

"This is nice," I whisper. Forgetting for the moment to be upset.

"Well, so you know, you're the only woman to ever ride with me."

That's actually really sweet.

"Thing is," he goes on, "I take ridin' as seriously as breathin'. Other brothers might not be the same, but for me, only my old lady rides on the back. *Only* my old lady. *Ever*. And Elise, that's you, darlin'. Always been you."

That's really very sweet, too. But, "I'm *not* your old lady, Beau."

"God, Elise." He kicks back the stand while starting the engine, revving a couple of times before taking off. I have no choice but to hold on, although I hold on to the edges of his cut instead of putting my arms around his waist and try to keep my thighs from pressing against him.

Part of me begins to melt into the sensation of his powerfully strong body molded taut against me while vibrating lightly from the powerful engine beneath us. It's too easy to melt around Beau if I let my guard down. We tend to get pretty melty around each other. And I know some would say melty is good. But some would be wrong, way wrong, and this would be why I have to fight the melty, to get my guard up fully in place.

He doesn't want me, he wants his revenge, and I'll be

damned if I'm just going to turn over, or in this case, melt, and give it to him. And with this last thought in my head, I realize the opportune moment I've been given when we slow for a traffic light, and I click that guard back up and lock it down.

"*You're a liar, Beau.*" I leap from the back, pretty much surprising the both of us, and take off running in a full-blown sprint toward an escape. Checking every so often over my shoulder to gauge how far away I've run.

My feet beat hard against the pavement, and I wish I had worn better shoes because I feel every step in my shins.

Soon I've lost sight of him completely and turn down another busy street. Cars speed and weave past me with horns honking in warning, as I try not to end up roadkill. Another opportunity presents itself. There's a random pickup truck sitting at a stoplight. I jump into the cab right as it begins to pull away from the red light just turned green.

"Please *go*." Panting heavy, I cry at the driver, slapping his dashboard with several rapid open-handed slaps in the universal gesture for hurry. "I was kidnapped."

But he doesn't go. Well he does, but only so far as to pull off into a McDonald's parking lot, locking the doors and he leans forward to fish his phone from the center console.

"She's here," he says to someone on the other end.

What have I gotten myself into now?

"No, she just jumped into my truck...Will do."

He hangs up and not a minute later the rumble of a Harley engine echoes behind us. I look out the side of the truck to see Beau dismounting his bike and walking up.

That's when I turn back to the driver, for the first time it clicking what's in front of me. The cut, he's wearing a cut. Big patch across the back says: PROSPECT.

Worst. Luck. Ever.

"What can I do to get you not to open that door?" I beg,

bringing out the big puppy dog eyes, trembling lip and hands curled into a prayer position at my chest.

Apparently, the man has no heart. He stays quiet, craning his neck to blast me with a Beau-esque glare that says: *Ridiculous woman.* If that look is a prerequisite to join a motorcycle club, or what everyone shortens to MC, then he's well on his way to getting patched in.

I lean into his body space, brushing my breasts against his arm, tickling his ear with my moist lips. "I'll do anything for you to not open that door." I use the same deep, sexy, throaty voice that I used on my clients.

No reaction.

"Please," I whisper.

Still no reaction. Okay, new plan. "I've got money. You could get yourself a kick-ass Harley."

And yet still, this guy won't even shoot me a glance. I only have one thing left to offer. "Free home-cooked meals for a year. Let me tell you, I'm a great cook. You don't want to pass this up."

He finally gives a reaction. Rolling his eyes, he asks, "And how would I collect on that?"

Okay, so he has a point. But aren't bikers supposed to be, like, morally dubious? Couldn't he take me up on one of my *other* offers?

Panicking, I try again, taking this conversation full circle. "I'm really good at sex. Promise—I'll rock your world." I mean, he's not exactly hard on the eyes, he could probably show a girl a good time—*what am I saying?* I don't want to sleep with this guy, I just really don't want him unlocking the door for an even more pissed-off-looking Beau.

So what does the prospect do? He unlocks the door for an even more pissed-off-looking Beau.

"*Traitor*," I hiss while being lifted out of the front seat and flung, yet again, over Beau's shoulder. Caveman.

"My patience has officially run out," he growls, dropping me hard on the back of his bike. "Try that stunt again, Elise, see what you get. You understand me?" When I don't answer he tilts my chin up. "I asked you a question. Do you *understand* me?"

"*Yes.*"

"Good." He kisses me then. And it's powerful, filled with a million different feelings and sensations. The melty kind. I hate him for making me want him again.

When he pulls back from the kiss, he shoves a helmet down over my head and climbs on the bike in front of me. But before we take off, he slides me forward so all of me is pressed up against all of him, and pulls my arms to wrap around his waist to hold on tight.

Frantically, I turn my head to the left and right, hoping to find an escape. That's when I spy him, a man on a bike. Dark sunglasses covering the top half of his face, and a black bandana printed with the bottom half of a skull, covering up the bottom. I've seen him before, at Lady's. The black leather cut means he's a biker.

He's probably a Lord. But I don't like the way he watches us. It's unnerving.

"Beau." I tap his shoulder. "Who's that guy?"

"Not now, Elise. I'm pissed."

That doesn't stop me. I keep tapping until he looks. "What guy?" he asks.

No guy, now. He's gone. *Poof!* Gone.

"I'm not kidding. There was a guy on a bike."

"Darlin', there's guys on bikes all over."

WHY DOES Beau have to have such good genes? Handsome. Sexy. Imposing. Confidant.

We hit the highway almost immediately. He really doesn't want to risk me hopping off again.

He doesn't talk to me. Doesn't even attempt to talk. We drive. The wind on my face feels freeing. The high is better than *almost* anything I've experienced with Beau. We drive until my hands cramp from holding on so tightly and I need him to pull over. Somewhere in Indiana.

"*Beau*," I shout as loudly as I can through the wind rattling and the pipes rumbling all around us. "Beau, I'm so cold and hungry."

He points to a highway sign: Food and Lodging Next Exit. We've been on the road for a few hours now, both of us using the opportunity to calm down. It shouldn't feel so good to be pressed against him, not after the way he betrayed me. Yet it does. Our connection constantly humming beneath my skin.

Considering I can't get rid of him, I use my time wisely, comparing old Beau to new Beau. How have the years changed him? Can I live with the changes? Maybe I should give up, quit fighting this, fighting him, now that I know he's never going to let me go. And truth be told, I've missed him. *Dammit*, I hate myself for admitting defeat. But as he rolls into the parking lot of a hotel—a nice one—and dismounts, I realize that's it. He's won. I've officially been defeated.

Big changes are in store for my future. Scary changes. He has shown moments of kindness... And his revenge was spoiled the day of my father's funeral. *If he was even out for revenge, Elise.* There is that possibility. I might have been so wigged out by the Houdini situation that I misjudged the situation. Beau and I had been close once upon a time. But then... why did he walk away from me all those years ago?

As I stand next to his bike trying to figure all this out, Beau brushes his knuckles gently over my cheek. Seems new Beau can still read me as well as old Beau used to.

"Come on, darlin'."

When I pull the helmet off my head, I know my hair looks awful, but Beau slides his arms around me, holding on like he thinks I'm the most beautiful woman in the world.

Feeling him, the way he treats me so tenderly, it becomes a hundred percent clear. He didn't betray me. He loves me. Beau loves me. Beau's always loved me.

Shoot.

But he did lie to me. Can I forgive him for that? Yes. I probably would've done the same thing in his position. *Stupid, Elise.*

Beau's lips descend breaking into my thoughts. His lips press to mine. Gloriously his tongue strokes my mouth, caressing my own.

I sigh. He hears my sigh, feels it, and smiles through the kiss, moving one of his hands to squeeze my butt cheek.

It's now that the hours of rubbing up against him catch up. Hunger completely forgotten, there's only one thing I'm hungry for now. I wrap my arms around his neck, hijacking the kiss.

"Slow down, baby girl," he whispers against my cheek. "We got time."

"I was an idiot, Beau. I'm sorry." I pepper kisses to his jaw. "Your life, the town, Houdini..." My arms tighten around his neck, lifting up on my tiptoes to align our bodies. I'm coming down from hours of friction. I need more of it.

Hooking my leg around his hip, I begin to rub against his crotch, and I moan, "*Beau.*"

"Right here, darlin'," he chuckles. Really, *chuckles*.

"So much for my life in Chicago."

"Glad you're finally gettin' it."

"Not yet," I breathe, pressing another weighty kiss to his lips. "But if you take me inside... I will be."

Beau Hollister's magnetism pulled me in, standing in a

parking lot with other cars filled with passengers of the adult and child variety. Kids shouldn't witness this.

"Take it easy, baby girl. I'll get you there."

"Beau," I warn. "Have you ever ridden for hours with your crotch rubbing against someone's ass, the bike underneath you vibrating?"

"Point taken," he returns, pressing another deep kiss.

"I just realized that you love me and I think I love you... Take me to bed or lose the ability."

Chuckle gone, he tosses me over his shoulder, through two sets of glass double doors, inside the hotel, coming to a stop in the spacious, brightly lit lobby. Slate gray walls, slate gray and white striped sofas, and a modern, sleek metal and glass chandelier hangs from the ceiling in front of reception.

"Miss, are you okay?" the receptionist asks.

"I'm fine," I reply, very aware of all the eyes on us.

Beau fishes his wallet from his pocket. "Need a room, *now*."

Even though I can't see her, I hear the fingernails clicking light speed against the keys on a keyboard along with her snickers. Within moments she says, "You two have a nice stay." Then Beau whisks us off to the elevator.

And I don't even wait for him to close the door to our hotel room before starting to strip. When he sets me on the floor, my shirt is on the luggage rack. My shoes and jeans are the next to go—tossed in a trail, bra, and panties a memory, ending up with me sprawled naked across the lush, fluffy white comforter before he ever kicks off his second boot.

His eyes flash with heat. Want. Desire. He peruses every inch of my body. "So eager," he says. Though I'm not sure if he means *me* or *him*. "My mouth or my cock, darlin'?"

I'm done waiting. "Any. All. Both. *Fuck*, I don't care. Just fuck me, Beau."

He drops to kneel in front of me, spreading my legs wide,

dragging my bottom to rest at the edge of the bed. My heels planted against his thighs, he cups an arm under and around each of mine, tilting my hips up into the exact position he's after. Beau uses his luscious mouth to pepper kisses up my inner thighs, nipping then laving his tongue over each spot his teeth grazed. He's not shy about showing how much he enjoys the feast, groaning.

I writhe and squirm, gripping handfuls of comforter just to have something to do with my hands. It's already too much, and he's just getting started. Beau's mouth turns magical, licking, sucking, and nipping exactly where I need his mouth to be. Pure blissful torture.

The next thing I know, the world vanishes. It's only him and me. *Oh, god...* It's all I can do not to scream. My breaths coming in heavy pants, my nipples tingling with carnal electricity.

My hips move, grinding down against him because what he's doing is great, but I need more. Beau's not in the mood to be rushed, moving his forearm to rest against my pelvis, stilling my hip movements, relentless in his slow punishment.

Head off the pillow, bent forward, mouth open—no sound. My entire body quivers.

Magic.

I can't hold on. Wave after wave of unadulterated pleasure rushes over me, making me come harder than I thought humanly possible. And considering the orgasms he gifted me before I high-tailed it out of town, that's saying something. Yes, it's safe to say the man has unprecedented oral skills.

While I'm still riding that euphoric high, I lose his mouth feeling him slide inside me.

Oh shit.

With every thrust, he moves us up the bed until my head hits the pillow, never once breaking his rhythm. I'm literally along for the ride. Then repositioning us, he throws one of my legs over each shoulder, bending in to kiss me before resuming the festivities. The kiss is sweet, tender, as he whispers against my lips. "Love you, baby girl."

From just his words I feel it building again. Overwhelming my senses. Every push, every pull builds my sexual world, expands my sexual universe. The entire bed rocks as he gives it to me the way he wants me to take it.

Strands of his thick locks fall forward. I want to run my fingers through all of it, rake my fingernails over his scalp until he gives me his approving grunts of pleasure, but he won't let me. He holds my hands above us as he continues the pounding, the frantic.

The slapping of skin is the sexiest sound I've ever heard. I feel another orgasm coming on. So close. But before I get the chance to get there, he stops, flips me over to my belly, and brings my hands up to hold onto the headboard. From there he lifts my right leg to hook backward around his thigh, and he grinds.

"Who do you belong to, Elise?" he groans.

Only a squeak escapes. The burn. The pressure. I need to let go.

"Who?" he asks again.

"You," I manage to whisper. "*Beau.*" The grind alone would do it, but Beau takes it to the next level reaching around to press his finger against my center while lacing the fingers of his other hand through mine still gripping the headboard so we're gripping it together. And he keeps grinding.

I can't... he just... oh *god*.

This is different from anything we've ever done before. Slamming my head back against his shoulder, I detonate, my orgasm bomb going off all around him. Again.

He won't let up. Won't let me recover. Pressing kisses

down my neck while he continues the pressure on my center. His manipulations become almost painful, so raw, so sensitive. Yet he won't... let... up... Pumping. Grinding. Until he rings out another two orgasms.

"Fuck... *Elise!*" He roars out his post-coital bliss, spilling inside me, over and over, it goes on forever. He turns my chin to look him in his eyes as he unloads. I love it.

Four orgasms in one night.

I'm spent.

The man's a miracle worker.

Why was I fighting this?

Falling against my back, he traps me between the headboard and his body for only a moment under all his body weight, before pushing up on one arm. He brushes strands of hair, which had fallen in front of my eyes, behind my ear with his other hand.

Beau lays us down, face to face, chest to chest. The way he never breaks his stare, it's so personal. So intimate. So much more than great sex.

I'm lost to him again.

"For the record... you done fightin' me?" he asks on a heavy breath.

God, he's beautiful, sweat glistening his brow as he smiles that crooked smile down at me. He already knows the answer.

I nod. My head being the only part of my body I seem to have retained control over. Never knew it could be this good.

"Why, Elise?"

His question confuses me, pulling me from the blissful state I'd taken up residence in.

"I need to hear you say it," he then says, and it hits me, what he needs to hear.

"I don't know if I can tell you yet."

"You can. You're thinkin' too much. I don't wanna know

what's in here." Then he brushes the back of his hand along my temple. "The head always messes shit up. I wanna know whatcha feel here." He moves his hand to press the skin over my heart.

What do I feel? Only that I need him in my life and for more than just orgasms. As superior as they are.

"Part of me might still hate you, Beau." I try my hand because I wouldn't be me if I gave up without a little fight. He likes the fight.

"Darlin'." He shakes his head then brushes a light kiss over the apple of my cheek. "None of you hates me. You're scared. I get it. I wasn't exactly upfront with all the information."

"Just give it to me now."

"Can we agree to you tryin' life as my old lady, first?'

"I'm here aren't I?"

"Don't know. Are you here or are you *here*? Because baby girl, I need you to know the parts I withheld, those are the unimportant parts. The feelings I've given you, those are what's real, what matters."

Suddenly fighting simply to give him a fight seems ridiculous.

"I'm *here*, Beau. But I'm not ready to give you any more than that yet." And that's true. I need to trust that we can make it for the long haul before I give him that part of me. We still have clap-back from his club and the town, wanting us to fail.

"Fair enough. Waited seven years. Can wait a little longer."

Hell, even if I *didn't* still love him after he gave me four orgasms? Yeah. I nod again. Snuggling closer against his chest. I'm good giving him that.

"Okay," Beau says, very seriously. As if we've decided something.

"Okay," I repeat, too tired to say more.

Then after leaning over to kiss my forehead, he tugs us both up the bed. As he folds down the covers, I arch my butt up to help him along, then we're lying side by side, me tucked up under his arm once he's brought the blankets back up to cover us.

"Now sleep. We got a lot to talk about. I wanna rest before we get into it, and I want us past it by the time we get home."

"Sure." I yawn, letting Beau flip me over to use him as a full-body pillow. He flings my arm across his chest and my leg across his thigh. I'm perfectly fine giving up all the control because I lack the energy to do anything but submit.

Pulling me closer, kissing the top of my head once more, he lets me alone to drift off to sleep.

When my eyes open again, it's to the sensation of Beau kissing my neck, sucking the skin into his mouth. There's no light filtering in around the curtains from the outside, so it must still be early morning.

"Hey, baby girl." He pauses his ministrations to greet me.

I finally get to reach up and run my fingers through that thick hair. Losing the hairband, his luscious peanut butter locks fall down around his neck. He presses into my hand, his low growl, an admission to his enjoyment of how I work my fingers.

"I think I wanna fuck you again before we talk." Beau brushes his lips along my earlobe.

"Weren't you supposed to tell me the truth while buried to the hilt inside me?"

He pulls back allowing me to see his whole face, but mostly my eyes fixate on that adorably crooked smile. "You remembered." It's a statement, not a question.

"Hardly an offer a girl could forget."

Beau rolls over on top of me, resting most of his body weight on his forearms. "Open your legs, darlin'."

I do, allowing him to settle between them. My inner thighs resting against his outer thighs. "You ready to hear the truth?"

Yes. I'm achy, but yes. I nod. No buildup necessary this time, just the promise of what's to come, namely me.

He positions himself at my entrance and slides in, slowly filling me up to the hilt. Nothing has ever felt as perfect as Beau inside me.

Before he begins to move, he holds my stare. "I never set you up. Think you know that by now, but it's important I get that out first." Then he moves his hips, withdrawing almost all the way before sliding in slowly again. Every inch of him extracting concentrated pleasure. "Was plannin' on tellin' you that day, so I could be there for you, support you at your father's funeral." He picks up the pace, only subtly, kissing everywhere his lips reach.

I think it's perfect until he throws a twist of his hips in hitting *the* spot.

"*Beau!*" I scream his name, digging my nails into his back. I might have drawn blood. I don't know. What I do know, this... this is perfection.

"I wanted us to show a united front. I needed the town to know they mess with you, they feel the wrath of the Brimstone Lords. I have loved you since high school, Elise. You should've been mine from that day in front of the Whippy Dip. Not Logan's. But you chose him then, so I hung back for you and for him. 'Course, by spring of your senior year you found your way back to me. You and me, we were already in love. Even if you hadn't said the words yet."

"But you didn't want me because of the baby."

He twists his hips again rendering me incapable of thinking straight. My mouth drops open, incapable of speech.

"You're wrong, darlin'. I wanted you and was willin' to raise Logan's baby as my own. Everyone was hurtin' so bad at the funeral, lookin' to me to make it right. I thought if I just gave them that day..."

My heart begins to pound as his pace picks up.

"Oh... *Beau*..."

"Elise, baby girl. You left that day... and never... *oh fuck!* Never... came back."

His rhythm begins to stutter as I clamp down around him. Starting my release. Triggering his release. We come together. Fast, despite making love slow.

And then we pass out.

It's later in the morning by the time I open my eyes again. I can tell by how the light that didn't shine earlier, shines around the closed curtains now. He's beautiful lying next to me, slumbering in a way that seems to have evaded me despite the mind-blowing orgasms he's pulled from my body.

If I stay in bed with him, I'll keep tossing and turning, only succeeding to wake the poor, clearly spent man from his restfulness. I carefully, slowly slink from the bed and his arms and move to the bathroom for a little me time.

Can I accept what he's told me and move on? Because I never want to be that woman, the one who brings up shit that happened twenty years ago just to hurt him. If he and I are going to make this work, I have to be able to put that time behind me.

The water jets in the shower help to reduce my stress some. Lying flush against the travertine tiles, they massage my body with spray from three walls.

What does holding a grudge do besides cause us both heartache? How much more time am I willing to waste? Our truth isn't easy, but it's ours. I have to accept it or let him go for good.

With the water pelting against my skin, I sink to the floor.

Realization hitting like a hammer strike: I'm not ready to let him go for good.

I've decided to forgive Beau Hollister.

When I step back inside the room wearing nothing but the fluffy, white towel, he's awake and his eyes alight with intense desire for me. To his credit though, he doesn't look solely at my body, moving those deep bourbon eyes up to meet my blue ones.

"What brought on that smile?" he asks. "It lights up the whole room, you know that?"

"I forgive you, Beau." I shrug, needing him to feel my sincerity.

He knifes up, a thickness to his voice. "For what? What'd I do this time?"

"You aren't getting it. I *forgive* you."

There's the lightbulb moment. "*Fuck.*" He runs his fingers through his hair gathering it like he's going to pull it into a bun but without his hair tie, lets the strands fall again. "You mean it? Because I can't go on with life thinkin' we're good only to have you spend your life fumin' away, waitin' to explode all over me."

"I mean it. I've spent all night thinking. And well, you didn't *really* do anything wrong. Aside from not supporting me at the funeral. Or telling me who you are."

"Who gives a fuck if I'm Mark or Beau?" He slams his hand down onto the bed next to him. "I'm still the man who loved you in high school. I'm still the man who loves you now."

"That's what I'm trying to tell you. Apparently, I *don't* care. So, if you want me, I'm telling you now, you have me. All of me."

Throwing off the bedclothes, Beau leaps from the over-stuffed mattress. Smile lines crinkle around his glassy eyes and the crooked one around his lips. In two steps has me, holding me in his arms. Tenderness to his touch, using a crooked finger, he tips my chin up. "Let's go home, darlin'. We'll go to the store, invite some friends over. I've got a kickass grill. Steaks sound good?"

"With bleu cheese, fried onions, and creamed spinach on the side?" I laugh as hot tears run down my cheeks.

Beau swipes at my tears, clearing his throat. "Can you cook creamed spinach?"

"Sure. I'm a great cook."

He shifts slightly, still buck naked, to unhook the towel covering me, letting it drop to the floor so our bare bodies press together. Although the scene becomes intimate, he doesn't act on it, moving his hands to my hips instead.

Beau presses his forehead to mine, squeezing his eyes shut. "Check us out," he says. "How very domestic of us."

"Domestic sounds nice."

"Domestic sounds fucking perfect."

14

BEAU

She mounts my bike with her whole self-pressed against my back, trusting me with her life as we start to ride. She's trusting me with her life, but I'm trusting her with mine. There really ain't much else in the world to fuck a man up other than a woman. Elise Manning don't know the power she holds. I got my brothers in the club and my woman on the back of my bike. Nothing else I need in life. Few wants, sure, but as for needs, this is it. Without either of 'em, shit, I can't imagine that life.

Even before she was mine, I knew she would be. I knew I'd make it happen. A few hiccups along the way, but now she is.

The drive goes faster than I want it to. Wind smacking my face, the rumble, and vibration of the bike underneath me, pushing the machine to its limits through every mountain pass from the time we crossed over the Kentucky border, about two hours ago. We're forty minutes away from home when my phone vibrates in my pocket.

"Get that for me?" I yell to Elise.

She slides her hand down to reach inside my front jean

pocket, stroking me a few times teasingly as she grabs for the damn thing. "It's Chaos," she calls back.

"Answer it."

She does. "You've reached sex god Beau Hollister's phone. Love slave Elise Manning speaking." The silly woman giggles.

Silence.

"O-oh. Okay. He needs to speak with you. Pull over."

This can't be good. As I signal, I cut to the shoulder of the highway, Elise hands me the cell.

"Brother," I say.

"Boss, you gotta get home, *now*," is all he says and hangs up.

While we'd holed up in our little sex den for the night, the brothers had continued on through to deliver Elise's belonging to my house.

"*Fuck*."

"What?" Elise asks, squeezing her reassurance against me, and she don't even know she's doing it.

"I don't know," I answer honestly. "But I got a feelin' it's bad. Hold on tight, baby girl." Handing her back my phone I burn out of there with such speed both our heads snap back. Her grip tightens around my waist with one arm as she shoves the cell back inside my pocket lacking her earlier playfulness, then brings her second arm around to really hold tight.

With her fingers cutting a death grip into my skin and her face buried against the back of my cut, we take the forty minutes in just under twenty.

My house has cops and the fire department and my brothers swarming the property—in the drive, on the porch, rounding from the back. Neighbors stand around watching the scene unfold.

Tommy and Chaos approach us at the same time.

"Elise." Tommy greets her sharply with a curt nod.

"What the fuck?" I ask, completely dumbfounded.

"You might want to keep her back." Chaos warns.

At the same time Elise yells, *"Oh my god!"* and jumps off the back of my bike, running for the porch before any of us realize she's doing it. The scene has us that fucked up.

When I reach her, she's shaking, staring not at the broken-out window or inside the open door leading to the fucking firebombed living room. No, she's caught up in the words spray-painted across the front of the house. *The whore or you.* The signature looks like an anarchy symbol, but with an H in the circle instead of the A.

Bedlam Hordes.

"What the hell do the Horde want with Elise?" Tommy asks me.

Hell if I know.

Over the past few years that Houdini character has held a grudge against me personally, causing problems. Fucker always escapes just before. We've caught several of his brothers, made them pay for his antics, but none have ever broken. We still don't know the pussy's identity. And he *is* a pussy making his brothers take his hits.

"It's okay." I offer her my arms, holding her as much for my comfort as for hers.

"Okay?" she says quietly at first, lip quivering. Then she pushes back from me as her volume goes up. *"Okay?"* she says again. "Does any of this look okay to you, Beau?"

I think she's about to lose her shit. I'm just waiting for the tears to fall, for her to bolt, when she completely gob smacks me twisting in my arms to address the lawn. "I'm *not* a *whore.* None of you knows what happened. None of you!" Elise then shifts back to me, Chaos and Tommy. "They ruined your home. Where are we supposed to live now?"

"Only thing worth savin' already got in my arms, darlin'."

She turns her gaze up to me. Looking with those big eyes that go straight to my heart and my dick. I clear my throat.

"We'll stay at the club. Safer anyway."

My woman is something else. She nods her head. "This has to stop, Beau. Fight for me." Biting her bottom lip, Elise fists my shirtsleeves, closes her eyes, and swallows. When she opens them again, when she finishes her thought, *shit*. "Help me to fight, *please*," she says. "Help me to be Brimstone, too. A Brimstone Lady."

I can't keep the smile, the pride, outta my voice. "You got it, baby girl." I tug her so close to my chest we could hold a dime between us. You'd think with my home in ruins I'd be more upset. But knowing Elise was with me, no one was harmed. The rest is just things. Replaceable things.

Chaos pats my back. "It's official. I'm a hundred percent in love with your old lady."

"The fuck, brother?" I ask teasingly, knowing full well he's got no idea what I heard in Chicago.

But it don't matter what I heard in Chicago, what with how Elise answers. "Sorry. I've had enough chaos in my love life. I'm content to let him." She motions to me with her chin. "Show me who's *Boss* in that department." Then she looks me dead in the eyes. "But *only* in that department."

She was tested. Her first official day as a Brimstone old lady she was tested, and in my opinion, passed with flying colors.

Duke steps around from the side of the house where he'd been listening. "Didn't think she had it in her."

"Know you didn't. Don't doubt me or mine again." My challenge goes out to all of the brothers.

"Never again, brother," he calls over his shoulder as he heads for his bike. "Let's roll out, leave the investigating to the professionals."

"You need anything more from me, Tommy?" I question

the man, with Elise still pressed up against me because my arms tightened around her when Duke showed, rather than let her loose.

"Not right now."

"Can I go, then? I need to get my woman settled. It's been a long day."

"Go. I need you I'll call. And I'll have Maryanne stop by tomorrow."

"Good deal." I pat his arm. "Let's go, darlin.' You and those kind lips."

"I know, *I know*. The kind you'd like to see wrapped around your cock... Not you too. Hollister hell, I tell you what." She laughs, shaking her head like she don't know what to do with me. I love knowing I can make her laugh, especially in the face of all this disaster.

As we walk, I pull her behind me and hold her hand to the edge of the drive where we both mount my bike, her arms move to hold me tight again. Helmet on, because I put it there, she presses her cheek against my shoulder blade, kissing me briefly. She kisses the leather, but I feel it all the way through to my core. It was the kind of kiss saying she's here with me and not just physically. She really is here with me.

After that, Elise keeps to herself the two miles we ride until rolling up to the front of the compound, where we wait while prospects Levi and Blaze open the gates for us.

"Good to see you again, Elise." Levi's lips tip up in that way he has, the one which has convinced many a girl to drop her panties for the kid.

"Find your own," I warn him.

"Just being friendly, Bossman," he quickly counters.

She slaps my shoulder. "Leave him alone."

My response is to turn and kiss her full on the lips. Once I know I got her attention, I pull back to lay it out. "Don't tell me how to deal with my brothers."

Elise rolls her eyes. Pursing those plump lips. She don't like what I have to say, that's on her. Though, she checks that anger pretty quick, takin' my hand once I've parked and offer to help her off my bike. So damn cute when.

The atmosphere feels different today from the last time she was here. The pieces ain't shown yet. Brothers who stayed behind to look after the place in the wake of my house being firebombed, lounge inside the main common room up at the bar or on the sofas watching television. A couple of hot mamas, those are the bitches who have been elevated from just a piece of ass, they live here semi-permanently and help take care of the men, but ain't anyone's old lady, they mill about doing what they're here to do—takin' care of the brothers.

Since Dawna passed, there's only one other old lady in the higher echelons of the club aside from Elise, and that's Trisha, Sneak's wife.

She's a pretty thing, bombshell blonde, tall and lean but not overly curvy. Not a secret given my old lady, I like curves. But she's still pretty and as sweet as they come, teaches third grade over at Lafayette Elementary. Recently cut that long, lush hair of hers into a pixie cut. Sneak wasn't happy about it, that's why I think she did it, to piss him off. Trish came to the club and found him in close proximity to a piece with that same hair. He wasn't cheating. The man's not stupid enough to throw away something so good. She was just a brazen piece and a case of bad timing. I was there. He already had his hand up to push the bitch away when his woman walked in.

Trish's blue eyes sparkle when she sees us, not having had the chance to meet Elise before all that shit went down.

"Oh my goodness, *you are real*." She squeals, reaching out

to pull a stiff as a board Elise in for a hug. "I thought you were like a unicorn or Leprechaun, or the product of a bad acid trip." And then, with my woman pressed up close and personal, she laughs out. "I'm Trisha, by the way. Sneak's old lady. Wife, actually." After which the crazy woman releases Elise.

Elise, for her part, rubs at her upper arms. "Have I met Sneak?"

"He was at the house," I tell her. "You just didn't see him."

"Hence the name Sneak?"

"I can already tell we're going to be great friends." Trisha beams at her, and Trisha's beaming is infectious, spreading to both me and Elise without us having any control over the situation.

Staring back and forth between Trish and me, Elise pulls a conversational one-eighty. "Do you have a grill here?"

"Out back, why?" she asks.

"Oh, because Boss here promised me steaks for dinner, and I am starved. Anyone else hungry?"

Several voices pop up from brothers around the common. "I'm hungry," and "I could eat." I didn't even know they'd been listening.

"Darlin', why don't you make a list of what you need from the store? I believe you promised me deep-fried onions and creamed spinach." Then I look to a prospect named Blue, whose truck she'd inadvertently jumped into at the red light yesterday. "You're goin' to the store for Elise."

"You got it, Boss," he answers without hesitation, fishing keys from his pocket.

"I gotta keep my woman happy."

"Then we all gotta keep your woman happy. *Hey Elise.*" He winks.

"Yeah but." I get in his face the same as I did Levi. "Only the ways I tell you to. Got me?"

"Come on, Bossman. You know I'd never go there. I might wanna father children someday. And fuck if you wouldn't make that shit hurt twice as bad. We know the rules, no fucking with another brother's old lady."

"The way you're salivatin' thought you might need a refresher."

Elise held her tongue during the whole exchange. That *ain't* in her nature, which means I'm in for some shit. She still don't even acknowledge me when she turns to hand off her list to Blue.

"Thank you, Blue," she says. "Excuse me for a minute, Trisha." Again, pretending I don't exist, she retreats to my room, well, our room now. I follow her out of the common and down the dark hallway wondering how long she'll keep it up.

I flip on the light switch and shut the door securely behind us.

She turns, a hand holding her elbow, rubbing her forehead with the other. "Why am I here?"

"What?"

"Why am I here?" she repeats.

Leaning back against the door, I cross my arms over my chest and give her a stupidly flippant answer. One I know I'll pay for. "Because we're living here for now."

She shifts on her hip, losing patience. I know by her long, exaggerated sigh. Received and not appreciated. "Yes. But why would you want to live with someone you clearly don't trust? I thought it was cute, that you were just being funny with Levi. But now I'm just insulted."

"Not following, darlin'."

"You're making me sound like the whore the town accuses me of being. Do you think I'm a whore, Beau?"

"You know I don't. But the men—"

"Won't touch me if I don't want them to or it's rape. Are your brothers rapists?"

"*Fuck no.* We don't hurt women or children."

"So then you're assuming I want them to fuck me, that I am a whore."

"I'm not gonna win here, am I?"

"What's to win? Every brother who smiles at me gets the same in-your-face lecture. You are the only man I want, Beau Hollister. You. But now everyone is just going to look at me like some home-wrecking whore who can't be trusted. So thanks for that."

"*Shit.* Baby girl, I *did not* mean that. It's just, you're mine now. Finally, you're mine. You chose Logan before, what's to say you won't change your mind about me?"

"Then you *don't* trust me. I didn't choose Logan over you. He spoke up first, wooed me while you stood back with your hands in your pockets." Her face scrunches up, with those damn glassy eyes, like she's about to cry.

"Calm down."

"Forget you, Beau. Things changed for us. And you know it. I wanted a life with you. For five years, I couldn't move past you. Not until I met Mark. And oh, who was Mark? *You.*" The tremble to her voice at the end guts me, the tears she fights so hard to keep from falling ruins me.

"God, I'm an idiot. Come here, baby girl." When she don't move I reach out, tugging her to me. "I'm so damn sorry."

Sometimes I feel like I'm drowning from the weight of how much I feel for Elise, how deep my love goes. The anchor of our past constantly pushing my head under relationship waters, to where I'm swimming hard to break through the surface, trying to catch a breath. I don't know what the hell I'm doing here.

Before Elise, I fucked around in high school. But when you're young and the town considers you a golden god, you dip your dick in as many holes as are willing. Then Elise showed up in front of the Whippy Dip, and my world changed forever. I knew then if it wasn't with her, I never wanted a relationship. Even when she chose my dipshit cousin. For the past seven years, I've continued to dip my dick in any and every willing hole, biding my time until this precious woman was in my arms. Now here she is, and I'm fucking it up.

The pissed-off expression hasn't left her face when I bring my mouth to hers. At least she don't push me away. Soft and easy, she presses those delicate lips against mine. Funny how I can begin to breathe again with my mouth pressed to hers. I don't push for more. This is her deal. But I won't deny being fucking ecstatic when she grabs fistfuls of my shirt, running her tongue over the seam of my lips for me to open to her.

Hell yeah, she does.

From pissed-off to turned on, in a matter of seconds. Dirty. Gritty. Arms and hands. Tongues and teeth. We're wild and frantic.

Never really cared much for kissing with other women. It was just a means to an end. With Elise, I could kiss her for a week straight before my dick ever touched her. Of course, we ain't waiting that long.

She wraps her legs around my waist, taking breaths through her nose so she don't have to leave my mouth. My hands on her ass, keeping her propped up, I begin the slow, backward walk to the bed.

As the backs of my knees hit the edge of the mattress, I twist to lay her down.

She breaks off the kiss, pushing at my chest. "Wait, wait, wait."

Now? I could drop my hands and hold her up with just

my cock, I'm so hard for her. And she wants to stop? But what choice do I have? "What's wrong, baby girl?"

"You've um—slept with pieces here, right?" she asks through pants.

"What? *Yeah*." I snap, not meaning to. Frustration from needing to be inside her makes me an ornery bastard.

"Can we flip the mattress first?"

"Why?"

"Groupie juices," she answers.

My hands still on her ass, I stop kneading her butt cheeks and cock my head, as I didn't see that coming. "What *the fuck*?"

Groupie juices? I throw my head back and laugh. And I laugh loud. Got-damn I love this woman. "Yeah darlin', let's flip the damn mattress so I can be inside you already."

"Nice to hear romance isn't dead," she laughs.

"Hey, I can be romantic. Just let me show you after we fuck."

"Doesn't that defeat the purpose?"

"No baby girl, it don't. Because now that I got you, I plan on keepin' you."

15

ELISE

It's been a week since the bombing attack on Beau's home. A home that we can't even consider renovating until the fire marshal and police detectives finish their investigation. There have been some adjustments to living at the compound, such as always having men, pieces, and hot mamas underfoot. I want a bowl of fruit loops, but find someone else got to them before me. We buy more and I hide them, only to discover someone raided my stash.

They're louder than I'm used to. Party more than I'm used to. And the constant cloud of smoke hovering above our heads in the common from all the cigarettes and other non-tobacco products smoked on a daily basis will probably end up causing me cancer.

Though I relish these quiet moments to myself—they come so rarely since we rolled back into town—I admit, missing waking up next to him this morning. Seems I've gotten used to his warm body wrapped lovingly around me, even in sleep. He left for work before I woke. I knew Beau would be gone, he and Duke and Chaos. Some kind of new acquisition. They didn't really go into it. I understand not wanting to jinx the sale by talking about it until the ink is dry on all the signatures.

As I lay sprawled out on the bed, deciding on whether to get up or stay here for a while longer, my cell begins to ring, making the decision for me. Reaching over to the bedside table where I left the phone plugged into the wall to charge last night, I look at the display. It's not a number I recognize, though, being local, I answer.

"Hello?" I say into the receiver.

There's no response at first. Then music. The kind that comes from mobiles parents hang over baby cribs.

So I ask again, "Hello?"

"Hello?" I hear *my* voice say back to me. It's a prank. Just a prank.

"Who is this?" I demand.

"Who is this? Who is this? Who is this?" The voice, my voice repeats, but each one goes higher and faster as if someone is playing my words back to me in fast forward. Then in that same high-pitched voice, I hear, *"You shouldn't go out today."*

Damn Hadley for giving out my number. And damn these townspeople for not letting go. Why can't they just leave me alone? I pinch the bridge of my nose and hang up. The phone rings back several times before it goes to voicemail. Stupidly, I listen and I wish I hadn't. It's more of that mobile music and my voicemail message on fast forward. Then abruptly a shrieking laugh cuts off the message.

Somehow the attacks on my car or the empty house, as bad as they were, felt tame compared to the violation of some stranger's prank over the phone. They found me in my bedroom. My sanctuary. Now I have nowhere safe. Nowhere they can't get to me.

Shaking, I walk out of our bedroom in an almost zombie-like state. Forgetting to tame the bedhead hair. Forgetting that I only wear Beau's Easyriders tee. Underwear. No pants.

No slippers. My feet stick to god knows what on the way into the kitchen.

The kitchen. The innermost room in the compound. Therefore, the safest room in the compound. But not even the smell of coffee cures my woes.

"Jesus, lass. Are you sick?" The voice I've never heard before.

I scream and twist to the knife block sitting on the counter, pulling an eight-inch butcher knife firmly between both hands.

"*Fuck*. Calm down."

Twisting back to the intruder, I swing the knife wildly, narrowly missing his chest as he steps toward me, in an attempt to disarm the feral animal I've become.

"It's okay, you're okay." He holds his hands up, not in surrender, but to reiterate his sentiment. "Elise, right? C'mon, lass. Put the knife down."

I blink and look at my hands holding the knife, then back at the man who inches closer until one of his arms secures mine to my side. He snatches the weapon from my hands and sighs in a '*crisis averted*' way, and slips it back into the block, before sliding onto a barstool where he picks up a steaming cup of coffee, sipping peacefully as if I hadn't just tried to gut him.

With my brain cleared, I look to the man to apologize but the words get lost. He's, well, he's buck-ass naked for one. And as much as I'd like to look away, it's like my eyes won't obey my command to do so. He's an amalgam of piercings—both nipples, gauges in his ears, and even down-home with a barbell through the head of his penis. And it's a hell of a penis. It's such a penis that I know he's a natural redhead, not by the hair on his head. This guy—walking, breathing sex appeal.

"My eyes are up here, lass."

Oh my god. Caught in the act of staring. My face burns. "Sorry about." I wave my hand in the general direction of the knives. "Trying to kill you. You scared me."

"Eh, day in the life. No harm, no foul." As he swallows another sip from his mug, I take the time to notice his light spattering of freckles that I'll bet turn the ladies on.

Somehow, I thought he was being humble with his, '*day in the life.*' The scar under his left eye suggests otherwise, along with offering a badass edge to his movie star face. As does the gunshot scar puckered over his right shoulder and one lower left side pelvis.

Awkwardness from potential homicide aside, we've done the whole introduction thing backward. I mean, learning a person's name should come *before* seeing him naked. He has me at a disadvantage. One I tend to rectify. "So—you got a name?" I ask. "I could give you one." And I throw out an eyebrow waggle for good measure.

Snickering, he stands to pour another mug of coffee, and good Lord Almighty, the back matches the front. What's the saying, could bounce quarters off his ass? "They call me Scotch," he says.

"*Of course,* they do."

"It's more for the drink than the accent if ya can believe it."

At the pause in conversation, I turn to grab a mug of my own. Spooning sugar and pouring a couple glugs of milk. After my first fortifying sip, I lean against the cupboard, holding the mug below my nose to breathe in the steam.

"What had you so scared there, lass?" Scotch *had to* go there.

"It was just a prank call. Probably some teenage punks. But it was—*weird.*"

"Weird?" he asks.

"Unnerving."

There's another question he's poised to ask, I see it on his face, but before he can ask it Beau's voice booms into the kitchen with us. "What the fuck, man?"

"Was just getting coffee, Boss. I was sitting here minding my own business when she wandered in."

"But why are you naked, brother?" Beau's tone softens. "We talked about this, not while Elise is here."

"I just got in last night. I'm not even sure what's up from down yet. Oh, and she tried to kill me with a butcher knife." Scotch rats me out.

Beau whips his head to look between Scotch and me. "She tried to kill you?"

No. If Scotch tells Beau about the call or how wound up it got me, he'll never let me leave the compound. The moment Scotch opened his mouth to tell Beau the truth, I talked my lie over him.

"I was just in a bad mood this morning. I'm not used to being idle, it's time for me to find a job." For my part, everything I've said is as much the truth as the lie of omission.

Snickering, Scotch winks at me over the top of his mug he'd brought back up to his lips. "Tell us lass, what type of job interests you?"

"Well, my BA's in hospitality, and I'm currently working toward my masters in finance." Craning my neck to face Beau. "I'm over the phone sex now that we're together." And I sip from my mug again, too.

"Come here." Beau tugs on the back of my nightshirt and brings me into his body until I hit his chest, wrapping those strong arms around me.

I actually girl-sigh, and notice Scotch rolling his eyes.

"What? I can't help it, he feels good."

"I've had several years of hearing just how good he feels. The walls are thin, lass."

"*Right*, now I've got that image burned in the back of my brain for eternity," I say. Not kidding.

That same time Beau's grip tightens and he yells, "*Jesus*, Scotch."

The Scotsman chuckles as he turns to drop his mug in the sink.

"Wait until you get an old lady," Beau threatens.

"No offense, Boss, but my cock is happiest when I spread the love. Wouldn't be fair to give all this to just one lady."

Okay so the teeniest part of me agrees with him because he is seriously impressive and I know impressive sleeping with Beau.

Scotch shuffles past us, patting Beau on the shoulder as he passes him. Then he pauses in the doorway and turns back around. "Hey, I bet she'd do well with the new club. Hired anyone yet."

"No." Beau releases me, pinning Scotch with a hard '*what the fuck are you thinking?*' glare.

What does that mean? No, he hasn't hired anyone yet or no I wouldn't do well with it? I'm smart. My GPA is spot-on. I could run the new club.

"Can I give you my resume?" I ask. His face remains devoid of expression as he listens to me, so I tease, "Hey, I'm even willing to sleep with the boss." Just looking for a reaction.

Still nothing.

"What's the matter, babe? At least check my resume before writing me off."

"You don't have to work at all, Elise. I can take care of us."

"Then what exactly am I supposed to do with my days? I've worked hard for my degrees."

"You'll be busy with the kids."

Wait, what? I shove away, wondering when exactly my Beau had turned into a sexist pig.

"Oh no, you did *not* just go there." One hand on my hip, using my finger to enunciate each word, I point at the air, in his direction. "You did not. We don't have any kids, and you keep this shit up we never will."

"Sorry, lass," Scotch mutters. As I chance a look over to the man, he won't meet my eyes and shrugs before withdrawing from the kitchen completely.

Whatever. He's throwing me off my game. I'm angry, I have to keep focused. I mean, stay home with the kids? I did not work my butt off to get into DePaul's graduate program to be forced into the role of the little woman. Elise Manning, soccer mom? I take a few steps away from Beau because *Boss* can't exist for me right now.

"I'm so disappointed in you," I whisper. And move to leave too. But Beau can't let it go, or let me go, reaching out to grab my wrist. At first, I think it's to apologize, but no. His eyes, his face says he's angry with me. Angry with me? Nothing raises my hackles more than someone who turns misplaced anger on me because he can't admit his own idiocy.

At that moment I completely lose my cool, snatching up the mug that I'd left resting on the counter, and throw the remaining milky, sugary liquid in his face. He gives the desired result releasing me, lifting his hands to wipe the coffee from his face.

"Dammit, woman!"

"More where that came from," I hiss.

"Fuck, Elise." He strips off his cut, tossing it on the counter, and begins unbuttoning his shirt to peel off the brown-stained transparent fabric. "Get to our room."

"Did you just send me to my room like a two-year-old?"

"If the shoe fits."

Okay, that went *too far*.

I try to remind myself there's a learning curve for Beau and me, that despite our history, we've spent too much time apart, and need to get re-accustomed to each other's quirks. But some things can't be blamed on a learning curve, maybe him being dropped on his head, but not the curve.

"You *will* be sorry," I warn with my finger pointing directly in his face this time. Then I stomp off to our room. *Not* because he told me to.

Inside our bedroom, my eyes go directly to the cell I'd tossed on the rumpled comforter before leaving after that call. A stupid crank call I don't want to think about what with Beau being an arrogant, sexist pig. Unfortunately, arrogance is a good look on him. Sexist pig, not so much.

The walls feel like they're closing in on me. Surround by Beau's *brothers*, no friends of my own. Stinking pranks. It's all too much, I have to get out for a while. Just for the day.

Maybe it's not smart of me, but I long for some alone time to clear my head. After a shower, brushing my teeth, and painting on a little light makeup, I walk back over to the bed and pick up my phone to check today's weather on my weather app—temps today should reach the mid-seventies.

My hair falls in soft curls cascading down just past my shoulders. I pull on a silverish-lavender-fitted satin camisole, then slide up my favorite faded jeans. Naturally distressed, even I have to admit they make my ass look freaking incredible. Between the choice of sneakers, black flip-flops, or my silver wedge thongs, I pick the thongs, grateful the boys hadn't unloaded my stuff inside Beau's house but piled it all in the garage.

After slipping the dental floss thin strap of my small, mirrored purse around my shoulders, I cautiously stick my head through the doorway to make sure Beau hasn't planted a guard on the other side, to keep me locked away inside.

In the twenty minutes I've spent primping, he hasn't even attempted to talk with me. I know he'd hate me leaving the compound wearing this ensemble without him on my arm. The boobs and ass look that good.

Honestly, don't get him. Expending all this effort to get me then damaging what we're building by turning into this guy I don't recognize. I'm not the kind of woman who wants to be dominated. Even though, I'll admit, I give him that in the bedroom. But I maintain how we are in the bedroom does not translate into our everyday lives. I love Beau, but what I want is to be his partner. Why won't he let me be his partner?

Keys in hand, again, I glance side to side, to make sure I'm not being watched, as I walk casually outside to my parked car, which the brothers who work in Duke's garage repaired and repainted despite my running back to Chicago. Because of Beau. And I can't let myself forget that.

The next hurdle, I have to make it past Levi and Blaze, who still guard the fence. Only a couple years younger than me, both have that sexy bad boy thing going on. But Levi has something special. If I was a different kind of girl, the kind the town accuses me of being, I'd flirt, and flirt hard.

So as I turn the ignition, I plaster on my biggest smile and best bubble gum attitude, pull out of the parking spot, and drive slowly over to the gate.

"Hey boys," I greet them after rolling down my window.

"Where you off to today, Elise?" Levi asks, leaning down close to my face despite Beau's warning. The man's a natural flirt. Exuding all that sexy, youthful confidence, he can't help it.

"Just the library," I lie.

"Aren't you supposed to have an escort now because of the Horde and your house?" Blaze cuts in.

"Not that Beau ever said." And that's the truth. He never

once mentioned an escort. "Besides, joining a club called the Horde? Really?"

Both men laugh. Blaze rubs his hand over the top of my head, messing my hair, and Levi tweaks my nose like I'm their little sister. *Hello*, I'm older.

Laughing along with them I say, "I doubt any of them can spell library, forget about going in one. They might spontaneously combust from all the intelligence assaulting them."

To that, the two men reward me with tipped up lips and nods of agreement.

"I guess it's okay. You need anything," Levi says, "You call straight away. It's our job to come running."

When I look into his big eyes, I have to ask myself why a man would choose this life. Prospecting, by all accounts, sucks. Forced to do every gross, menial job the brothers can think of, to prove their loyalty.

I realize I've been staring when he reaches over to tug on one of my curls, and I clear my throat. "You know Levi, you're going to make some girl really lucky someday."

A big dimple appears at the corner of his smile as he runs a hand through that dark, wavy hair.

"Nah, nah, nah... just because Bossman is content tethering himself to one pussy for the rest of his life, don't go jinxing the rest of us. No offense."

"None taken. You're young, too young to understand you're only chasing down different pussy every night because you haven't found the one meant for you, yet."

As he opens the gate he says, "Then let's hope I stay too young to figure that out forever."

All three of us laugh as I drive through the gate. Still laughing, I shake my head at the little punk as I turn onto the road, tossing a salute to the men before they disappear from my sight.

That went well.

What they don't know as they happily guard the gate at the compound two miles outside of town, is that I just drove through town, past the library. I take the highway until I hit the interstate. Then I take the interstate. I want a Starbucks.

Three hours later I get a text from Beau.

Him: Where R U?

Me: FK U

Him: Calling.

Then my phone rings. "Beau," I answer.

"Would you like to tell me why you left here without an escort?"

"Not really. Here I thought I was an adult who could go where I wanted, whenever I wanted." Feeling proud of that response, I sit up a little taller in the seat and click on my blinker to merge into the left-hand fast lane to pass a tractor-trailer.

"That was before you became Brimstone. Elise, get home."

"No. I'm fine."

"Darlin', where are you? I sent Blue down to the library, he said you weren't there anymore."

"Never went. Changed my mind. I'm allowed. You don't have me barefoot and pregnant yet Beau Hollister."

"Is that what this is about, the job?"

"Yes." I grip the steering wheel tighter. "That and the fact that you baited and switched. The man I fell for wasn't a Neanderthal. I'll stay home and take care of the kids?"

"Well, Dawna—"

"I'm not Dawna. I'll never be Dawna. I'm Elise. I'm always going to be Elise."

"Don't you think I know that?"

"No Beau, I don't think you do."

"Dammit, come home now."

"I can't—not yet."

"Elise, where are you?"

"I might be outside Nashville."

"Nashville?" he screams into the phone. "What the hell you doin' in Nashville?"

"I wanted a Starbucks?" Here I am, reverting to answering him in questions.

He, however, doesn't answer me. He hangs up. Part of me aches for him, for making him worry or whatever, but the other more dominant part at this moment is pissed right the hell off. I feel like a prisoner the way he won't let me live life. The man seriously needs to chill with the overprotective bit. How would the Horde even know where I am? It's Tennessee for crying out loud.

16

ELISE

The city life. I miss it. Big cities come alive in a way Thornbriar doesn't and never could. And bonus, it takes me away from the bad juju Beau and I have swirling between us. One of the things I loved so much about Chicago, Nashville has, too. The buzz. The hum. That thing which makes a city, a city.

He gets mad but doesn't stop to consider all I've given up to be with him.

I turn into one of the numerous parking lots around the city and pay my fifteen dollars to park. Slinging my purse around my shoulder, I flip down the vanity mirror so I can finger-comb my hair that Blaze mussed, then get out, press the key lock, and set out to walk the busy streets. There are catcalls and flirty eyes from men holding doors for me. It feels good like I'm getting more of myself back. The me before my world fell apart, and I mentally imploded. Unfortunately, all I can hear is Beau's voice in my head, ruining the buzz for me. What I hear is Beau in the bathroom at Moe's bar. *"There are consequences for your actions, Elise."* Maybe I shouldn't have worn these jeans without him. Wait, no. I've never had to answer to anyone for what I wear and I'm not going to start now.

As I walk, contemplating all this, I eventually come upon a Starbucks, *yay!* where I go inside to wait in the not too long, not quick enough order line. After ordering my mocha frap and a chocolate muffin, I sit at a table by the window watching people walk by.

It's all good for about twenty minutes until I see a man leaning against a parking meter. He's tall, black hair, good-looking enough, and has targeted me, standing right outside the window. Not that I plan to act on his attention, but when he catches my eye and winks, I'm glad I wore my good top. There might be a puff to my chest watching him lean against a parking meter watching me. Damn those bedroom eyes, serious bedroom eyes. Different from any of the other men of Nashville today holding doors or whatnot, he's a bad boy. And let's just say, those eyes and the vibe he gives off takes him from good-looking enough to seriously hot. *Yowzah.* I like how this day is turning out.

Of course, I'm with Beau, but I spent so many years cloistered from everyone except for the fringes of humanity, the attention feels nice. This is innocent flirting anyway, right? Nothing to cause any permanent damage in my relationship with Beau. It's fun, the game we're playing, where I get to be slightly naughty with the broody and kind of dangerous-looking stranger.

I smile at him, then drop my eyes demurely, looking up through my lashes.

His eyes narrow on me. No longer the flirtations of a seriously hot, kind of dangerous-looking man. They're hard, downright threatening. What the hell is that about? We were having fun. Weren't we having fun?

There's a flutter in my belly, but in the *so not in a good way,* way. More, the *look away slowly to not look like he's kind of freaking me out* way. I drop my eyes from his for real. Now playing the role of a demure, otherwise occupied Elise, *for real*. As I turn away I notice for the first time, this black-haired, used to be hot now downgraded back to merely good-looking enough man wears a cut.

Shit. What now? He's not someone I've ever seen before. Is he a Lord? Coincidence that he's from a different club entirely? Could he be Horde? Since I don't want him to know he freaks me out, I keep my head down pretending to check something on my phone. When I chance another glance back, the man is gone.

Pure, unadulterated relief washes through me for about five seconds, or until the front door to the Starbucks opens and the black-haired, cut-wearing man along with three of his buddies step inside. I know they're his buddies because they're all three wearing cuts, and on the back of those cuts, patches. Bedlam Horde.

Worst. Luck. Ever.

Trying and hopefully not failing to *not* show panic, I send off a quick text to Beau.

Me: Might been right. SRY I caused U such trouble.

Him: Elise?

Me: PRBLY not coming home. Ever. Horde. Everywhere.

Him: Fuck! In public? Don't move. Fuck!

Me: Starbucks.

Him: I know. Tracking location.

"This seat isn't taken?" The black-haired Horde asks me in not exactly a nice tone but probably the nicest he's ever used. Now I don't think he's even so much good enough looking as scary enough, because he's right next to me.

"I'm finished here," I tell him, lightly, calmly. As if I don't have a care in the world by recognizing the threat he brings to mine. "You and your friends can have the table." When I stand to leave, he clamps a hand around the back of my neck, pushing me back down into the seat.

"Not so fast, sweetheart. Someone wants to speak with you."

"I'm not from around here." I try to play it off. "You must have the wrong girl. I have one of those faces."

"Oh, Elise. What was Bossman thinking, letting his *piece* take off alone? Always thought he was smarter than that."

"I really don't know what you're talking about."

When I try to stand up again, instead of a hand, I feel the blunt end of cool steel against my back.

"I'd rethink that decision, sweetheart," he warns.

He's right. I rethink it and sit back down.

"Good girl."

My eyes close for quiet contemplation, mainly reflecting on what an idiot I am, and even though he's made some really backward comments today, Beau is a good man and I think I'm ready to admit I love him. Sad that he won't get to hear those words from me, that we'll never get our shot to really be Elise and Beau because as I stated earlier, I'm an idiot.

I continue to lament my life choices with my eyes squeezed tight. If bodily harm comes to me, I don't want to see it coming. Though eventually, he stops harassing me, to speak with his buddies. That's when I chance opening them again on a whispered sigh and really, I'm glad I do.

As my gaze shifts outside, while trying my best to formulate an escape plan, I zero in on at least a dozen men wearing —and for like the first time ever I notice straight off—biker cuts. Brimstone Lord Biker cuts, where they gather off to the side of the store.

Without calling attention to him, my eyes cut to a man

almost outside of my visual horizon, so totally out of the Horde's. The man slips out of his leather, folding it and stuffing it into a saddlebag at the back of a bike. He moves inside the Starbucks, not on Horde radar, who incidentally continue to talk amongst themselves.

Only my attention follows the man as he moves stealthily through all the tables and customers to the back by the restrooms. There I see his hand pull down on the fire alarm. The alarm buzzes loudly. Strobe-like warning lights flash. While patrons and employees scramble out of the store, Lords file in. Black-haired Horde grips my arm tightly, flanked on all sides by his Horde compadres.

They're outnumbered and outgunned, yet it doesn't stop the gunfight from breaking out. I don't know who fires first. All I do know is someone throws a chair through the front window, the black-haired Horde falls, and I'm flung like a rag doll over someone's shoulder. The patch on the back of his cut, even upside down, I can see the flaming devil and the words Brimstone Lords.

Then I'm safe, tossed into the back of a black SUV with the windows blacked out, and I feel the car hum to life and gun into traffic.

I'm surrounded by black. Even blacked-out glass separates the front and back seats.

When we do finally stop, someone flings the door open and drags me from the backseat, not gently, inside a large, corrugated metal warehouse. But just like back home, it turns out to be a clubhouse. Unlike back home, I'm not made welcome, offered a drink, or any such use of manners.

The room fills to capacity with pissed-off bikers, club pieces in various stages of undress huddled in a corner, and at least one man laid out across a sofa bleeding. Is he bleeding because of me?

The biker continues to carry me, while I remain flopped

over his shoulder, through the common into a kind of holding cell. Which is really an empty room where he drops me, again not gently, onto the floor.

I sit, back resting against the blank white wall, hands resting on bent knees, lightly banging my head against the wall just to pass the time.

Eventually, I fall asleep. There's no way to know how much time passes before I'm woken by someone shaking me.

"Elise." *Shake.* "Elise, get the fuck up."

My eyes pop open. "Chaos?" I tilt my head studying him, not fully awake yet. "Where's Beau?"

"You've done it this time, little girl."

I've done it. I didn't mean to done it. How do I keep doning it?

He helps me up from the floor, leading me from the room with a hand to my back. Nobody talks to me, not even Chaos. As we walk through the compound, I even see Duke, president of the Thornbriar chapter. I do not see Beau.

Outside Blue sits in the driver's side of Beau's red pickup. Yet still no Beau. Chaos helps me in then moves to mount his bike. Bloodhound, Levi, and Scotch leave the compound next, mounting their bikes. Last to come out, looking über pissed right the hell off, is Duke. When he mounts his bike, all the men start their engines and peel out, escorting me and Blue, two riders to the front of us, and three to the back.

Beau didn't come.

Blue doesn't talk. The men don't stop. As the scenery changes to denser forests covering bigger, rockier mountains, the sky darkens revealing an aerial sea of twinkling stars. Yet I can't shake the foreboding feeling taking hold in the pit of my gut. And really, is there a worse foreboding than gut foreboding? The answer to that would be an unequivocal *no*. And since that answer comes in the form of an unequivocal no, I drop my gaze from where I've been staring out the window to my hands, close my eyes and pray to the universe that I didn't just screw up my second chance with Beau to the point that there's no way to unscrew it.

When we finally pull into the Thornbriar compound, Levi won't look at me. Blue parks the truck then hops out. He runs around to get my door. Taking me by the arm he leads me inside through the common and straight to my room where he opens the door and shoves me in, closing the door again sharply. Beau's not in here, either.

I shower, dress for bed, choosing one of Beau's tees because it smells like him *and* I'm a glutton for punishment and climb under the covers. He doesn't come home all night. When I wake up in the morning, there's no body indent. His side of the bed remains just as cold as the night before.

To this, I decide to stay in the room away from angry bikers for as long as I can hold out and sulk.

At some point during the day, Trisha pops her head inside the room.

"Just checking to see if you're still alive," she says, not nearly as welcoming as before, but at least she's not a brother of the club.

"Kind of wishing I wasn't, right now," I admit, honestly.

"You'll get through it." Her eyes soften. "Hungry?"

"No. But thanks."

She leaves. I continue to lick my wounds in bed, staring at the wall. Occasionally, my phone.

When the clock on my phone flips to ten—that would be *p.m.*—Chaos walks in the room this time, slamming the door against the wall with a loud *bang*, making me jump. "Quit your hiding. Duke wants to see you." Then he leaves.

Right. Duke. Just who I really don't want to see now. Maybe turn me back over to the Horde?

That wish notwithstanding, I do as he says and get out of bed, then throw on a bra under my T-shirt and a pair of yoga pants before heading out to the common area. Duke keeps his office in a room to the right of the bar.

"To think he's throwing away the club for you." A woman, she's a hot mama—one of the available women who live here semi-permanently in exchange for caring for the men—steps in my face.

"Throwing the club away?" She's got my attention, which proved by the ugly smirk on her face, she knew she would.

"Boss's the VP. How do you think your actions look on him? How long you think Duke's gonna put up with your shit? He fucked me on the regular. Right up 'til you came back to town. I never gave him these problems."

"He's the VP?" I ask, choosing to disregard the disturbing information in which Beau *fucked her* "on the regular."

"So selfish you don't even know what position your *man* holds. It's on his patch. Hasn't been home, has he? Don't be surprised he smells like pussy when he does get back. A lot of girls willing to take your trash."

"He's not my trash. I love him."

"Funny way of showing it."

As much as I don't want to stay talking to her, I let out a longish, exaggerated sigh because what I want even less than spending one more second with the sparkling conversationalist happens when we hear Duke call, "Manning. Get the fuck in here."

Right.

I breathe out heavy once more, sucking up my courage and walk with my head hanging, looking at my feet, and enter his office. I'm not sure what I thought the office of the president of an MC would look like, but this really looks like an office. Computer monitor, keyboard, phone. Lose papers, files, cabinets for those files. He leans against the desk when I enter.

Duke's naturally intimidating in that badass president of an MC way, what with his dark, so black it's almost blue hair just starting to streak with silver at his temples. He wears it messy and longish, long enough to curl around his ears. And like all the movies portray, as an MC President he sports a kick-ass mustache and goatee, thick, black with more silver in his beard than his hair. He's big and buff, full of tattoos, and never wears sleeves.

The thick chain which goes from his belt loop to his wallet rests on the desk. His motorcycle boots he's planted as firmly to the floor as his palms against the desktop. Like I said, naturally intimidating. But now, on top of all that, his gray eyes glare beadily at me with his mouth set in the meanest scowl I've ever seen up close. His scowl could make a grown man wet himself, yet while taking all of him in, I see a dull gold wedding band still glinting slightly from his left ring finger. It's humanizing in a way that makes him just a bit less scary.

"Take a seat," he growls. Yes, growls.

Despite that greeting and the fact that he doesn't look happy, he strangely doesn't seem as pissed right the hell off as yesterday. To keep him from going back there, I take a seat right away, sitting with my head down again, hands folded in my lap. Even without his earlier pissed vibe, I sit feeling on the verge of tears.

"Got anything to say for yourself?"

I shake my head no.

"Elise Fuckin' Manning has nothin' to say?"

Again, I shake my head no.

"Well, this is a first. As for yesterday, Rage, the Horde president, denies any knowledge or involvement with those men detaining you. Said they went rouge, but that's bullshit.

A president controls his club. With that knowledge, what do you thinks gonna happen here?"

"I need to collect my things and probably move to California or somewhere far away, where I can't hurt Beau anymore?"

"The Lords just declared war on the Horde. Not just Kentucky. When we had to send our Nashville boys in to rescue you, shit got serious. You think we're really just gonna let you go?"

My head whips up, eyes flash to his. "Wha—what are you gonna do with me?"

"That's up to Boss. You're his old lady."

"I don't think I am, not anymore…" My nose begins to prickle. "I'm just not sure where I'll go."

"Have you eaten at all today?"

"Not really hungry."

"You need to eat."

I don't want to eat. I don't want to argue or be a nuisance, either. "I'm very sorry." I shoot him a sad smile. "For what it's worth, I do love Beau. I'm just not a very good old lady. I'm sure he's out finding my replacement as we speak."

Duke laughs at me. It's humorless, but he laughs, shaking his head. "Go. And eat. They're watchin'. I'll hear if you don't."

People keep wanting me to eat, I'd think it would be better on everyone if I just wasted away. Yet, because I don't want to be called back into his office, I stop off in the kitchen to grab a granola bar from the pantry, waving it around in the air as proof of my following Duke's order— even though no one's there to see it—before heading back to my room.

But I don't eat the bar. I lie in bed, unable to sleep. They declared war because of me. Even though I'm not sure what war between clubs ensues, I doubt it's sending each other nasty notes in the mail and leaving flaming bags of poo on rival doorsteps.

It's really late when the door to the room creaks open, so late it's early. I hear boots fall. Clothing hits the floor and his side of the bed finally dips. I smell cigarettes and booze, but not pussy. And I burst out crying.

"Shh..." He wraps his arms around me, tucking me against his bare chest. "You don't wanna be doin' that now."

"I'm so... *sorry.*" I cry against his tattoo of my name while he strokes a hand down the back of my hair. "I really... didn't think the Horde... would be in Nashville. I was just getting away... for the day. Baby... I didn't even know... you're the VP. How did I not know? You... you have a *patch*!" I cry even harder.

"Elise, darlin' stop."

"You... want me... to leave? I told Duke... I'd move... to California."

"Baby girl, I don't wanna live in California."

"No... I meant—"

"Know what you meant. But I've told you this before, so you gotta get it now. Our life is together."

"When are you gonna say when? I started... *a war.* I'm not... worth all this."

"Not worth this? I got Helen of fuckin' Troy in my bed, and you think you ain't worth it? Here's somethin' else for you to get now. Nothin' in my life worth fightin' for more than you. Nothin'. And I didn't want you at the new place because it's a titty bar."

"I can handle it..." I sniff loudly. "I actually have tits."

"Don't I know it. But darlin', we might be legit, but we ain't boy scouts. You get what I'm sayin'? This is still an MC and even though we moved away from that other bullshit, shit gets real, we do what we gotta do. And shit can mean anything. Think you can handle that?"

"Will I go to jail?"

"No. You'd be responsible for a legit business. But brothers act how they act, do what they do. You'll know things that could impact any one of us. Me. You prepared for that burden?"

"Are you afraid I'll... l-let you down again?"

"Elise, you never let me down."

"You're wrong. Yesterday, I did. I made you look bad not just here... but with another chapter. So bad you didn't come to get me... or come home."

"I wasn't with another woman if that's what you're worried about."

"It's what I deserve."

"No, it's not. Don't ever say that shit. But here's what's gonna happen. Give me your hand." I hold my hand out to him, thankfully my crying jag calming down. "No, your left hand," he corrects me.

I don't see what it matters which hand, still, I lift my left to him. Beau reaches down with his unoccupied hand tagging his jeans from the floor. One-handed, he fiddles with the jeans wrestling a small black velvet box from one of the pockets, using his teeth to help him open the box. I'm shocked motionless as he proceeds to slide the most beautiful ring I've ever seen in my life—a raised princess cut diamond, probably two karats, surrounded by what looks to add up to two more karats of pink, chocolate, and canary yellow diamonds in a platinum band—on my ring finger.

"*Beau.*" The tears start up again. "I've never seen anything like it."

"But?" he asks, warily.

"No buts. It's exquisite."

As he visibly relaxes a broad, beautiful smile tips the corners of his lips up.

"If you're workin' for the club, we're gettin' married."

My face falls. "Oh, okay."

"Baby girl, what's wrong?"

"Nothing. I got it. Goodnight."

"Goodnight? We just got engaged."

"So I can't testify against you or whatever."

In one move, Beau releases his hold but pins my arms above my head as he rolls on top of me. "Is that what you think I meant? No. Never. I meant if you're in, you're all in. I want every part of you."

"*Oh.*"

"Yeah *oh*. Since the day I met you at the Whippy Dip I knew I was gonna marry you. But part of your punishment is that it happens faster than you probably plan on."

I'm quiet for a moment, maybe two. Those strong hands of his release mine and bring them to hook around his neck while he traces a line of sweet kisses down my jaw. With every press of his lips, I feel safer, yet more scared than I ever remember feeling in my life. What am I getting myself into, really getting myself into? This I want to ask; this deserves an answer yet instead of throwing myself under that bus I chicken out. "When did my dad join the club?" I question instead.

He answers immediately. "Wasn't an official member. Especially at that time, the club needed someone they could trust, which your pops was more than willin' to fill that role. But with havin' a practice in town and all..." Beau's arms loosen just a bit as his words trail off. This I find disturbing on some level, because well, we just got engaged. His arms shouldn't be loosening for any reason.

If I were any other woman, I'd realize that his words trailing off and arms loosening probably means he's uncomfortable or even sad. Unfortunately for him, I'm not another woman. I'm me. And in being me, I venture forward with another uncomfortable question, and I know for sure it's uncomfortable when he tenses just the briefest of seconds before he regains control of his emotions. "How is it that you're the VP? Aren't you a bit, well, a bit young to be a VP?"

"Yeah," he laughs humorlessly.

"Yeah? That's it? Care to expound?"

"Not really, not tonight."

"Beau, I just agreed to marry you, and still you don't trust me?"

"No, not that, darlin'. Just, especially tonight with you just agreein' to marry me, this shit's... *unpleasant* to say the least."

"Okay," I mummer and turn away, tucking my hands under my pillow to lift it closer against my face.

"Shit—alright. Okay." He sighs sadly before starting up again. "You remember your pops' friend Rex?"

I turn back to him and nod. "I met him only a few times. Whenever he and my dad hung out, they'd do it away from the house."

"Not surprised. Your pops wanted to keep you away from all that shit."

"Shit?"

"Rex was your pop's best friend all his life. When they were teens and your pops went off to college, Rex became a prospect with the Lords. Their lives took 'em in different directions, your pop to medical school, a husband, and eventually a father. For Rex, his eventually led him to becomin' our prez."

When he stops talking, I suck in a breath.

"He was also Duke's older brother," Beau finishes.

"Really?"

He nods. "Really. The club was located farther outside town then. Almost to the edge of the county." He stops talking, pressing his forehead against mine. We're about to get into the real heavy. Then Beau sighs. "The club was into some bad shit back then, baby girl. Bad shit. I won't go into it, but if you ever watched any TV shows or movies about outlaw biker gangs, that'd be about right."

Inside, I'm freaking right the hell out. But somehow, somehow, I know that if he senses it, he'll shut down and likely never open back up. To keep our conversation flowing, I push back any thoughts of a freakout and nod my head to tell him I understand and to continue.

"We were at war with the Horde for years over territory, this was before I came in at the end. Shit got real, too real. Brothers ended up dyin', a lot of brothers ended up dyin' includin' *their* vice prez and Rex. Hell, the only one of his lieutenants left standin' was Duke and that's only cuz he'd taken a leave of absence. Dawna's cancer had come back and he'd been stayin' outside Chicago while Dawna got some specialized treatment from that big cancer hospital up there."

"I know the one." My response feels as stupid as it sounds, as the big cancer hospital is hardly the point of this story.

If my stupidity bothers him, he doesn't show it. "I'd been hangin' at Lady a lot back then, drinkin' my pain away." He continues on. "Logan dead, you just gone. The baby. It was all too much. I was lost. Couldn't go back to school. Everything just—well, since I was such a hanger-on, some of the brothers looked to recruit me. I was all alone and they offered me a place, a family. I took 'em up on it. Was a prospect when the big shit went down. I won't go into what I saw or what I had to do to stay alive. You don't need those images in your head and I never want you to think of me as anything but the Beau you know. This ain't up for negotiation. Take it or leave it."

"Okay," I agree right away, figuring I'll eventually find out, but if he's not in the mind frame to share yet, who am I to force the issue? "I'll take it."

A beat. Then two. Then three he stares at me as if waiting for me to argue, and shakes his head. I can see the *'what am I going to do with you'* question dancing in his eyes.

"Duke had to come back to take his place at the head since they were all gone. But he promised Dawna that if he took over, they'd get outta all the shit they'd been into because he needed to be there to take care of her. He needed lieutenants who wanted outta the life. Who wanted the family but not the shit. I got patched in when he took over because of how I handled the shit I had to do. Mick, who shoulda been Duke's VP got sent up for takin' out a cop in a bar brawl. That left me to take the spot 'cuz Duke knew I didn't want the shit like he didn't. Chaos and Blood got patched in a few months after me. And a few months after them came Carver and ended with Sneak. We called a tentative truce with the Horde while they regrouped. Although we never trusted 'em to stay down. Eventually, brothers either left or decided bein' outta that shit was a better place to be. So here we are."

"I don't know what to say."

"Nothin' much to say. It is what it is, darlin'."

I suppose he's right. That was then. That's not the club they are now. So be it.

"How soon we talking?" I ask, changing subjects. "The wedding?"

Swiping a finger along the apple of my cheek, he leans over to kiss my temple as he laughs lightly through his nose, seeing my subject change for what it is.

"Soon," he says, showing me that crooked smile of his.

And that's it. He gave me heavy without making it too heavy. I love him, I'm sure of it, and I think it's about time he knows.

"I love you, Beau," I say confidently, and lean up to kiss him.

Beau closes his eyes just a moment, squeezing me tighter. "Say it again," he pleads.

Since I don't mind, I say it again. "I love you, Beau."

"Love you too, darlin'."

17

BEAU

"*Holymotherfuckinglordoftheuniverse!*" she cries out in one long, jumbled mass of profanities. Loud. So loud, I think prospects guarding the gate can hear her.

My ring on her finger, life is falling into place. It didn't take much to divest my fiancé from all her clothing. Just a nightshirt and panties. Every time I look at her like this, it's hard to believe she's finally mine. She's the most beautiful woman I've ever seen in my life. Her eyes are closed now and I prefer she keep them open so I can drink in their depths when she comes. Just knowing why those soulful, blue beauties are closed, I'll let it pass this time.

Starting at her navel, I licked and sucked my way down, kissing on each thigh until she whimpered. Then I put my mouth to her, the woman so ready her back arched off the bed, fisting the sheets, she ground against my mouth, my tongue. Those thighs trembling the closer she got to the edge.

Needing to up my game, I dragged my thumb through her wetness. But when I pushed it into that tight, puckered hole of her ass, her legs snapped together so fierce, I thought she'd snap my head clean off my neck.

"*Holymotherfuckinglordoftheuniverse!*" she cries.

This is how life should be. The smell of her, the taste of her on my lips, I trace a trail of kisses up her abdomen, over each swell of breast, taking extra care with each pink, pert nipple, up her collarbone. Then again, more attention to the dip of her throat, licking and nipping the way she likes it, over her chin, jaw, behind her ear until finally, I reach her mouth, kissing her hard, deep, and wet so she can taste herself, how amazing she tastes.

"On your stomach, baby girl," I whisper, as I've decided to change tactics after making her come so hard already. This is gonna be fun. She flips over and I crawl on top of her. Spreading her legs, I slide my knee under her thigh to give me more leverage and slide inside her. We both groan as I fill her slowly, inch by inch, until I've filled her completely. Before I begin to move, I tilt her chin back kissing those lips again, taking that mouth deep again. Then begin pumping slow and rhythmic. This ain't no race, I'm not fucking Elise tonight. I'm making love to my fiancé. My fucking *fiancé*.

It's a beautiful word for a beautiful woman. But I end up losing all that rational thought as she pushes her sumptuous ass back against me, grinding, trying to take as much of me as she can get. My girl is a voracious lover. Hungry for my cock, always so hungry for my cock.

Easy from our sweat-slicked bodies, when I start to get close, I flip her around onto her back without disengaging from her tight heat to pull her calves up over my shoulders. This way I know I can go deep.

"*Beau*," she practically sings, and I've never loved the sound of my own name so much.

"I'm here, baby girl. Come for me. You got it in you."

"WHAT THE FUCK IS THAT?" Chaos, of all people, grabs Elise's left hand, shoving it in my face.

"Manhandle my fiancé again, I'll put you in the ground." Although I keep my tone light, he's known me long enough to read the words loud and clear.

"You're rewarding her? *Christ*." He turns to look at her. "You know I think the world of you, doll. But you're shit for an old lady and bad for the club."

I have no idea if Elise responds or was even planning to respond. I have no idea if Chaos opened his stupid yap again. Not when all I can see is red, and crack him so hard in the jaw blood and spit fly from his mouth. He stumbles backward hitting the bar which stops him from stumbling any further.

"Say another word, we got issue, brother. I love Elise. I'm marryin' her and I want you standin' up with me when it happens. Nashville was an honest mistake. Even Duke realizes it."

And then Candy, the hot mama I'd been fucking before Elise showed back up in my life has the nerve to get in my face, resting her hand on my chest. "Bossman, you can't be serious. You're gonna marry her? I did everything you ever asked. You needed it, I got it. Wanted to fuck, I dropped whatever I was doin' for you exclusively, but you make *her* your old lady—now *your wife*? That's fucked up."

"Shut it, Candy." I swat her hand off me like it's a mosquito, she's just as annoying.

"I thought after what she did, you'd come back to me," she whines.

"Did I ever lead you on?"

"What?"

"Did I ever lead you to believe we had anything more than fuckin' between us?"

She sucks in a breath. "No."

"Did I talk about takin' an old lady?"

Now she lets that breath out. "Yes."

"Tell 'em who, Candy. They already know but I need you to say it."

She says nothing.

I give her arm a light shake. "Now."

"Elise."

"So then why *in the hell* do you think it's okay for you to come at me the mornin' of my engagement to the woman I always said would be my old lady, layin' *your* shit at my feet?"

"I just—"

"Get the fuck out, Candy. You wanna fuck other brothers, that's your deal. But hear me now, you pick this shit up—toss it out, carry it with you—I don't give a damn. But you keep it outta my life, away from my woman. You don't say one goddamned word to her. You don't look cross-eyed in her direction."

"Beau, it's okay baby. After what I did—"

"No, you don't." I cut her off. Putting a stop to this *now*. "Don't you ever take that shit on. What you did was a mistake. This world—my world—is new to you. So no, it's not fuckin' okay." I turn to point my finger in Candy's face, actually poking the skin of her cheek to drive my point home. "Know your place, woman. You're a hot mama, a good fuck and loyal to the club. But Elise is a great fuck, the best I've ever had. Loyal to me, and she's not just an old lady. With Dawna gone she the top lady. I know even she didn't realize her place, what agreein' to marry me means. But now, no one's in the dark. So what do you have to say to Elise?"

"Fuck. I'm sorry. Welcome to the club." She puts no

warmth behind that lame apology we all know she don't mean a damn word of, but I can see my woman squirming next to me, so I decide to drop it for now.

"I'm takin' Elsie to see the new club, meet the girls we're keepin' from the acquisition and set up for some new hires."

I grab her hand, tugging her along behind me. My brothers, other hot mamas, leftover pieces from the night before, they part for us like I'm Moses, all staring at her. At me. Yeah, I'm the VP, but I don't usually throw that power around. But fuck it if Chaos and Candy didn't bring that asshole out in me. If prez would've wanted her gone, well she and I would've sold our stakes in the businesses and moved somewhere, maybe out west. That's how serious I am about this lady. But he was there. He talked to me, talked to Elise. Someone gets in my face over this, I will knock them down literally or figuratively. You don't mess with mine.

"We're taking the bike?" she asks, as we move through the lot in front of the compound.

"Think you know the answer to that." I'm gonna enjoy today's ride. Wanting to create a business environment, being the new manager, she decided to dress like a manager in this sexy as sin black pencil skirt which she has to hike way the hell up her thighs to be able to mount my ride. As her thighs straddle me, her barely-there lacy thong presses up against me, her arms wrapped around my chest. I feel those tits pressed against my back.

Not that she don't get me hard just by looking at her, but I know those tits sit cupped in a matching barely there lacy bra, both white. Which she wears underneath this fitted white blouse with pearlescent buttons keeping it secured. Buttons she didn't begin to button until the third button down to give me a peek of cleavage. She accentuates her hourglass figure with a thin black belt. Yeah, this gets me *hard*. Revving my engine—

pun intended—I look down needing to adjust myself, and notice the cherry red sex kitten heels she's wearing. The only color she's wearing aside from the same cherry staining her lips.

We're out of the compound riding toward town when she yells to me, "I'm nervous."

"Nothing to worry about, darlin'. Your resume is good. Best we seen—truth."

"Fuck me," she says.

I hear her but ask, "What?" thinking she means it like she forgot something. She don't.

"Fuck me," she says again. "Calm my nerves."

"Where you want it, baby girl?"

"Here. On your bike. Pull over, bend me over your bike Beau, and calm my nerves."

Never let it be said that I don't keep my woman happy. With just the trees to watch us, I pull the bike over to the shoulder of the road. She immediately jumps off the back. I dismount and pull her in for a long, wet kiss before pushing her head down against the seat so her ass sticks up in the air. With those heels she's the perfect height.

"Let me get you ready."

"Already there," she whimpers, and I reach my two fingers inside her thong to check.

This is why I love her on the back of my bike, she's dripping for me.

"I just need you."

"You got me, darlin'," I growl.

Never ceases to amaze me, Elise. I unbutton my jeans, pull the zipper down and tug them around my hips only. Kicking her feet apart to widen her stance at the same time tugging her thong to the side, I plunge in hard and fast. She gasps loudly from the intrusion, yet shoves back greedily against me. We go at it, pounding. Punishing.

"Harder!" She demands, practically screaming. "Oh gawd, harder Beau!"

I laugh. "I go any harder...my cock is liable...to punch a hole...through your abdomen."

Then we hear it, both our heads turn to the rumble of a car engine in the distance. "Don't you dare stop." She keens.

Same, I tell her, "Come on, baby girl. Gotta finish this."

The rumble gets closer. Not big on going to jail, but no way I'm pulling out if we don't finish before the car catches us. Still, I shift down, pounding as hard as I can physically pound. I feel it, the moment she tenses, her walls undulate, then she clamps those tight pussy muscles around my throbbing cock. And that's all she wrote. I lose it, spilling into her as she continues the vice grip, milking every drop from me. Fuck, I can't hardly move, but that car is close. We don't even have time for a proper comedown before I pull out with a hiss from Elise at our quick separation.

And I don't even have a napkin or anything to wipe myself down with, tucking back inside my jeans and zip, then help her stand. We only just have her thong back in place, her hands smoothing down her skirt when the car passes us.

It couldn't have been any closer. She laughs. I laugh, falling into each other.

"You want to go back, clean up?"

"No," she answers, surprising the hell out of me. "The squish as I walk feels sexy. I like knowing you're inside me."

Wow.

"Woman, you can't say shit like that to me or we will never make it into the club today."

She only shrugs. "I love you."

"Never gets old hearin' that."

SEVERAL OF THE waitresses and a few of the dancers fawn all over me. I push them away telling them what seems like for the hundredth time, "Not me you have to impress. I'm a man who likes tits, I'm already impressed. Boss-lady," I point to Elise, who seems a little startled by this new nickname, although there's amusement and excitement dancing in those eyes. "She's the manager. She's the one you need to impress."

You can see it, each one of those women thought coming on to me was a way to further their careers. Guess I can't blame them, for a long time—too long a time—I was single and up for being impressed. Kind of biting me in the ass, though, as I keep tryin' to let it be known, understood, that I'm totally, completely, officially off titty radar. Unless we're talking Elise.

"Can I get you anything?" Heidi, a pretty, little blonde waitress, one of them failing to clue in and continuing to lay it on pretty thick with me, finally turns her attention to the manager.

"Yeah," Elise answers, sharply. "Can I get you to keep your hands off and quit eye-fucking my man as he's already explained he's taken, and I control your employment?" Don't see that very often. I know she trusts me, so this show of possession is for the women here. She's setting up dominance. MC must be rubbing off on her. And I gotta say, this jealous bit is as sexy as fuck.

"I wasn't…" Heidi fumbles.

Elise stands from the table. She folds her arms across her tits, and cocks her head, pinning Heidi with a hard, take no bullshit, stare. "Save it. I hear you're good, those double Ds and tight ass will get you good tips and bring back regulars who'll want in your section, hoping to get in your pants. But try that shit again, you *will* find yourself sans job, got me?"

"Yes, Ms.—"

"Manning," Elise says.

Right at the same time, I shoot out, "Hollister."

"Manning," she says again. Now looking at me. "We aren't married yet. My license still says Manning."

"Your license still says Illinois," I correct her. "Why have 'em gettin' used to Manning when in a couple weeks they'll be changin' it over to Hollister, anyway?" I wink.

"Couple weeks?" she yells. "Did you hit your head? I figure at least a year."

"A year? Oh no, no, no. Already wasted five of 'em."

"So then what's another year?"

"Time we'll never get back. Bet Hadley wishes she had another year. Sure as shit know Duke wishes he had 'em."

"That's unbelievably sweet, Beau."

"I'm a sweet guy."

"You're an arrogant guy, yet your point has merit. I said yes, which means I'm sure about you. About us. So really, what the hell would we be waiting for?"

"You tell me, darlin'."

"It takes time to plan a wedding?" It's cute when she answers me in questions. Nervous habit I hope she never loses.

"You want big?" I ask.

"No, actually. Well, strike that—yes."

I wince.

She chuckles. "Not what you think. I want a pig roast, with a whole pig. And I want you to invite everyone who's important to you. Brothers and old ladies, as long as you don't invite your parents or Candy."

"Elise."

"No, Elise. Your parents hate me, and Candy was your long-term fuck toy."

"What I was gonna say is you got nothin' to worry about because George and Margo will not be gettin' an invite. And please give me some credit here. I might be redneck, but invitin' former fuck buddies to my weddin' seems too redneck even for me." That brings out the sweetest smile in the world and she sighs.

Can't fucking marry her fast enough.

N ever. I've never pictured myself watching a pole dance, especially up close and personal. Yet here we are. No judgment. I mean, I'd been a phone sex operator. Though, I never saw myself as a biker's old lady, either. Life certainly has thrown me some curve balls.

The way she swings upside-down using one leg, no arms. These women aren't sleazy. They're acrobatic with sick core muscles. Two dance to pay for Masters programs, and one for medical school. And they've impressed me.

Seriously. *Slick*, the MC's newest acquisition, has some pretty fantastic dancers, with some pretty fantastic abs.

Before Beau sat me down in my very own office, at my very own desk cluttered with blueprints and contracts this morning, talking me through the brothers' vision for the club, I'd never been inside a titty bar. No reason to. I have them so why pay money to see others? Their vision though, now that the renovations have started, is off the charts cool. Like I'd do girls nights out here just for the décor kind of cool.

First off, the walls have been painted black. Tables and

chairs in a black lacquered finish as well. To the right when you walk in is the bar. The bar has a serpentine ripple to hold the maximum number of bodies, classy black high back bar stools with a grate pattern along the high backs sit intermittently along the ripple. Opposite the bar is the VIP section with high backed leather, half-circle pleated seating. Each individual seat has a small square table set in equal spaces apart from each other to set beers or shots down on.

The VIP section is semi-private for lap dances. Then there's the stage. Three stages actually. The main one is the largest, an oval with a prominent pole and plenty of room for exotic dancing. Then there are two smaller satellite stages for private bachelor parties and the like. Blue light cascades down over everywhere. All glassware is frosted to look like ice so they appear to glow under the blue lights.

Even the new waitress uniforms look like class. Our version of the little black dress, shimmery satin, sleeveless with a bustier bodice, fitted and only dropping an inch below their bottoms. A slit up each thigh, almost reaches the crotch and there's a shimmery black satin pocket sewn on the front between the two slits to hold the float and tips. The pocket blends in with the rest to reveal a seamless look.

The women are allowed to wear the shoe of their choice as long as the heel is three inches or higher and black. As I said, class. The men already had the concept down. Had started gathering materials and stores such as tables, chairs, glasses and uniforms all kept in a warehouse while searching for the right location. Smart. Really smart. Because as soon as they signed on the dotted line, renovations started. Which is why, after only owning the place for a couple days, they're so far ahead. For a real high-end titty bar, which this place is, we require a high end atmosphere, dancers and wait staff. Only the best for our customers.

Once Pepper, the girl we'd been watching, our med

student, finishes her dance, I rush the stage because in this moment I couldn't be more excited if I were in Disneyland instead of a titty bar and she was Cinderella instead of our headlining dancer.

"Would you consider teaching classes?" I ask, although the asking sounds more like down on my knees with hands clasped against my chest begging. "Because I seriously want to put a pole in our bedroom like, yesterday." My eyes cut to Beau's wide ones as he listens with an air of rapt excitement. "I think it would be good for the club, teaching classes, not the putting a pole in my bedroom, pulling in a female clientele. That's a whole lot of untapped revenue. Plus, if women know what it's about and how good a shape they'd be in, I see less dramas showing up on our doorstep from women who might not like their men hanging out here. I read in the paper, just last week a man and a bouncer were sliced by a broken bottle because the guy's wife showed up at another club. Drama and expense we don't need."

"That's fuckin' brilliant," he whispers into my hair, arms wrapping around my waist from behind. "Why didn't I want you workin' here?"

"Because you're a caveman who wanted me barefoot and pregnant, and afraid titties would offend me."

"Recoverin' caveman," he counters. "And yes, I still want you pregnant. But I'm so glad to know titties don't bother you."

"I have them. Even been known to whip them out when my man's being a good boy."

"Don't I know it...but I'm never a good *boy*, darlin'. I'm all man." He shoots a grin. It's big and it's wicked.

"Compromise, then. We'll put a daycare in the back. Show our kids that boobs aren't a big deal."

"Fuck no!" he protests.

"Why?" I do not like the direction this conversation is heading one bit.

"*Why?* And rob my boy this father-son bondin' moment? They're tits not udders. It's a big moment in a boy's life when he discovers the true beauty of a pair of double Ds."

But, "That's just contributing to rape culture."

"Not my boy. He will know how to respect women and that no sure as fuck means no."

"What if we have girls?"

He shrugs. "Boobs are just boobs. Seein' as she won't be datin' until she's twenty-five and I reserve the right to hand-pick the bastard, it'll be up to her old man to show her the beauty."

"I'm sorry, you're going to *handpick* her boyfriend at *twenty-five*?"

"Yep."

"That's older than I am now, you realize. Older than we could possibly be having said daughter. And my father never chose who I dated."

"Elise, darlin', look how that turned out."

Okay—*ouch*. Now I'm pissed. "Horrible," I reply. There's a smugness creeping over his face that makes me want to punch him. "Because I ended up with a caveman biker who can't seem to remember women won the right to vote, own property, fight in wars, run countries." This last part I say in my best Scarlet O'Hara, as I clasp my hands over my heart, batting my lashes at him, "Whatever would we do without a big, strong man to help us decide how many breaths to take in a day?"

Pepper, who'd been listening, snickers.

"That'll be enough," he warns.

"Will it? Will it be enough because my man decides for me it's enough? What happened to you? This is not the Beau I knew in high school."

"You're right. I grew up."

"More like fell down—in IQ points."

"Might as well face it, that Beau's gone. Probably forever. Best remember that's not the Beau who won the girl, this one is."

"What? That Beau *did* win the girl," I threw at him. "He just didn't want her enough in the end."

"Elise, laundry."

"Yeah, whatever." Along with one long, frustrated breath —which when I feel him tense behind me I know he understands—I pinch the bridge of my nose, feeling a headache coming on. How the hell are we supposed to make it for the long haul when all we seem to do is fight? "Pepper, think about classes. I'm heading to my office. Paperwork to go over. Contractors, new girls, inspections."

This club could be my dream job, if Beau would only let up. As of right now, he's made it a nightmare. Done dealing with his caveman antics, I yank out from his hold. In my mind I'm storming off to my office. The way I pull away, he knows he's upset me. In reality, to the rest of the club, nothing should appear off.

But apparently the caveman doesn't take the hint that I'm done with him for now, as I only just sit down in my chair behind my desk when I hear, "I wanted you, and you damn well know it."

"Get over yourself, Beau. I'm done arguing."

For once, he says nothing, standing in the doorway with his hands on his hips. On any normal day, I'd internally cheer. Today, though, today his silence and the look of confusion infuriates me.

"I'm not stupid, this caveman you've got going. It's about Logan. Logan happened. What's more, I don't regret it. I regret how things ended up, but we—the three of us—had some really great times together. And you can't keep punishing me because your damn cousin beat you to the punch. You... you *lunk-head*." Great. Fantastic. He has me so frustrated that I'm stumbling over my words. What a way to make a point. I pause, taking in a deep breath to clear my head. Only when I feel ready do I give him the rest. "*You* became my rock, the person I turned to while Logan derailed. At least until everything fell apart. And yes, I will concede that I kept us apart, too. But that's done. I'm here now. You're here now. We don't have to live under the shadow of Logan because there isn't one. Not anymore. Not for a long time."

After my lengthy, and in my opinion, well executed speech, the only reaction I get? Beau blinks. "We done?" he asks. "I like screwin' my woman so much more than fightin' with her."

And I like the idea of being screwed. Though with all the pounding it's taken today, my vagina will be sore tomorrow. Still, our conversation is far from over. "I just—I just need to feel like you respect me. That I'm your partner, not some burden."

"*Hey.*" He moves finally, coming behind the desk to turn my chair to face him, and tilts my chin up with the tip of his finger to look me in the eyes. "You are always my partner, baby girl. Always. Never in your life could you be a burden. Even if I had to carry you on my back or wipe your ass for you, you'd never be a burden."

Well how about that? Old Beau's sweetness showing through.

"You say that now," I tease, "Until the time comes you honestly find yourself wiping my ass."

"We're lifers, Elise. Not gettin' rid of me that easy. Now," he says, purposely changing the subject. "I believe one of the concessions in hirin' you was that you're willin' to sleep with the boss."

204 | SARAH ZOLTON ARTHUR

"Okay." I smile innocently up at him, batting my eyelashes for the full effect. "Get Chaos in here."

"Not funny. Not even close to funny."

Oh, I think it's incredibly funny.

"This bein' your first day," he continues. "You wanna look over contracts or break in this desk?"

Hmm...contracts or penis? Contracts or penis? I don't bother to answer, unbuttoning my blouse instead of words. He smiles that crooked smile I love so much and turns to lock the door, pulling his tee up over his head as he returns to me. My vagina will definitely be sore tomorrow.

But I decide I very much like office, on my desk, in the middle of the day sex. Maybe as much as bent over a bike with my skirt hiked up, on the side of the road sex.

MY MAN LEFT me to it, satisfied I'll be able to handle the rest of my first day on the job, probably because I satisfied him in more personal ways before he left to go open up the bar. Per his instructions, either he or one of the prospects will be along this afternoon to pick me up and bring me home. Well, home-*clubhouse* not home-*home*, which I'm more than ready to get back to even if home-*home* happens to be only two houses down from David and Lenore and three houses down from George and Margo. Too many rules at the clubhouse, too many chances for me to mess up again. And truthfully with how Chaos reacted to our engagement this morning, I don't know when I'll be ready to deal with him again.

Four hours neck-deep in paperwork since he took off earlier, there's a single rap on my office door before Clint, one of the bouncers who with his overly bulging mass really only has two career choices, those being bouncer or professional football linebacker, sticks his head inside the room.

Since first walking in this morning, I knew looking at Clint would be one of the fun parts of my job. Of course, I'd never let that secret out with Beau around, or either Clint or I or both might find ourselves no longer employed. And I want this job, but Clint needs it. He and his lovely girlfriend Sirena—and I know she's lovely because he showed me a picture—are expecting their first baby.

In my defense, it's not my fault. Clint keeps his head shaved bald, and there is just something about a bald head. With his super dark skin and eyes so brown they appear black, he's the kind of man you stand back and admire with a low, slow, "*daammnn*, son."

Which is exactly what I realize I've done when he clears his throat and cocks an eyebrow at me with a, "*Really*?" and laughs at me, shaking his head.

Yes, I'm embarrassed but never let them see you sweat, right?

I clear my throat right back and ask, "What can I do for you?"

"Jeff, Stella and I are heading out to lunch and wanted to know if we could bring you back anything?" Jeff and Stella are the bartenders. They're here setting up the bar in the most ergonomic placement. Seeing as I know nothing about bartending, I figured letting the professionals set up that area was the smartest decision I could make in regards to keeping the booze flowing freely for our customers.

"That'll be great. What are you guys eating?"

"Mexican."

"Carnitas. Bring me back carnitas."

"Got it, boss lady. Shep will be on in fifteen. If there's any trouble until he gets here, just call."

"I can't assume we'll have any trouble in the fifteen

minutes you're gone. Boss is just overly protective." Even though the club's not open for business yet, Beau had the bouncers come in to keep an eye on us womenfolk because apparently, we can't keep an eye out for ourselves.

"Sirena works in an office with security guards. Don't take chances with her, either. Let me tell you somethin' about men, when we have somethin' worth protectin', we protect it. Any and every way we can."

One more thing to like about the man. "That's really sweet. I can't wait to meet Sirena."

His face actually darkens with a blush. "I don't know sweet, but it's true. Anyway, carnitas it is. *Right.*" Then he pats the door a couple times signaling the end of our conversation and withdraws from my office leaving me alone again.

My guess, Beau probably thought getting me sorted out this morning would take longer than it had, so he didn't schedule another bouncer to come in until after lunch because he probably figured he'd be here. But with our earlier—*erm*, activities—I think he probably forgot because there's no way Mr. Overprotective would ever leave me without a big, strong man to keep me company.

My cell phone rings, startling me. I don't recognize the number so I let it go to voicemail. It rings a second, and then again. Same number. Before letting it go to voicemail the third time, I press the green button to answer.

"*Tisk, tisk, tisk.* I told you not to go out," the deep, distorted voice on the other end says to me before I even say hello. "There are consequences, Elise."

Freaked, I hang up right away. The phone rings one more time, but I don't answer. Resting my forehead to the edge of the desk, I breathe in and out slowly to calm myself down. This pranking business is getting out of hand. Tommy, which means Beau, should probably hear about it. And he's going to be pissed I didn't tell him sooner.

The club is supposed to be empty except for me since I sent the waitresses and dancers home a couple of hours ago, and now my bouncer and bartenders have gone to lunch. When I hear a noise, like someone walking around, I glance down at my clock, anxious to meet Shep, and thankful for him to have gotten here early. So I smooth my hair down to make sure I look presentable, and shove up from my desk moving out to the main room of the club to introduce myself.

The space is empty.

I go through checking all the rooms off of the main, starting with where employees clock in. Empty.

This is so strange; I know I heard walking. When I cross back through the main to get to my office, that's when I see a box, a wrapped gift about the size of a shoebox. I hadn't noticed it during my first sweep which gives me an immediate unsettled feeling. And I have the feeling I'm playing right into someone's hands, but I have to see what's in that box. *I have to.* Damn my insatiable curiosity.

Slowly as I lift the lid, at first it doesn't register because really, who expects to see this kind of thing in a gift box? But once my brain makes the connection, I scream, drop the lid and stumble backward.

Do not hyperventilate. Do not hyperventilate.

No matter how badly I want to heed my own advice, the fact remains there is a heart in the box. Who expects to see a heart, a real live heart, in a box? And since I don't know enough about anatomy, I have no clue if it's human or animal. All I do know is whoever left the box left a note inside.

You cut out my heart, now I cut yours.

The box stays, I run. Back to my office immediately, dialing 911. Dispatch tells me to lock my office door until officers can get to me, which sounds like a plan. She stays on the line as I'm obviously scared out of my pants. And since this is a smallish town, it doesn't take long until the shrill of police sirens can be heard outside.

From there it's even less time when I hear Tommy call out, "Elise? Elise you here?"

Safety. What a feeling. I could cry I'm so happy. Unlocking and throwing open the door, I yell, "In here, Tommy." Then end the call with dispatch.

Four uniforms stand in the main room of the club. Tommy reaches me, wrapping me first in a friend hug before ever going into cop mode. "In the box," I whisper into his chest.

This would be when he morphs from Tommy Doyle friend to Tommy Doyle cop. Using gloves, which I did not use, he lifts the lid on the box muttering, *"shit"* when he gets a good look at what's inside. "Why're you here by yourself? What was Boss thinking letting you here alone?" And I can tell he's not really asking me but more speaking his frustration out loud. Until he's speaking them into the receiver of his cell. Beau's booming meltdown comes through loud and clear.

Tommy's busy going over my statement for the third time when Beau shoves his way in, and he's pissed. But despite that, he folds himself around me holding me tight, full body to full body.

"Sorry," I speak against his neck.

"What're you sorry for, darlin'?"

"You look pissed. Lately you get pissed, I get blamed."

And I chance a look in his eyes. The love I see there keeps me transfixed.

"Hell yeah I'm pissed." Beau's words have passion but lack the anger I'd been worried about. "But not at you, baby girl. I'm pissed that someone did this to you. I'm pissed that no one was here to protect you. I'm pissed at myself for droppin' the ball with you."

"I'm scared."

At my admission, he hugs me tighter until the short bursts of air he forces heavy through his nose start to draw out and become softer, as he calms down.

"Won't happen again. With my life, I promise it won't happen again." He touches his forehead against mine briefly before dropping delicate kisses on my cheeks, forehead, chin and then finally my lips.

We both turn our heads to the sound of Clint's voice yelling. "What the fuck?"

At the same time, who I assume to be Shep shows up muttering, "Holy hell." And then there's the rumble of bike engines in the background. It looks like the gang's all here.

"Can't have 'em inside yet, Boss. Crime scene," Tommy tells him.

"Gotcha. Shep, Clint. Outside." There's no way I'll let go of Beau, but thankfully, there's no way he's letting go of me either. Linking our fingers, he leads me out into the parking lot where Shep, Clint, the bartenders and several Lords including Duke, Scotch, Blood, Levi and to my surprise Chaos wait for us.

I look at Chaos, bruised chin and all, before anyone to tell him outright, "I didn't do anything this time. It wasn't my fault." At my words, he flinches as if *I'd* struck him.

"Elise," he starts, but I hold my hand up to stop him.

"I just wanted you to know, is all." Then I bury my face against Beau's shoulder soaking up his warmth and protection. His arms, one around my waist and one around the back of my neck hold me so tenderly I almost break down.

Almost.

But I can't, not here, not now in front of all these men. I'm a Lord old lady. Time to prove my mettle. I vow to do this by not only *not* crying, but shifting in Beau's arms to look each man in the eye, speaking clearly and confidently. "I was in my office working, filling out paperwork the whole time. I didn't do anything stupid."

Surprisingly, Duke is the first to speak up. "Elise doesn't leave the compound without protection." Then he looks at our bouncers. "Someone is always on her at the club. Until this shit ends, and know it now, it will end soon, she needs to pee, clear the restroom and stand outside the stall until she's done."

"That's hardly necessary." I try to protest.

While Clint tells him, "Got it" with a curt head nod.

"Elise sweetheart," Duke continues. "Boss claimed you as his old lady which makes you Brimstone. But when he slipped that ring on your finger that elevated you to an entirely different level. We take care of our own, but go after a wife or kid, that brings a wrath forged in hell. Whoever did this will pay, and pay dearly. Can you handle that?"

Without delay, I nod my head. "*Yes.*"

Beau told me when shit got real they handled it.

Shit can't get more real than a heart in a box.

"Levi." Beau orders. "Check with Tommy. See if she's cleared to go. Grab her purse from her office."

"On it," Levi answers quickly, then takes off inside the club.

"Are you taking me?" I ask Beau quietly. "He's on his bike."

"Yes ma'am. But he'll come too because I need to be back here talkin' to Tommy. From here on out, when I'm not with you he's got Elise duty."

"Okay."

"*Okay?* Thought you'd at least argue with me a bit."

"Baby, someone left me a heart in a box with a note saying they were going to cut mine out. After just getting engaged this morning, I'd like to live to see my wedding day,

and I'd like to be around to give you those hypothetical children *un*-hypothetically."

He turns me in his arms again to face him, tugging my
hair gently to tilt my chin up. With his other hand copping a
feel on my bottom, he kisses me full on the mouth deep, long
and heavy in front of all his brothers. Surprisingly to no
catcalls. It's not lost on any of them what went down today.

Dare I ask, what next?

19

BEAU

S he's naked underneath me, moving, gripping the sheets, biting her bottom lip to keep from screaming out my name again. It might be our fourth time today, and I know I have to give her body a rest, but takin' her tonight means she's alive and unhurt. We went through so much to finally be together. Now is the time we're supposed to get our happy. What he almost took from us, being by herself, anything could have happened.

Thankfully the douchebag only dropped off the box, but just knowing he could've gotten to her, I could hardly think straight, which Elise was in tune to. When I got back tonight after dropping her off at the clubhouse and heading back to Tommy and my brothers at *Slick* so we could attempt to figure shit out, she sought to calm me down by bringing me to our bed and making love to me.

It works. Just as she knew it would. As she comes, I let go right along with her. Collapsing onto my back after my breathing calms down, and pulling Elise over to tuck under my arm.

"You were brave today," I say against the skin of her cheek after placing a kiss there.

"I was scared," she counters.

"Bravery ain't the absence of fear, you know that. I'm so damn proud of you."

"But I should have told you about the pranks."

"Fuck, *yeah*. You should've. But if I hadn't been a dick to you that mornin', maybe you would've."

Her kiss to my neck, I take as my answer. Then tilting her head to look up at me with those shimmering topaz eyes, she smiles a smile filled with so much love and hope, it takes my breath away. "Why don't we go on a real date tomorrow night?" she says. "We can go to the city, whichever city you want. But let's go, forget just for a night. What do you think?"

"Darlin', you keep smilin' at me like that, you could get me to storm the gates of hell and spit in the face of the devil, himself. That's a mighty powerful weapon you got spread across those lips."

"I take it's a yes?"

"The brothers'll think I'm crazy, what with all that's goin' down, but Duke'll understand. And if Duke does, the brothers will eventually."

Elise moves her head, tearing that smile away from me but replacing it by snuggling her cheek against my chest, arm slung around my middle, bare breast pressed against my ribs. Sighing as she snuggles once more. "I love you, Beau Hollister."

All the day's shit gets washed away with those five words.

Once she closes her eyes, it don't take long for sleep to catch up. Been a pretty exhaustive day so I can't blame her for crashing. As for me, not sure I'll ever find sleep again. Even though she's safest here, no safer place for her, when I close my eyes I see that note and everything, everything I could've lost today comes hurtling back at me. Instead I hold her close, always on alert. Her own private sentry standing guard even if I'm laying down to do it.

Middle of the night, clock says three a.m., I been watching her sleep for a while, twisting tendrils of her hair around my finger and untwisting them gently. Stroking the side of her head. Someone has the nerve to disturb us, knocking lightly on the door. Then displaying his death wish, Carver shoots his head into the room, just his head between the door and jamb.

"I know." He cuts off before I go at him. "I wouldn't be here if it weren't important. You gotta come see this Boss. Has to do with the Elise situation. Toby just got home from closing down *Lady's*. He found it at the gate... You just better come see."

Then he ducks out, closing the door behind him. With a kiss to her temple, I extract myself from her hold, from our bed. She rolls over on her side, using my pillow as a body pillow but don't stir. Knowing she'll be fine, I shrug into my jeans from last night, pull a T-shirt over my head and slip on my boots before I head out to the common, making sure to close the door quietly behind me. Don't want one of my brothers to accidentally see her gorgeous body naked while she's sleeping.

They're all waiting for me in the common. And not a one of them looks happy.

"What?" I ask. "What am I missin'?"

Duke, of all people, walks up laying a hand to my shoulder. "We got a message tonight."

"A message?" My eyebrows pull together.

"Brother, you can't freak out. Freaking out will not keep her safe. But I warn you, it's pretty gruesome. Tommy's been called." He takes a long breath in then lets it out even slower. "*Shit*," he says. And turns to walk out the front of the compound. I follow, my brothers filing in behind me. Somehow, I feel more like a death row inmate taking his final walk than I do the VP of a motorcycle club.

We keep walking past the rows of parked bikes and couple of pickups to the front gate. Blue and Blaze pull back the chain-link. Sitting in the middle of the drive there's an old, metal, milk can. The kind dairies used to use at the turn of the last century to hold the milk they'd eventually fill the smaller glass jugs with. Waist-high and equally as round, I'm not sure how anyone could have breached the compound to set this sucker down without one of us hearing.

Duke hands me a pair of gloves. "Put these on first."

I slip them on just before unlatching the lid and lifting. "What the fuck?" Throwing my hand to mouth, I stumble back attempting to reel in my shock and not vomit in front of my brothers. "Is... is that?"

"Sorry Boss," Carver says off to my side. "I wanted to warn you but you'd never have believed me. And you needed to see this before it gets tied up in red tape."

He's right, I did need to see it. And he's right, I'd never have believed it. Shayla McCrery shoved inside the can filled with water. Pale and waterlogged. Who would believe this? She'd wanted Logan something fierce when we were in school. She was a hot little piece back then, probably would've had him for a time if Elise hadn't shown up in front of the Whippy Dip that day. I'd hooked up with her a few times because, why not? A fact I'm painfully reminded of by the note floating next to her head. *Sloppy Seconds*. That's all it says. That's all it needs to say.

"No one saw who dropped it off? Where were the prospects? Who was guarding the gate? Elise has to fucking feel safe somewhere, and if we can't make it here, what am I supposed to do?"

"Blaze was taking a leak, and Blue heard something bothersome coming from further down the fence. He snuck away to check it out. The man was doing his job. And a man is allowed to relieve himself. This was in no way a fuckup." Duke makes sure to remind me.

It's at this point sirens rip through the air, flashing red and blue lights up the nighttime sky. Tommy, along with several county sheriff deputies spill out of cruisers surrounding the entrance to the compound.

He walks straight to me. "*Got-dammit*, Boss. What the hell is happening? Twice in one day?"

"You think I want this? My fiancé was threatened this mornin' and now there's a dead woman in a milk can, a woman I've had sex with."

"Who is it, Boss?" he asks, this time more angry friend than police officer.

"Pop the lid. Look for yourself. It's bad though, man." Tommy pulls on a pair of rubber gloves from a bag by his feet and pops the lid on the can, sucking in a sharp breath when he registers who's inside.

"You've gotta be shitting me," he mutters to himself, shaking his head. "She was a bitch, especially to Maryanne, but she didn't deserve this."

"No... she didn't."

By now the sirens have woken up every hot mama or piece who spent the night, and Elise standing outside barefoot, with sex hair, shivering in nothing but my tee, being held back by Levi and Blood.

"Beau?" she calls out. One terrified word.

"Go to her," Tommy tells me. "Just make sure I get your statement in the morning."

Don't have to tell me twice. I take off feigning as much confidence as I can muster before reaching my woman.

Levi and Blood move off to the side, allowing her passage, and when they do, she takes off full sprint, crashing against me. I immediately wrap my arms around her, using one hand to pet her hair while tryin' to calm her down. "Shh... it's okay, darlin'. You're safe."

"What happened this time?" she cries into my shirt. "Another message for me, isn't it?"

"This one I'm afraid was for me, baby girl."

"What is it? I can't tell from here. What was the message?"

How do I tell her? I decide to just rip off the Band-Aid and tell it to her straight. "Shayla's dead, darlin'."

Elise presses even closer at the news, but don't say a word. So I give her the rest. "Stuffed in a milk can filled with water. She drowned. There was a note. It said... see, what you need to know is that she and I hooked up a few times. Nothin' serious, just hookin' up—"

"What'd the note say, Beau?" she cuts me off.

"Sloppy seconds."

She gasps, going stock still in my arms.

"*Baby girl?*"

"It was Houdini, wasn't it?" she whispers, stifling a sob.

"Why you think that?"

"She drowned in a milk can. One of his most famous escapes."

That didn't even register. I feared it might be him, but...

"And, he called me sloppy seconds. In the cemetery, remember?"

Shit. No, with everything going down, that's something I did not remember.

"Why is he coming after you? Why me? What'd we do, Beau?"

I don't know how to answer her, and it makes me even more pissed off. We take off walking back inside the compound, my arm around Elise as we move through the common back to our room. I kick my boots off and drop my jeans using only one hand because I refuse to let go of her. Then I climb back in bed and tug to bring her down on top of me.

Carefully, I rip my tee up over my head and peel away the one she's wearing until we're skin to skin, and tuck the blankets around us like a cocoon. No barriers between us. I know she's scared, hell who wouldn't be?

For a good long while she holds tight onto me, her body trembling. Seems like she trembles for hours, neither of us finding sleep. Eventually, though, she begins to settle, and still, neither of us has spoken a word.

It's time. "I don't want you goin' into work today, darlin'. Please don't argue with me. I know we can't let this control our lives, but it is for now. Two attacks yesterday. A woman's dead. Stay here."

"I'll stay home. Call Clint, have him stop by to get the key. I don't want those girls left alone for any reason while they're setting up."

"I'm right there with you." Then I lean down and kiss Elise with everything I have in me. Don't even try to hold back the emotion. Not today.

With both hands, she rests them against my bare chest, pressing her lips harder against mine as I continue to hold her. She's not holding back her emotion, either.

"All I ever did was love you, Beau," she says after she breaks away from my lips. She glides her hand up from her tattoo over my heart to hold my cheek in her hand. "And I don't regret that. Not for one minute. Just... when do I get the chance to really show you? To give you the home you want?"

"One thing you need to remember. As long as I have you and you're safe. As long as we're together, I *am* home. You're my home, Elise. No matter where we end up in the world, you stick by my side, and I'm home. We'll work on normal, on that weddin' and babies when all this has settled down. But I'm always home with you, darlin'."

"Do you think Logan cursed us or something?"

I bark out an easy laugh. "No, I don't think he's cursed us. I just think some jackoff is usin' him against us. Someone knows our history and is takin' advantage."

One rap on the door cuts our conversation. It opens and Duke strides in as I make sure the blankets are tucked securely around my woman. He stops next to the bed. "Heard voices, knew yer up."

"Whatcha need?" I ask him, eyeing my president suspiciously.

"I think we should send Elise away for a few days."

"No. *Absolutely not.*"

"*Boss.*" He uses his hands to usher a calm-down order. "I know you don't want to, but we'll send her to the brothers up in Chicago. She was safe there. I already contacted Blood's sister. Says she'll be happy to take Elise in. We'll go secret. The boys are on alert."

"If she goes, I take her. I'll borrow Tommy's Explorer. Have him drive it to the compound. We switch, one of the brothers takes him back to the station, as long as he keeps down so no one sees him leavin'. Don't want them catchin' on and comin' after us."

"Can do that. But we'll need you back here. You get the night, then it's back or he might figure shit out. He knows you wouldn't be away from Elise."

"Right."

Duke walks out then and Elise leans her forehead against the dip of my throat. "I don't want to leave you," she says. "I'll go if you ask me to... but I'm scared to be away from you." The last part she whispers, tearing *my* heart out with each word. I did this. Every bit falls on me because I invaded her life, brought her back to live here, even when she tried so many times to get away. If I'd just have let her be. *Shit.*

"Don't." Her voice drops low, serious, admonishing me. "I know you too well, Beau. We had a rocky start and yes, I was resistant. Not because I didn't want you, but because of how much I did, and still do. I'm your home? Well, guess what? You're my home, too. You said it yourself, we're lifers. Don't take on this guilt. Don't take away my life, okay? Just... *don't.*" Her eyes tear, the wet falling against my chest.

"We're better together than we are apart, baby girl." All I have in me to say, as I clear the thickness from my throat feeling her sad, hot, tears streak my skin.

Even though I know I should send her away, that she'd be better off to cut ties with me completely, we both know how true my words are. She might be safer, but she'd have no kind of life. Neither would I. Existence. Apart, that's the best we could hope for. Because it's all either of us had before. And as selfish as it makes me, I can't go back to that. Not after getting a glimpse of the promised land.

She relaxes against me, but I'm not through. After pausing to get the rest of my thoughts together, I do what has to be done. "We're better together, but Elise, I'm askin' you to go to Chicago."

She gasps like I've smacked her across the face. I hurry to continue.

"Not forever, just 'til we can get a handle on him. I swear if you need me for anything, you call me. But if somethin' happened to you, just... darlin' I wouldn't survive it. And I know how weak I sound tellin' you. But straight-up honesty, losin' you would send me over an edge there's no comin' back from. You understand what I'm sayin'?"

She nods. The hair from the top of her head rubs against my throat, filling my every breath with the smell of that coconut shampoo she loves to use. Fuck if that ain't a gut clench. Fuck if I don't know if I'm making the right decision sending her away. Because fuck, I got a feeling this shit's gonna last longer than any of us foresee.

"I'll go to Chicago, Beau."

"I love you, Elise Manning."

"Hollister." She laughs through her tears still streaking down my chest. "Why get used to Manning when in a couple weeks it'll be Hollister?"

I tilt her chin up gently, pressing a deep, slow, open-mouthed kiss against her lips, using my thumb to swipe away the tears from her cheek. Once she settles back in, it don't take long for her to sleep again. Crying I hear, is exhausting.

Gently I shake her awake. It's early, only six, but still dark which we need for this to work. Tommy left in Levi's truck. I wanna be at least a couple of counties away before first light hits. She's disoriented, as she would be. I've spent the last ten minutes packing her bag, hating every damn minute of it. Because I know it means we'll be separated without being able to promise a return date. However long it takes, it takes. *Shit*. Life is gonna suck without her.

"Come on, baby girl. Get dressed."

Her groggy eyes find mine as I hold out a pair of black yoga pants to her.

"You can shower at Liv's place."

Elise shoves my hand away, shaking her head. "No. I've changed my mind. I need to stay with you, Beau. Okay? I'll stay in the compound. Anything you need, I promise. Just let me stay here. *Please*."

God, she sounds so desperate, she's tearing at my heart but we both know she can't stay. It ain't safe. "You gotta go darlin'. I hate it. I know you hate it, but you gotta go."

Defeated, her eyes cast down as she gives an almost imperceptible nod. Though she makes no move to dress, forcing me to squat down in front of her. I slip one pant leg over her foot, and then the second over the other, pulling them slowly up over her calves. Finally finding her legs, we stand together so I can tug them up the rest of the way. My hands graze her hips. She sucks in a breath and holds my hands there briefly before letting go. Without a word, I take her bra from the bed to slide it up both arms into place and secure it at the back, wrapping my arms around her like a hug to do it.

Elise rests her cheek against my shoulder, kissing my collarbone lightly then lifts her cheek and her arms above her head, waiting for me to drop the tee down over her head. Flip flops on her feet, we leave our room. Her bag in one hand, her hand in my other, she lets me lead us through the hallway into the common where all my brothers wait for us.

Levi, back from dropping off Tommy, walks up first. "It won't be long." He hugs her.

Next, there're hugs and arm pats from Carver, Blood, and Duke whispers, "Take care, sweetheart." Then more farewells from Toby, Blaze, Blue, and a few other brothers.

We're just about out the front door when Chaos stops us. He turns to Elise. "Be safe, sweetheart. Stay with Livvy, she's tough, she's got your back." He's got one of those model faces women fawn over, even with the bruise I gave him yesterday. Easy to read. And the way it reads he's ten kinds of uncomfortable.

Chaos rubs his hand along the back of his neck. "I'm sorry for what I said to you. Boss is lucky to have found a good woman to love him as much as you do."

This is a big moment. I slide my hand around Elise's waist, to tuck her under my arm, and shoot him a look to tell him we're good, we're solid. Chaos ain't known for apologizing to anyone. In true Chaos form, he has to lighten the mood by being a jackass about it.

"I can count on one hand the number of people I've said that to. You really should feel honored."

"That Beau has had four other women to love him as much as I do?" she teases back.

I give her a squeeze.

"I'm just teasing baby," she says, almost solemnly. The levity used with Chaos gone.

"I know." That thickness is back again. My voice fucking cracks. "I know," I recover. And I can feel everyone's eyes on us. It's time to go.

WE MAKE THE DEADLINE, exactly two counties away when the first light hits. Elise has been quiet, choosing to look out the window instead of talking to me. This cut cuts deep. We only have so much time left together for a while.

"Don't be mad at me, baby girl. I'm not sending you away because I want to."

"I'm not mad. Promise. Just tired. It seems since my father died, we haven't been able to catch our breath. Right when we think we've got a handle on one problem, another crops up."

"Do you trust your man, darlin'?"

She turns to stare at me.

"Do you trust me to take care of you?"

"Of course," Elise answers without hesitation.

"Sometimes I don't trust myself," I say. It's honest, but not what I'd intended to say.

"Pull over," she demands. When I don't, she says it again. "Pull over."

This time I do as she asks, pulling into the next park and pool we come to. Park and pools, or, the lots where folks who live on those long winding roads off the highway, it'd add an extra hour on the trip to pick up, meet to commute the rest of the way into the city for work. They're relatively empty this time of morning.

Elise climbs over the center console to straddle me, a knee to each side of my hips. She presses her hands to my cheeks, looking directly in my eyes.

"Sorry I got a little freaked this morning. If anyone else had asked me to leave, I'd have outright refused. But you, Beau, you, I trust with my life. If you say I need to go, I go."

"Good to hear your faith in me."

Hands continuing to hold my face, Elise strokes her thumbs along the apples of my cheeks. "Just promise you'll come home safe to me. I lost my dad." Then she stops to breathe, her eyes closed. When she opens them, they're bright with unshed tears as she searches mine. "Baby, you're all the family I have left."

"You finally think of us as family?" I twist her hair around my hand at the nape of her neck to tilt her head up and press my forehead to hers. For some reason my breathing gets heavy, saturated with the emotion she's just thrust at me. I'm the luckiest man in the world.

The corner of Elise's lip tips up right before she leans in to kiss me.

"Fuck yeah you do," I gloat and kiss her back.

Our hands roam as we go at one another hot and heavy. She shifts on my lap which knocks her knee into the seat-back lever. When she lifts her knee to readjust, it catches on the lever and the seat flattens backward, thrusting her forward so her forehead smashes against the bridge of my nose.

"*Shit,*" I bite out.

Elise giggles as she pushes up from me with one hand while trying to rub the bright red spot on my nose.

I gently slap at her hand. "You gigglin' at my pain?"

Her giggle turns to a full-blown laugh, and she throws her head back. But when she begins to crumple forward again, I put my hand to the center of her chest stopping her forward momentum.

"Whoa, whoa, *whoa*—keep that noggin away from my face."

"Does it hurt?" she asks seriously, although she's serious with laughter in her eyes.

"It's tender," I whine, rubbing the spot she'd tried to rub a few minutes ago.

The laughter fades from her eyes, leaving only the serious. "Let me kiss it and make it better," she says. Then Elise brings her hands up to hold my face and leans in to press her lips in three spots down my nose, letting her lips linger for a long moment against the skin between each.

After the last one, I let out an exhaustive breath and tilt my head up so our lips connect. Like my nose needs any more abuse. This time it's me who's responsible, smashing our noses flat. Our eyes close. One of Elise's hands moves from my cheek to finger the hair at the back of my neck, keeping my lips pressed to her. It's slow and sweet. Elise's kisses feel like life and happiness and future. I can't get enough of 'em and know I'll never grow tired of 'em. Fuck, I'm gonna miss this woman.

All too soon, she pulls back, her eyes open and looking right into my eyes. I'm two seconds from going full-on broody when she blows my mind once again.

"Thank you," she says. "For loving me. Thank you for never giving up."

Dammit. I don't wanna let her go.

B eau rolls the Explorer to a stop outside Moe's bar, double parking in front of a row of bikes. Several Lords spill out to greet us as if they've been waiting for us. It's weird to see the Illinois rockers again. Seeing as the last time I had, Beau and I were in a completely different place in our relationship. As in, according to *me*, we didn't have one. All my doing, running scared. I even kneed him in the balls.

At the memory, I snicker. Beau glances at me out of the corner of his eyes, smirking. I know he remembers it too.

The men stand guard while Beau and I are escorted inside. The smoke is not as thick as the last time I'd been here, but in my opinion, still too thick for this of morning and chokes off the fresh air. I fan in front of my face, and cough.

Rick, the bartender, waits to speak until the door closes behind us. He turns on me. "You're a lot of trouble, little girl."

Then with a chin lift to Beau, Rick asks *him*, "Sure you're not ready for some new snapper?"

I gasp, first from being called such a derogatory word as

'snapper'—as if I have nothing more to offer than what's between my legs—and second because, well, I finally admitted to Beau that I love him, and thirdly, this isn't my fault.

Beau turns some seriously angry eyes on the man who, really, should know better. "You sure you wanna live?" he asks back.

Rick holds up his hands like he's surrendering. "Hey, I'm just saying, plenty of pussy to fuck without all the headache."

"Keep sayin' it, and you won't have to worry about my headaches 'cuz you'll be dead. Got me?" Then Beau turns to me. "We're waitin' on Liv. Got some business to discuss with the brothers in back. Stay here, yeah?"

"Yeah, baby," I answer, because this time, I'm not about outrunning Beau, but am all about staying safe and alive.

Very suddenly he fists a handful of my hair to pull me in for a brief, yet highly expressive kiss. Not one of his sweet ones from this morning, but more possessive to show these men exactly what they're in charge of protecting.

Yes, I get all that from a kiss.

Then just as abruptly he drops his hand and walks out of the main bar area to a room off the back by the hallway leading to the restrooms. And he does it leaving me breathless for a moment. The sound of a snicker reminds me that I'm among people and I pull it together.

"I'm Crass." The snickering man introduces himself.

"No doubt," slips out without my meaning it to. Me and my mouth. But luckily, he barks out a laugh in lieu of causing me bodily harm.

"You got looks and sass." The jerk reaches out to run his thumb over my lips. "Can't tell you how badly I wanna fuck that mouth right now."

"Um…" Before he gets a wild hair to act on his desire to violate my lips, I slowly back away from him.

"Don't worry. You're the founding chapter VP's old lady, you're safe. Doesn't mean I can't fantasize."

"I'd rather you didn't if it's all the same. Beau—erm—Boss is the only one who gets to have relations with any part of me, and he'd probably break your neck for looking twice my way."

He laughs again. "Beau? Seems I really mistook the situation."

"Uh, how did you take the situation?"

"Thought maybe you started as a piece who worked her way up the ranks. Did your time as a hot mama. If the gash is good enough."

Dear God, what is wrong with these men? If snapper isn't bad enough, now they throw in *gash*? That's reprehensible. "I take offense to the term gash, and I was never a piece or hot mama. Never."

"Can see that now. A hot mama even elevated to old lady, would never call Boss by his given name. Now you're really safe. You girlie just earned my personal protection."

"Why? If you don't mind me asking?"

"Let's just say I know a little about having it and having it taken away."

I understand a great deal about this man now. "Sorry," I say with nothing else to add because I am.

But he doesn't answer me, instead, he turns to slam the whiskey Rick had slid on the bar next to him while we were talking.

His signal to the end of our conversation. But now having had it, I feel safer being here until Beau can bring me back home.

We only sit silent for about five minutes when Livvy walks in. Same gorgeous strawberry blonde locks as before, but today, as compared to how she'd dressed the first time we met, she's dressed down. In a pair of dark jeans, which make her butt look fabulous.

And I know I'm not the only one who thinks it, as every pair of eyes left in the bar follows that butt as it makes the walk toward me. The woman paired those jeans with a black leather halter top not even long enough to cover her abs and black biker boots. She just rewrote the definition of hot while here I am, standing at the bar wearing an oversized tee and yoga pants.

"Girl, we have a lot of catch-up coming." This is how she greets me. It's nice to see her again, though I wish our reunion could be under better circumstances. Thin, toned arms wrap around me once she reaches me.

"Yes, I guess we do."

"So I guess this means Beau doesn't have to die?"

I throw my hand over my face laughing my fool head off. What a memory. An actual happy memory of me and Liv singing karaoke. She joins in with her high-pitched chipmunk chitter.

"No," I force myself to say. "No, I really don't want Beau dead. I shouldn't have fought it, but I was scared. In my experience, it was easier to try to dislike him, than to admit I had feelings for him, which five years ago, ended in hurt. A whole lot of hurt."

"But you've stopped fighting it?" she asks soberly.

"*Yeah*. He had to remind me that he's worth taking a chance on again."

"Take it he is."

"Liv, he's so worth it, I feel stupid for having fought it for as long as I did."

She opens her mouth to respond but the men take that opportunity to file out of the backroom, Beau in the lead, beelining straight for me. Only once he takes me fully into his arms does he acknowledge Livvy with a chin lift. "Liv."

"Hey, Bossman. Good to see you again."

"Wish it was for shits and giggles. Thanks for takin' my girl in."

"Always… *always*."

"Boss." The president of the Illinois chapter approaches us. The patch on his cut says *Tag*, which I heard the men back home talking one day about his accomplishments. Apparently, Tag is short for Toe Tag, making said accomplishments quite clear. Glad he's on our side. "Boys don't have all day. You got the escort now. The women need to leave the condo, they take a man with them. Crass here just volunteered. He's a good man. Knows his shit. He'll stay with them at all times. He'll call backup for any outdoor excursions."

"Crass, good to see you again." Beau pats his arm. "I don't have to remind you the precious cargo you're protectin'."

The man eyes both me and Livvy then nods his understanding. "Fully aware."

WE'RE DEFINITELY a sight to behold. A Harley riding, black leather motorcade rumbling down Lake Shore Blvd. Though only Beau, Liv, and I in Tommy's Explorer, and Crass on his bike, pull into the parking garage. As we exit the vehicles, the men take up positions, Beau to the front of us, and Crass bringing up the rear. Seems a lot of extra trouble when Houdini shouldn't even know where I am. But it makes my man feel better, so he'll get no complaints out of me. He already shoulders more stress than one man should have to, no one can accuse me of adding to it. Not anymore. Nashville stressed him because of me. There will never be a repeat of Nashville. Not if I can help it.

Liv swipes a key card to gain us entry into the building.

Her high rise has so many condos, the building so large, there are two elevators per wing, four wings total—north, south, east, and west. Livvy lives in the north wing. As soon as we enter, Beau pushes the button for the fifteenth floor, meaning he's been here before. As the doors shut, Liv digs her keys out of her purse.

"You remembered," Beau says to her. She nods but gives no further insight on what he's referring to. Though I can't deny the bite of jealousy from my man and my friend having some sort of shared history.

"Get that look off your face," he says. I look to Liv to determine what look she's wearing. "Not her. You."

Oh. Me? "Wha-what look am I supposed to get off?"

"The one that says you think I had sex with your friend. Woman, do you honestly think I'd have you, my old lady, my *fiancé*, holed up with some piece of ass I'd bedded in the past?"

"No. That's not it. It's just... I spent so much time fighting you. You had moments with Liv that I wasn't a part of because I was too scared to trust you." The tears start stinging my eyes. "And now you have to leave me. What if something happens, Beau?" God, I feel weak breaking down in front of Crass.

Beau tugs me into his arms though, holding on tight. "Shh... nothin' gonna happen, darlin'. I'll come get you in a couple a days."

"He killed Shayla," I whisper. "Something happens to you I'll have to live knowing I wasted those precious days. Or what if something happens to me? I was selfish and kept those memories from you."

"You still trust me?"

"Yes."

"Then trust nothin' will happen. This is just precaution."

"But what if—"

He cuts me off. "What if my aunt had balls? Then she'd be my uncle."

"Or your aunt with balls." I wipe my nose with the collar of my T-shirt.

Snickering, he agrees, "Or my aunt with balls."

"I just love you so much, Beau," I whisper against his throat.

Thankfully the doors open for us. I stare straight ahead, refusing to make eye contact with the witnesses to my emotional breakdown.

"Lucky bastard," I think I hear Crass mutter as we exit. But that's as much as either of them say about it.

Liv unlocks the door inviting the three of us inside her home. It's a beautiful space, mid-century modern. Decorated in mushrooms. I love it. As much as I'd love to admire the space for a moment, Beau excuses us, leading me by the hand down a narrow hallway.

Yes, Beau knows exactly where he's going and where he's going is Livvy's guest room. What I expect is frantic, throw me on the bed, hardcore *'I'm not going to see you for a few days and I'm angry this asshole Houdini is putting you in danger'* fucking. What I get is so far from that. It's the opposite. He doesn't fling me. He scoops me gently into his arms as he kicks the door closed with his foot. Then he lays me even more gently across the bed, my hair fanning out over the pillow as if he's staging a perfect memory to get him through.

When he moves his body over mine, it's a slow, deliberate glide. And then... and then he takes my face in his large hands, stroking the apples of my cheeks with his calloused thumbs, the fingers on each hand holding against my neck and ears. He tilts my chin up just enough to capture my lips in a full, deliciously deep kiss. Again, nothing frantic. So much can be read from a kiss. And up 'til now I thought I'd read all his greatest works.

I was wrong.

If a picture can be worth a thousand words, this kiss has to be worth a million, all of them expressing, "I love you... you are my life" in a way saying the words never could.

Message received. Message so damn received, emotion clogs my throat and tears sting the corners of my eyes. Not sad like in the elevator. These tears emanate from some other emotion, altogether, and it's altogether overwhelming. We are the air and trees, neither good without the other. We are the embodiment of need and love.

Slowly, and only breaking the kiss when he has to, to lift my T-shirt up over my head, but resuming the beautiful torture the moment the hem clears my lips, Beau undresses me. In the time since our reunion, we've had all kinds of sex. From kinky fucking, to hardcore banging quickies. We've made love. But this—this has that something special which cannot be labeled. Something I've never until this moment knew existed. Nothing short of the most beautiful, touching moment of my entire twenty-three years. So beautiful, so touching, I'm unsure if I'll feel a moment like this ever again.

As he loves me, because there's really no other word for it, as he loves me with kisses and our bodies connected, the buildup he builds within me can't be described. Not as a tightening coil, or as a raging fire, or even a slow burn. I'm at a loss for how to describe it, but just know it's there building between us, for me, for us. Giving me the chance to process every emotion he's communicating and giving me the chance to answer back.

When I finally hit my breaking point and tumble over the edge, I feel him filling me as he tumbles right along with me. And as I fall, it's not on a scream of his name or a shout out to the Lord Almighty, but on a whispered gasp, concealing a promise. And it's nothing short of the greatest orgasm given by anyone in the history of orgasms. Of this, I'm sure.

Beau still doesn't speak, so neither do I. He rolls over, keeping his hand at my backside. He keeps us connected. We lay on our sides, my leg hitched up over his hip, face to face, chest to chest.

"You need me to pull out?" he whispers, finally breaking the silence.

Still too raw with emotion, I shake my head. I need to feel our connection for as long as possible.

"Good," is all he answers. Then the room falls quiet again.

Well before I'm ready for it, a soft knock resonates against the door followed by Livvy's soft voice. "Boss, Chaos is on my phone. He says he needs to speak with you right away. Says there's been a development. I'm sorry."

"*Yeah.*" His voice cracks. "Yeah, I'm comin'."

He shifts pulling out of me, disconnecting us. Yet instead of letting go, I hold on tighter.

"Darlin'." He coaxes my arms loose, or at least tries.

"*Beau,*" his name hiccups through my lips on a sob.

"Shh... it's all gonna be fine, baby girl."

"I know. Or I *should* know... it's just... my head understands it's temporary. So then why does my heart feel like we're really saying goodbye?"

Pain washes over his face. He doesn't need it. He doesn't deserve it. How do I stop feeling this, though? I'd turn it off if I could. But it's here. All the time. With every breath. It's like my body knows what neither of us is willing to admit: I'm about to lose the love of my life.

Nevertheless, he extracts himself from my hold. As always, gently. Beau kisses my fingers at the knuckle before dropping my hand completely.

We both dress and when he leaves, I follow closely behind.

Even worse than the knowledge that my Beau will be

leaving me is the pity stares from Liv and Crass directed solely at me, and they hit me square in the gut. Thus, they become the hardest looks to stomach.

Shit. Without a word spoken, I know our trip to Chicago has turned into more than a couple of days. Damn my instincts. My heart knew. Now the rest of me does, only to be confirmed even further by the blank look which slides over Beau's face as he listens to whatever Chaos has to say on the other end of the phone.

And the minute he hangs up, in two steps, I'm once again crushed against him, held in the arms I hope to be held in for the rest of my life, however long that might be.

"Darlin'," he starts. Just that one word dregs the fear up from the bottom-most place in my soul.

He gives off the vibe of a man about to spill something so vile he worries I may never completely recover. "Darlin'," he says again. "They determined the heart's human."

I suck in a sharp breath knowing he hadn't hit me with the worst yet.

Oh, how I wish I'd been wrong.

"They identified the owner of the heart. Baby girl, her friends hadn't heard from her and got nervous. Called Tommy to knock on her door, check things out."

"Who?" I ask, but he keeps on talking as if I hadn't asked my question.

"Apparently Shayla had been killed first. He sent them out of order for some reason. We're still lookin' into it. They found her danglin' upside down from her feet inside a Plexiglas tank filled with water."

A tank?

"Who?" I practically shriek.

"*Hadley.*"

My breath leaves in a gush as my knees buckle beneath me. Luckily Beau has a firm hold, keeping me upright. My ears know what they just heard. My ears know, yet the rest of me vehemently rejects the knowledge.

"Wa—was there a note? There was a note, right? From Houdini?" I ask, my body shaking even as I try to control the shakes. "I did an essay on him, the magician, my junior year of high school." Then I swallow hard. "Mrs. Gentry's class. You remember her?" Though, I keep rambling, not giving him a chance to answer. "Houdini—he had a famous escape, the China Box escape, or something like that. Sounds like what you described."

He nods his affirmative.

"But darlin', I swear I never had relations with her."

"No, you wouldn't have to. If—damn my head hurts—if," I clear my throat instead of swallowing again, and pinch the bridge of my nose. "If Shayla was... if she, um, died first then it's not about you or only you. My dad got with Hadley and didn't have time for me anymore. So maybe the love he gave her came as sloppy seconds? Or maybe, I mean everyone knew how hard his death was on me. Maybe my love for him was sloppy seconds?" As those last words leave my mouth, a horrible thought hits me. "Logan, he didn't have a fling with Hadley before my dad, did he? I mean, we all know he wasn't faithful to me. You think that's why she wouldn't let my dad see me? Guilt?"

"Don't know, but we'll be lookin' into it. Damn shit that bastard's causin' us still, he didn't appreciate how good he had it."

As I try to process this newest blow, Liv cuts into our semi-private conversation. "Do, uh, do you really think this Houdini guy is going after Logan Hollister flings?" she asks.

"It has to be more than that," Beau answers her truthfully.

It hits me. Right here, right now I know his play. "Club connection," I tell them.

"Pardon?" he asks.

And Liv says, *"What?"*

"I haven't figured out the why of why Logan's been involved. But if we can prove Hadley had a fling with Lo, then he's going after club connections that had relations with Logan. He's hitting the Lords by hitting those connections."

"So the bastard has to be someone who knew Logan when we were younger." Beau deduces for us.

"Seems that way." Crass, who'd been totally quiet up 'til now, finally chimes in. Arms folded over his massive chest, he looks contemplative, and I know he's not just been paying attention but formulating. "Also seems like we need to find out about anyone else who might have jumped your boy's bones with a tie to the club. You and your woman, Boss. Doc and his woman. The first chick fucked someone in the club, I'm guessing?"

Beau's firm-lipped glare gives enough confirmation for Crass to continue. "Shit, there a way to figure out who all he fucked? Think it was just those two or you think he was a stupid prick for going out on that beautiful lady of yours?"

"He was a stupid prick for doin' it just once, but I got a bad feelin' about this."

As Beau talks, I take notice of Liv becoming very agitated. *Very* agitated. Opening and closing her hands into fists at her sides. Scrunching up her lips, nose, and brow. She catches me watching and stops. Fisting one of her hands to bring it up, she chews on her thumbnail. "You really think he's targeting women who slept with Logan Hollister?"

"Yeah, why?" I ask.

"I had a one-night stand with Logan Hollister," Liv blurts out to all our dumbstruck faces. Me personally, my mouth hangs open from the gut-punch of betrayal. "Swear I didn't know he had a girlfriend," she rushes on, so I must be wearing every emotion I feel, and not slightly. "We met at a game senior year. Sat next to each other at Wrigley. I was in a vulnerable place, and he offered to make me feel less vulnerable for a time. He was charming and handsome, so yeah, shit… I took him up on his offer. Please don't be mad at me, Elise."

No. This can't be blamed on anyone but Logan. And so I attempt to pull myself together. "It didn't seem he was in the habit of telling women that he had a girlfriend." I laugh humorlessly.

"I know it was him because my brother had been down on club business with our father, your whole town was freaking out about his death. He sent me a picture with a caption that said something like, 'Didn't this guy sit by us at the game?'"

"Shit," Beau grumbles. "*Crass.*"

Crass nods his head. "With my life. Word."

Whatever the unspoken promise that's passed between the two men, I can't think about because Liv, my friend, continues to chew on her thumbnail, which has me worried.

"Livvy, is there something else?"

She ignores my question, turning her gaze to Beau. "Don't tell Chaos," she whispers.

Chaos? I thought Blood?

"Can't keep shit from my brothers, Liv. And I wouldn't keep it even if I could."

She doesn't respond with anything save slumped shoulders and such a defeated face you'd swear Beau had walked up and popped her shiny red balloon with a pin just to watch her cry. One thing I've come to learn about my man, he has a reason behind everything he does, which means Chaos needs to know. Whether she likes it or not. And by the looks of her, she does not.

I left my woman crying inside the apartment being consoled with an arm around her waist by a mournful Livvy while Crass stood as a sentinel behind them. With a nod, I closed the door but didn't leave until the locks clicked into place.

Now back at the clubhouse, the six of us—Duke, Chaos, Blood, Carver, Sneak, and me—sit around the oval table in our meeting room off of Duke's office. I'm in my spot to Duke's right, as his VP and right-hand man.

Chaos leans back in his chair to Duke's left while we wait for our president to bring the meeting to order. Next to him sits Blood. Then next to me, Carver. Finally, at the opposite end of the oval sits Sneak. Sneak, being the last of Duke's lieutenants to join is forced to sit the furthest away from the president.

Every man here has earned his place, despite our youthfulness. This room, with all its dark wood-paneled walls stained darker by years of smoke buildup and troubled times, used to bring me peace from just stepping foot inside. The one window, a reinforced window behind the president's chair above his head, shows straight beams of light hitting dead center, highlighting the very ideals we hold most dear. Dropped in the middle of the thick oak table, our founding members commissioned the carving, the emblem we proudly wear on our backs, the flaming devil head with the words *Brimstone Lords* scrawled in old English lettering above the head, and the words: *Live Ride Brotherhood* below it. Brotherhood. This is the one word we'll all need to remember in times to come because it's the binding fabric of our club and the very thing that psychopath is trying to tear apart. I would've preferred to drop the Liv bomb on Chaos in private before bringing it to the table so as not to blindside the man. Tried several times to call him on my drive back from Chicago only to have every call sent straight to voicemail. No time to pull him aside here at the club as I'd only just walked inside when Duke called the meet.

Eyeing each of us, Duke starts. "What're we doin' about this bastard?"

Before anyone else can chime in, I got to get this off my chest. "We figured out his play."

All eyes turn to me.

"Me, Elise, Liv, and Crass, we figured out the pussy's play, and it ain't good. He knew my cousin Logan. Don't know the why of it, but he's targetin' any woman with a club connection who might've slept with Logan Hollister. Clearly, Elise had. Know Shayla had, back in high school before Elise came to town. Possible Hadley before she got with Doc. Follows the pattern." Several breaths being sucked in sound around the room. Hate this part, but it's now or never. I lean forward catching Chaos's eyes before quickly swiping to Blood and put it out there. "Livvy slept with Logan."

"What the shit?" Chaos yells. His chair crashes to the ground from the force of him standing.

His hands slam the table in front of him at the same time, also the same time as Blood shouts. "No fuckin' way."

"Sorry brother." I look to Blood, although the brother I'm talking to sits to the left of Duke. "She admitted it before I left. Crass won't leave the women. He's promised with his life to keep 'em safe. All the men have sworn to keep vigilant. It sucks, but y'all know I wouldn't've left Elise if I thought they couldn't keep her safe."

"So what now?" Carver asks.

"We gotta draw him out. Try to find out any woman connected to the club who mighta had sex with my idiot cousin, and draw him out."

"Couldn't have been too much of an idiot to have all these women sleep with him. Must've known what he was doin'," Sneak unfortunately opens his yap which brings us back into the uncomfortable portion of the meet.

And fuck if I wanna do this but I have to ask, "Sneak, brother, do you know if Trisha had been with Logan at any time? Hate to ask, but we gotta know any potential targets, and we'd need to hide her out quick-like if she had."

"*Shit,*" he mutters. "Last thing I wanna do is question my wife about other men she's fucked. Lemme talk to her. She's in class right now. I'll go down at her lunch hour. *Shit,*" he mutters again.

"Right, then. We need to round up every brother, prospect, and hanger-on. Need all information about their women, and we need to talk to any piece or hot mama. Let's hope none of the other gals let Boss's cousin in their pants." Duke's final order. "Now get the fuck out of here."

Good thing we got responsible workers in our club businesses because not one of us six will be getting any work done 'til we can solve this. Houdini's going down. Come hell or high water, he's going down.

Once I step back into the common, I stand off to the side

leaning against the wall closest to the bar and watch a very pissed-off Chaos already on his cell phone talking real low. Yeah, I know who's on the receiving end of his frustration. If I'd just found out about Elise, I'd be doing the same. So, I wait patiently until he hangs up, then walk over casually to him, dropping a hand to his shoulder. "Speak to you outside?"

He grunts and nods.

I take off, and he follows.

When I turn on him, but before I speak, he starts, "Liv and me got history."

"Walls were thin in the condo," I admit.

"*Right*. Blood, Liv and I, we grew up together. My pops wasn't a brother, which I know you know. I tried to stay cool, but Liv is... *Liv*. No staying cool around that, brother. She laid it out for me, how she felt, what she wanted from me. But how uncool would it be to move in on your best friend's sister? I did what I thought was right, and I shut it down."

S'ppose it'd be as uncool as moving in on your cousin's girl.

Me and Chaos ain't so different except Logan cheated and is dead, and I never slept with Elise back then, no matter how badly I wanted to.

"She was obviously hurt. Made damn sure I knew she'd met someone. I thought it was bullshit. Now I find out it wasn't? Fuck, Boss, she gave him that? She gave that dipshit cousin of yours what should've been mine?" He runs an agitated hand through his hair. "Thought it *was* mine." Then he begins to pace. "I lost my shit. What I knew, she'd never been with another man. I claimed that as mine." And he stops his pacing to look me dead in the eye, his tone turns hard. "All this time, and it *wasn't mine*." At those last words, he shoves a thumb to his chest. Finally, he drops his head and his hands to his hips.

Defeated. My brother looks utterly defeated. "That was the night Tank got dead, Boss. Blood called me freaking out. I had to have his back. But to have his back meant turning mine on Liv, rolling out of her bed to do it. We got our revenge but had to move out fast. Couldn't go back to Chicago for a while and by the time I thought I could, she wouldn't take my calls, so I thought it best to let her get on with her life."

"Don't have to tell me about tryin' to stay cool. Newly twenty, and I was willin' to raise that dipshit's baby as my own if it meant Elise and I could be together."

"Houdini can't get to her, Boss. Not a world I want to live in where Livvy isn't breathing in it somewhere."

"She's safe. But we got work to do to keep her safe."

22

BEAU

I t's been a week since the meet at the clubhouse. Early
this morning, I got a call from Sneak asking me to come
down to my house. All Sneak's sneaking brought him to a
lockbox inside Dave and Lenore's home, Dave and Lenore
being Logan's parents. The lockbox had been hidden on the
top shelf inside the closet in Logan's room. I'd totally
forgotten about the thing until he reminded me.

Although he wanted to just bust the thing open, the room
as a whole, even inside the closet looked spotless. No dust or
cobwebs, meaning Aunt Lenore frequented the space. So
she'd notice a busted lock on a lockbox that hadn't previously been busted. As I said though, I remembered that
lockbox because before his world began to unravel, he'd
given me the spare key to that box. A key I know ended up in
my junk drawer inside my kitchen.

My little bungalow, the one I'd painstakingly restored
with my own two hands, remains a bombed-out, third-world
massacre as we ain't had time since getting the okay to start
renovations to actually find a contractor to renovate. With
Elise here now, I ain't gonna bother with the repairs. I need a

real home for my woman, and I need it fast. We're lucky the bulk of the damage stayed to the front portions of the house —the living, dining, and master bedrooms.

So now we're at Dave and Lenore's home inside Logan's old room while they're at work. We went in through the back. And as I spent most of my life coming and going from this place, I actually knew exactly where they keep the spare key. Nice to not have to break in.

Sneak pulls the box down handing it off to me. As I twist the key in the lock, Sneak shoots me a look, one that I know means he's hoping as much as I am that there are some answers locked inside to help Elise, Liv, and any other woman who might've crossed paths with my cousin.

Logan wasn't always the asshole he'd become. Inside the box, there are a bunch of compartments. In the top compartments, he'd kept mementos reminding me of that time before he became the supreme asshole when we were best friends and had our whole lives ahead of us. I didn't have it in me to look too closely at those memories. And ain't it just a kick in the teeth that next to all those good memories he stored the evidence of his downfall. We pull out a bag with probably two grams of coke, a rolled bill, straight blade, and a mirror.

He had a full ride to UK, why would he have risked it by getting into this shit? And that ain't the worst of it. Fuck, I wish it'd been the worst of it.

"Your cousin was one serious fuck," Sneak says while staring down at a photo he's holding in his hand. No shit. It's one of maybe fifty or sixty pictures of naked women who seem completely unaware they were having naked pictures taken.

The coke stays, we ain't about that life. The pictures, unfortunately, have to make their way back to the compound with us. I stack them into a manageable pile, feeling the stench of his sins sully the Hollister name more with each one I touch. I'm the fucking disappointment? If they only knew.

Sneak closes and locks the lockbox, placing it back up to its home inside the closet. Then we leave.

Neither of us speaks until we're back at my bungalow where we'd parked our bikes. I turn to Sneak, rub my hand down my face, and mutter, *"Sheeit."*

Sneak bobs his head but doesn't reply. That about sums it up. We mount our rides and head back to the compound.

Once back on Lords' soil, I send him to round up the boys while I unload on Duke. Goddammit, this ain't gonna end well and I can't help feel somewhat responsible. He was *my* cousin. I should've known, should've stopped him.

Fuck.

Duke predictably leans his head out of his office. "Brothers, *rally.*"

Some clubs call it church. We don't hold church we rally to discuss club business. When the club president calls rally, you don't hesitate to rally. This is why as I turn to head into the rally room, I see Blood shoving his exclusive hot mama from his crotch where she'd previously had his cock, sucking him off just moments before. He might not be happy about it, but he don't complain either. It's just the way it is.

When we're all seated inside the rally room, me to his right and Chaos to his left, Duke calls the group to order. "They found some shit."

My brothers understandably grumble.

Still, he continues, "We're giving Boss the chance to look first, seeing as his old lady might be in one of these."

They wait somewhat less than patiently as I move through the stack. I flip each one down on the table as I pass it, but stop once I make a hit. I'm sure they expect it to be Elise.

It ain't Elise.

Who it is, is Livvy. A very naked, unaware Livvy. Chaos'll lose his shit when he sees, so I make sure he don't see, not yet.

I continue turning pictures over until my growl fills the room. There's my Elise, probably the last time she and my dipshit cousin were together, face troubled, body naked. Extremely naked. That picture stays with me. I slip it into my jeans pocket then flip the rest of the pictures of naked women side up along the table for my brothers to see. All forty-eight of 'em (there'd been fifty).

"Apparently when my shithead, and surprisingly cokehead cousin decided to cheat on Elise, he went all out. We collected these pictures from the bottom of a lockbox in Logan's room. Not one of these women looks to know they've been made in print. Look closely brothers, it's worse than we thought. But…" I look to Sneak. "Trisha thankfully ain't one of 'em."

"Yeah, I talked to her. Good to not see the proof, though."

Ain't it the truth? I nod, wholeheartedly agreeing with him. It sure as shit would've been good to not see the proof of Elise and that jackhole together.

"Cokehead?" Chaos asks.

"We found the shit in the box," I respond.

He scowls. Grunts of disapproval ripple around the table because every brother here fought a bloody war to free the club from that life. Because of that shit, Duke found all his brothers dead or in lockup. He was forced into the presidency with only newly patched in men and recruits patched in early at his back as his lieutenants. Some of the brothers might smoke a bowl here or there, and not a one of us here don't love his booze, but you touch any harder, you're out. Just like that, no warning. We take your cut, black out your tat and send you on your way.

Shayla's picture is the first to be singled out. Next, as we'd feared, Hadley had a fling with Logan. The naked, hard-nippled proof stares back at us. We also single out Candy, one of our hot mamas, a couple of pieces who've been hanging around for years, and at least one old lady of one of our hangers-on. The rest of the women we couldn't identify yet.

"Round 'em up," Duke orders.

Chairs scrape across the floor as the men take off to hunt down the newly identified potential victims.

"Chaos, a word." I tug him to my side and wait for Duke to leave. As a picture speaks a thousand words, I reach inside my pocket to pull out the one of Liv. "You didn't ask but…" I hand him the photo.

He closes his eyes and sucks in a long breath. Temper in check, he grabs it and chances a look. "When you didn't say anything… was really hoping she wasn't in there, you know?"

"Didn't say anything because I knew Blood would want the picture to keep the other brothers from seein' his baby sister naked. But it ain't right for Blood to be seein' his baby sister naked. That's for your eyes."

"Thanks, brother," he says while continuing to glare at the photo.

"You'd have lost your shit in front of him. There's too much work to do. Ain't got time for that drama."

"You're being cool about Livvy. Don't think it's a betrayal?"

"She's not a brother's old lady. That I'd beat the shit outta you for. But this. Can't help who you fall in love with. Not a brother's sister or say…your cousin's girl. Make me kind of a hypocrite, don't ya think?"

"She won't have me."

"Gonna let that stop you? Don't think I haven't noticed

your lack of female company since you reconnected in Chicago. This woman means somethin' to you, you do what ya gotta do to see it through. Yeah?"

Chaos crumples the picture in his hand. "Yeah, brother. *Yeah*."

"Good. Let's go catch this fucker so you can get on that."

23

ELISE

"You gonna tell him?" Liv surprises me, showing up in the bathroom so early in the morning. She drops to her knees behind me gathering my hair into a ponytail in one hand while rubbing the other over my back in slow, comforting circles.

Am I going to tell him? I sigh. Why does life have to be so damn complicated? The badass biker in his faded, worn jeans, tight T-shirts, scuffed motorcycle boots, and black leather Lords cut is all I've been able to think about for the past six weeks.

Six weeks since he held me in his arms for the last time. But as beautiful as his deep brown eyes or his peanut butter hair tied back in that sexy bun are to me, they're not what I'm missing with my head bent over the toilet heaving nothing more than stomach acid now that I'd already emptied out everything else earlier. Tears sting my eyes from the force of my retching and being hunched over for so long.

No. What's on my mind is how much I miss his sense of humor. He's the kind of man who would help me through this by making me laugh so hard I'd completely forget about the nausea.

"It's just the flu," I tell her.

"Honey, you don't have the flu. What you've got is a parasite. A parasite you caught when a river of Beau Hollister emptied into your reservoir." She leans away, taking her hand from my back to open the cupboard under the sink, pulling out a long thin box. "Here." She places the box in my hand and begins rubbing my back again. "Pee on this. Once we have confirmation, we'll get you set up with an OB."

I don't have to pee on a stick for confirmation. I've been through this before. But I push up off the floor and wipe the sweat from my brow with the hem of my nightshirt.

While I do that, Liv takes the box again, pries open the top, and pulls the test out. She stands close as I drop my undies and sit, then she shoves the uncapped stick at me, and I shove it in the urine stream.

"Says results can take up to three minutes to show, depending on how much pregnancy hormones are in your system." Liv reads the directions from the back of the box.

The test doesn't take three minutes. Or two minutes. Or even one minute. When I pull the test back to look at it there's a giant pink plus sign staring at me. A pink plus sign. A plus sign. *Giant*. No. Not giant, this dwarfs giant, carrying the entirety of my life on its pretty pink points.

What am I going to do?

"You gonna tell him?" she asks again.

What *am* I going to do? I know what I'm *not* going to do. "No," I reply. "Not now. He's got too much on his plate to worry about this, too."

"I think that's a mistake."

"Duly noted." I continue to stare down at my hand, at the first test I ever wish I'd flunked.

"Serious, Elise. He needs to know."

"Serious, Liv. I haven't heard from him in six weeks. I'm sure he's kept silent thinking he's keeping me safe, but that shit's not cool. And if things are so bad that he can't pick up a damn phone to talk to me, well then he doesn't need to bear the weight of this."

Liv leaves so I can finish up and wash my hands, then I head back to my bed and pull the pillow over my head to block out the early morning light streaming in between the slats on my blinds.

She's a good friend, showing up with hot tea and toast sometime later.

"Love you," I say because I really do. I was never blessed with a sister, what I was blessed with is Liv. And to think I avoided her for so long. I was an idiot.

"Love you, too." She drops a cell and a torn piece of paper with a number written on it on the bed next to me. "This is the number to my gynecologist's office, obviously they provide obstetric services as well. I didn't know who you went to."

"If I call that makes it real."

"Sorry honey, the puking, and pink plus sign made it real. That's whether or not you call. Calling will just ensure you're both healthy. Maybe in the future, avoid unprotected sex with your sexy biker to keep from any repeats. "

I take a bite of lightly buttered toast. "I know. I'm being ridiculous, it's just that—" then I swallow my bite and sip my tea. "I've been through this before. And it didn't end well so." I shove the rest of the slice in my mouth, clearly avoiding her eyes.

"You're scared. I get it. Chaos filled me in on some of your and Boss's history. But honey, Boss won't turn his back on you. He wants this with you. A home. A family. You're giving the man his dream. So let's take care of that dream, so we can see it to fruition."

There'd been a time when Beau told me he wanted this life. But six weeks of zero contact, when I know he's talked with Crass. I'm beginning to think he's had a change of heart. What man in his right mind wants to give up his freedom to be tied down with a woman and baby, especially when that woman has a killer after her?

It takes me several minutes after Liv leaves my room to go take another call from some horny loser who can't sex up the real thing, to get out of my own head. Then I press the number she brought me onto the keypad to call. After ten minutes, the sweet-sounding receptionist on the other end has me set up with an appointment for next week. Thursday.

24

ELISE

Next week. Thursday...

L iv stands next to my head, snickering under her breath at me. No. Strike that, her laugh is not *at me* per se, more at how uncomfortable I am. It's all fun and games until you're the one squirming on an exam table wearing nothing but a paper gown with your feet up in stirrups.

Dr. Coty, as she introduced herself, rolls a condom on a thick wand and bends down to insert it up my who-ha for an internal ultrasound.

A regular ultrasound wouldn't do? Uh *no*, I asked.

"It will, but an internal ultrasound will give us a better picture. With your history, we want to make sure everything is good."

How could I argue with that? I brace as even wrapped in a condom, the wand feels cold. It's a shock to the system, and I shudder. Not one of my better Thursday afternoons.

"Everything looks fine," she finally tells me after several heart-pounding minutes. "Don't forget to set up your appointment for next month before you leave. I'm going to go, you can go ahead and get dressed." As suspected, I'm at seven weeks gestation. And as promised, she withdraws the wand, throws the condom and her rubber gloves in the trash, and walks out of the room.

The nurse loads me down with a bag full of prenatal vitamins and other stuff they say I'll need and we stop to make my next appointment at the reception desk before leaving. Though, I cross my fingers that I won't still be in town next month. Then we head downstairs to the main floor lobby where Crass said he'd be waiting. We told him this was Liv's yearly appointment because I didn't want him to know about the pregnancy yet. He talks to Beau several times a week.

Both Liv and I scan the seating area for Crass. Neither of us sees him.

Something feels off.

We walk over to wait by the restrooms in hopes that he's just inside relieving himself. When after ten minutes, he hasn't joined us yet, we decide to check outside by a small circle of benches where the smokers gather. What we find are three older men, two balding, and one in a wheelchair, no Crass. Panic sets in and I make one of my stupider decision letting Liv search the left side of the parking lot, while I take the right.

"Hello, Elise." The whisper is the last I hear before a sharp pain strikes the side of my head… *and blackness*.

Good, *good. My eyes creak open, which means I'm alive.*

First I register the pain, although duller now then the initial strike and foggy vision. I blink several times in an attempt to clear the vision and wait for my brain to slowly get back online. Pain. Foggy vision, and—constriction? Yes.

Constriction. I try to move my arms to figure out why there's a constriction, only my arms won't move.

But my chest burns. Because I've never *not* been able to move my arms before. It burns as my heart beats faster and faster with every second that passes. Even as I will myself to take long, meaningful breaths, my nose and lungs only allow short, shallow pants. Too short and too shallow to do any good. I feel about ready to pass out.

Keep it together, Elise. Think, why won't they move? Why is it taking so long for me to think? *Okay, I got it. They won't move because straitjackets are made to keep one's arms from moving.*

Chest pain. Tightness. I really can't breathe.

He didn't kill me, but I'm going to die. I'm going to die. I'm going to—stop it. You're pregnant. It's not just you in the room. Calm down, now.

Yes. I'm pregnant. I have to act like a mother now. Focusing on the baby helps me to settle. Those long, meaningful, greatly desired breaths start to slowly replace the pants. *In through the nose, out through the mouth. Still alive, and breathing. What next?*

The fog's lifted from my eyes but they're somewhat blurred by tears. And I can't wipe them away. Still, I scan the room to take in my surroundings.

There's nothing in the room but four windowless walls, peeling wallpaper, and me on the floor. In a straitjacket. Cracks in the ceiling, crumbling plaster, and rotted through lumber allow small pockets of natural light to filter inside since the place lacks artificial light. I'd be surprised if electric had ever been hooked up.

But no Liv.

Without a doubt, I know who's behind this. It's his most famous escape. God, why couldn't I be chased by a biker who calls himself Olaf, and likes warm hugs? Since I'm alive, I know I'm meant to be last. So then, where is Liv?

The panic begins to form a ball in my gut again, but panicking won't keep my baby safe or save my friend.

Okay, think, Elise, think… How do I escape from a straitjacket?

The first thing that comes to mind is to wriggle. Escaping isn't as hard as I thought it'd be. The trickiest bit comes from contorting myself into crazy positions until I can reach the buckles and actually unbuckle them.

The whole process takes what feels like ten minutes. Once I'm free I try the door. It pops open and I proceed cautiously because he's either set a trap or never expected me to free myself.

Liv's not anywhere in the four rooms of the dilapidated farmhouse. I don't spend too much time snooping around. I probably should look for clues or evidence as to Houdini's actual identity. But I don't want to get caught if he should decide to drop by for a visit.

I shield my eyes from the bright sunlight. It's still daytime outside, or daytime again for all I know. A long, empty, dirt drive connects with a gravely road in the distance. I run toward that road with everything in me.

As I'm bent over gulping down air I hear a loud engine. A beat-up, rusted-out orange Chevy pickup rumbles past, popping stray rocks out from under the tires. The old man behind the wheel stops, rolling down his window.

"Need help, little lady?"

"*Yes*. I was kidnapped and escaped. Do you have a cell phone?"

Maybe he doesn't believe me, or maybe he picks up escaped kidnapped victims as a matter of course, but if the man feels any concern for my situation, he doesn't show it.

"Sure," he answers as if ready to share a little town gossip on an easy Sunday afternoon after church. "Keep it in the glove box for emergencies. Climb on in," he drawls even slower like I hadn't just told him I'd been *kidnapped* and *escaped*.

Without hesitation, I round the hood of his truck, and press the handle to open the door but with all the rust, the door sticks. And it takes several good tugs to crack it open. Cautiously relieved tears stream down my cheeks when I finally climb on in and pull the door shut.

My savior leans over and pops open the glove box while he continues at the same speed he'd been traveling before down the dirt road. The signal bars hit three bars while I punch in Beau's number.

"Hello?" he answers gruffly. It's so good to hear his voice that I forget to answer. "Hello?" he asks again.

"Beau?" I half whisper, half cry.

"Darlin'?"

"It's me, Beau. We need help."

"What's wrong, where's Crass?"

"I don't know. H-he got to us, Beau. Liv and Crass are gone. I woke up in a straitjacket... maybe he meant for me to escape, maybe he didn't," I keep rambling. "But they're gone, and I'm in a truck with a nice man who picked me up... I'm scared, Beau."

"Listen, baby girl, put the man on the phone with me. I'm commin' for ya. Got my word. We're mobilizin' now."

"*Okay*. Here." I hand the man the phone. "My fiancé wants to talk with you."

After the cab fills with several affirmative sounding grunts and head nods that Beau couldn't possibly see, the old man flips the cell closed and hands it back to me. "Put this back in the box, little lady." I do immediately. At the same time hearing the snap of the latch on the glove box the old man speaks up. "I'm supposed to take you somewhere public and stay with you, so we're heading to IHOP." The pickup rolls to a stop at a four-way intersection. Dirt having replaced the gravel about a mile back. He idles a few moments and the truck vibrates. Then the old man pulls away from the stop sign. "Feel like pancakes. You feel like pancakes?"

No, I don't really feel like eating pancakes, I don't really feel like eating at all. But as I'm currently expecting and the man continues to be so gracious about the situation he's found himself in from just doing a good deed and stopping—a good deed he'll probably think twice about repeating from now on thanks to me—who am I to rain on his pancake parade? Thus, I answer with an emphatic, "Pancakes sound great."

About twenty-five minutes later, the old man, who'd introduced himself as Lester Greene, sits across from me pouring a berry-flavored syrup over his second stack of all-you-can-eat pancakes while I continue to pick at the only three stack I'd ordered.

My friends could be dead for all I know.

Crass, he'd lost a lot in his life. We'd had some pretty intense late-night conversations over whiskeys for him and ginger ales for me once I suspected I might be pregnant. I'd come to care for him in these seven weeks like the brother I never had.

And Liv? What would I do without Liv in my life?

The room suddenly goes quiet, the silence pulling me from my thoughts. I turn my attention to the door along with the rest of the patrons. That's when I see Blue, Levi, and Blaze scanning the room and let out a gasp of pure relief when Levi's eyes lock with mine. A Lords cut commands a room. Any room. And these three men, even being prospects, are no different.

Lester Greene stands once they reach our table. The wrinkling around his eyes and pursed lips tell me that even at his age, he's willing to go to battle to protect me, even in the face of badass bikers.

"You the man I talked to on the phone?" he asks Levi.

"No Sir, he's been detained on important business. He's put us in charge of gettin' Elise back to safety," Levi says.

Lester Greene turns to me. "You know these boys? You okay with going with them? I'll have the cops here before they can drag you out to their bikes."

"Yes, these are my friends. I'm good with going with them. Thank you so much, Lester." I stand from my seat and walk the two steps to where Lester Greene partially guards me. A farmer in his dirtied farmer's overalls and red and black-checkered flannel shirt, no weapon, wielding only his sense of decency as his sword.

Respect for Lester Greene. So much respect for Lester Greene. I swipe my thumb over his aged skin, briefly resting my forehead against his soft, silver hair, then kiss his cheek.

"We owe you anything for takin' care of our girl?" Blue asks.

"No son, you do *not*." Those weathered eyes, which had looked so soft on me moments before, turn hard and glaring at Blue. "A man should never need compensation for doing the right thing. And taking care of this lovely young lady was and remains the right thing."

Levi's quick to smooth things over. "Not trying to ruffle any feathers, here. We're just grateful to you and want to show our gratitude. At least let us pay for breakfast. It's the least we can do for you getting our Elise back to us."

Without waiting for a response, Levi pulls his wallet from his back pocket, secured to his belt loop by a thick silver chain, and drops two twenties on the table. It's way more than the price of our breakfast, and Lester only glances ruefully at the bills but doesn't pick them up, which means our waitress will have a good tip day.

One last goodbye to Lester Greene, and Levi guides me by the hand out to Beau's pickup. Blue leads and Blaze takes up the tail. I'd say I have badass biker-in-training bodyguards, but who am I kidding. I've seen these guys in action. They might not be full brothers yet, but they *are* full badass bikers, nonetheless. And in the same formation they walked me out of the restaurant, Blue mounts his bike, taking off in the lead, then Levi and I follow next in the truck, and Blaze on his ride takes the rear.

We've only just turned right out of the parking lot and driven maybe a mile down the road when Levi's cell starts blowing up. At the first red light, he answers.

"*Shit!*" His response sharpens the edge I've been on since I came to in that old farmhouse, an edge that had only started to dull when my bikers showed in the IHOP.

He hangs up, dialing Blue. His one-word clipped into the line, "Shipyard." Then he hangs up on him without a sign-off. Repeating the same with Blaze, "Shipyard."

When the light goes green, the boys speed off, weaving in and out through traffic. "Hold on tight," Levi finally addresses me, shifting down more like navigating the Daytona International Speedway than a busy boulevard. "Change of plans, Boss needs us at the shipyard. When we get there, you stay in the truck and keep the doors locked until one of the brothers you know comes to you. Get me?"

Get me? Here I sit, totally freaking out inside, those pancakes a regret waiting to happen. And he expects an answer? The gurgle my stomach makes suggests that regret might appear sooner than later.

"Elise? You get me?" He repeats himself.

His tone startles me out of the fear stupor. I swallow back the breakfast on the verge of resurfacing. I'm a Brimstone Lady, I can't lose it, at least not yet. "Get you."

"Nope. Beau says I need the words from you, or it don't count."

Really? At a time like this, Beau's going to worry about

me lying to him? Fine then. I give him what he wants to hear. "When we get there, I stay inside the truck 'til one of the brothers I know comes to get me."

"Good girl," he says.

Fear replaced by irritation, I reach over and punch his shoulder. Not hard, but satisfying. "Don't be patronizing. Remember I'm older than you, buddy."

He only laughs. So I narrow my eyes at him. *Bikers.*

When he turns into the shipyard, the scene looks right out of a movie where the protagonist finds his way to one of those bike rallies, there are so many Harleys scattered everywhere. Also scattered everywhere are their riders, so many Lords' cuts. All in black leather, all sporting the flaming devil head, only some with Illinois rockers, some with Kentucky, and even some from as far away as Missouri. I didn't even know they had a Missouri chapter.

Both Blue and Blaze park then hop off their bikes. Before he leaves too, Levi turns to me. "Remember, Elise, doors locked. Only brothers you know." That's all I get. He swings open the door and slides out, slamming the door behind him.

I, being the ever-dutiful biker old lady, do as directed by my badass biker friend who was given his command by my own personal badass biker, and reach over to lock his door after making sure mine is secure.

Now the waiting commences. I watch through the windshield of Beau's truck as the bulk of the men take off toward a pier at the end of one of the shipping lanes.

Please let Livvy be safe.
Please let Crass be safe.

25

At Elise's call, my stomach dropped. We've been in the city for a few days now, she just never knew it.

Blood tracked a hot trail up Chicago way, no doubt now, Houdini'd been comin' after Liv. We thought we could get to him before he got to our women. Clearly, we underestimated the son of a bitch.

As upset as Blood got with word of his sister's kidnapping, understandably, Chaos went ballistic. An out of his mind, blinded by fear and rage, kind of ballistic I couldn't sweep under the rug as mere friendship any longer.

Blood knows now.

Duke knows now.

Neither has confronted Chaos yet because he'd probably kill them second degree for doin' it before we get her back safely. Lord help us if we don't get her back safely. He won't make it if she don't. And I know he won't because I wouldn't make it if Elise didn't. Women. Biggest practical joke God ever played on men. Get us to care. Feed us the need to protect. So much that a woman gets under your skin, really and truly under your skin, there's no digging her out again. A real man'll give his life to make sure hers is good.

Life would be so much easier if we were all the heartless fuckers most women accused us of being. Yet knowing I have my Elise to go home to, I wouldn't want it any other way.

Going off the messages Houdini left us, we'd looked up the magician Houdini's greatest escapes, and knocked the ones he'd already done off the list, or the ones too benign for him to use against our women. This was about the time I'd gotten the call from a scared Elise, and Blood got the call from a paid informant that he'd seen some outside the normal operations going down at the shipyard.

Duke, Blood, me, and Chaos raced down to the end of the pier where a together-enough-to-catch-it Chaos thought he'd seen the glint of something metal. He'd been right.

The metal comes from a chain wrapped around one of the pylons holding the pier up in the water. More brothers file in, each grabbing a length of chain, and we haul up whatever's attached to the end of that chain. Several times I look to Chaos, whose face has gone blank. Completely blank.

The final tug sees us successfully raising the end of the chain, wrapped around a large, soggy wooden box about the size of a beanbag chair. Water drips in heavy rivulets to the ground until we set the box carefully onto the solid plank board, where the water begins to pool around our feet.

One of our brothers from the Missouri chapter hands off a crowbar to Chaos. He immediately begins to dig under the outside slat of the wood and pries it up.

Two more slats broken away.

He throws the crowbar to the ground where it bounces and clanks, then he reaches inside to pull a trembling, soaking wet, yet very much alive Livvy out of the lake water, filling up half the box. Between the water in the box and pooled at our feet, she had to have been completely submerged. She wasn't coughing which means we got to her before her lungs gave out from holding her breath.

Thank God.

One arm under her knees, the other around her back, Chaos pulls Liv to his chest planting a very public, very unchaste, highly un-platonic kiss to her slightly blue lips. He keeps on kissing her until she whimpers into his mouth, and he pulls back. His breaths come heavy.

Her breaths come as heavily as a women's pulled from a wooden box that had been submerged underwater would, which ain't that heavy at all.

"Blanket," he calls out.

Another brother appears from the crowd with an old Indian print woolen blanket. Chaos only lets her go enough to wrap her securely.

"We got to get her to a hospital. I'm taking her to the truck. You grabbing Elise, Boss, or she coming with us?"

"I'll grab her. Levi'll ride your bike back home."

Blood opens his mouth to protest, but I stop him with a hand to his chest and a head shake.

"Not now. You gotta have words, do it back home. Let him have this. Let *them* have this."

He scowls at me and glares at Chaos, yet he nods his acceptance and heads off to follow Chaos and Liv on his bike. The hunt's still on to find Crass. We leave the Illinois and Missouri brothers to handle that for now while we make sure Liv won't suffer any residual effects.

I jog to the truck to collect Elise. It's the most beautiful sight I've seen in weeks. She's sitting in the cab, thin arms wrapped around her middle, her eyes on Chaos and Liv. She don't notice me until I reach the door and knock, making her jump. Elise turns toward the window, visibly relaxing for only a second before she throws open the door to launch herself into my waiting arms.

"*Darlin'*," I whisper into her hair.

That's all it takes for her to break, tears well and fall freely down her rosy cheeks. Then for the first time in seven weeks, my lips find hers, their home. She's so beautiful. My arms stay locked around her shoulders even as I pull her away to allow Chaos to gently set Livvy inside the cab.

"Liv?" Elise calls to her. But Liv won't take her eyes off Chaos.

"He's got her. Let him take care of her. You'll see her back home at the compound, yeah?" I end that last statement waiting on his reply.

Elise squeezes me tighter when he nods.

"Yeah." Chaos says and nods a second time before rounding the hood to fold himself behind the steering wheel.

We let them go. I walk a shaken Elise to my bike and lift her to plant her on the back.

"Someone will get your stuff from Liv's. We're headin' home now."

Now I'm fucking confused. I wake to Elise's mouth wrapped around my cock, sucking me hard. And this, after spending the night making love until we passed out from exhaustion. Seven weeks apart, we deserved our time to reconnect.

My balls pull tight and I'm about to let loose a fucking great orgasm when out of nowhere, she throws her hand over her mouth, stumbling off the bed, and runs to the bathroom. She barely makes it to the toilet before the retching starts.

Elise groans in pain. I fall behind her to hold her hair back. The sound just about rips my heart out. And she keeps spilling her guts into the commode until there's nothing left but dry heaves.

Fuck.

She's gray with sweat beading along her temples, dew-dampened skin over the rest of her face.

"Baby girl, you feel sick or you think you ate somethin' bad?"

"Neither," she says. Grabbing my hand, she pulls me to sit next to her, our backs resting against the bathroom wall tiles. It's there she lays me out. "Beau, baby, I have to tell you something."

I freeze.

Think my heart might've just stopped. "Go on," I prod.

"Seven weeks ago, Beau..." she breaths in a deep breath and lets it out slowly before she continues. "Seven weeks ago, you took me to Chicago, gave me a proper goodbye, but didn't bother to use a condom."

What the fuck?

"Are you tellin' me you're carryin' my baby?"

"Yes."

"You're havin' my baby?"

"Yes."

"I'm gonna be a daddy?"

"*Yes.*"

"Ho-*ly* shit!"

"Beau," she starts, and I know I should probably handle this differently, but shit, she just told me she's having my baby. I shove up off the floor and run out of our bedroom into the hall still buck-ass naked.

I shout down the hallway for anyone who's close enough to hear me. "I'm gonna be a fuckin' father!" To that, there comes the hoots and hollers of congratulations from my brothers.

Elise sits on the bed, my T-shirt draped over her newly

pregnant body, knees bent, her chin resting on those bent knees, her feet crossed at the ankles. "So you aren't mad?" she asks.

Really?

"Mad? Darlin' this is all I've ever wanted with you. You wearin' my diamond, my baby in your belly. Bit unconventional, but now I just got to get my gold band around your finger, and we'll be set. Beau and Elise Hollister livin' the life we were meant to live. Raisin' the kid we were meant to raise. This is so damn good, baby girl."

"I'm scared to death. We both know I was young, but *Jesus*, Beau. I wanted that baby."

"Know you did. I wanted it too, 'cuz it was a part of you." Elise don't look me in the eye as I slide on the bed next to her. She don't as I lift her onto my lap to wrap my arms around her, either. I press a soft kiss on her cheek.

"What if..." The pain in her voice slices through me. I know where she's about to go.

"This baby's gonna be fine, darlin'. We'll make sure you get to all your doctor's appointments I'll keep you fed healthy. We got this."

"You can't guarantee that. You can't promise we'll have a healthy baby at the end of it all."

"Nobody can make that promise, Elise. I won't even try. But I know it has to work out for us this time."

"Why?"

"Because I have faith. It's our second chance to get it right. In what? Thirty-three short weeks, we're gonna be holdin' a sweeter than anything you've seen in your life baby girl who looks just like her mama."

"Or a baby boy the spitting image of his daddy."

"Speaking of gettin' my girl fed properly." I ignore her wishful thinking. "Throw some pants on so your man can cook for you."

"Food? I don't know… I'll just end up puking it back into the toilet."

"Which is why I gotta get you fed again. Please don't argue. Your stomach feel queasy now?" She shakes her head in the negative. "Then you need to make up for what you just got rid of." And that, as they say, is that.

Me in my jeans I slip on, and her in my shirt and a tight pair of yoga pants, I lead her by the hand down the hall through the entry into the main common. 'Course I don't expect it, but damn does it feel good when my brothers begin slapping my back and hugging Elise, giving us both their sincere congratulations.

Then Duke clomps in the room from his office, boots hitting hard against the wood floor. He keeps advancing until he stops in front of us. "So you're giving us a legacy."

"Yes?" Elise hesitantly answers.

He snickers, lighting the cigarette hanging from between his lips, talking around it. "A second-generation Lord," he says then he turns his head to blow the smoke away from Elise's face and offers me one. I want one too, but wave it away because I should probably quit, what with the kid on the way.

"Oh, well then, yes."

Duke's next words belie the badass mountain of a man speaking them and reiterates the reason I joined the club. "Can't tell you how special…" He trails off. "My Dawna, she couldn't have babies. Radiation killed her eggs as a kid. Married her knowing we'd never have that. Don't regret it, but still, yours'll be the first legacy to be born to this club in years. Pleased as fuck it's you and Boss giving it to us."

"I gotta admit, I'm pleased to be givin' it." I pull Elise close and hold on tight.

"Know you are, brother." He tugs me with one hand to the back of my neck, forcing me to let go of Elise, in order to hug me. Duke pats my back, telling me in an unusually low drawl, "Congratulation. Dawna would be so happy."

Fuck. This is huge.

Then, as if he hadn't just blown my mind, back with his normally booming voice full of gravel, he claps his hands together. "Little prince or princess of the Brimstone Lords. God help ya, brother, you get a girl. Might need a deal with the devil if she looks anything like her mama. Beauty like that... when it's good to have your brothers. The pricks you can't get, we'll have your back."

"Forget *looks* like her mama, heaven help you she *acts* like her." Chaos comes out of the kitchen carrying a tray of food. Haven't seen him look this light in ages.

"Was thinking it, just didn't want to spoil the moment for 'em," Duke tells him, which makes me laugh. Elise says nothing.

"Ah, Elise doesn't mind, do you, sweetheart?" Chaos says. "Just good-natured ribbing. She knows I think the world of her."

"You're lucky I like you," she jibes with her own light-hearted dig. "Speaking of people I like, how's Liv? Where is she?"

"She's good, hospital only kept her a few hours. Told her to rest. She's in the bedroom. I made us some food." He holds the plate up. "She's just not ready to see everyone yet." Then he shifts, looking ten kinds of uncomfortable. "Blood won't talk to me."

"Did you expect anything less?" Duke asks.

"Not really, but shit, he knows Liv'll need his support and the stubborn ass wouldn't talk to her at the hospital. Just stayed long enough to see her alright and took off. He wants to get shitty with me, I can take it. But I can't let his stink touch Livvy. She wants to see him, she's been asking."

"Give it time," I offer. It ain't much, but it's something. "He'll come around. Your sister and one of your best friends? Then to find out it started years ago?" I give a low whistle. "He'll be lickin' those wounds for a while. You just stick to carin' for her, get her mind healthy."

"Plan on it."

"If she wants to talk, even just about stupid girl stuff, I'm here," Elise says.

"I'll remind her."

"I mean it, any time." Elise sinks back against me. Her whole demeanor changing. "What about Crass?"

Dammit, I hate having to tell her this part. I know how close the two of 'em got. Been tryin' to shield her from the blow for as long as possible.

"Got him up in the trauma center at Rush. His brothers' been keeping us informed since they found him." Duke shakes his head. "Sorry, sweetheart. Blunt force trauma. He's been placed in a medically induced coma to hopefully help him heal."

I tuck her in close under my arm as she sucks in a sharp breath.

Her eyes begin to water. "Then I have to go to him. Beau, you have to let me go to him."

The pleading in her voice makes me feel like shit for denying her. But my hands are tied. "Sorry darlin', can't do that. Houdini's still out there, and you're carrying our baby." I bend my head to kiss the corner of her mouth. "I want him safe just like you, but I'm selfish and need for this baby to be safe. You need to help Liv recover here and tend to our family growin' inside you. Crass'll understand. I know. And you know it, too."

"It just doesn't feel right." She hangs her head.

I know it don't. Especially not to someone with as big a

heart as Elise. Crass was all business when it came to the women, but Livvy's updates made me feel as if he'd really put himself into the big brother role for the women. Although Liv has Blood, Elise has no one, which means she's feeling this deep. But again, no matter how deep she feels him, we've got us a little one to protect now, and I damn well intend to protect *her*.

"Get that food back to your woman before it gets cold," I order Chaos and don't miss the smirk he shoots my way at the use of 'your woman' as he moves past us. Of anybody here, I know how good that one feels. With Elise under my arm, I start for the kitchen again. "Come on, gotta get my baby mama fed."

"I hate to disappoint you, but baby mamas don't wear their man's ring. I have a diamond on my left finger that says I'm more than a baby mama."

Damn, she's cute when she's feisty. She's cute when she's right. My woman is just plain cute. And I'm one lucky son of a bitch.

Depositing her on a bar stool, I go to the fridge and grab out a package of bacon, cheddar cheese, a tomato, and lettuce. I might not be a trained chef, but I can whip up a pretty mean BLT.

From one shelf lower I grab a bag of raw broccoli cuts and a dill dip. Setting my haul on the counter, I open the cupboard for the bread and a can of Sour Cream and Onion Pringles.

The smell of frying bacon draws several of the brothers into the kitchen. I set Scotch to work slicing tomato and Sneak, toasting bread.

"Trisha's out in the common talking with Hannah." Sneak rambles while pushing down the toast into the toaster. Hannah is Blood's exclusive hot mama who lives here on a permanent basis. "Just wanna say thanks a lot, brother."

"What'd I do?" I look over my shoulder at him while flipping the bacon.

"Knocked up your woman. That's whatcha did. Got lucky Trish didn't want babies until other old ladies in the club started popping out kids. She didn't wanna be the only one not partying and wanted our kids to have *cousins,* shit that woman comes up with. God dammed pain in my ass is what she is." Four slices of toast pop from the toaster. Sneak grabs them up and tosses the pieces on a paper plate, then he loads the toaster with four more slices of bread.

"Anyway, she wanted our kid to have *cousins* to grow up with. And since there were no other old ladies popping out kids, I didn't even have to think about it. Now that you knocked up Elise, she's gonna be all over my shit. So thanks for that. You know I can't say no to my woman. Now I'll have to impregnate her and the Lords clubhouse goes from biker compound to fucking Romper Room daycare."

Scotch lays his knife down next to the slices of tomato and pins me with a deadly serious glare. "Kids start taking over, Boss, I'm transferring charters. No offense, Lass," he says to Elise.

"He says that now." She goads him. "But you all wait, he's gonna fall head over heels for some woman and will be eating his words when she ends up preggers with a Scotsman's baby."

"Curse you, woman," Scotch growls back.

We might chuckle laugh, but Elise throws her head back to really let loose. It's a beautiful sound and even more beautiful sight.

I'd be remiss to say Crass and Houdini ain't perched right at the edge of all our thoughts. But being here, right now, laughing and cooking with my brothers. The woman I've loved since I was eighteen on a stool in my club, wearing my T-shirt and my ring, giving me everything she's giving me, waiting for that food we're cooking, being here right now is abso-fucking-lutely *perfect*.

Damn, but I hope it lasts.

I'm in the bathroom, leaning against the vanity, staring into the mirror, trying to figure out what to do with my rat's nest of hair when a couple of thoughts hit me. What started out as lunch for Beau and I turned into two hours of food and conversation with several of his brothers and Trish had joined us. Trish who indeed got on Sneak's shit telling him in no uncertain terms in front of God and everybody that since I was now with child, he'd better get to work knocking her up as well. My hand automatically drops to rub my yet nonexistent belly.

Part of me wants this just for us. For me and Beau alone to give the club a legacy, the prince or princess of the Brimstone Lords. But then, that would be selfish. Our kid deserves other kids to grow up around. It would be a good thing. A really good thing.

But what right do I have to feel happy when my friend Crass has been placed in a medically induced coma fighting for his life because he promised to protect mine? And I can't even go up to see him. Why is my life worth more than his? I

276 | SARAH ZOLTON ARTHUR

don't have the answer to that except the brothers, including Crass, all think I am.

Then there's Livvy. God, as if being kidnapped wasn't bad enough? To be thrown inside a wooden box, nailed shut, secured around the perimeter with a metal chain, and lowered into the frigid water of Lake Michigan? The seals on the box kept the air pressure intact enough to withstand it filling up with water immediately, but she would have drowned if we hadn't found her.

She'd run out of air in those last seconds. She held her breath. *Held* her *breath*. She still hasn't left Chaos's room. I have no idea if she's willing to talk with me, and I have no one to blame but myself.

I started this.

Whatever reason Houdini has to hate me, Beau, or the memory of Logan, I started it the day I picked Logan Hollister. Hadley is dead. Liv could have died. Crass still might. My friends suffer needlessly, dragged into our mess because I had a crush on a cute boy.

My eyes close to the sting of tears forming in them, but strong arms wrap around my waist, there's a nip to my shoulder and a kiss to my jaw. My eyes open to my badass biker resting his chin on the spot he'd just nipped. His eyes catch mine, twinkling with his love for me. I push back into him, intent to soak up the warmth he's offering. I love this man with everything in me.

"Carver got ordained," he says.

"I'm sorry, what?"

"Carver. Got ordained. He went online, Church of Purple Snowflakes or something. I don't know, all I know is it's legal for him to marry us. And before you bust my balls, hear me out."

I nod subtly.

"*Right*. First. We were plannin' on gettin' hitched anyway, and we were plannin' on sooner than later until Houdini struck again. Now that we're havin' a baby, it needs to be sooner because when I take you to your doctor appointments it's as your husband. Saw the ultrasound picture you'd stuffed behind the strap of your bra. Fell out when I was takin' it off you. Didn't know what it was, fell face down. I got distracted. Just picked it up, looked at it."

I reach up behind me to comb my fingers through his mess of hair. No bun, no hairband to encumber my movements. "I'd forgotten I stuffed it there, what with the kidnappings and all. I didn't want Crass to see it because I didn't want him to know before you."

"'Preciate it. What I don't appreciate, it said Baby Manning." In a sudden movement he flips me around and sets my bottom on vanity, then gently forces my chin up so he has my attention. "That baby, my baby, is a Hollister. Period. We're a family. A unit. Won't be long before we're back in our home. Anyone livin' under my roof lives there with the last name Hollister. Caveman, I know. You'll deal. With me so far?"

Again, I nod. Less subtly, as the mood calls for.

"Good. The next, well, the next is for you and me, but also for the brothers, for Liv. For Tommy and Maryanne, and anyone connected with the club. We've had a rough patch. Time for some fun, to let off some steam. With Houdini still on the prowl. With Crass's condition. With Livvy in kind of a bad place in her head, we all need a reason to celebrate. You agreein' to a wedding is you givin' that to them, all of 'em. Think you got it in you to give 'em that?"

I might have given him shit about the Hollister name. I'm still me, I have to give him shit on principle alone, but what he says, about giving them a reason to celebrate? After everything they've done for me...

"Okay," I kind of mumble. That seems the least I can do.

"Promise baby girl, it'll be the pig roast of all pig roasts. Since the compound'll be swarmin' with brothers, won't be a safer place for you on the planet. Maryanne's comin' by the club to help you plan seein' it's not safe for you to leave without an escort, and the boys are pretty busy right now. It's the best way."

A COUPLE of hours later Maryanne shows up bearing gourmet coffees from the little coffee shop downtown and a bottle of alcohol-free sparkling wine to celebrate my good news. News Beau clearly shared, because I haven't had the chance to thus far. She let her displeasure on that be known in no uncertain terms.

"Can't believe it's finally happening," Maryanne says for like the fiftieth time while we're sitting at the pool table we'd turned into wedding planning central. We've got Beau's laptop open creating custom biker chic invitations. He wanted those silhouettes of naked chicks sitting, leaning on their arms behind them, one knee bent, one high-heeled leg stretched out long in front of her. The kind you see as decals on the back of pickup trucks.

We nixed that idea pretty quickly. None of the boys have a clue to the design we do come up with. We even found a coupon online for forty percent off the first order which is great seeing as they're custom, and we have to order two hundred of them.

All our badass bikers should be pleasantly surprised because I know they're thinking tuxedos, tulle, and yards of pink and cream. Bump that. I'm a Brimstone Lady. So much so that Mar and I keep going, page after page, until we find the bones of the dress I've been searching for on a site that does custom orders.

"Maryanne, I want you to be my matron of honor. You and Trish and Liv standing up with me. That is if Liv'll do it."

"She will. Give her time. I mean, the shit she went through…"

"Give who time?" We both turn our heads. *Livvy*. Oh, thank goodness. She's watching us from the mouth of the hallway to the back rooms wearing one of Chaos's Lord's T-shirts knotted at the hip to show off her perfect figure and a pair of denim cutoffs, faded with a fine layer of fringe around the legs and at the pockets. It's the first she's ventured out since her rescue.

"How are you?" I ask in lieu of a response.

"Chaos says I'm not allowed to answer *I'm fine*. He says I have to answer truthfully, or he's forcing me to a shrink. So, I'm not fine, but I'm better than I was."

This is not a moment for words. This is a moment for hugs. And she's just going to have to suffer through it. I shove up from my chair tucked between the wall and pool table and scurry the three quick steps to her, pulling her into my arms.

"Love you, Liv."

"Liv, I'm Maryanne," she says by way of introduction as she wraps her arms around both Liv and me. "I can't be left out of hugs. It's a sickness."

I can always count on Maryanne to give the tension break we all need.

"What's going down at the pool table?" Liv asks, pointing to our workstation once we've let her go.

"It's where all the cool kids hang," Maryanne answers.

I laugh, feeling that lightness Beau talked about, and shake my head. "Planning a wedding. Beau got bent because the ultrasound picture said baby Manning."

"Let me guess," Liv says back. "Anyone livin' under my

roof has the last name Hollister." She drops her voice and pulls out her best country twang to sound like Beau.

"How'd you know?"

"Chaos was bitching at me last night. *The nerve of you having them put the name Manning instead.* I tried to tell him it doesn't work that way. No matter how many times I told him you don't choose the baby's last name until it's born. While it's inside the mama, it's got the mama's name. He thinks you could force the issue."

"*Men*," Maryanne grumbles.

"Men," both Liv and I agree.

"Would you stand up with me?" I ask her.

Those big blue eyes of hers go even bigger.

"Think you're up for it?"

"Oh Elise, I'd be honored. This is… this is… *amazing*." And she burst out in tears.

"Honey, please don't cry." My arms circle her waist as I try my best to console her. "I want you and Maryanne to pick out a few different ideas for bridesmaid dresses. We're going for biker chic. Then you can show the choices to Trisha."

"Aren't you a bridesmaid short?" Maryanne asks.

I throw her a '*what?*' glance.

She throws a frustrated '*come on*' back my way. "Beau'll have Tommy. He'll have Chaos. Sneak. But he's not getting married without Liv's brother standing up with him. You said Carver's officiating."

"He is."

"Well then, who you gonna ask?"

"Who won't Blood mind standing up with?"

"There's a hot mama he talks about all the time. Although I'm not sure she actually sleeps with the men. More helps take care of them for a place to stay. You've probably seen her around," Liv says. "Her name is Hannah. I'm pretty sure he's sweet on her, and they're definitely friends."

"Hannah? Oh, right. Long hair same color as mine and great big boobs." I tap my finger to my lips as I think about it. "I do know her a little. She's friends with Trisha and dances at the club. I wonder if she'd do it since we don't really know each other well."

"You could always be a bitch," Maryanne cuts in, "and ask Candy to stand with you."

"Girl, she's not even invited. Terms of me saying yes. No Candy. No George and Margo."

"Like George and Margo would show if they were. You *Hollister whore.*"

Maryanne would be the only person on this planet allowed to call me that without threat of ass-kicking. So to that, I rub at my eyes with my middle fingers, flipping her the double bird.

"I guess we'll never know because they're *not* invited." Although completely irrational, I can't help the sudden wave of hormonal emotion crashing down on me, and drop into a chair as I burst into a fresh round of ugly tears. "My baby's never going to know grandparents. *Never.*"

"What about your mom?" Maryanne asks.

"Haven't heard from her since I moved here in high school."

"That's harsh," Liv says like I don't know disowning your only kid isn't the epitome of wrong.

"Sure she's happy at UC Medical, living a great life as a Denverite."

"She's a doctor, too?"

"That's where she met my dad, in medical school."

Then Liv slides into the seat next to mine to rub my back. "Well... maybe this baby won't have grandparents."

Maryanne pulls another chair up to the pool table. She rubs my back too, so I'm surrounded by the love of my girls, my sisters.

Liv rests her forehead against my cheek. "But it'll have aunts and uncles, even if not by blood, who'll love him or her unconditionally. *Okay?*"

"Okay." I sniff.

"Baby girl, why you cryin'?" Beau makes a beeline over to where I'm sitting. I never heard him come in. Maryanne scoots her chair over to give Beau room. He drops to his knees in front of me, brushing my hair away from my eyes, searching them as he holds my face. "Plannin' this is s'posed to be fun."

"No grandparents," Maryanne offers.

"*Huh?*" he replies.

"Her dad's gone, your parents suck, and she hasn't talked to her mama in seven years. *Pregnancy hormones.*" She ends in a whisper.

"I know they suck. It all sucks. Wish Doc was here to meet our little miracle." He absentmindedly rubs his hand over my belly. "But promise, Elise. Promise our kid will have all the family he or she'll ever need and will never go a day feelin' unloved."

"We're having a baby," I tell him.

"We are."

"We're getting married."

"We are."

Why do I feel like the other shoe is about to drop?

I t's not easy organizing a wedding while in lockdown. But
Liv and I haven't been allowed to leave the compound
since we got back from Chicago. I'm not complaining.
Getting kidnapped and having your friends almost die tends
to put the world in perspective.

Trisha's had a harder time adjusting, only being allowed
away from the club when she's at work. She and Sneak have
even been staying in his room down the hall from ours.
Despite Trish never having relations with Logan, Sneak was
so freaked out by what happened to Liv, he promised her
they'd start work on a family that night if she'd agree to
move into the club until the Houdini threat was neutralized.

That was seven weeks ago. I've been cleaning all day,
getting the spare rooms ready for our outside guests arriving
tonight. Brothers from as far as Texas are about to descend
on the compound to celebrate mine and Beau's impending
nuptials tomorrow.

I will never forget Beau's eyes when the invitations
arrived in the mail. Black cardstock. A raised, embossed
flaming devil head, proud and prominent, at the top of each.

The words *Brimstone Lords* spelled out in old English lettering across the top. *Live. Ride. Brotherhood.* Etched below. A perfect replica of the patch the brothers wear, not only across their leather cuts but also inked onto their backs as a sign of devotion. It was that moment as he read the words we'd picked, inviting his brothers and friends of the club to join us, because there couldn't be a brotherhood without family, that he understood I got it. I'd told him before, of course. But sometimes words are just words. Those invites were my testimony to my devotion to him and his place, and by extension, my place in the club.

My concerned biker keeps trying to get me to take it easy because of the baby. But with so much left to do, how could he expect me to slow down? I'm the VP's old lady. Period.

By the time I finished the last room, he'd taken to physically forcing me to "Sit your ass down," which I did for his peace of mind. The prospects had made my white bean chicken chili per my precise directions. Only I wasn't allowed to leave my stool as they prepared it.

Now after the "Fuck, this shit's good." And "Damn, Boss's one lucky bastard get a girl can cook." I'm having a great time listening to glory days stories of biker rally pasts. Someday, when all this Houdini nonsense is behind us, I hope he'll want to take me to one, so we can make our own memories.

Beau was right, we're giving them exactly what the club needed after Liv's kidnapping. She's over talking with a visiting old lady from the Illinois chapter, while Chaos engages her old man in conversation. He won't go far from her. Constantly shooting eyes her way, refreshing her drink, using the excuse he needs another one whenever he sees her low.

All's not totally right in our world, though. Blood shoots her and Chaos glances too, but his come from an entirely different place. He still won't talk to either Chaos or Livvy. He only agreed to stand with Beau at our wedding tomorrow so long as he's not standing directly next to Chaos.

I know Duke's losing patience with him. Even he can't deny how Chaos is with Liv.

But as fun as biker rally stories, and as intriguing as Liv and Chaos watching are, I'm wiped. I'm wiped and don't want dark circles around my eyes in my wedding photos.

"Gentlemen." I stand, pushing away from the bar where we've been sitting. "Growing a child is tiring, and I need my beauty sleep."

"Brothers. I'll be back." Beau stands, too.

"No. Stay. Have fun."

"Woman," he whispers. "I wanna help my old lady to bed, I'll do it."

Well okay, then.

The moment he gets me inside the room with the door shut, he presses my back against the wall locking me there with his hips, his mouth taking mine hard and hungry. This will be the last time he gets to fuck Elise Manning. Tomorrow he'll be fucking Elise Hollister.

My tiredness fades, replaced by desire as he kisses me, clawing at the button on my jeans, ripping apart the zipper.

His hands go from caressing my face to shoving the jeans down my legs along with my panties, taking care to not put too much pressure on my tiny baby bump just starting to show, at fourteen weeks. A baby bump, I take from his actions, he finds sexy as hell.

It's still hard to believe he's all mine. The baby is mine. The family I so wanted most of my life, is mine.

While I turn my clawing fingers to his fly, he moves us, walking me backward to the bed. Our lips still connected. The backs of my knees hit the edge of the mattress and I fall gently onto my back, hair spreading out over the pillow, ending the clawing to his fly. It doesn't matter. His hands work just as well for the job.

Before the frantic starts up again, Beau catches my eyes and holds them. "Love you darlin'. Love you with everythin' in me."

His words have the power to undo me. I take a moment to slow breathe to keep myself from bursting into tears, giving myself permission to just stare back. He really does love me. It's written in every wind-cracked line on his face.

I blink, closing the moment. He descends slowly to recapture my lips. The kiss is powerful and torturously delicious. "The brothers can continue without me," he whispers against my jaw. "What I've got in here is so much more pressin'. We'll get back to the frantic after we make it through the slow and I plan to make the slow real good for you, baby doll. Because you deserve it. My Elise."

The morning starts a little tense as Elise frets about all the setup which needs to get done. Always the Brimstone old lady, she takes the responsibility even when she's supposed to concentrate on getting herself ready.

It don't matter how many times I assure her the brothers have our backs. That we'll have a fucking fantastic wedding. I force her to lay back down, heading out to the kitchen to bring her breakfast in bed. I make a decent French toast. Sprinkled with powdered sugar. Served with a side of sliced strawberries, sausage links, and an alcohol-free mimosa with alcohol-free sparkling wine and orange juice.

I leave her to check on the setup when her girls show up to start hair and shit. She's calm. And I'm at peace knowing I gave her that calm.

Finally, we arrive at the big moment. It's about damn time. I've been waiting seven fucking years for today. Blood's kept a little distance from our group, but Tommy, Chaos, and Sneak have been standing at my side for the last ten minutes, giving me shit about my life as I know it is over now that I'm about to be hitched to an old ball 'n chain.

Screw them. Tommy and Sneak would lay down their lives for their women without thinking twice about it. As for Chaos, Liv will be wearing his ring as soon as we're clear of Houdini. Maybe sooner.

I miss my chance to tell him that. The house band from Lady's starts the first bluesy rock chords of the wedding march. I turn completely around to watch her walk down the aisle because I don't wanna miss a second of her walking toward *me*.

Fuck. The most beautiful woman in the world, my woman, my bride, stands at the end of that aisle on Duke's arm, she's wearing the sexiest, most biker wedding dress ever designed —fitted head-to-toe white leather. The top of her dress, a vest like one of our cuts, but it's corseted and plumps her tits to absolute perfection. The bottom skims over her curves, including that slight baby bump, only to flair out at her shoes. Her hair's done up in this braided side bun thing, which honestly takes my breath away.

My eyes never leave her. Her eyes never leave me. As she and Duke pass our brethren guests, laughter erupts from each row. Once they get to me, I see what they've been laughing at. Elise has a flaming devil head on the back of her dress, but the devil head has a pink bow tied to the top flame as if it was hair, with the words: *Brimstone Lady* written in old English above it. Below it, *Bossman. Elise. Forever.*

Don't know how she pulled it off, but damn if I can't stop from laughing too.

Carver looks to Duke. "Prez, say your peace."

In a black dress shirt, his cut, black jeans, and his boots, like all my groomsmen, he turns to speak. With his normally unruly goatee and unkempt black hair, just beginning to silver around the temples, trimmed for the occasion, he shows his respect for me and Elise and our day. It means a fuck of a lot.

The laughing dies down completely.

"Take care of him, sweetheart," Duke says. "He's a good man, and Boss, Doc ain't here, so it's been a sad privilege to act in his stead. Take care of this girl and the family yer creatin'. What you got is precious. Don't ever take it for granted."

I look from Elise, who started with the tears the moment her dad was mentioned, out to all the brothers gathered to celebrate with us today. I know Duke's right.

"Nothin' in the world more important," I tell our prez, specifically. And then I repeat myself louder for the rest. "Nothin' in the world more important."

He guides her hand into mine with another firm nod and backs away to sit in the front row.

Carver starts to officiate once more. "We've faced a lotta shit recently. As a club, as a family. This little lady hasn't made it easy on Boss since he decided to woo her again. But honestly, can't picture any other woman on the planet able to handle him the way she does. Made for each other these two. So, Boss, you got something you wanna say to this beauty standing next to you?"

"Boy, do I ever," I say, to the soft laughter of the room surrounding us.

Elise shifts to face me at the same time I shift to face her, still holding her hand.

"*Darlin'*. Seven years ago, when you showed up in town in front of the Whippy Dip, I knew I was fucked. Saw it. Saw it as sure as I'm standin' here now that my world would never be the same. And damn if I wasn't right on that."

More laughter from my brothers.

"You sure pulled me through the wringer. Thing is, I don't mind a damn bit 'cuz all of it brought me to right here, right now. So now, don't matter my world's never gonna be the same. Far as I see it, that's a good thing so long as I have you along for the ride. We walk this life path together, nothin' else matters. Even through—"

"Your first kid datin'." Tommy cuts me off.

"Teenage pregnancy scares." Chaos adds.

"Shotgun weddings." Sneak finally finishes, to the amusement of everybody but me.

"*Piss off.*" I squeeze Elise's hand a bit tighter. "But yeah, even through all that shit, Elise, you and I are together, we'll deal. Always."

She blinks at me a few times, laughter and tears together before she starts. "I don't even know where to begin. Everything you said is true. I put you through the wringer, even when I didn't mean to. I did it. But you haven't always made things easy for me either, Beau Hollister."

Elise is beautiful whether she's smiling or crying like she is now. She wouldn't agree. But where most women's skin turns splotchy, hers blushes. The way she scrunches her nose and bites her lip, one of the cutest ways I've seen a woman cry.

With tears streaming down her cheeks, squeezing the stems of her bouquet of daisies until they start to bend, she swallows, gulping back some air, and then swipes her thumb under her eyes before continuing.

"But none of that matters anymore," she says. "None of it. My dad's gone. My mom stopped talking to me years ago. Yet here we are, getting married. And in seven months we're having a baby. You gave me you, Beau. And in doing so, you gave me a family. In every sense of the word. If having a family means kids dating, teen pregnancy scares, or shotgun weddings, so long as I got your hand to hold while dealing with it…" she stops then whispers with a shuddered breath, "I love you, Beau."

No one's laughing now.

Carver clears his throat. "Ah... yeah. Boss, how 'bout you recite some vows, brother?"

I nod and repeat his words.

"I, Beau Hollister, promise to love you, Elise Manning, for the rest of my life. Takin' in account what it means to be a good husband—to be a friend, a lover, a provider, a protector —to be a true partner even if bein' that partner comes as a bossy caveman. We'll always reach where we gotta be."

Carver turns his head to look at my woman. "Good. Now how 'bout you Elise? Ready for some vows?"

"*God yes.*"

I can't help smiling ridiculously wide. And no, my eyes aren't watering. I'm a man. Our eyes don't water, even for something like marrying the love of my life. I know I look like an idiot, but my woman, she's ready for her vows. She wants to be mine. Means a lot. No, means the world.

She repeats his words, with some adjustments of her own. "I, Elise Manning, promise to love you, Beau Hollister, for the rest of my life. Taking into account what it means to be a good wife—to be a friend, a lover, a provider, a protector however that comes about and whatever that means to us within the construct of our marriage—to be a true partner even in the face of you being a bossy caveman. We'll always reach where we gotta be."

"Got a ring?" Carver asks me.

I turn to Tommy who hands off the gold bands to me, then take my woman's left hand. As I slip hers onto her finger, I say the words. "This ring symbolizes what you mean to me darlin'. So with this ring, I thee wed."

Elise takes the second ring from my hand, then as she slides it over the knuckle on my left ring finger, she gives it to me. "This ring symbolizes what you mean to *me*, babe. So, with this ring, *I* thee wed."

"Love hearin' that." Carver addresses the guests. "Now,

with the power granted me by the Church of Divine Waters, I'm proud to be the one to pronounce you husband and wife. Beau, brother... Kiss your bride."

He don't have to tell me twice.

Throwing my arms around her shoulders and her waist, I haul her in close and kiss the shit out of my wife. Hard. Wet. Deep. And long, until the congratulatory catcalls turn pornographic.

She's breathing heavily by the time I let her go.

As we turn around to face all our friends, Elise leans her weight into me. Carver announces, "Brothers, ladies, let me introduce to you, Beau and Elise Hollister."

There's ruckus clapping and boisterous laughter from my brothers as I drag her back down the aisle behind me, calling over my shoulder, "Go ahead and start the party. Gotta fuck *my wife*."

Once we're back in our bedroom, she glares at me, hands on her hips. "I should be mad at you Beau Hollister, for telling all our wedding guests you're going to fuck me," she says before she lets loose that smile I fell in love with. "But I'm just too damn happy to care at the moment. So, you got lucky, mister."

"Not as lucky as I'm about to get, Elise Hollister, so get over here and kiss your husband."

"I don't want to ruin my hair. Undo your pants and sit on the bed."

Fuck, we'll go with that. I unbutton, unzip and tug my pants down to my hips as she hikes her dress up to around *her hips* and shimmies out of her sexy, lacy thong. I'm already hard as a fucking rock and judging by the way she mounts my lap, straddling my thighs, gliding herself down my erection, she's more than ready herself.

We don't move right away, pausing to stare into each

other's eyes. I breathe her in, taking in the early smell of sex mixed with her perfume. Her chest heaves up and down as she unbuttons the plunging neckline of her dress. Those gorgeous, voluptuous tits spill out just begging for my mouth.

And *that's* when we begin to move.

Her hands around my neck, Elise's head falls back as I grip her hips, grinding her heat against my straining cock. When we've found our rhythm, I move one hand from her hip to push down against her pubic bone and suck hard on her nipple.

The noise she makes—*fuck*. It becomes a breathy cry of my name. *"Beau."* But I'm not ready to let her have it yet. There's still more I want to do to her before I'm ready to share her and the day with our guests.

Gone from the festivities for almost an hour and a half, we eventually stroll back into the main common from our room, arms linked, and her head resting on my shoulder while I take most of her body weight. And her hair, well, let's just say is slightly worse for wear.

My brothers pat me on the back while Elise gets a lot of cheek skims.

Once we arrive, the party really begins. Food and drinks all around. The hog roast to end all hog roasts. I eat like a man who fucked hard and needs to refuel. Elise picks delicately at hers, dreamily and careful not to drip sauce on her dress. Though, it's leather so it'll wipe right off.

As soon as she's finished her meal, Maryanne sneaks up from behind to snatch the paper plate from Elise's hand, setting it on the bar top behind them, and drags my woman to the makeshift dance floor where she's bum-rushed by her bridesmaids.

They laugh and dance.

A hand grips my shoulder, and I turn my head to see

Tommy. "*Shit*, I got me a wife," I tell him, then take a long pull from my beer.

"Yeah, you got a wife…" Silence hangs between us for a minute while we both let it soak in. "Just a piece of paper, brother," he offers. "Nothing different than you already been doing. She was already your family."

"Know you're right, but somethin' about havin' that paper feels weightier." I sigh and slump back against the bar. "Can't believe you had the balls to do this when we were twenty-one."

"My balls have always been bigger than yours," he laughs, punching my shoulder. "But no doubt, she'd been here, you'd 'a done it, too. Seriously, she's already been sleeping in your bed every night. Who you turn to first when you've had a shitty day?"

"Elise."

"When you've had a fucking fantastic day?"

"Elise," I repeat wearing a bit of a smile.

"What I'd be shitting my pants about is that in seven months you're gonna be responsible for a baby. A fragile human life. Small—"

"Shut it, Tommy."

"Delicate."

"Shut it, Tommy."

"Completely vulnerable."

"Shut it, Tommy!"

The bastard laughs at me and he keeps laughing until Elise makes her way from the dance floor back over to us.

She kisses my cheek while I tuck her under my arm, skimming my hand across her dress to rest on her belly. The second my hand makes contact all those nerves vanish.

Tommy can laugh all he wants because right here, right now, I know without a hint of doubt that I'm holding all I'll ever need in my arms.

My wife and kid.

Whose balls are bigger now?

"You good, baby?" She snuggles closer into me. "Because you look about ready to puke."

"Nope. Good now."

"You happy?" she asks.

"Never been happier, darlin'. Tommy here was just tellin' me how he and Maryanne wanna start tryin' for a family now, too." I tell her, watching my oldest friend take a drink of his beer.

He chokes, coughing up and spitting out beer all over the floor.

That'll teach him.

Tommy's horrified face is priceless. That's what he gets for giving Beau shit about our impending bundle of joy. I know he was, they've all been doing it. But please, a baby for Maryanne? If something that important had been discussed, she would've already told me about it.

Today has already been everything I've dreamed it would be and gets exponentially better when Chaos strolls up to us holding my cell phone. "Elise, sweetheart, you got a call. Should probably take it."

I stare at the phone, hoping, praying it is who I think it is. Then I excitedly answer, "*Hello?*"

Hearing that low, gravelly, voice, I could totally cry. "Elise, girl," Crass says. And because it's me, my eyes immediately tear up. Like I haven't done enough of that today.

"Oh my god, I've been so worried. How are you?"

"Better."

"You home?" I ask.

"Not yet."

"I wanted you here. You deserve to be here."

"Chaos told me about Liv. Girl, I'm sorry. So damn sorry."

"Don't." I have to put a stop to this right now. "Don't you dare apologize. You were almost killed trying to protect us."

"Still didn't—"

"Shut it," I cut him off. The men around me snicker because yes, I just told a scary, badass biker to shut it. "Who's taking care of you once you get home?"

"Me. Sure some of the brothers or old ladies will stop by. I'll manage."

"Nonsense. Come down here. I'll send some boys up to get you. Me and Liv will get you on your feet in no time."

"Sweetheart, not my charter."

"I don't care. I... you..." It's a struggle not to get emotional again. "Just let me help."

"Never had a sister."

"Yeah, well, now you have two. Beau and Chaos can make it work. Let me know when you're getting out."

"Gotta go. Congratulations, girl. Tired. Tell Liv I said hey."

And he doesn't even give me time to answer back, just hangs up on me. But he's awake. He's awake and talking and I can't ask for more than that right now.

After tucking the phone into the pocket of the bodice of my dress—because *heck yeah*, my dress needed pockets and I was damn well going to have them when I ordered the thing —my husband takes my hand, lacing our fingers together, and leads me out to the makeshift dance floor. The Lady's house band begins playing the Etta James rendition of "At Last."

I wouldn't call what we're doing dancing so much as a slow, intimate swaying. With my cheek pressed against his chest, Beau sings the words softly in my ear for only me to hear. He can't carry a tune in a bucket, but no song has ever sounded more beautiful. *Ever*.

The man is full of surprises. I had no idea he'd even dance

with me today, let alone that he'd be the one picking our wedding song. We continue to sway as if wrapped in our own plastic bubble, separating us from the rest of the world. At almost the final notes of the song, a commotion breaks out by the front door of the compound, breaking our bubble.

We walk over together, hand in hand, until Beau spies the cause of the commotion and shoves me behind him. "What the hell are you doin' here?" he yells at our unwelcome guests.

"So, it's true, you really married her?" Margo's words come out more accusatory than questioning.

"Get out."

"You promised me, Beau," I whisper.

"Darlin' you know damn well I didn't invite 'em," he replies. "Get. *Out*," he growls at them again, when they haven't moved.

Several of the brothers begin shuffling the wedding crashers to the door when George manages to break away, stepping up in his son's face.

"Please, Beau. Be reasonable. You can't marry her. She's trash. She's a whore."

My husband doesn't even get the chance to take a swing at his father. Oh, someone does, just not whose fist I expected to see connecting with the man's chin.

Out of nowhere, Liv lets fly. And since she was raised in the life, Liv knows how to throw a punch.

I jump out from behind my husband, half screaming, half laughing. "*Oh my god, Livvy*. That. Was. *Awesome*."

"Don't you ever talk that crap about my friend again," she snaps at him right at the same time Margo shrieks.

But Margo's shriek doesn't come from an '*Oh my god you punched my husband*' place. And we all know it by following the line of her finger pointing at my small, yet noticeable baby bump.

"Since this is the last time we'll be speakin' to one another, I'll tell you." Beau takes a menacing step forward. "I've already married her." Another step. "She's my wife. It's done." And another, until he's standing toe to toe with a visibly shaken George, who smartly steps backward. Though his retreat is thwarted by at least five bikers giving Beau his say.

My husband puts an exclamation on the conversation by pointing a finger at George's chest. "We're expectin'. It's too bad you're such an asshole who can't let go of the past. A past that was *not* her fault. Because in seven months you could've been enjoyin' your first grandchild from your only son. But you'll never have that honor because you never earned it. These people." He pauses to gesture around to all our guests. "These people will fill in. They've already made Elise feel welcome, and they're looking forward to spoilin' our kid rotten. Don't think your absence will be missed. Now get out so me and my wife can enjoy our day with the people we love."

"Son, this is a mistake." George almost sounds pleading instead of contrary. *Whatever.*

That's the last he says because Blue and Levi take hold of each of his arms and drag him back toward the door.

When Liv and my other bridesmaid Hannah approach Margo, she turns abruptly, clutching her purse to her chest like she's in a bad neighborhood and afraid of being mugged, and runs out after her husband.

"So sorry that happened, baby girl. Especially today. Never wanted their stink to touch you."

I shrug. "You still love me?"

"You even have to ask?"

"You still want this life, this family, with me?"

"Ain't no life, no family *without* you." He rests his forehead against mine, his arms holding me, brushing his lips along my jaw.

"Then whatever. Pothole in our road. But I'm warning you, Candy shows up—it's on."

After kissing the tip of my nose, he takes off to see that George and Margo have actually left the property.

I find myself leaning back against the bar watching Liv get the accolades she deserves for stepping up the way she did when my phone rings. The display says Maryanne Calling. That's odd seeing as she's here.

But when I scan the room, I don't see her.

"Where are you?" I ask after pressing accept and putting the phone to my ear. No hello.

"*Elise.*" Maryanne's voice comes through the connection low and scared. She crying.

No, no, no... this can't be happening. I frantically begin searching for her with my ear still pressed to the cell, running from room to room.

Then there's a rustle and the voice I hear next is not Maryanne. "Times up."

That stops me in my tracks. "You... you can't have her. She's never been with Logan." I've heard this voice twice now. There's no forgetting his voice. Houdini has Maryanne.

"I make the rules, Hollister whore. Even trade. You for her."

"She can't be hurt in any way." I negotiate while tears run down my cheeks, thickening my voice. *Don't panic. Don't panic.* "She's alive and unhurt."

"You have my word."

"She stays alive and unhurt even after we've made the trade."

"Ah, smart girl. Agreed. Of course, I'll have to knock her out for a bit. But I promise she'll wake unharmed."

I swallow hard. "*Where?* Where do you want to meet?"

"There's a service road to the very back of the compound property. Start walking now. You've got ten minutes to get here, or she dies. I remotely think you've let on to Bossman or anyone else, she'll be dead before they reach her."

"You have my word."

On that parting line, he disconnects. I check to make sure no one is watching, then I run into the kitchen to slip out the back door toward the field.

When cut grass turns to terrain too bumpy for heels, I kick them off mid-run because ten minutes isn't a lot of time. And the whole time my hand stays lying flat against my mildly convex belly.

The air chills considerably as a dusky wind picks up making the outside feel just that much more ominous. And like he said, there's a service road, just a dirt road, up ahead of me where two figures stand. One, clearly a man. One, the silhouette of a woman in a dress on her knees.

His eyes train on me, watching my every step and when I'm about fifty feet away, he touches the prongs of a stun gun to Maryanne's shoulder, and she drops.

She's just stunned... she's just stunned, I remind myself over and over, all while continuing to run to him. My side burns from running, and my gut aches because well—*it's Maryanne*. God, I wish I hadn't eaten that pork. I feel like I'm going to throw up.

"Please don't stun me," I beg once I've stopped maybe two feet away, rubbing my belly. The sun just beginning to dip behind the mountains, casting light and shadows along the road behind us. Houdini's eyes drift down.

"Well, well, well... this is a development. Ain't it funny how life works?" he asks. No, it isn't funny. His chilly voice gives me flashbacks from the cemetery. "Was gonna stun you, but... Now I'll have to blindfold you."

I can't decide if I want to punch him or scream, but either

of those ends up a death sentence for me but especially Maryanne.

"You're not going to kill me?" I ask, shuffling slowly toward my oblivion.

He grabs my arm, pinching until it hurts. "Not *here*. Plans have changed. Fucking perfection."

He drags me stumble along behind him down the bumpy service road to an old Bronco. Most of it is black with a red front passenger door. The back bumper has been jimmy-rigged, made up of a solid strip of particleboard held in place by thin wire and one of the taillights has red electrical tape covering where the plastic cover should be. It's well, it's the Frankenstein's monster of SUVs. And I doubt it's his.

Before he allows me inside the monstrosity, he opens the back hatch and pulls a dirty green bandanna that had been sitting half draped over the grooves of an old flat tire causing dust to puff up in the air from both the bandanna and tire when he snatches it.

"Can you beat it against your leg a few times before you wrap it around my face?"

His look tells me no he cannot.

"I'll sneeze the whole time if you don't. It'll get annoying for you and me. Please, I've been cooperative thus far."

Houdini glares at me, yet surprisingly, he does actually beat the excess dirt from the rag before tying it tightly around my eyes. Next, I hear tape ripping and smell the plastic smell of duct tape a second before the sticky gets stuck over my mouth. Finally, he duct-tapes my wrists together behind my back before pulling me a few steps. There's the sound of a door opening and then I'm shoved roughly onto a seat. Judging by the length of the seat, it's the backseat of the Bronco.

He's not going to kill me yet, and I have to keep my wits

about me. Memorize time and turns, isn't that what they do in movies?

Unfortunately, as he drives, I find I'm nothing like a movie heroine because I quickly lose track of both time and direction. Without a way to know how long or how far we've traveled I can only say it feels like we've been traveling a million miles for a million years.

God, poor Beau. After the shit start we'd had, all those obstacles between us. Today was supposed to start our happily ever after. I mean, haven't we earned it?

When the Bronco finally skids to a stop, I hear voices, both deep male voices, but they're talking too quietly for me to know what they're saying, especially with the blood pumping so heavy against my eardrums and them being outside the vehicle.

Two voices? He said he wouldn't kill me yet, but will he— I swallow hard—*hurt* me? Will the other guy? My body tenses when I'm pulled from the backseat. Luckily, for the time being, only to be transferred to another vehicle, another backseat, before we start driving again. The gut-wrenching fear did a number on my bladder, though.

"*Houdini,*" I chance a call to him. Of course, with duct tape over my mouth, it comes out sounding more like a murmured, "*Ouini.*"

His response is to growl low, guttural. Yet he does rip the tape from my mouth. I didn't really expect him to, but thank goodness for small miracles.

"Houdini," I chance again. "Please... I have to use the bathroom."

His answer, another growl. Though after about a minute, I feel the vehicle veer as if taking a shoulder, then stop. My door opens, and I'm pulled not gently from the seat. He drags me roughly over what feels like pinecones and twigs against my bare feet about twenty-five steps before he stops us. My dress tugged up over my hips. My panties ripped away from my hips.

"Squat," he finally orders.

So this is happening. Me. Peeing in front of my kidnapper.

I stand when I've finished, and he simply pulls my dress back down until gravity takes over. There are so many other ways this could have gone down.

"Why did you kill Hadley, Shayla?" I decide to ask before he tapes my mouth again. Because I know once we reach the car, he's going to tape my mouth again.

Even though I don't really expect him to answer, he snickers through his nose. "Had to get your attention. Got it, didn't I? Now shut the fuck up before I change my mind about killing you."

Okay, so I promptly shut *the fuck* up.

With my headache intensifying, I'm thankful he seems to be in a hurry to get wherever we're going. As I'm not sure what hurts more, the incessant pounding inside my skull or those pinecones and twigs stabbing my bare feet that he drags me back over them, until finally shoving me back inside the vehicle. Though without, I note, tape on my mouth.

Another million miles over another million years, all in total silence, only the hum of the tires skimming over the pavement fills the void. I can't seem to work up the courage to speak with him again.

Eventually, with the sound of crunching gravel underneath the tires, the car rolls to another stop. Houdini yanks me from the car, crunching gravel now under my feet, then *we* stop. Keys clink and rustle. He yanks me again, and we walk until he shoves me not exactly gentle at my chest with the backs of my knees hitting something, I assume furniture, and then my bottom falls and hits a soft cushion.

The place smells musty like it's been closed up for a while and in need of a good airing out.

"Get comfy," he grumbles. "You're gonna be here a while."

Yes. Big, bad Houdini uses the word *comfy*.

That's the last he says to me before he leaves. The door slamming shut clues me in to him leaving. And for some inexplicable reason, instead of trying to plot my escape or at very least to contact my husband... *Oh man, my husband. He's got to be worried sick.*

All I can seem to think about is whether or not Houdini has a power cord compatible with the phone hidden in my pocket. In case the battery runs out, I could charge it. How could I contact Beau with a dead phone?

Answer: I couldn't.

Thus, concerning myself with power cords in these uncertain times doesn't seem so ridiculous. However, I need to focus. To escape.

I blame the stress.

Stress makes us think crazy. Worrying about power cords would definitely qualify as me thinking crazy. Just not ridiculous.

Easier than falling apart, my mind shifts through whether or not the prospects put the food away before the men undoubtedly took off to find me so we don't get rodents or bugs while I'm gone because I cannot live with rodents or bugs. And because I have to have faith that the men *will* find me. Then I move on to wondering about Maryanne, if she'll be able to get the grass stains out of her pretty bridesmaid dress.

Alone in the room, I can almost pretend I'm not someone's captive when the door opens.

"Bed," is all he grumbles. *Uh-oh.*

Houdini picks me up and cradles me like a groom might cradle his bride with one hand behind my back and one under my knees, giving me no choice but to loop my arms around his neck to keep from spilling to the floor, or at least feeling like I'll spill to the floor. Who knows if Houdini would let me fall?

He sets me down, gently this time, onto the bed, not removing my blindfold yet tearing the tape from my wrists. It stings. They sting. Again gently, he rubs at my wrists leading me to let my guard down, which really, is a total my bad. So my bad when in my lowered guard, he unbuttons the vest of my dress then pulls the zip of the skirt down the side, stopping where it stops just below my hip. I freeze while he shoves the leather off my shoulders then stands me up to let the bottom half slip to the floor so I'm almost bare to Houdini wearing only my lacy white bra.

Uh-flipping-oh. Double on that uh-oh when he runs his finger down from my collarbone, between my breasts to rest at my baby bump where he stops, resting his whole hand to cover my bellybutton the way Beau does, and he grumbles low, "Fuck Elise, you got a beautiful body, even knocked up."

I don't want to thank him. That might encourage him.

"Sleep," he orders. "I'm wiped."

For the briefest of seconds, I think he might let me lie back without wrist restraints. No such luck. Softer than the duct tape, I feel the satin he binds my wrists together with. This time, he binds them to my front. Although soft, he binds them tight. *Tight.* Super tight. That cutoff line just before tourniquet tight. It won't make for a comfortable night, but I shouldn't lose my hands because of it.

The uh-oh gets worse when I hear clothing drop to the floor, the covers rustle from the other side of the bed, and his weight and body heat slide in next to me. I start to really get nervous then when he flips me to my right side, his knees cocked against my knees to curl back over his, and he drops his arm over my waist to rest again on my belly.

Scary, murderous Houdini spoons me.

A spooning Houdini freaks me out so badly I blurt out, "I thought you were gonna cut my heart out."

As the full weight of my stupidity hits, I suck in on my bottom lip and bite hard, bracing.

Who the hell reminds a scary murderer that he intended to cut your heart out? Me, only me. About now I'm beginning to think I might deserve to have my heart cut out.

On a soft laugh, he grumbles again. "Sleep. We'll talk tomorrow." After which he nips the skin behind my ear, sucking it deep into his mouth. So deep I know he's marked me. It turns my stomach. He wants Beau to know he's had his mouth on me.

A quiet sob breaks from my throat.

With a brief arm squeeze, he releases me. "Sleep."

What choice do I have? It's been a long, exhausting day and until he decides to end me, I'm still growing a child, so I force my mind as blank as my mind can go,

And I sleep.

My phone rang. Busy shooting the shit with my brothers, I didn't even bother to check who was calling, just pressed the accept button while bringing it to my ear.

My blood froze.

"Fuck you," he growled into the phone and hung up.

And that's how I found out Houdini got to my wife.

"*Shit*." I hissed, whipping my head every which way, looking for my bride. A bride I didn't see. Not anywhere. "Anyone seen Elise?" I shouted at the same time Tommy walked up.

"Have you seen Maryanne?" he asked.

For the briefest moment, I relaxed thinking the girls were just off getting into trouble somewhere 'til Maryanne stumbled inside the clubhouse, and she looked dazed, crying, and with grass stains on her dress.

The word, "*Tommy*," tumbled from her lips before her steps faltered, and she began to go down. He had her in his arms before she hit the floor.

"He has her," she said, voice quiet. "He *has her*," she said again louder, more panicked. *"He has her,"* she screamed now, clutching Tommy's vest, so hysterical her face contorted to the point she didn't even look herself anymore.

At the sound of glass shattering, I turned to see a trembling Livvy, sparkling wine puddled around her feet. Watching Liv tremble, my life with Elise flashed before my eyes. What we had. What we're supposed to have, raising our baby. *This can't be happening.* We took all the precautions. I thought my heart stopped beating while simultaneously beating so ferocious in my chest I was about to have a heart attack. "This can't be happening," I choked out. No. I had to get my shit together. Breaking down wouldn't get her back.

"Where, Maryanne?" Tommy stroked her available cheek with the back of his hand.

"Out back. Service road at the edge of the property," she murmured because of the other cheek she had pressed hard against Tommy's throat.

"On it," Chaos called as he took off out the door, Blood, Sneak, and Carver on his heels.

Then Duke looked up from where he studied Maryanne and called out to gather the prospects. "Blaze, Blue, Levi mobilize."

Blue and Blaze appear next to Duke. "Where the fuck is Levi?" he barked.

"Don't know, ain't seen him in a while," Blue answered.

I slid up next to him. "Don't got a good feelin' about this."

He put his hand to my shoulder. "No Boss, me neither."

"Mar, you okay baby?" Tommy asked, still holding her close.

She only slightly nodded.

"I gotta go," he told her. But his face said if he could hold on tight for the rest of their lives, they'd stay in that spot on the clubhouse floor for *the rest of their lives.*

She nuzzled deeper into Tommy, an almost hug because she wouldn't let her fisted death-grip of his dress shirt go *to* hug him.

But before he set her off his lap, after the kiss he dropped to her temple, she stopped him. "Tommy, save my friend." Only those of us surrounding her heard, but we sure as hell heard.

"Let's go, Boss, bring the phone. We got some friends, some higher-ups, maybe they can track the call."

"Rise and shine..." grumbles in my ear. For a second, with the warmth at my back, I can almost imagine the voice belonging to Beau, the warmth belonging to Beau, but it's only one second past that second to send me careening straight into my fucked-up reality. And yes, there's no other way to describe it. "Up," he says again, pressing his lips against my jaw.

"I have to pee," I tell him, bringing my bound wrists up to my face to scratch my nose. The problem being he thinks I'm trying to remove my blindfold, slapping my hand away.

"Not yet!" Bursts from his mouth.

I feel his heat ratchet up by a gazillion degrees and his muscles go taut in that arm he slaps my hand with. Then because I've ticked him off, he rolls me to my back and climbs on top of me wrestling his thighs between my locked knees.

"Time to have a little fun."

This would be how I end up with a Bedlam Horde named Houdini kissing wet kisses down the dip of my throat. And how I end up with a Bedlam Horde named Houdini rubbing his calloused fingers all over my breasts, over my white, lacy bra. And finally, how I end up with a Bedlam Horde named Houdini grinding his thankfully boxer brief-covered crotch against mine.

Before my brain catches up with my mouth, my mouth whispers against his hair, "I can't."

He stills. Rolls off me. Inconceivable, yet him rolling off me gives me hope that he can be reasonable. Yeah, no. Not a Bedlam Horde named Houdini.

"See we're gonna have to have our talk first. Coulda gone down differently, but what did I expect from the Hollister whore?"

I gasp at his crude comment, I guess because I'm not fully awake yet. A crude comment is the least I should expect. He roughly grabs my hand in a way more attuned to what I should expect from him, and yanks me up to a seated position, twisting my legs so my feet hit the floor.

"Why are you doing this?" I finally pluck up the courage to ask but do it knowing how I take my life in my hands.

"Why do you think?"

"My guess, Logan slept with your girl or maybe your sister, and you're taking revenge on Beau because they used to be close. If that's the case, I gotta tell you, they drifted apart years ago."

"Drifted apart my ass," he grumbles as he runs his thumb along the apple of my cheek, sounding lost in thought until abruptly with the scary gruff to his voice back he barks, "Alright sweetheart, this how you wanna play it, we'll play it your way."

I really don't want to play. So, I tell him. "I don't want to play."

"Yeah, you do." He laughs through his nose. "My move."

The word *move* hardly leaves his lips before the dirty bandana that's been covering my eyes since yesterday is ripped from my face. It takes about seven blinks before the black splotches disappear only to have me stare right into a pair of brown eyes I'd recognize anywhere. Brown eyes which used to look on me with warmth now hardened in an unnatural way. Oh, but I remember the hardened brown, too. The last time I looked into those eyes they held the same unnatural hardening. I don't... I don't understand.

"*Lo*?" I scramble back from him until my shoulder hits the headboard. "H-how is this possible?" Tears prick the corners of my eyes, for a brief second because it's Lo, and he's alive. Then my brain catches up, and the tears aren't for Lo any longer. "You died. You killed yourself. I don't... how is this possible?" I ask again. Shame and fear, and disgust with myself for ever having loved this man, replace any softness I would have shown him.

"Makes me sick, you layin' with him," he says while running his fingertip down the length of my arm.

Not thinking nor caring that I'm about to piss him off, I goad him, because what do I care at this point? I'm dead anyway. "You cheated on me Logan, not the other way around. I never che—"

"*Bullshit*," he cuts off. "Think I'm stupid? I saw you ride off with him, remember?"

"We just went for a ride. I slept with *you* after homecoming."

It's like he doesn't hear a word I've said. He lunges at me, fists around my throat, he squeezes to just short of choking me.

"I wouldn't've needed those women if you woulda kept your legs closed. Just kept your legs closed, Elise. That's all you had to do. You were mine."

Now his fingers squeeze to just over choking. Not enough to make me pass out, but definitely enough to hurt.

"How is this possible?" I croak, my voice breaks partly

from the fear of his hands around my throat, and partly from not pulling in enough breath.

"Mine," he grumbles.

"How is this possible?" I croak, louder.

"Mine," he grumbles again.

"How is this possible?" I manage to screech in his ear. The sound is enough to shake him from whatever crazy trance he's in. His fingers loosen, going back to just short of choking.

"Alright baby, you wanna know I'll tell you." Logan's voice goes eerily soft. Right before the serial killer strikes at the main character in a movie, soft. "I was so about you, all about you. But you, the phone calls, the visits. Your sweet little ass spent more time with that dipshit once he went away to school than before he left, makin' me the chump. I don't much like bein' the chump, you understand. So I found a guy who knew a guy and helped me find release."

"What kind of release, Lo?"

"Tardust, snow, dream—blow, baby. The best kind of release."

"Logan—no—please tell me no."

"Cleaned up since then, don't pretend to worry. Course, didn't clean up fast enough to save my full-ride or place on the team. Random testin'. *Bullshit*. I come to my sweet girl-friend needin' her to make me feel better and what do I find, my girl and my boy—my cousin—hell, coulda been my brother for as close as we were, not just standin' at your back but stabbin' me in mine."

It's at this point Logan drops his hand from my throat and pushes back. Not far, but far enough to pace the carpet back and forth, clearly agitated. "Stab me in the back," he murmurs.

"He didn't stab you in the back."

Logan lunges at me, stopping shy of touching me with anything but the tip of his nose against the tip of my nose.

"He did. *You* did. Tellin' me you're havin' my baby with *him* at your back. What the fuck was I supposed to do with that? Sleepin' with that prick with my baby in your belly. That's the fuckin' definition of a whore, Elise."

"I never slept with him, Lo. Not once. Never. Before I thought you died and for the five years after, I never slept with another man. You, however, didn't give me that courtesy."

"You're a liar *and* a whore. But as I see it, he took what was mine so now I'm takin' what's his. Fair's fair."

"Please, Logan. Tell me how you're alive when the town buried you."

"Hard to identify the body with the head blown off. Was fuckin' this girl, her brother was Horde. He helped me pick the dick out at a mall in Lexington. My body type, hair color. Rage helped me kidnap the douche, but I had to be the one to take him out. Didn't think I could do it. Crazy thing about that, Elise. Didn't realize just how easy it is to point and pull a trigger. My fingerprints on my dad's rifle. Benefit of bein' *the god of Thornbriar*, the town was too stunned for those losers to do a proper identification. Then Rage helped me disappear. Enter Houdini."

"You're crazy," I whisper.

"No baby, not crazy... *free*." He walks over to a dresser turning his back to me to pull open the drawer so I take the opportunity to look around and realize I know exactly where we are. Exactly.

Same log frame bed. Same Navajo print blanket covering the soft pillow top mattress. Same tacky woodland prints hung on the walls. Same. Everything is the same. Except for the man. The man had changed. The same, but so very different.

I cannot believe he brought me here, to the first place I'd given myself to him. That's when he turns back around throwing a pair of drawstring shorts and a T-shirt over his shoulder. He reads my face, knows I know.

"Yeah baby, long time since you been here. Let's get you dressed." Normally I don't much take to being ordered around, but as I'm at a disadvantage sitting half-naked on a bed with a crazy nutzoid, out of his ever-loving mind Logan, I quickly stand, stepping into the shorts he's crouched down for me to step into and allow him to pull them up.

He ties them resting low on my hips. And after unbinding my wrists, he slips the tee over my head, knotting it at my lower back as I pull my arms through the armholes.

With my wrists bound again, I'm led out of the bedroom. "I'm married to him, Lo. You can't have me."

"I don't want you bitch. That ship done sailed. I mean, I'll fuck ya. Still got a hot little bod. Always had a tight little cunt. Don't look used, so I bet you're still pretty fuckin' tight. No, I'm takin' the baby. Imagine it, Elise, the baby of the VP of Brimstone Lords bein' raised by the Horde."

"I'll never stop fighting to get away, you know."

"Not sure what you'd be goin' back to. Bossman's dead. Either way, he's dead. Givin' you this one chance, come willin' and Maryanne lives. Livvy lives. Trisha lives. Fight me, I take 'em out and make it painful. Won't realize the meaning of suffering 'til I'm done with 'em."

Deep breath in. Deep breath out.

I close my eyes, picturing Beau's molten liquid eyes and crooked smile. I remember how it feels to run my fingers through that thick peanut butter hair. To feel his arms around me. His beard tickling my shoulder when he kisses my neck. To rest my cheek on my name tattooed over his heart when we're lying in bed together. And at the very last, I remember how a duck walked into a bar.

"Decide now," he orders.

There's no way for me to escape right now. Not until he trusts me again. And if he's proven anything this morning, it's that he's crazy enough to pick off my friends, one by one.

No, I never. My friends have to stay safe.

Swiping the wetness from my eyes, I agree. "I'll go."

Houdini, because I can't call him Logan anymore. He's fallen so far from Logan Hollister or *my* Logan Hollister, that man, well, he's as dead as the town thinks he is. Houdini blindfolds me again, along with replacing the binds around my wrists before leading me out of the cabin. "Safer if you don't know just yet."

I assume this means he doesn't want me to know which way we're heading. After shoving me inside the car again, he runs back inside the cabin muttering something about another clip. I'll further assume he's not talking about something to keep my hair pulled back.

Suddenly and very unexpectedly my door cracks open to a whispered, "*Elise*."

Tears sting my eyes again, even as my heart rate kicks into overdrive. I know that voice. I know it. "Levi?" I whisper back.

"No time. gotta get you out, sweetheart." And he yanks me from the car at the same time removing the blindfold. "Bend low, keep quiet and run," he orders, as he pulls me by my bound hands along next to him.

So many questions swirl through my brain, number one being where's Beau? But I'm not stupid enough to open my mouth. Levi says keep quiet he'll get quiet.

We run.

In the distance we both hear an angry, "*Fuuuk!*" to which Levi responds by dragging me faster, and I must admit, with my being barefoot, he's much more agile running over rocks, twigs, tree roots, and other forest debris. My feet feel shredded. But if he can get me back to my Beau, then my lips will stay zipped without one word of complaint.

His words come at me ragged. "Taking the river. There's a ferry not too far, get us Ohio side. Hidden. Sit," he orders then.

Levi says sit, I sit.

Beau would be shocked to see how well I take orders. Along with his proficiency in the rescue arts, badass biker prospect Levi apparently already developed that badass biker ability to read minds as well, since he says exactly that to me.

"Boss always says you're shit for taking direction," he tells me this as we're sliding down the craggy embankment landing our feet at the squishy mud shoreline of the Ohio River. A shoreline smelling of rotten plant life, which kicks in my pregnant woman gag-reflex and paranoia, as I'm sure at this very moment, the rotten seeps into the open cuts on my feet infecting me with some crazy E.coli or salmonella or tapeworm larvae in every step.

I refuse to freak out about what I might already have contracted and instead, roll my eyes and mutter an annoyed, "Whatever," back at him. An annoyed whatever we both know I don't mean.

And it's not until we begin to slow from a run to a quick-paced walk that I realize my feet have gone completely numb. I'm not sure when it happened, when I stopped feeling the pain from my shredded feet. The cold mud put a stop to that.

Numb feet infested with E.coli, only I could use them as a means to calm myself down. It's what's on my mind when I look over at Levi pulling his cell from his pocket. Being right on the river, there's enough open space for a connection. I could cry when I see the name, the number he connects with.

"Got her," he says into the receiver. "On the river. Heading north. A cabin off route eight. She's right here."

Then he thrusts the phone in my hand. "Make it quick," he once again orders.

"*Beau?*" How I prayed to hear his voice one more time. His name, I whimper. Not that I want to cry, I'm just not sure I can help it. "Beau," I repeat stronger, as I bend my head to use the fabric at my shoulder to wipe my eyes.

"Elise, god darlin' it's fuckin' good to hear your voice. We're comin' for ya. Stick close to Levi. Shit! Christ! *Shit!*" Beau's voice breaks. "I… if you… *shit!*" he says again.

I know what his sentiment means. I won't make him say it.

"I'm okay Beau." I stare out over the river, while I try to reassure him. "Guess I owe you a wedding night?" I give my first gift to him, lightening the mood. We can't have him breaking down in front of his brothers.

"Woman, when we're done, I'm takin' you away for a month where you'll do nothin' but lay in bed naked, givin' me my weddin' night."

Levi tugs my arm and spins his finger in the universal gesture for "Wrap it up."

"I'm being ordered to wrap this up. But Beau, you gotta know Houdini—it's, he's—he's *Logan*." The line goes silent at the same time Levi jerks us to a stop.

"He can't be baby girl. Lo—"

"He is," I demand, cutting him off. "He kidnapped me. Took me to the family cabin on route eight. He escaped death."

"Houdini," that's all Beau clips back.

"Yes, just like Houdini."

"Put Levi back on."

"Okay, love you, Beau."

"Love you too darlin'."

Levi grabs the phone from my hand without me even offering it up. Because he did just rescue me from my crazy ex-boyfriend. A man who we all thought killed himself years ago. A man we found out murdered several people and wants to fuck me until my baby is born so he can steal the kid to raise hating his or her father and arch-nemesis in a rival club. Because of all that, I'll let it slide.

After hanging up, Levi tells me, "Beau wants us to continue up to the ferry" and starts off walking again while shoving the phone back inside his front jean pocket. "Come on," he follows that. "Time to hustle."

It takes us another twenty minutes of hiking before we find ourselves in a crouch behind a tree at the wooded shoreline. We watch as the ferry unloads passengers on the Ohio side of the river, which means we'll be waiting a while.

With little grace, I plop my butt onto the damp ground and hold my bound wrists out to Levi. I think he forgot they've been bound this whole time. Since I kept up, and as I vowed, didn't complain once. He reaches inside his boot to pull out a switchblade. He flips it open and slices through ties. The delicate red fabric flits down into a mud patch, soaking up enough brown to turn a dulled red reminiscent of dried blood.

Absentmindedly, I rub at my wrists. As I watch Levi flip shut the switchblade, I notice his skin full of welts and bruising and his T-shirt torn at the sleeve. Belatedly it hits me that when he rescued me, he wasn't on his bike.

"What happened?" I ask, fingering the torn cotton like expensive silk.

He watches my fingers but doesn't push them away. "Got sidetracked by some Horde outside Dover."

My hand immediately stills, gripping his shoulder. Levi got sidetracked by the Horde? By himself?

"*Are you okay?*" Though whispered, I shriek. If I hadn't heard myself do it, I wouldn't have known it possible.

"Just a little banged up. My guess, Horde won't be too happy with me, though."

"Why?"

"Let's just say there's five of them outta commission for a while."

"Five?" I whisper a shriek again. "*Five.*"

He locks his hands together over his bent knees and drops his head, smiling possibly one of the sexiest, most panty-melting, cat-ate-the-canary grins I've ever seen. So hot, I don't know how to channel my reaction. Yesterday I married the love of my life, I shouldn't have a reaction *to* channel. And I have no excuse, except to say he's a badass, rescued me, he's beautiful and I'm human.

"If I wasn't totally in love with Beau, I'd kiss you right now."

His smile evaporates. "Maybe keep that to yourself."

"What, is badass Horde dropping Levi scared of Beau?"

"*Yes,*" his answer comes without hesitation. "I want my patch, but more importantly—I want my life."

"Okay then." I chuckle. "I'll keep it to myself."

"Good. But Elise…"

I lift my head to look him in the eyes.

"*Thanks.* I know why he loves you. Someday when I'm ready to find the right pussy, way, way, *waaaay* down the road, I'll know what to look for."

Two choices. I could laugh or I could cry. I pick laugh and punch him in the shoulder, just a soft punch to show I get him. Then we hear the rumble of the ferry engine cranking to life across the river, effectively ending our Levi and Elise bonding moment. We push up from the ground, and I wipe at my behind while I stretch, bending slightly backward. It's time to go home.

32

W hen my eyes pop open, they open to dark. The darkest of dark. Darker than the cave Beau had taken me to at Carter Caves, and soundless. Only the sound of my breathing, my blood pumping in my ears, my heartbeat kind of sensory deprivation. About two point five seconds after that, my freak out commences. About two point five seconds after that, I realize how cramped my quarters are, as in just big enough to hold my body. Then about two point five seconds after *that,* I shut the hell up.

My head hurts. My heart hurts too. My guess, for very different reasons.

So here's what I've got—the darkest of dark, sensory deprivation, and the softest padded satin surrounding me. It doesn't take a genius to figure out where I am. A coffin.

I don't know how much time passes since I woke up and came to that eerie realization, but all I can do is sit with my memories, waiting, hoping someone will find me in time, that my Beau doesn't lose his family today. I rest my hand on my small baby bump. Mommy's little parasite.

The ferry. Levi and I watched it glide back across the river toward us. I guess we both let our guard down. But the ferry was coming. We'd be safe. Away from Houdini. Neither of us thought anything of it when he grabbed my hand and pulled me to start for the dock. "Let's go."

He'd sidled over so his feet rested in the water to prepare to help me climb on board the boat. And then it all happened so fast... so, so fast.

Houdini was there. He'd found us. He'd found us with his gun out, trained on Levi. And Levi dropped. Well first his body jerked several times, I screamed bloody murder because I think I had, in fact, witnessed a bloody murder, and then Levi dropped.

Scared immobile. I'd been too stunned to move because my badass biker buddy might have just died to save my life. Then my flight instinct kicked in but kicked in too late. By the time I turned to run, Houdini had already caught me.

I felt it when the butt of the gun connected with the back of my head. It hurt for a second, after that second, nothing hurt. Not until I woke up here. In a freaking coffin. The real Houdini, the magician Houdini's most difficult trick. The one he never got to perfect before his untimely demise.

Come on, Elise. I know I have to listen to that inner voice inside my head. All this reminiscing serves no purpose, save messing with me enough to get worked up again, thus using up my limited oxygen stores. And as I'm not keen on using up my limited oxygen stores, I force my eyes to close, to think of Beau and how he looked at me as I walked down the aisle toward him. The love, the pride he wore for all his brothers to see, but it was all for me, just for me.

Then I let myself drift off to an imaginary world where Beau and I relax on the beach, the setting sun still warming our skin while we hold each other watching the ocean waves lap, break after break, eating away the sandy shore until the salty water finally laps our toes.

Tears sting my eyes.

I wanted that imaginary world. I still want it, but the chances of ever getting it slip further and further away with each passing minute. So I let it go, imagining another, where I rock our baby on the swing out front of Beau's house, leaning against his chest. Beau's strong, comforting arms hold the both of us.

And I begin to sing. Softly. I pick a lullaby my father used to sing to me when I was a little girl. He'd sing it those nights I'd wake up scared from some unidentified monster hiding in my closet or under my bed, or when the thunder rattled the house so fiercely, my child mind thought it would crash down around us.

I sing because I would have sung to my little parasite when he or she woke scared from some unidentified monster hiding in the closet or under the bed. Or the nights when the thunder rattled our little bungalow so fiercely, his or her child mind would think it would likely crash down around us.

As I sing, my words muffle out from a loud thud. A heavy, loud thud. Like maybe the edge of a shovel hitting the coffin lid, thud?

"Hello?" I call. But my voice comes out softer than I mean it to, probably due to the sheer surprise of hearing the thud in the first place. "Hello?" I call out louder this time.

"Elise?" I hear my name called back. Muffled, but called nonetheless.

"Beau?" I yell this time. *"Beau?"* A screech now.

"Calm down baby girl." *Thud.* "I'm here." *Thud.* "I'm here, darlin'." *Thud.* Voices grow louder. *Thud.* "Elise?" *Thud. Thud. Thud.*

"Here!" *Thud. Crack.* Blinding light, so blinding, so light I have to close my eyes to shield them, missing that first glimpse at my Beau. That is until I hear the *thunk* of his boots hitting the wood, his broad, strong body shielding me, I see the light dim through my closed eyelids then open them. And I have never seen anything so beautiful, so wonderful in my entire life.

33

BEAU

Seven months later...

"Come on darlin', you got this."

"No. I don't," she cries. Yes, cries. Squeezing my hand so tight, *my* eyes tear. "I don't got this Beau. Get them to turn back on the epidural. *Pleeeaaassseeee!*"

"Can't Elise," Dr. Brennan tells her, her voice full of authority.

"Yes, you can! My husband is a scary badass biker who will fuck your world! Turn the goddamned epidural back on!"

"Baby's crowning," the doctor tells her.

"Fuck. Your. World," she yells right as Dr. Brennan pulls at my hand not being crushed by my wife.

"Come, Beau. Your baby's head is out."

Uh... I thought my job was to stay by my wife's head letting her crush the circulation from my fingers. Not sure I can deal with—that thought gets cut right the hell off as the doctor drops my hand only to force my head around and down to see my kid squeezing out of my beautiful wife.

Shit, that looks painful.

Not for the first time in this pregnancy, I shoot a thank you to the universe that I'm not the one in her place, especially now on the bed with her feet planted against the mattress baring down. I'm a big man. I can only assume...

"Arms out Hollister," the doc orders. Then she forces my hands to grip my kid's shoulders, and together we pull him or h—holy hell it's a him!

"It's a him," I tell my wife. "It's a *him,* darlin."

"A him," she whispers, sounding absolutely spent.

ELISE'S BEEN out for a while. Me and my boy been spending some quality father-son time bonding. He's learned a lot so far. How his mama and I met. How he's the first legacy born to the club in years. I thought babies squirmed a lot, but not him. This little guy seems content to just be held in his daddy's arms.

"Never thought we'd get here," Elise surprises me, murmuring into the darkened room.

"Hey, baby girl. How you doin'?"

"Better."

She presses the remote button to move her bed into a more seated position.

I stand from the chair me and boy have occupied to move to her bedside. I can read her look clearly and slide him from my arms to hers, kissing her first and then placing a gentle one to the top of his head. She kisses his head, too.

"We have a family, Beau. Can you believe it?"

"Yeah, darlin' I can. You gave this to me. I knew the day I met you in front of the Whippy Dip, if I was ever lucky enough to be here, it'd be with you."

Before she can respond to my confession, there's a soft knock on the door.

"Open," she calls. And there, the rest of our family, Tommy, Maryanne, Chaos, Livvy, Sneak, Trisha, Carver, Blood, Duke, Scotch, Blue, Blaze, Levi, and even Crass pile into our little room. Blue, Blaze, and especially Levi wearing full patches. Fuck if they hadn't earned 'em.

Especially Levi. Took bullets for my woman. Sacrifice like that forges a bond never forgotten.

I heard the gunfire. We were close to the rendezvous point. Tommy next to me, I took off running toward the sound of the shots only to see him drop. I went cold but pushed on, hoping to get to Elise in time. Houdini already had her on the one-car ferry, the driver shot dead.

"Logan," I called out to him. He stilled, and I didn't know where to look, to him or to Tommy bent over a prone Levi trying to save his life. I made the choice. "Lo, come on. You don't gotta do this. Let her go. I won't come after you, just let her go."

"Don't know who you're talkin' to, Logan's dead, Boss. Don't you remember?"

And as he pulled Elise in front of him to shield him from my bullets aimed in his direction, I knew he was right.

Logan *was* dead.

While we hunted Houdini and Elise, Levi fought for his life. We'd gotten to him in time for Tommy to call it in, air-vaccing him up to Cincinnati where they rushed him into surgery. Then the waiting began. He'd stayed on life support for a few days. Once we'd found Elise and she'd been checked out and cleared by a doctor, she refused to leave his bedside.

Since I refused to leave her side, we spent our first week of marriage in a hospital room.

Didn't matter, she was safe in my arms.

Dr. Brennan was another new addition. She came to town before the wedding. Thornbriar needed a new doctor, she said she'd been passing through and decided to stay. Convenient since Elise couldn't leave the compound. She's pretty. Curly, naturally red hair and bright green eyes. The hair she always keeps pulled back in a bun, even when we'd see her at the grocery store. And her eyes are always assessing. Not sure what she thinks of the club, but if she has any prejudices, she never lets on. And the woman shows no fear, even in the face of my wife threatening her badass biker would fuck her world.

"Hey guys," Elise says warmly, through her smile. "Come on in."

Liv takes up position next to Elise's head, placing her hand on Elise's shoulder. "He's beautiful, sweetheart. Just beautiful."

"Yeah..." Elise's eyes go dreamy. "Everyone, I'd like to introduce you to Gunner Levi Hollister."

"Gunner?" Chaos stumbles over boy's name like he can't quite figure out the taste. "Where'd you come up with that?"

Elise stares down, smiling at our son, and then turns that smile up towards Crass.

"That... uh... that'd be me..." he grumbles to the laughter of the group.

"You want to hold him?" she asks Crass. "Beau, let him hold him."

I take our boy from her arms, handing him gently over to his namesake, Gunner "Crass" Duncan.

As he stares down at my Gunner, Crass says, "That boy is the spitting image of his daddy."

To which I respond by takin' my boy back and holding him up against Crass so their faces are flush next to each other, and search back and forth between them. "Yeah," I snap, "and when I find the fucker, I'm gonna fuckin' kill 'im."

Eight weeks later...

"Holymotherfuckinglordoftheuniverse!" Elise yells in a whisper so as to not wake a sleeping Gunner. I got back from my run just a half-hour ago. We been out lookin' for Liv. She hadn't been heelin' as well as we thought. Chaos is goin' crazy out of his mind.

Soon as I got to the clubhouse, though, seein' as I ain't tasted my woman in eight weeks, I grabbed her and the boy from our room there and sped for home.

Eight weeks. Six of 'em because she gave birth. That ain't something guys share. It's a joke the brothers who've gone down this road before us don't wanna spoil. I had no idea when I knocked my wife up that come post-delivery, we'd be in for a six-fucking-week dry spell.

This would be her second *Holymotherfuckinglordoftheuniverse* since our festivities began. While she finishes her scream, I roll my hips then continue pumping hard, my face in her neck until I find that euphoric release of my own. I stay planted inside her for a few beats trying to control my breaths.

"*Wow*," she says.

Yep. That says it all. Instead of returning her wow, I kiss her slowly, much more slowly than how this evening started out.

"I'm gonna go clean up," I tell her as I roll out of bed heading for the bathroom. It's nice to be back at home. With some added protection of the big and little variety, including cameras and a security system since Houdini got away, and birth control so we don't end up with another Gunner yet. Just as I get back to her, knee to the bed, boy starts his wailing from the other room, loud and obnoxious, through the baby monitor.

"I got him," I tell her before she starts to get up. "You go ahead and get dressed." Then I bend to the floor grabbing up and tug on my boxer briefs before heading out the door to our son's room.

A few minutes later I lay down in bed next to Elise where she immediately takes Gun and the tiny formula bottle from my arms. Cradling him in hers, she feeds him.

"So Gunner," she starts. "A ham sandwich walks into a bar and the bartender says—hey! We don't serve food in here."

Not the End

THANK YOU FOR READING! I hope you loved meeting Beau and Elise. The next book in the Brimstone Lords MC series is DUKE REDEEMED. Find out who the sexy biker president can't stop thinking about and takes to his bed.

CLICK HERE TO READ DUKE REDEEMED >>

Don't miss more badass MC brothers from The Bedlam Horde, starting with DEVIL'S ADVOCATE: VLAD

I appreciate your help in spreading the word, including telling a friend about the Brimstone Lords. Reviews help readers find books! Please leave a review on your favorite book site. A review on Amazon helps the most.

SIGN UP FOR SARAH ZOLTON ARTHUR'S NEWSLETTER: Sassy, classy and a little bad-assy newsletter

Now, how about reading the first chapter from DUKE REDEEMED...

FIRST CHAPTER from DUKE REDEEMED
Dr. Brennan/ Caitlin

THE CURVACEOUS WOMAN MOANS LOUDLY, limbs wrapped around him. She rubs her indecently clad skin over most of his body, kissing on his chest and neck as they stand outside his club room while I pass them on my way to Elise's. His hand on the knob pulling the door shut.

Their presence in the hall perfumes the air with alcohol, sex, and really bad decisions.

No shirt, wearing only a leather vest exposing all his expanse of beautifully ripped chest dusted in dark hair and covered in tattoos. His arms. His chest. I'd bet any amount of money, his back too. All covered in tattoos.

Beyond the dusting of hair on his chest, he hadn't bothered to button up his jeans. I swallow down the lump in my throat, embarrassed that I'm unable to tear my eyes away. Even more embarrassed that I stop moving altogether, to openly gawk at the man. But when I say he's beautiful, I mean, *He. Is. Beautiful.* In that gruff, gritty, could kick your ass without breaking a sweat kind of way.

My eyes follow the line of coarse hair trailing down from

his navel, a runway pointing to the root of what promises to be a long, thick good time. When I move my gaze back up, I find him glaring at me through heated eyes. Not the good heat, the lip licking, '*I want you*' way which would work for me, as I clearly want him.

No, he looks at me with a something else kind of heat.

My lips part and I feel myself beginning to sweat under his intensity. I clear my throat knowing I have to gain back control of the situation. I ask, "Is Elise inside?" Pointing to her door two doors down.

He says nothing, just stares at me like I'm the dim kid in class.

Control, Caitlin. Get back the upper hand, I silently motivate myself. In order to do that, I train a condescending smile across my face and raise one brow. Then I ask again, slowly and drawn out, "Is Elise in her room?"

His face turns harder than it had looked only seconds before, I'm sure not understanding the audacity of someone, especially a woman, speaking to him in such a manner. "Watch it," he grumbles.

"Come on, Duke." The woman hanging all over him, whines in a breathy, '*just had great sex but I'm ready for more*' kind of voice. And that's my cue to get the heck out of here.

"Never mind." I wave him and his attention away. "I'm sure she is. Have a nice day." Then I turn my attention from the man and force myself to walk like I'm not trying to escape which is especially hard pulling a plastic cart on wheels behind me. The cart keeps catching on my heels, causing me to wince each time because having a heavy cart attack my heels hurts.

I only give a light knock on Elise's door. If the baby is sleeping, I don't want to bother him yet. As I wait for her to answer, my back to him, the back of my neck burns from his stare. I feel it. He's there, watching me.

And even if I didn't feel him watching, I'd know it the way Elise pulls open the door and steps into the doorway. She glances at me briefly, but only briefly because her eyes dart over my shoulder and stick. A sort of half-smile smirk dusts across her face before she moves back out of the way.

"Hey Elise, how are you?" I ask as I move into her room.

Today I'm at the Brimstone Lords compound for Elise's six-week checkup, post-baby Gunner's delivery. Her husband is out on a run. That's what the men call them, even though I know he and two other MC brothers are out searching for Livvy Baxter. They're lucky, as in lucky to be alive, as she and Elise were unfortunate players in that crazy, murderous Houdini's psychotic show. Bad business, that was. I got the details first hand, but even if I hadn't, their stories were the top news stories all over the country.

"Good. Thanks for coming down," she says in what I can only describe as a forced cheer. I've been coming around here for close to a year now, and Elise Hollister is usually quite open with me.

I pause before replying, waiting to give her the opportunity to come clean on whatever has her troubled. She stays silent. On a sigh, I shake my head once and pick back up. "Not a problem. I know the drill. Any cramping? Started your period yet?"

"No cramping, and yes, period here and gone."

While I look for a place to set down my purse, she hops up on the bed. Then I walk to her bathroom to wash my hands. "Good. That's good. So, how's our boy been?" I call through the door left open, though not loud enough to startle the baby.

"Busy. Can't wait for him to get home." She giggles. At least that seems genuine.

"I meant the *baby* boy."

"Beau can be quite the baby."

Now we both giggle quietly as I can see the little bundle of joy wrapped up and sleeping soundly in a bassinet.

"*Ugh.*" I blow out an exasperated breath. "That's all men."

"Don't I know it. I live in a biker compound."

"I'm going to check you first and then I'll check Gun. Let him sleep a little longer."

I turn around to the plastic bin on wheels that has all my equipment inside, unlatch the locks and flip the lid open. What I need is right on top.

Once I've pulled the portable stirrups out, I order Elise to strip down for me while I secure them to the side of the bed with clamps, then gesture for her to lay down. This is one of those naked appointments, as she calls them.

Her feet up in the stirrups, legs spread, bottom to the edge of the bed, the appointment is as comfortable as I can make it. Her body visibly tenses, as everyone's does, when I don my gloves and lube her up. She shudders at the speculum. No one likes a cold, metal cylinder shoved up inside their lady bits. But as most of my female patients are, she's a trooper.

She's healed nicely and the insides look good.

After Elise is dressed, I hand her off a script for birth control as well as an already filled case. The woman needs to start them ASAP. When her biker husband gets home, after already having had to go six weeks without getting any, I know where his head—both his heads—will be at.

But neither Elise, Boss nor I want her preggers with baby number two just yet. And from what Elise has shared, her man isn't the best with condom usage.

"Any big plans tonight?" Elise asks while slipping her yoga pants back on, an innocent question, but it jars just the same.

Much to her chagrin, I have to wake the baby to check him out, too. He squirms and coos. Not the case at his last checkup where I neglected to blow on the stethoscope to warm the metal. Gunner wailed. A meltdown of epic-newborn proportions.

Boss looked ready to rip my head clean from my body. And it wasn't because I made his son cry. It was because I made his son cry after we'd finally, *finally* gotten him to *stop crying*.

Two weeks straight of colicky baby crying, the new parents were about ready to crack. We'd nixed the breast milk but had to figure out a formula that wouldn't cause gas.

With too many choices, on about formula number five, we hit. Enter me and my stethoscope mishap. Despite being a miserable boy, I miss the newborn stage.

Gunner is a happy baby now. Incredible what a change in diet did for his constitution. They're doing a great job with him. Thus far he checks out completely healthy.

We leave her bedroom. She and a wide-awake, wriggly Gun walk me through the common area, where the glutton for punishment that I am, looks for Duke again. The MCs president. I've known him as long as I've been coming here. As Elise's doctor, at first. But being a family practitioner, I started caring for a few of the brothers as well.

But not Duke. He's strong and charismatic. Personally, I think he's so tough, he scares the illnesses away. And for some reason, he can't stand the sight of me. He legitimately bristles whenever I come around. Then we end up snapping at each other or are reduced to speaking in sarcasms, like in the hallway earlier.

A damn shame because when he has those tattoos on display, and he's in full MC President mode, exuding all that power and badass-ness, even though he's normally not my type, *lord help me*... I'd put hand to forehead and swoon if I didn't think Elise would want to know why. I'm not in the mind to give up that ditty of information about myself just yet, if ever.

She continues out into the paved courtyard with me, and we stop at the trunk of my Jeep Grand Cherokee. I flip the hatch door and begin to heft boxes inside. My Cherokee color is Cayenne, and it's sexy as hell. I let Jade pick it, she liked that it matches our hair. When we moved to the mountains, I upgraded from our little sedan. I didn't think a sedan would be safe on slick winter mountain roads.

"*Caitlin,*" Elise says to grab my attention. *Oops.* "Any big plans tonight?" she asks again, I assume because she asks it with a bit of emphasis. I've been in Thornbriar for months and still haven't managed to form any real friendships. Acquaintances, sure. Yet every night when I'm done doctoring, my butt is at home on my sofa watching television with my four-year-old. Most people don't even know I have a daughter.

She's at daycare during my office hours. I usually stop by the grocery store before I pick her up to avoid the inevitable "I want... I want... I want" in a preschooler's whine. I love the girl but that gets annoying.

My little Jade, anyone who has seen her eyes knows why I gave her that name. It's our extremely Irish heritage. She's the spitting image of her mama. Both my parents were born over there. Jade had been born when I was living there taking care of my grandmother before she passed. Though, my little girl happens to be much more popular. She's going to her first friend's sleepover tonight. So no, no plans. A Friday night and I'll be where I usually am.

"Nope," I answer Elise. "My ass will be sitting on the couch watching the History Channel."

"Why don't you come hang? Trish is coming over with Sneak. Maryanne will be here too because Tommy is working and won't be home 'til late. We're having a girl's night in."

She pauses, then, "And I think Duke'll be there, too. I mean, as an FYI." Although her words sound benign, spoken in a casual tone, she keeps peering over my shoulder, out toward the gate and main road.

"Do I need to bring anything?" I ask, peering over my shoulder as well. When I turn back to look at her, she's wearing a troubled face, I guess, which wipes any thoughts of 'Duke being there' out of my mind.

Though, she clears it quickly enough. From troubled to blank. "Just your cute face and an appetite for junk food and gossip," she jokes. "The prospects have already done the shopping. There'll be alcohol for those of us who can drink and fakeohol for those who can't. And we're making our own pizzas."

"Wow… um… sure. If you think it'll be alright with the guys."

"Please, you'd be doing them a favor, not having to keep me company." She shifts Gun in her arms. "Most of them would prefer to be off getting laid."

She just had to tell me that, right? Now I have images of sexy bikers getting laid, or rather one sexy biker, in particular, getting laid, sifting through my head. "Right. Then what time should I be back?"

"Seven is when the other girls are showing. Is that too late?"

"Sounds perfect to me." I finish packing up my car and move to say goodbye to Elise and Gun when she grabs my elbow softly to stop me from leaving. "What's up?" I ask.

"Nothing… uh… be careful, okay?"

That's an odd sendoff, adding to her odd behavior out here. I take advantage and ask, "Be careful of what?"

"It's really probably nothing."

"Let's assume it's something, what would that something be?"

Elise moves in closer and drops her voice. "When you come here do you, uh, do you ever get the feeling of being watched?"

What? "No. Not that I've paid attention. Have you?" It's been less than a year since she'd been kidnapped by Houdini and buried alive. The choice came down to saving Elise or catching Houdini. Boss saved Elise. That means that psychopath is still out there somewhere.

"Well yeah. When I leave the compound and sometimes when I stand out here for too long. It's just leftover anxiety, I'm sure."

"Have you told Boss?" I ask.

"*No,*" she says way too quickly, almost a whispered shout, startling the baby. "He'd freak. He'd come back. He'd tell the other brothers."

"Yes, but Elise." I pause. My turn to lay a hand on her arm. "You were kidnapped. He needs to know."

"Beau is off trying to find Liv. I want my friend found. And more than that, I want him home. We've spent so much time apart. I want my family back together. Under one roof. It's selfish, I know. But if he comes home now, he'll only have to leave again. Plus, I never leave the compound without a guard, so I'm cool, you know?" She tries to sound unaffected, but I can see through her façade.

I open my mouth to tell her what I think of that idea when she cuts me off. "Please don't say anything."

Do I agree to that when I don't agree? But she's my friend, I think. Or at least starting to be my friend. I can't betray her trust, even if for a good reason. Letting out a slow breath, I decide on how to answer. "Okay, for now. But you need to tell him. If not for you, think of Gun."

This answer seems to appease her, she smiles a genuine smile, even if it doesn't reach her eyes. Then she nods and steps back. I take that as my cue to climb inside my car and actually leave.

A prospect stands out front by the fence, he pushes open the gate for me and shoots off a two-fingered salute as I pass through. This new crop of prospects is something to behold. If I were a few years younger and didn't have a child, I'd work him like a stripper pole, not that I've ever worked a stripper pole. But I'd heard the saying numerous times from Elise and her friend Maryanne Doyle, and it seems apropos here. His small name patch, the one on the front of his vest stitched just above his heart, says Jesse. Though, I believe his mother did him a disservice with that name. She should have called him *Eye Candy*.

They must like him. Gate duty is pretty important, especially in their world. From the way Elise explained it, all prospects start off doing the shit jobs that no one wants. Unclogging toilets, cleaning up vomit after a party, cleaning up after the party. Making a four-a.m. food run when a member has a sweet tooth. They like you, trust your loyalty to the club and the brothers, they'll move you up to the gates. From gates, it's protection. You prove your grit, then you get patched in. There's no timeframe.

You might be cleaning puke for two years; you might only be on the gate for a month.

The whole dynamic is pretty fascinating.

Jesse looks like he'd show a girl a good time. Too bad there's only one man I'd honestly consider going biker for. And I have to remind myself that he can't stand the sight of me. God, that gritty voice gets me every time. Not blood, but liquefied want courses through my veins. Pumping through my erratically beating heart. No other way to describe it.

Plus, and this is important, it has been *so long* since a man has done that to me. Not since Aiden, Jade's daddy, left Jade sad and me broken-hearted for a new life and a new woman he'd been talking to online in Australia.

What kind of man leaves his toddler daughter to move to another continent?

But we survived.

I hope Mr. Sexy Biker won't be there tonight. Seems since I first took Elise on as a patient, I close my eyes and dammit if it isn't him, those lines, probably from his years of smoking, surrounding a pair of gray, bordering on silver, eyes that stare back at me.

Apparently, I'm more obvious about my attraction to him than I mean to be. Usually, Elise drops little tidbits of information about him when I'm at the compound and he's around, trying to pique my interest. "He's only like, thirty-eight years old. That's a lot of good years left to uh, do whatever one might do with a man like Duke." Or "He likes his pieces, but Duke hasn't been in a relationship since his wife died. He's very loyal."

I actually never thought she'd try to coordinate a meetup where Duke and alcohol were involved. I mean what else could that FYI of hers mean?

A shiver runs the length of my spine just from thinking about thinking about him.

"Mama!" Jade rushes to me, slamming her tiny body against my legs, and wraps her arms tightly around my knees, which me being five foot nine and all legs, is where she reaches.

Scary how the mind can wander so much that a person can lose consciousness to the world around them. I don't remember driving here. I don't remember getting out of the car. I don't remember walking through the parking lot or inside the building. None of it.

My girl and her preschool were my destination, but holy

cow, I need to be more careful. *And* to stop lusting after someone I'd never stand a chance with. I'm no biker babe.

Shaking my head, I chuckle at that thought. Me, as a biker babe? The idea is even too ludicrous for my imagination.

Get your act together, girl.

After disengaging Jade from my legs, I take her hand and we walk back to get her bag and sign her out.

"Miss Jenny, I'm going to a sweepover at my fwiend Macy's house. It's her birfday."

"So you've said," Miss Jenny answers, chipper as always.

"I'm sure about a million times today." I joke.

Miss Jenny rolls her eyes but then shakes her head yes, laughing as she does.

We gather Jade's bag, lunch pail, and jacket, sign her out and say goodnight to the staff. Then my little bundle of energy beats me to the car where I've unlocked the doors from my key fob.

She's already sitting in her car seat in the back, waiting for me to buckle her in, by the time I reach her.

"I'm not 'posta eat dinner wiff you. Macy's mom is makin' us birfday burgurs before the cake." My princess kicks her dangling legs excitedly.

"Well then, let's get home and get your bag together so you can have those birthday burgers. Okay?"

We ended up packing half her room into her overnight bag, but she was so excited to be going to an actual sleepover, she didn't want to forget anything.

Now I've got sweat-drenched hands gripping the steering wheel tighter than the situation warrants. It's just girls' night in at the clubhouse. A chance for me to make some friends.

After dropping off Jade, I swung back by my house to gussy myself up in that using makeup to make me look naturally flawless way. I don't want any of those bikers to think

I'm there for anything more than to hang with the girls. But I don't want to look like Medusa either. It's a fine line.

Jesse is no longer on the gate when I pull up. Another prospect lets me through. I might not know all of them, but they all know me from my time taking care of Elise.

I walk in wearing a white fitted babydoll Tee under my black lamb's leather jacket, black skinny jeans, and ballet flats. My hair is down, all the buoyant curls springing in a sort of tamed hysteria. They've never seen me with my hair down. I kind of feel like Sandy from the end of Grease. At the *first* double-take from the first biker, I pause long enough to look over my shoulder and coo, "Tell me about it, *stud*." Then I keep walking as if I'd never stopped, to begin with.

GET IT TODAY! Duke Redeemed (Brimstone Lords MC 2)

You can find Sarah Zolton Arthur on:
Amazon Facebook Instagram Goodreads Twitter BookBub
TikTok

ALSO BY SARAH ZOLTON ARTHUR

Adult Romance Series

Brimstone Lords MC

Bossman: Undone (Brimstone Lords MC 1)

Duke: Redeemed (Brimstone Lords MC 2)

Chaos: Calmed (Brimstone Lords MC 3)

Scotch: Unraveled (Brimstone Lords MC 4)

Hero: Claimed (Brimstone Lords MC 5)

Blood: Revealed (Brimstone Lords MC 6)

The Bedlam Horde MC

Devil's Advocate: Vlad (Book 1)

Devil's Due: Sarge (Book 2)

Devil's Work: Dark (Book 3)

Immortal Elements Series

Flight: The Roc Warriors (Immortal Elements Bk. 1)

Soar: The Warrior's Fight (Immortal Elements Bk. 2)

Run: The Viking Pack (Immortal Elements Bk. 3)

Adventures in Love Series

Skydiving, Skinny-Dipping & Other Ways to Enjoy Your Fake Boyfriend

D.I.E.T. (Dating in Extreme Times)

WTF Are You Thinking?

Holiday Bites (A Lake Shores, MI World)

Baby, It's Cold Outside Book One

Always Be My Baby Book Two

Standalones

Summer of the Boy

The Significance of Moving On

Audio

Summer of the Boy

Skydiving, Skinny-Dipping & Other Ways to Enjoy Your Fake
Boyfriend

Flight: The Roc Warriors

ACKNOWLEDGMENTS

Thank you to the best sons a mom could ask for. You two are truly my best friends and I couldn't do this life without you. Thank you for being my biggest cheerleaders. Guess what? I'm yours, too! Finally, thank you to my favorite baristas (Hello, *coffee*). I literally couldn't do my job if you weren't doing yours so perfectly.

It takes a village to raise a novel, and you all are my villagers. The people who helped turn a project I was proud to have completed into a project I'm proud to present to the world.

ABOUT THE AUTHOR

Sarah Zolton Arthur is a USA TODAY Bestselling author of pretty much all things romance, but she loves to get down and dirty with her MC bad boys. She spends her days embracing the weirdly wonderful parts of life with her two kooky sons while pretending to be a responsible adult.

She resides in Michigan, where the winters bring cold, and the summers bring construction. The roads might have potholes, but the beaches are amazing.

Above all else, she lives by these rules. Call them Sarah's life edicts: In Sarah's world, all books have kissing and end in some form of HEA. Because even outlaw bikers need love.